The Irontrace Saga: Malice

T.S. Night

Cover & Interior Design: Stanley Customs

First edition

Trade Paperback ISBN: 979-8-9986492-9-5

Content Warning:

MANY READERS MAY VIEW TRIGGER WARNINGS AS SPOILERS. IF YOU WANT PLOT-SPOILING TRIGGER WARNINGS, PLEASE SEE THE ENDNOTE BEFORE READING.

This novel contains graphic scenes of surgery, medical peril, dystopian peril, and emotionally intense situations that may be triggering. Readers with chronic illness or medical sensitivities may not want to read this book.

READER DISCRETION IS ADVISED.

Author's Note:

While this book draws on a wide range of real-world medical knowledge, it is a work of fiction, set in a dystopian future that does not reflect current medical practices or ethical standards.

The procedures, diagnoses, and medical systems throughout this work are speculative and dramatized for storytelling purposes.

DO NOT interpret any part of this book as medical advice. If you have medical questions or concerns, consult a licensed healthcare provider.

I've done my best to balance realism and imagination. If you're a medical professional reading this, I hope you forgive the liberties I've taken in service of building a whole new world.

- *T. S. Night*

For the ones who make breathing possible, thank you.
To those who struggle, hold on. It always gets so much better.

To: ♥Nathan Cantone♥

<u>09/12/2050 0543</u>

I am begging you, Nathan, please come. There's a guard or guards out there. I don't know, I'm too unsteady to go check. Love you.

<u>09/12/2050 0559</u>

Why haven't you come? You have to hurry before Ivan gets back! They'll take my phone again soon.

<u>09/12/2050 0704</u>

Did Ivan get you too? I can't understand why you've abandoned me.

<u>09/12/2050 0704</u>

You are KILLIN' me, wife. -I

<u>09/12/2050 0704</u>

Recipient Unavailable

0

Three Weeks Earlier

It's a lounge-on-my-husband-until-I-rot kind of afternoon. And I am thriving here.

"Yet another reason I'm glad my execution got postponed!" I rip my sunglasses off to gawk up at him. Dumb move. The sun nearly blinds me.

He laughs, fiddling with my soggy mass of red curls. My typically overachieving Ivan is comically bad at doing hair. He's been trying to twist it into a bun for about ten minutes.

"Your execution wasn't postponed. It's canceled. You're the darling of the healthcare renaissance. So anyways, The Bastion has kept track of my mile high stack of awards and merits." He wiggles his eyebrows with a hilarious lack of humility. "Each added to the bank account they were supposed to give my parents as a 'thanks for letting us imprison your kid, we finally killed him off' gift. But since you, my brilliant wife, removed the Agora that held me prisoner, *we* get the money."

"Gracious. I married you for that face. These biceps." I give his impressive upper arm a squeeze. He grins. "Turns out you're smart and loaded. This is gonna work out long-term."

"What a relief. I don't think I could ever get all the hair you've shed out of the apartment. I'd just have to move at this point."

Suddenly having several million dollars is very much an Ivan thing to surprise me with. In the three months I've known him, he's taught me some of the most heavily guarded secrets of 2050.

He's on a black ops team of genius engineers called the Irontrace Squadron. They protect and maintain an operating system called The

Kernel. It's the brains of the artificial intelligence models that have taken over our lives. Our dear world leaders in The Bastion enthusiastically murder anyone who disagrees with them. Recent disasters that have plunged the world into pandemonium were caused by a psychopath named Anthony Moulson. Ivan's honesty about everything makes me trust him completely and love him fiercely.

For now, we're on a beach.

"Happy belated two-month wedding anniversary, Commander Rhys. We should-"

He puts a finger on my lips and smiles, making a silent 'shhh.' "Come here, I've got a present for you."

We've been laying in the late August sun for about an hour. The chilly water takes my breath away when we splash into it, dissolving into playful laughs.

"Dive with me." He takes a deep breath and ducks under the waves, gently pulling me under the clear blue water beside him.

He pulls my left hand between our faces, pointing to the panic button on my engagement ring. *What are you doing, baby?* I yank my hand, but he won't let go. If he accidentally hits it, it'll call the rest of the Iron-trace Squadron. They've barely recovered from when I was taken a month ago.

He points to, then taps on the row of emeralds on my wedding band before blowing his breath out in a swirl of bubbles and pulling me to the surface.

"What was that about?" I blurt, wrapping my legs around his hips to float.

"It worked!" He nods toward the shore with a cocky grin.

I gasp. He and I are climbing out of the waves, walking towards our beach blanket. But we're not...we're very much out here beyond where the waves break. "How, Ivan!? Who? What are they?"

The Story on the beach wears my same bright pink swimsuit. Her long red curls drip water as she laughs, holding her Ivan's hand. He smiles and kisses her forehead. I see the same scar on his face trailing down his neck, more scars on his chest and back from battle wounds through the years. He wears my Ivan's black swim trunks on his tan, sculpted frame. They're our mirror images, but alive, having their own conversation.

"Digital clones. Stretch your hand out, my love." My hand strikes against a slightly bouncy, shimmery surface. "Murderous Moulson and his minions of destruction can hear and see us everywhere. I told you, I'll beat him. I can't focus until you're safe. I built this shield, SAM, Safety and Mitigation, you can activate from your emeralds. Moulson is wily. He'd know if you go missing while he's watching."

I smile and lean back, letting my torso float. "You built digital clones of us, so we can hide from Moulson. He won't notice when we disappear into this shield?"

"Correct, my beautiful genius. They have vital signs and thermal signatures. If he sees them, he *will* think it's us. Plus, we're hidden from everyone else in here too." He folds me tighter against him.

"Even better!" I lean closer, but it makes us sink several inches below the water. We pop back up, laughing and sputtering. "You couldn't have made this SAM thing waterproof?"

"It's a prototype. I'll make some tweaks. Let's get back to shore before you drown us."

"Did you swim much in the waterfalls while you were growing up?" His effortless backstroke while I'm furiously doggy paddling beside him shows he's as good at swimming as he is well...everything else.

"No. Part of our tactical training is deep water scenarios in case The Helm gets flooded. They've tried to drown me every few weeks since I was nine. I had to figure out how to save myself and complete increasingly harder water survival challenges with each passing year."

Stupid Bastion! Who does that to people, let alone children?

"That's less of an idyllic story than I expected, sorry."

"Idyllic and The Helm have never been in the same sentence. Anywhere. Ever. Until I tossed you over my shoulder, drug you into my apartment, and you fell head over heels for me."

"Oh, is that what happened?" I laugh.

"More or less. Tell me what you learned about Moulson while we're in SAM."

"He's not a scary man. He looks kind and intelligent. Then he speaks. It betrays how evil he is. He uses those transcranial magnetic pulses to pause people or something? He said it takes away their attention and memory. It was super creepy. No one fought back." I stop swimming and float. "Even you Irontrace and the Air Titans. You just...you can't see that Moulson is lying. He told me his whole life story. Mark Guthrie isn't real. His name is Anthony Moulson."

Just talking about it makes my heart pound. I've felt cruddy in general since I got back and this isn't helping.

"I'm right about this. Please. You have to believe me."

Ivan pulls me on him to tread water. "I have to say, I've looked into the background check on Mark Guthrie. He's solid. From what I found, Mark is who he says he is." I open my mouth to fight him on it. No. *MOULSON IS GUTHRIE!* Ivan continues, in a single breath, "But I believe *you*. If you say Guthrie told you he's really Moulson. That's what I believe too."

This conversation is ruining our trip to the Cove. We've only got two hours. I don't want to talk about Moulson. What if I'm wrong? Did I imagine the whole thing?

"New approach. You ask me questions. I'll talk," he says, trying to break my silence.

How did The Bastion let Anthony Moulson assume a fake identity as some guy he calls Guthrie? Irontrace are geniuses—how has he tricked you all? Should I tell the world who he really is? Will he really kill you if I do? How close am I to being handed a second death sentence for keeping this secret?

"What's he done to your brain?" I ask.

He frowns. "I know what Moulson looks like. I can picture him. But when I look at Guthrie, his face shape is different. His eyes are the wrong color. Looks and sounds nothing like Moulson. He seems like a chummy old friend."

"I wish you could see it. I feel like I've gone insane."

"If anyone can pull this off, it's him. I'll figure out how he did it, don't worry. When I watch you or anyone else from my workstation, I'm pulling data from a ton of sources. Radar, satellites, hacked drone cameras, and The Bastion's optic sensors they have everywhere."

"Creepy. Not you. The Bastion."

He crinkles up his face and laughs. "Thanks for clarifying. I was watching Rosa's feed-"

"Wait. *You* sent Rosa?"

"Yes. Not sure yet why Moulson lied and said he did."

"Is she in The Bastion too?"

"Nah, Mom's like the other robots from Atlas Caverns."

The water is finally shallow, but I stumble. "She's a...*mom*...your mom? What? The other what?"

He makes a faux frown at me, but his eyes sparkle. "Baby, can you not tell the difference between humans and robots?" I shrug, wide-eyed. "She's the robotic parenting model that took care of me at The Helm. Everyone who works in Atlas Caverns is a robot too. Did you think we train Irontrace engineers and then plop them in there as cashiers and to wash laundry?" *I did, actually.* "I mean, Rosa is well-made. Do you know what Rosa means?"

"Pink in Spanish?"

"You're not wrong," he concedes. "Not in this case though. R. O. S. A. Rhys's Operating System Auto-mom."

My jaw drops.

What is this world I eloped into?

Robots perfectly mimicking humans. They're all around me in the secret facility we live in behind a waterfall. In a heavily guarded forest. With my husband who doesn't legally exist.

Ugh. A sense of unease turns my stomach. Can Moulson hack them to and use them to attack us?

Ivan's brow furrows at my blank face. "Story?"

I bend over to pick up a hand-sized white clam shell from in the waves. Mom loves these as soap dishes. Mom. Robot mom. Robot mother-in-law?

"Rosa is the closest thing I've got to a mother-in-law?"

"She is. Sorry. When you went with Rosa that last day, it was like a hole was torn in reality. You were just gone. The council members decided to execute you before I got there. That would have been the worst decision in the history of The Bastion."

A sharp laugh escapes. "When they locked me in for execution, I told them you'd never forgive them."

He glares in the direction of the city. "I wouldn't have. They knew I was coming for you. They approved it. Then decided to kill you. I can't believe I'm saying this, but it was good Moulson got there when he did."

I nod. "I'm going to grab my water. I think I'm dehydrated." I think it's been too much sun. I'm lightheaded and my heart is still racing.

Ivan jumps in front of me, hooking his arms around my knees and pulling me onto his back. This is a much nicer way to get to the truck.

I shift up on his back to kiss the surgical scar I gave him about a month ago. It's an eight-inch U-shape low on his neck, between his shoulders. I'll be giving the same scar to hundreds of Irontrace.

"How long does this SAM shield last?"

Digital Story and Ivan lay on our beach towels in the sun. Ivan strides past them and pauses beside the tailgate of his truck.

"Until you squeeze your ring again and blow their pixels away." He turns sideways so I can climb in. "Leave 'em alone. Let's stay hidden."

I throw him a beach towel as he hoists himself up behind me. He dries his face then wraps it like a cape around my shoulders, pulling me in front of him.

His dark eyes take on a mischievous glint when they meet mine. Yep, he makes the dread go away.

Then his smile falls.

"Did you? Do you feel that?" He jerks back to stare at the ground. "The beach just shook."

We freeze. For a heartbeat, nothing happens. Then the beach ripples and rolls.

"An earthquake? In Ohio?" I drop low. I've never been in an earthquake, but it seems safer than falling over the edge of the truck bed.

"Moulson!" Ivan shifts me onto his lap, wrapping around me like a shield. "Squeeze your emerald. They look too happy."

Digital Story and Ivan go from laughing in the cracking wet sand to scrambling straight for us. As they leap at us, they disappear into thin air.

"Do we stay here?" I ask through gritted teeth.

The roar of the waves has kicked up so much it sounds like the Cove is hissing at us, warning us to flee. A collection of shells I threw in the toolbox rattle as the truck lurches. I hope they don't break. I'd have to add them to the ever-growing list of lovely things Moulson has ruined.

"We should get out of here before the sand liquifies. Come on." Ivan scoots towards the cab, pulling me with him as the truck suspension creaks.

"Before it what?" I flop in the window and land in a tangle on the bench seat. Ivan slides over the edge to hop along the running board and climb in the driver's door.

Inside the truck, it's a rollercoaster. Ivan was so excited to buy this huge lifted black truck, but now it's riding waves of sand like it's nothing more than a child's toy.

"The sand gets saturated with water, loses its strength and behaves like a liquid, you know, quicksand, nightmare type stuff." He turns the truck on and shifts to drive, slowly powering forward through the shifting sand. "Do you wanna get dressed before I call the control room?"

"Waitwaitwait!" Water drops fling on my truck window as I rush to put my hair in a clip. My Irontrace patients don't need to see their surgeon in a halter top swimsuit.

He grins, watching me throw on his black Irontrace T-shirt then shimmy, struggling to pull my shorts over my wet swimwear.

"Stop it with that face!" I tell him. Keep making the face. *Always* make that ridiculous, irresistible face. With one eyebrow arched and those lips twitching at me.

"The world is undeniably a dumpster fire. But I promise to always stop and appreciate how glorious my wife looks in the flames."

I laugh and toss his extra shirt at him. He swipes the media console on the dash and a screen turns on, connecting us to the control room. "Commander Rhys, checking in."

"Get back quick, Ivan," Senior Commander David Delac says.

"Is this worldwide or regional?" Ivan asks.

"Local. Moulson hacked into artificial intelligence models that maintain deep fluid injection sites in central Ohio."

Trees sway violently along the hilly edges of the Hocking Forest. Massive, shallow-rooted pines topple over, ripping other trees down with them. Ivan grabs my arm to catch my attention then points to a landslide. We gasp in unison at the boiling mass of nature pouring down the hill.

Boulders gain speed and tumble into more trees and debris, pulling the mess with them to crash into an open field below. Black angus cows clumsily run in panic through their meadow with lush grass and late summer wildflowers. A white horse jumps the fence in terror, galloping along the road.

The road in front of us buckles and wide cracks open. Cars swerve wildly off the road. Ivan brakes hard, pulling into the grass.

Suddenly, everything goes still.

"Darke fixed it!" David yells. "Turn up monitoring on all AI models. And someone find Anthony Moulson!"

He might be in the control room with you, but you think he's Mark Guthrie! The words die on my lips.

"See you soon, Delac," Ivan says.

"Put some real clothes on before you come in my control room," David barks.

"Will do." Ivan disconnects from the call and blows out a deep sigh. "I've never been out here for a Moulson attack. You good?"

"Yep. You?"

He nods, distracted by a message on the dash.

"Kinda feels like the world is falling apart when he does that," I say.

Disasters didn't happen until about three months ago. Life under The Bastion was close to a utopia if you didn't ask too many questions.

Or try to use your brain. Not anymore. Moulson has crippled the world in his personal vendetta against The Bastion.

"I'm not sure what the magnitude was, but that was a long earthquake," he says, putting the truck in gear.

"Ivan, you don't have a driver's license. The road is busy. Let me drive."

"I printed one off before we left. Delac approved it."

"You can't just print off a license. You have to learn how to drive."

"That's what I'm doing." He smiles.

Our hilly, curvy roads in the foothills of the Appalachian Mountains are a test for experienced drivers. If Ivan wasn't Ivan, there's no way I'd agree to be his passenger. I have to admit; he's doing a decent job so far.

"Oh no." I point to a busy intersection where the road curves away from the Cove. Several boulders rolled into the road. Some crashed into passing cars. Most of the drivers appear uninjured and are driving away from the wreckage.

Except one.

There's a swarm of emergency vehicles around a dark green dually truck that's flipped over. The passenger side is almost entirely caved in from the impact of a car-sized boulder. My view into the windshield and driver's window is obscured by the white pillowy airbag curtains.

A girl about my age sits on a stretcher beside it. Her long blonde curls spill from a messy side ponytail. A medic is trying to put an oxygen mask on her, but she pushes his hand away.

"Stop! Ivan. Park the truck!" I grab his thigh. "That's Richelle."

1

"Richelle!" I fling myself out of my truck door. She's more than just a cousin. She's like my second sister.

"Story?" she says my name in more of a startled yelp than a word. "Where have you been?"

I give her a quick up and down assessment as she leaps from the stretcher. "Sit down! Are you injured?"

"You disappeared!" She crushes me against her in a bear hug.

"Are you hurt?"

"No, I'm doing good. Really good." She doesn't sound 'really good' to me. Richelle is normally the picture of happy confidence. Today her jade-green eyes are bright with tears.

The left side of her face has several abrasions. Her neck is mottled with the stress hives she and I get. A medic is trying to guide her back to the stretcher and she's being about as cooperative as a rabid skunk.

"The EMS bot said I can go home. Stop touching me!" She twitches away from his hands.

The monitor on her stretcher glows with green letters: *Patient is stable. Release to family.* Good! That's why she was able to hug me with her typical farm-girl strength.

"You said you don't have family to go home to. We legally have to transport you to the hospital," the medic tells her, warily eyeing her hands.

Ivan and I swap confused looks. Richelle has family. My family. Her six brothers. Her mom. Her dad. Though knowing The Bastion and AJA, it's a depressing coin toss whether her dad has been executed.

"I'm not going to the hospital!" she hisses. "Story, I'm sorry. So sorry for what Otto did to you." Interesting! She calls her dad Otto now after his betrayal.

"We have to follow protocol," the medic says. "You were living in your truck. It's totaled. You're coming with us."

What in the world? Her family's farm is one of the largest properties for several counties. It's not just space to live. You could easily disappear on those rolling hills.

I duck between her and the medic and lay an arm across her shoulders. "Richelle, you live in your truck?"

She turns to the medic. "Fine. Take me to the hospital."

"I'm going with you," I tell her, before turning to Ivan. "I'll be okay in SAM, right? No one can take me again?"

My stomach knots. Every instinct screams this is by far one of my dumbest ideas. Smile. Be tough for Richelle.

"You'll be safe wherever you go with SAM."

"Do you think it's safe for me to go back to Lancaster?"

"The investigation is ongoing. Her dad and brother who tried to abduct you are still in custody." He curls his fingers around my chin and tips my face up. "Richelle's been fully cleared. She wasn't involved with their attack on you."

Oh, Ivan, why can't you have just told me no?

I'm really going back to Lancaster. I can do this for Richelle. I think I can. No matter how hard I try, my eyes won't meet his questioning gaze.

"She shouldn't be alone. I'll ride in the ambulance with her."

Eyeballs, work with me! When they finally meet his, concern tightens into a hard look. For a moment, I see how intimidating my husband must be to everyone else.

"As a Commander of The Helm, where you're employed, I forbid it. Get back to your lab and work, Dr. Rhys."

That makes my heart race in a whole new way. Some women would be unhappy at the thought of being "forbidden" to do something by their husband. He's Ivan. He doesn't boss me around or make me feel lesser than him. We're partners in life. And right now, neither of us wants me to get broken ribs again from a trip to my hometown.

"Yes, Sir," I mutter, surrendering to the smile I reserve just for him. He squeezes my chin affectionately before releasing me.

"C'mere." He leads me to the stretcher where two medics are preparing Richelle for the ride. "Excuse me, guys, we need a minute. Hey, Richelle, I'm Ivan."

Her eyes sweep up and down his massive frame. He's wearing damp black swim trunks, a black button up linen shirt, and black running shoes with the laces tucked in the sides. She gives me a goofy smirk. "Secret man?"

"He's not a secret anymore, Richelle. He's my husband."

She does one of those hysterical laughs people call a guffaw, then nods approvingly. "Pleasure to meet you, Ivan..."

"Rhys," he supplies.

"Ivan and Story Rhys. I like it. You better deserve her." She wags an accusing finger at him.

"I think we're gonna be fast friends, Richelle. I've heard you're good with horses. And fixing things?"

He can't possibly be serious. No way. David will kill him.

Richelle steadily meets his eyes. "I grew up in a saddle. I can repair any engine you put in front of me. And I build and mend fences strong enough to keep Otto's bison burger herd contained."

A silent look of understanding passes between the two of them.

"Medics, my wife is a doctor. Can she sign to take Miss Ross to her clinic?"

"Thank you, Ivan!" I throw my arms around his ribs and pull him down to pepper his cheek with kisses. He's unfazed, swaying to the side without missing a beat. Richelle and the medics gawk at my smoochy spectacle. It probably makes them have serious doubts about my medical skills but releasing her to me would be less paperwork for them.

"You're willing to accept responsibility for her as your patient?" A man in a red medic uniform steps close to me, pulling out his phone.

"I am," I say, letting go of Ivan.

Handling a stable patient recovering from a car crash may be the easiest patient to ever roll through the doors of my Helm clinic.

"Sign here." He hands me his phone with a PDF open for transfer of care. "Miss Ross, let my coworker help you up."

I confer with him on her condition and assessments while his coworker unstraps her.

Richelle asks Ivan, "Dude. What happened to your face?"

Yup! She's fine.

Richelle asked us dozens of questions about life at The Helm on our way back. Explanations ensued on why my twenty-five-year-old husband is just now learning to drive.

She and I tried to stifle our shrieks as he flew around curves on blind hills that made our stomachs drop. He sprinkled in details of who he is and why his work is classified. Richelle squealed happily when he said if she proves herself trustworthy, he'll find her a spot working with me.

"You didn't kill us, great job, baby!" I tell him when he parks.

"Told 'ya we'd be fine." He winks, hopping out.

"So, this Helm hideaway place you all live is carved into old Ash Cave?" Richelle asks.

Ivan nods. "Yes. Doesn't feel like you're in a cave though. You'll see. It's nice in there."

"I'll keep an open mind," Richelle says.

She's so brave. I wish I could be like her. The first time I entered Hocking Forest, I was scared. She walks in beside us like she's heading into a coffee shop. Maybe if I'd been walking in with her and Ivan it would have felt different for me too.

Dad and Nathan Cantone, Ivan's buddy and right-hand man, are waiting for us at the Agora boundary.

"Really, Ivan?" Dad calls to us. "How many more stray Ross girls are you going to bring here?"

"Did you just call your own daughter, my wife, a stray?" Ivan thunders back. He and my dad have some kind of complicated relationship that's getting weirder lately.

"You know what I meant," Dad retorts with a chuckle.

"Enlighten me." Ivan cocks his head to the side, taking the reins for his beloved horse Obsidian from my dad.

"Nice to see you, Richelle." Dad smiles, walking his horse in a tight circle.

"Richelle, you ride my horse, Cloud," I tell her, giving Nathan a quick "Thanks," when I take the reins from him.

"Uncle Alan, is this a problem?" Richelle asks. "I don't need to be here. I don't need help. I have friends I can stay with. I'll go."

Ivan pulls me up behind him on Obsidian, then whispers over his shoulder, "Are you sure you and Richelle aren't sisters? I seem to recall a nearly identical conversation with you in May." He tries an awful impression of me, but his deep voice keeps cracking. "I don't need help. Don't kidnap me, Handsome Forest Man. Sorry I'm drooling down your back in this lightning shield you built me."

We're lost in a fit of happy newlywed laughs until Nathan pulls us back with a quiet, "Ivan."

Everyone is staring at us.

"I don't think it's a problem, but I'm not in charge," Dad says.

Ivan glances between Nathan and Dad, then speaks in his authoritative Commander Rhys voice. "Story needs to hire a real staff. Richelle, do you pinky promise to keep all this a secret?"

"I swear on my life!" she says, smiling.

"Do you accept a job here as Story's, let's call you a Trusted Advisor?" he asks.

"Sure do," Richelle says.

"Richelle, Otto really screwed things up between our families," Dad warns, obliterating her grin.

Ivan rocks his hips forward in the saddle and Obsidian walks. "I've already considered that. If I think, even for a second, you're going to betray her, I'll-"

Richelle cuts Ivan off, "Same to you, buddy! You've known her for like ten minutes. I've loved her since we were both in diapers. I'll turn you into hog food if you hurt my Story!"

Ivan laughs. "You'll do well here, Richelle. Let's get back."

As we approach the entrance to The Helm, Lark sprints at us.

"Story! You took out Francois' Agora!" she shouts. "He showed me. It looks great! Now he can do anything."

"I did...I sure did!" I stammer. Francois! Not cool. I wanted to talk to her about this, but I'm not sure how much she understands her health issues being caused by a malfunctioning Agora.

"Do mine next! Fix me! He said it was super easy and didn't hurt much. Can you do it before I start school? Or fall break? Please do it by winter break. I want to play in the snow and go sled riding without it going crazy. When? When can you do it?"

"Dad and I have to find the right doctor first, Lark." I slide off Obsidian's rump to walk into the entrance of The Helm with her.

My heart breaks watching her dance around, singing a song about "no more Agora." I don't have the heart to tell her that Agora removals are considered experimental. The Bastion said we have to bring them a mountain of case studies before ASTRA will approve her surgery.

Ivan and Dad wear the same smile, laced with silent despair. Thanks for the help, guys, really appreciate it.

She grabs Richelle by the hands, twirling her in a circle. "Did you hear that? Story is going to fix me! I'll never be put in a coma again! No more comas! No more hospital! No more MNP!"

2

My lab whiteboard is filled with names of commanders who need their surgeries done. Lark's name is written at the top, as always. Relentlessly chasing a way to save her has been the North Star of my life, leading me here.

"I've done two of these surgeries so far, Richelle. You need to learn about them as my Trusted Advisor. If you're cool with it, you'll be helping me plan, prep for, and manage my surgical schedule."

She sits at my desk, toying with a bin of dry erase markers. Having attached several of them into a long stick, she points to the list of names.

"So, these thirteen patients are the people running this show?"

"Kinda. They're commanders at this Helm. The Bastion said to get the people in charge done first."

"What if you slice their brains accidentally and kill all the bosses?"

"I don't do brain surgery, but yes, it's a risky procedure. The Agoras are a death sentence if not taken out. The Bastion wants Agoras out as soon as possible."

"Didn't The Bastion put them in there?"

"Yes."

"Then why do they want you to take these Agora things out?"

Moulson. I don't know what he did. He somehow persuaded them to let me remove Agoras. Ivan's theory is that Moulson either bombed them into submission or blackmailed half of The Bastion.

I shrug. "I'm getting to save lives, so I'm happy."

"These are some high-ranking guinea pigs. Don't mess up." She wags a finger at me. Thanks, Richelle. That's helping my anxiety.

"Tomorrow is Senior Commander David Delac's surgery," I say, drawing a star by his name. "Ivan's been going on about how awful that job is. He already works fifteen hours most days between tactical training and the control room."

She snaps her marker stick in half and says, "Ew."

"Speaking of ew. Look at how these awful things progress." I do a quick search for David's patient record and project years of MRI and angiogram scans onto the theater wall monitor.

I explain the images to Richelle, starting with the first scan from when David was ten, healthy, and Agora-free. Then the scumbag forest wardens and their ASTRA implanted the one-inch flat square neural chip low on the back of his neck. A week later, it had begun sending out its deadly tendrils. The Agora was bioengineered to extend sharp filaments and create a tangle of arteries and veins called an arteriovenous malformation, or AVM.

"So, Bastion put these in there like GPS murder blobs?" she asks and I nod yes. "If they go outside their boundary, it kills them?"

"Yes. It's a way to imprison them to get free labor from geniuses. See how these tendrils in his neck are ready to sever his vertebral arteries if he leaves the boundary?"

For the first time in our twenty-two years as best friends she's speechless.

"This is similar to what Ivan's Agora was like. His surgery was fairly easy. I hope David's will be too. INES. Wake up."

The large surgical robotic console beside me lights up and a woman's voice speaks. "Hello, Dr. Rhys. What are we doing today?"

"Please help us prep for an Agora removal tomorrow. Show an overlay of how the vessels should flow in this area in green. Show the neural chip and its tendrils in red. Highlight the AVM in yellow."

Richelle gasps when INES displays a map shining a spotlight on how wrong everything is in the back of David's neck.

"Done, Dr. Rhys."

"INES, make a note of the images I'm uploading to you right now. We need to pay close attention to the area with chronic changes from clotting and old bleeds."

"Yes, beautiful," INES replies in Ivan's voice.

"This is a weird robot. Why the voice change?" Richelle asks.

I laugh. "INES is an Ivan creation all the way. He built it to be arguably the most advanced surgical robotics system in the world, but he programmed it to speak to me in alternating voices. When INES uses his voice, it addresses me with pet names." Just talking about him makes my stomach leap.

"That's adorable. He can't keep it professional when it comes to you. I'm not getting 'I'm a super serious commander murder-y dude' vibes from him. Can't judge a book by its cover I guess."

"That's because Ivan's not a murderer."

She stretches, hitches to the side halfway through it, and pulls a face. "I'm pretty stoved up from the crash. I'm going to see if I remember how to get to your apartment and take a hot shower. Thanks for bringing me here. Night."

"I'm glad we're back together. Later!" I call over my shoulder to her. Focus.

I need to study for tomorrow. My third surgery. This is a huge deal. The other two were emergencies. This one is planned and The Bastion knows about it. He'll come in my OR awake. Talking. Then INES will use its anesthesia system to sedate him.

"INES. You ready for tomorrow?" I've lost it. Why am I asking a robot how it feels about something?

"I am. Will there be anything else?" INES asks.

"No. Thank you. See you in the morning. Power off."

"Night, then." The console goes dark.

The theater screen monitor powers on.

"Ivan?" Midnight surprise time from my love! Tonight is getting interesting. I smooth out my clothes and swipe my hair to the side. Wonder what he's gotta say. A video feed flashes on. What kind of sick joke is this?! I'm face-to-face with the piercing stare of Anthony Moulson. His ice blue eyes are identical to Lark's.

My mouth falls open. His twists into a predatory grin.

"I hate a cliché, but hands up, Story. Don't touch any panic buttons."

New prototype suggestion. Hands-free way to get help.

"How's your research coming?" Moulson asks.

Ivan, I need Ivan. How can I get him to help?

"Dr. Rhys. I'm a busy man." His singsong voice is disgusting.

"You're interrupting my research!" I blurt.

He scoffs. "Research? Spend less time on beach towels with Ivan. I was disappointed to have to herd you back here with the earthquake."

"I'm working with *INES. Right now.*"

INES console lights up. Yes!

"Good evening, Dr. Rhys," INES says. Moulson's face clouds.

"INES, power down," he orders.

"Dr. Rhys, do you want me to recognize and respond to that voice?"

"Shut it off," he says.

I clear my throat then say, "INES. Irontrace 3-9-1. Go to sleep."

INES cycles through a repeating fade of black gradients. It appears the console has shut down. It definitely didn't. "Moulson, you're interrupting my research."

"Work faster. Remember, if you aren't focusing, I'll stick you in a lab somewhere with no Ivan to distract you. Get Kate's surgery done." Oh, this is lovely. He's still calling Lark by the birth name he gave her.

"We can't do Lark's surgery without a lot more data."

"Stop calling her Lark! Her name is Kate. Kate Moulson! She's my daughter. I named her!" He stabs a well-manicured finger at the screen.

Don't flinch.

He can't get you. That's why he's so mad.

He may be her birth father, but he's a mass murderer. Any claim that DNA could give him has been severed.

I square my shoulders, stepping closer to the monitor. "Her name is Lark."

He smirks. "For now. How's married life?"

I pick a tiny piece of lint off my black scrub shirt and flick it towards the floor.

"Is Ivan treating you well?"

I twist my hair in a bun, grateful my surgeon-steady hands don't betray my racing heart.

He narrows his eyes. "I was hoping we could be friends. I see you're choosing to keep this business only. Get back to work. See you soon."

The monitor he was on powers off. He's gone. I did it! I stood up to him. Ha!

Immediate regret. A cold sweat hits. Why would I talk to him like that? He wants Ivan dead. I should've just pushed my panic button. What if he retaliates? A horrible wave of nausea hits. He's watching. In here. On the beach. In our apartment. Everywhere. I can't escape.

And now I've made him angrier.

My stomach revolts and I barely make it to the medical waste bin. It's empty, thank heavens. But still, this wasn't my finest moment. I sink onto the top step. The cold steel floor soothes the fire on my cheeks. Maybe I'll just lie here. It's after midnight and I haven't slept in what, eighteen hours? Moulson wins for today.

I'm a planner. Time to tank my fragile mental health even more by dwelling on what could happen next. That's considered planning, right? Let's run through some scenarios of what tomorrow could bring.

The Bastion finds out I know Anthony Moulson, the world's most-wanted man, is masquerading as Mark Guthrie and I didn't tell anyone because he threatened to kill Ivan. They execute me. Not ideal.

Moulson sends a drone and kills Ivan. I die of heartbreak.

I can't do research fast enough and Lark's malfunctioning Agora ruptures. Near instant death for her.

One of us doesn't make it, no matter which way this goes. I can't plan my way out of this one.

"Whatcha doing, baby?" Ivan's voice comes from INES' console. "INES pinged my employee ID number, but I was fixing a broken air traffic control unit. Kinda critical. Why are you laying on the floor?"

"Hi. You're watching me too?"

"Too?" he growls.

I raise my hand in a silent thumbs up.

"Ivan?" No answer. Great. I scared my new husband off.

Suck it up, move. I pull myself up with the rail and walk to the bathroom in the corner of the lab to brush my teeth. This was a horrible way to end such a great day.

When I emerge feeling much fresher, Ivan is typing fast into the console that makes up INES' brain.

"What happened?" He rushes down the steps.

"I got really tired, and the cold floor felt nice. I think I'm a bit sunburned from the beach." He wraps me in the most all-consuming Ivan embrace. I slide my hands under the back of his shirt. Once they're hidden from view, I push the emerald to activate SAM. As expected, digital Story and Ivan appear.

"Okay, now tell me what really happened, my love," Ivan says.

"Moulson turned on a monitor and was in here being a creep."

His panicky grip squeaks the air from my lungs. "What!? Are you okay? What did he say?"

"First thing he said was not to hit my panic button. Then he said to spend less time on beach towels with you. He said he herded us back with the quake. Did many people get hurt?"

He scrunches up his face but doesn't speak.

"Ivan, did anyone die?"

"No. He hit mostly unpopulated areas. You need some rest." He holds my face in his palms, gently rubbing my cheeks with his thumbs.

"What time will you be off work?" I ask.

"I don't know, maybe around noon. They assigned me extra hours in tactical sims and fitness training tonight."

"Noon! Twelve hours from now, noon?"

He kisses my forehead. "I have to make up time for going to the beach. I sent all of INES' recording data to my workstation. I'll come up with some extra safeguards tonight."

"Thank you."

"Can I walk you home? I have a few minutes."

"Sure. Richelle should be there already." I reach to shut SAM off and he catches my hand.

"No, not yet. This is our last time together before I step in as Senior Commander. My schedule will be absolute garbage then. Let's make the most of our walk back." I laugh when he drapes an arm over my shoulders, turning me close to him.

"It can't be much worse than it is now," I tell him confidently.

"I promise it will be, sorry." His voice makes me pause.

"Don't worry, my love. It's only two weeks." Surely, those words won't come back to bite me. For now, it puts a smile on his face. I hope it lasts.

3

"Nohohohooo." I swipe the screen of my phone to shut my alarm off. Six o'clock came around way too early. David's surgery is in four hours, and I want to go prep.

If I can move. This cocoon of blankets Ivan tucked me in last night stayed wrapped tight. It would be a crime to undo his work, at least for a few more minutes.

"Story?" Richelle mumbles from Ivan's side of the bed.

"You can go back to sleep."

"Nah, time to go watch you cut a brain open for the first time."

I can't help laughing as I wiggle free. "Again, that's not what we're doing. I'm gonna get ready."

David's surgery should be the easiest one I've done. Ivan's is a blur. Any memories of it are like a shadowy panic attack that only ended when I sent him to recovery. Francois' surgery was complicated. He'd crossed the boundary that day, causing an Agora injury that I had to fix on the fly in the OR. Scary, but I did it.

I can do this, too. I can save our friend. When I come out of the shower, dressed and ready, Richelle hands me a cup of iced coffee.

"First Trusted Advisor job of the day? Caffeinate the surgeon!"

"Thanks," I say, taking a long swig.

Immediate regret. The taste of my beloved coffee turns my stomach. My summer of nonstop horror must've given me an ulcer.

"Mmmm. Tastes great, I've gotta get to work," I say, abandoning the cup on the counter.

In the lab, Dad is surrounded by his top picks for surgical staff.

My friend from the clinic, Commander Mai Voss, shoots me a sneaky wave. She's the top engineer for cutting-edge ORION nurse units.

"You're here!" I mouth to her and grin.

My packed lab is a breath of fresh air. The more the merrier to keep Moulson out of here. Two hours pass as Dad and I run through an overview of the surgery with our new team.

"Morning, David," I say, flicking my eyes to the screen above him. Green check boxes are filled in next to Patient Education, Consent Signed, Discharge Instructions, Recovery Plan.

"Morning. Story, you sure you're feeling up to this after dying last month?" David asks from the operating table.

"I'm fine. Promise." I've already proven my skills under pressure. Ulcers & anxiety can't stop me.

"Girl, what?" Richelle exclaims from the platform steps, prompting the room to collectively turn our way. "Did Otto do that?"

"No, it happened when I got arrested for treason," I whisper.

"Don't whisper in front of your patients, Dr. Rhys," David says. "Who's your friend?"

Richelle hops up the steps and leans over David, her strawberry blonde braids hanging between them.

"Hi! Richelle Ross. Don't worry, I'm not going to watch your surgery. Blood is super gross. No desire to see that. Not much blood though, right, Story?" She pauses to glance my way. I nod. A conspiratorial look takes over and she whispers to David, "She's supposed to be good at this. You'll be fine. Probably. I don't know, honestly."

Wow. She's really bad with patients. Confidently bad though. Maybe that counts for something and she'll figure it out. David's heart rate is gradually increasing on the monitor. His baseline of mid-sixties is now hovering in the high eighties. I should make her leave the poor man alone soon.

"Ivan hired you, right?" he asks.

"Yes! I went from farm girl to Trusted Advisor for Story. But I'm thinking of being her bodyguard." She fakes some terrible karate kicks in the direction of David's shoulder. He watches her, unflinching. "Touch her and die, you know, that kind of stuff."

His heart rate is now in the low hundreds. Hard to say if he's going to kill us both or loving her wildly un-Irontrace-like antics.

"I see why Ivan likes you," he says once she stops.

"Richelle, I need to finish prepping him. Can you head back to my desk so we can get the sterile field ready?"

"Sure!" She doesn't. Instead, she leans over and tilts her face parallel to David's. "Listen, we need to form an alliance. You give me all the dirt on Ivan. I'll give you all the juicy deets on Story. Deal?"

He nods slowly. "I guess?"

"It's a date. See ya soon, Davey boy." With a quick ruffle of his hair, she bounces down the steps.

He looks at me, lips twitching down at the corners.

"Time for your party hat." I stretch his puffy bouffant cap and put it on his head. "Sorry about Richelle. At least you never have to guess where you stand with her."

It's got to be weird to be an Irontrace. No family. I'm the closest thing he's got to a support system right now.

"You ready, David?" I ask, trying to sound calm and steady, not like I'm about to slice his neck open.

"Knock me out. This thing could blow any minute." He doesn't look my way. He's openly staring at Richelle while she flips through an upside-down angiogram manual.

"Here we go then. INES, initiate patient anesthesia and positioning protocols."

The ceiling above the operating platform resembles a steel honeycomb. Its vacuum-sealed chambers sterilize and hold INES' many attachments. David's eyes widen as the arms lower in a slow dance.

He needs a distraction. "So, you've been here since you were ten years old. Where do you want to go once you're free?" I ask him.

The anesthesia module administers the mix of sedation meds in his IV as he replies, "I'm from a village outside of Vancouver called Glass Bay. Since the day my parents sold me to The Bastion, I've wanted to kayak up there-"

"Sedation target achieved," INES says. Three arms shoot down to work on his next prep stages.

"Dad, time to scrub. Ivan's broadcasting this with a thirty-second delay to facilities all over the world."

Moments later, we're ready. Our eyes meet and he hands me a scalpel. *Showtime.*

My dad has been training surgical robots, up-and-coming students, and other doctors for longer than I've been alive. His professor voice rings out, and I see his eyes crinkle, betraying a grin hiding behind his surgical mask. "Welcome to the Rhys Method of AVM removal."

Psht. If it was an 'AVM removal,' that would be a whole different story. Calling it what it really is, an Agora removal, would be much harder to explain.

"Can I give Dr. Rhys the introduction she has earned?" Moulson's voice cuts through my OR.

My scalpel drops silently to the floor. The rustle of my surgical gown as I jerk to dodge the scalpel from landing on my foot is not so silent. He's here. Where? Breathe. You have to look like a professional. You *are* a professional.

"I'm Councilman Mark Guthrie, the newest member of The Bastion." *No, you're not! You're Anthony Moulson.* "Myself, the rest of The Bastion, and hundreds of healthcare and education facilities are tied in today to watch you make history."

"Did you get consent from my patient for this?" I snap.

"They did. I confirmed it," Ivan says from the control room video feed. "David wanted to make you famous."

David! A little warning would've been fantastic.

"Thank you, Senior Commander Rhys," Guthrie continues, "The exceptional surgeon we're about to watch is a trailblazer. For decades, human surgeons were banned from operating rooms, limited to training surgical robots to work in their place. Dr. Rhys viewed this as unacceptable. Driven by a fervor to save her sister, she bravely cast herself into the role of the first Bastion-approved surgeon since 2025. Learn from her. Join her. Put humanity back in healthcare."

Applause breaks out from the monitors. This surgery has to go perfectly. I already dropped a scalpel. That's a hit to my baby credibility.

Don't let Moulson know he got to you. Suck it up. Be brave. Make precise cuts.

"Thank you for joining us. Please feel free to ask questions as we go," I say. Dad's eyes are clearly pleading with me not to drop this one too as he hands me a second scalpel. "Ivan, are you there still?"

"I am," he says. "Ready to detonate the Agora. Now?"

"Yes."

"Done. Makes me so happy to blow those things up." Ivan laughs. You can practically feel the smoke coming out of The Bastion's ears to watch their creation have been so easily destroyed.

I hold my breath and stare at David's monitor screens. The detonation worked. Vitals are stable. No change to his brain, nerve, or muscle function. First hurdle of the surgery is done.

"You're happy to blow anything up, SC Rhys," I say. Knock it off. Now's not the time to joke with Ivan. A ripple of laughs from the spectators puts me at ease. "Looks good. Thank you."

"No problem. I'll be here if you need me."

Now it's really showtime. Don't mess up. Dad, INES, and I spent the next four hours and twenty-one minutes working through a flawless Agora removal. Dad fielded the dozens of questions that came in. I gave technical explanations of removing the AVM, the neural chip, tendrils, and closing with a bioengineered rapid-heal skin graft.

My mask pushes up in my bottom lashes from a huge grin. Moulson didn't break me. He didn't fluster me. I saved my friend, David. He'll be back as Senior Commander again in two weeks. I'll travel the world, getting the data I need to prove the Rhys Method works and assemble a dream team for Lark's Agora removal.

I'm so happy I could *puke.*

4

Since my poisoning, my whole body has been off kilter. That seems to track as a side effect of dying. To put my mind at ease, I'll run a stat HCG for a fast yes or no answer.

I hit *Submit* to order the lab work then stick my arm in the blood draw tunnel on INES.

"Dr. Rhys. Remain still." INES expertly takes a sample from the antecubital space in the bend of my arm. As the tube whirs up into the ceiling, INES flashes a pressure bandage over the site, then says, "Stat results will be available in ninety seconds."

"Ninety seconds," I mutter. "Might as well be an hour."

I've been cooped up in here all day. I feel like if I don't go for a run I'm going to spontaneously combust. "Stretch, I'll do some runner's stretches."

INES beeps. These results won't change anything. They'll confirm that I've got stomach issues from anxiety and then I'll laugh with Ivan about this over margaritas tonight.

"Look? Don't look?" I bounce back and forth on the balls of my feet. I spent twenty days in and out of a coma. No wonder I have no idea what's up with my body. It's easy to lose track of your calendar when you missed three weeks of life.

"A quick peek won't hurt anything."

I click on the *Available Test Result* banner that pops up. A squeal of terror and excitement and something I can't define escapes.

Stat HCG: HIGH 229,301. Value indicates patient is seven weeks, two days pregnant.

Pregnant!

Bad timing. Awful timing. Great. A new anxiety to dwell on. A voice like an auctioneer takes off in my mind, racing through what complications my recent health issues could've caused.

The slam of my lab door opening so hard it crashes into the wall behind it nearly makes me faint. Ivan doesn't even look at me. He barrels past in a full sprint to INES main console.

"Hi!" I tug his shirt, trying to turn him to face me. He doesn't budge. Doesn't talk. The only sound is his lightning-fast fingers on the keyboard. "Hey, I need to talk to you."

He spins, leaning in like he's going to kiss me but instead, whispers onto my lips, "Stop, wait, please." He turns back to the computer console.

Unbelievable. He's got to stop working for a few minutes.

"Uhm, Ivan. I did some labs."

He whips back around and wraps me in a frantic hug. He whispers in my ear, barely louder than an exhale. "Seriously. Stop. Turn on SAM."

This is not how I saw this moment going. Maybe Moulson is coming for me again and he's freaking out. Nothing could have gotten Senior Commander Rhys to leave the control room unless the world is ending.

I lean around his shoulder to catch part of what he's typing.

```
mv /labresults/StoryRhys/statlabs /home/ivanrhys/.statlabs
chown ivanrhys:ivanrhys /home/ivanrhys/.statlabs
chmod 600 /home/ivanrhys/.statlabs
chattr +i /home/ivanrhys/.statlabs
```

Gibberish.

He logs off the console and exhales with a huff. Maybe he just needs a minute to breathe and gather his thoughts from a rough first day as the big boss man? He laces his fingers on the back of his head, taking several deep breaths. After what feels like a small eternity, he pulls my hand up to his mouth to kiss it.

"Hello, my love. What did you want to tell me?"

The smile behind his keen eyes and upwards tilt at the corner of his full lips is fairly bursting with expectation. Yet he's patient, watchful. He knows already. How?

Well, now I don't feel like blurting it out.

"What did you do there with INES?"

"Work stuff."

"Sounds stressful." I turn to sit on the platform steps again.

"Not really." He walks down several steps and faces me, tucking a stray curl behind my ear. "Congrats on another successful surgery. I was in a worldwide conference call just now. The Bastion is raving about their new darling surgeon."

"Sounds important. Should you still be in there?"

"Oh, it is important. I'm currently derelict-ing my duty to be here." He grins and nods.

"You're gonna be in trouble." I try to sound like I'm scolding him, but he's grinning like a fool, staring at me, which makes me do the same.

"Impossible. I'm the boss now. Come. You need a better spot to sit."

"Why?"

"Because I love you and want you to sit on nice things like my lap. Not those cold stairs, covered with pathogens of unknown etiology."

I walk past his outstretched hand, just to drive him crazy. It works. He laughs, grabbing me from behind in a bear hug.

"You sound like a doctor," I say as we stumble more than walk to the couch.

"I dabble in healthcare. One thing I'm exceptionally good at is reading lab results."

I'm gonna make him work for it. "Seen any interesting ones lately?"

"I respect patient confidentiality. Especially of my employees here at The Helm."

Slick, Ivan.

"Does that apply to spouses?"

He shrugs. "Grey area. There's only one Irontrace who ever loved someone enough to demand permission to get married. The husband is an open book to her. His wife," he drops his voice to a whisper, "don't get jealous, but I've heard she's *stunning*." I crack up. "He doesn't have clearance to view her medical record. He'd never ask her for such permission because he respects her autonomy far too much."

"How would he know if she gets lab work then?"

"If he's halfway decent at ensuring her safety, any file created with her name or other metadata attached would automatically send him an emergency alert."

I scurry to my desk. "Give me a few days. I'll do policy research and write up a stack of forms for her to fill out so he can access her medical information." I shuffle through papers, stopping to scribble a small note.

"No pressure for the lovely wife to reveal her secrets. I love a good air of mystery. Keeps life interesting."

"Sorry to disappoint. I don't want to have secrets from you." I step in front of him, offering the paper.

My love, we are having a baby. I love you so much I could puke. Again.

He pulls me forward to stand between his knees and smiles up at me with a perfect Ivan grin.

"Story." His voice chokes up. He stops to clear his throat. A warm, happy feeling settles in my chest when he hugs me around the waist, resting his cheek on my lower stomach. "Story. You've had a bad few months, health-wise. You're kind of a mess. How are you feeling?"

"You nailed it. I feel messy. We're going to Australia in a couple of weeks to train new surgeons. I'm stressed. Nauseous. Tired. My heart is...I think this is why I've been having palpitations and feeling light-headed."

"What can I do for you?" He pulls me to sit with him.

"This." I flop into his arms. "I'm also incredibly happy. It's like fire-works inside me. You're my favorite person in the world and we made a whole new person. Can you believe it?" I jerk bolt upright. "You'll have a blood relative in your life again! They're tiny right now. But it's your flesh and blood, Ivan."

"Okay. You're okay, right?" He pauses until I nod yes. "The timing is really not my favorite." He grimaces, but then his beaming smile spreads back over his face as he wipes my happy tears. Good to know I'm not in turmoil alone. He's a mess too. "If you're happy and okay, then this is perfect. Like, *perfect* perfect. We can never be truly ready for some things in life, right? We'll take it as it comes. We'll adapt."

I laugh at this first attempt of fatherly bravado.

"You were a dying bachelor ninety days ago. Now you're married, healthy, and having a kid. Are you okay?"

"Okay? Hah. I'm okay. I'm waaaay better than okay. Everything is fine, it's going to be a-okay." His expansive vocabulary has been replaced by "okay" apparently. "I'm thinking, I'm processing. Okay. Are you done in here for the day?"

"Yes."

"Are you tired, hungry, thirsty?"

"Yes," I say. He laughs. "I could also puke. You're in the danger zone."

"What can I do for you?"

Fix Lark. Arrest Moulson. Buy us a house.

"I know this isn't the best suggestion because you're Senior Commander. But do you think I could just be the clingiest wife ever? We've been pulled apart too much. I can't stand it anymore. I want to be stuck on you like this."

I spin facing him, wrapping my arms and legs around him. He's trapped but looks like he's right where he wants to be.

"Sounds perfect to me, my octopus wife." The familiar embrace he wraps me in holds my ribs and shoulders a bit too tight. It feels like my lungs can't quite expand all the way. If anyone else hugged me like this, I'd have a panic attack. If Ivan stopped hugging me like this, it would feel like he's giving me the silent treatment.

Besides, who needs oxygen saturation of 100% when you could have an Ivan hug?

"Okay. I made plans," he announces.

"For what?"

"Safety. I'll set up a workstation in your lab to guard you. I'm creating a supplementary detail for when I'm not available over the next two weeks. Air Titans will take care of your transport. No more horseback riding. Plan whatever apartment renovations you want."

"You thought of all that in less than a minute?"

"And more, but let's get you food and drinks first. Are you telling your family?"

"We're having a baby. There. I just told my family. No one else needs to know yet." His lips curve into a hopeful smile that sends fresh tears falling. "I don't know if my coma and poisoning hurt the baby. I wish I had more info."

He looks thoughtful. "You would've been barely pregnant when they took you. I'm thinking if the baby has made it to seven weeks and your HCG is that high then the baby is fine, but we don't have to wait around and find out. Do you want a health panel run?"

"I do."

"Piece of cake in 2050. I'll write one now."

"What do you mean?"

He guides me to my feet, leading me to the INES console. "For the first fourteen years I was here, I worked in, then ran the biomed engineering, medical devices, and genome lab. It was too much once I became Commander. I had to give it up."

"I knew you're a doctor!"

"I do not have a doctorate in anything. Therefore, I'm not a doctor. Plus, Commanders get to blow stuff up. They said that and I abandoned my lab so fast my chair spun." He stops typing and turns to me. "What do you want to know?"

"Everything. Every data point you can get."

"You sure?"

"Yes. Is that okay with you?"

"Of course. I'll use your blood sample from earlier."

"Thanks."

He works quietly for a few minutes. Finally, he sighs and turns, putting his hands on my shoulders. "Okay, INES did it. Found fetal DNA in your blood sample. I tested everything we possibly could. You ready?"

"Yes."

"By the way, congrats!" He pauses, both eyes widening at the screen.

His jaw twitches so hard he may have cracked a molar. That is no good. Something is very wrong.

"Girl! Baby girl. No identified health concerns. Black hair. Olive skin. Brown eyes. She's my mini-me, sorry, love." He grabs me in a fierce hug. "What am I saying? I'm gonna be a dad! Gotta get used to that. Oh, she has curly hair like you. I hope she has your brains and heart too."

Picturing this perfect little Ivan and Story creation is too much. I wrap both arms around his ribs and bounce with excitement.

"We're not done yet." He bites his lip, peering at the screen with a lopsided squint. "Baby boy too! Healthy little guy," he says, pride swelling in his voice.

My arms drop from around him. I love his sense of humor. Just not right now.

"Not funny." I bump him over with my hip to look at the screen.

"Not joking, baby." His deer-in-the-headlights expression sobers me instantly. "We're one step at a time people. He has red hair like you. Well, not right now, but he will."

I'm on the verge of collapse. When the world is running along perfectly, a twin pregnancy comes with risks. Complications. Twins? In 2050? How will I do long days in surgery in my third trimester?

"Baby, you still okay?" He pulls me against him.

No words come out. I just mumble happy, scared, grumbles into his chest.

He continues, "No issues identified with organogenesis for either baby. They're as healthy as can be at this stage. You are too."

"Can I be in SAM while pregnant?"

"Yeah, you're all fine." He's scrolling fast from top to bottom, reading the results over and over. He stops and picks me up in a burst of excitement. He carefully spins with me. "You're *all* fine. What a day!"

"So now you're an OBGYN too?" I tease.

"I should add that to my resume. We need a code word for..." He waves his hand to motion from my head to feet.

"They made it through everything with me. We need a super tough code name. Athena, Ares, Catherine, Tecumseh, Minerva, Aurora,

Persephone-"

"Holly!" he blurts.

"Holly?" I laugh. Weak little red berries?

"Those plants are super hardy survivors. Holly leaves are a bit stabby like their surgeon mom. The berries? Bright. Beautiful, like you."

"Holly." My lips curve into a grin, testing it out.

"When I first came here as a kid, it was a nasty Ohio February. I was scared to fall off Obsidian on patrols because he would slip on icy sandstone. I walked beside him for hours and got back late every time. It was miserable. I didn't understand how my parents could just give me up, sell me like that."

Danger. Full hormone meltdown coming.

"When I'd see holly plants peeking out of the snow, ice, mud, it was a reminder that if those tiny plants could make it, I could too. I just had to stay alive and better days would come. Now I'm here with you."

"Can we not use Holly for a code name?" I ask. He shrugs and nods before I quickly add, "I'd like that to be her real name. Your indestructible little Holly Rhys. Got any boy names?"

"You are just gonna name all these kids right now, huh?" He laughs and twists one of my curls around his fingers. "Hmm, there's berry plants here, huckleberries. They grow in awful soil. They come back quickly after fires or other disasters. I've read some random legends about knights rescuing damsels in distress getting huckleberry garlands to wear into battle as tokens of thanks. Huck?"

I grin. "Holly and Huck."

"Ilex opaca is the scientific name for the holly around here. I'm building Project Ilex to keep you all safe."

"You are *such* a nerd, baby."

"I'm *your* nerd. I'll use this massive brain for you any day." He points to his head, making sure to flex his arm like some kind of superhero scientist in the process. *That is COMPLETELY unfair to his pregnant wife...* "Don't worry at all. If you're really good?" I nod fast. "Then we've got this."

The confidence in his voice fools me into believing him.

Almost.

5

Watching Lark and her best friend, a young Irontrace named Francois, ride their horses takes up the rest of my evening. I try to stay present in the moment, but it's impossible. My life is unrecognizable from this time last year. I feel light enough to float away from happiness. Being married to Ivan still seems unreal sometimes, and our secret I'm carrying has planted a smile on my face I can't shake.

"Five more minutes please!" Lark yells, trotting her horse through the water of Cedar Falls.

"It's nearly dark. I've given you five extra minutes ten times," I yell. She's so happy. A third of her life has been spent in hospitals. Can't blame her for squeezing all the fun out of each day.

"Fiiiiiine! But this was the best day ever. Did you see Storm and I canter under the falls? The water almost knocked me down. Can we come here again tomorrow? I saw pretty rocks I have to come back for. I'm gonna use them to make a late wedding present for you and Ivan."

I admire Lark's endless ideas. She's a smart, creative kid, and her thoughts flow faster than the water over the falls.

As she spouts more plans, Commander Nathan Cantone's whispered voice over my shoulder makes me flinch. "Story, we're going to hand walk the horses back with you and Richelle. Ivan will break my neck if I leave you out here and ride back."

Ivan would today. That's for sure.

"Thanks, Nathan," is all I say. I'm tempted to tell him to warn me next time instead of mysteriously appearing at my ear from behind, but Richelle breaks the moment.

"I've dreamed of sneaking around the guards into the forest my whole life," Richelle says. "Who knew the key to getting in here was you falling for your hunk of a prisoner?" She elbows me and laughs.

"*Former* prisoner." I snort, wrapping my towel over my shoulders. The sun has set and it's getting chilly. My engagement ring softly buzzes as a check-in from Ivan. "I'm fine, baby," I whisper, squeezing the button on it to let him know I'm okay.

"Story, we should sing our vacation song!" Lark skips over to me, her dutiful horse plodding along behind her. "I know it's not a road trip, but we're in a special place. Let's teach it to Francois." She taps her reins on her palm and belts our family's car song:

"When we're driving on the road,

Stacked suitcases about to explode,

Dad missed the exit once, then twice,

The surprise detours were nice,

Mom hit a bump, splashed drinks everywhere,

How did this gum get in my hair?"

Lark goes silent, leaving me singing far too loud by myself.

"Story." She chokes out, gripping my waist.

"Lark?"

"It's not your fault," she says.

Not my fault? "Hey, hey, hey, what's wrong?" I ask, panic rising in my throat. Why bother asking? "Richelle!" I hiss.

Lark's hands fly to the back of her neck over her Agora and her breath shudders. *No! This can't happen out here.*

I hug her tight to keep her from falling. She tears at the Agora, her raspy breaths giving way to sobs of agony.

She's wrong. This is my fault.

What if those are her last words to me, ever? What if she really thinks it is my fault? Why am I out here instead of doing research? Every moment of my life should go to finding a way to save her.

"Lark, honey, I'm here." I drop to my knees, grappling to get control of her hands.

When she's in pain like this, panic sets in. Her instinct is to get rid of the source of pain. But when dealing with fragile arteries and veins that make up an Agora, the last thing she needs is more tissue damage. I catch her hands and tuck them under my elbows.

Over her shoulder, I see the MNP's artificial blood vessels growing, spreading out from her Agora. The black tendrils snake relentlessly across the back of her neck. How far will it grow this time before we can stop it?

"It's moving too fast," I breathe to myself.

"What can I do?" Nathan drops to my side.

"Call my dad," I say.

Francois hands his first aid kit to Mai. She tears it open.

"Francois, Mai, come help me build a stretcher. Let them focus on Lark," Richelle commands, digging through the fallen logs.

"Lark, you're okay," I say, checking her pulse.

Lie. Nothing about this is okay. No person—let alone a child—should have had a tangled web of neural chip and bioengineered, angry AVM tissue implanted in such a delicate, devastating area. There's nothing we can do to help her out here.

"Breathe with me, Lark. We'll have you back to the clinic in no time." I wiggle to shift her on her left side. "Here, cuddle up like this. We've got it now. You're gonna be fine. They're making you a bed right now."

A new wave of pain hits and she straightens out, nearly falling from my arms. We have to get out of here, but I can't move her yet.

"What is in this bag?" I snatch the first aid kit from Mai and dump it beside me. Neovascular repair meds. Various bandages and wound care items. Useless. She needs a hospital. The repair meds can't hurt though. I press them in Mai's hand. "We've gotta do something. Load a peds dose and give it in her vastus lateralis. Hand me the morpentanyl."

"Story, it's your dad." Nathan holds the phone in my face.

I don't look at it. I place the resp mask over her nose, mouth, and chin and give her an inhaled dose of pain meds. That dose would render my legs useless, but it'll lower her pain just enough to break her free from the spasm she's locked in.

"Let's count to ten, Lark. You'll feel better. One, two, three..." By ten she's still miserable, but the terrifying rigidity has left her spine and limbs.

"Ivan said you're 0.9 miles from the upper entrance of The Helm. He can walk you through building a travois as a stretcher," Dad says.

"Already done!" Richelle and her little team run over. They'd rigged the thick beach blanket along two logs and then lashed it in place with clips and paracord from Francois' saddlebags.

Cantone nods approvingly at Richelle. She may be a goofball, but she's never let me down. I'm so grateful she's here.

"How are you feeling, Lark?" Dad asks, in his calm doctor's voice. He has to know she can't answer him.

The Agora tendrils seem to be reaching farther and wider than normal this time. "Lark, it's okay. I'm here. We're going to pick you up and get you back," I say, stroking her hair.

"Put her on the stretcher, and sprint." Dad's voice cracks.

"No. Don't focus on speed. Get here safely. If they run, they could slip and injure Lark," Ivan says through the phone speaker. "I sent a support team. Start back on path 4B, Cantone. They'll be there any minute."

Mai, Richelle, and I transfer Lark to the stretcher and arrange a beach towel over her.

"Help," she pants, clutching my hands to her forehead.

"We'll have you back in no time," I promise. Years of being Lark's rock give me strength to help her on autopilot. But my body is at war with me right now. My stomach lurches hard enough to fold me in half. "Grab her!" *Now is not the time, babies!*

"Sorry Story, you must be so upset," Mai says as she and Richelle transfer Lark from my lap to their stretcher. "We've got her. We've got both of you."

"What's happening?" Ivan snaps.

"Story is having a uh...some kind of moment over there," Nathan stares at me while I fan my face.

"I'm fine, Ivan," I say. "It's going to be a bumpy ride, Lark. We're putting some stretchy bands around you so you won't fall. Just lay still, we'll be back soon." I help Mai finish wrapping the cords to restrain Lark. "Francois, pony the two horses to your saddle. Everybody grabs part of the stretcher. Let's go. Three, two, one."

Mai and Richelle have the head of the stretcher; Nathan and I are by Lark's feet.

"Up you go, you want me to tell you a story?" Richelle asks Lark. Lark doesn't answer. She's on her side, silently crying into her hands. My poor little Lark. I have to fix her.

"Cantone. Check your messages," Ivan barks.

Nathan swipes the phone screen with his free hand, then bumps me with his shoulder. "Let go, Story. I've got this end."

"No," I shoot back.

"You have to." He shows me a text from Ivan.

Story's hands stay free. She touches nothing. She carries nothing.

He puts his phone in his shirt pocket then grabs the log end I'm holding. "We got this. She weighs like sixty pounds. Go. Hold her hand." He gives a reassuring smile that does absolutely nothing to reassure me.

"Thanks." I jog a couple of steps to be by her head. "Lark, it won't be long and we'll get you feeling better."

The pain on her face deepens. She knows I mean another hospital stay. I rub her shoulder, unsure if it's to soothe myself or her. She peeks one teary eye open to look at me in the moonlight. The black tendrils of the MNP under her skin now reach from the back of her neck to her collarbones.

"Did you have fun today? I had the best time with you." I don't think I've ever cried at Lark during one of her Agora episodes. Tonight, my tears fall freely. "You'll feel better and start fourth grade in a few days. I saw the letter Mom put on the fridge about your teacher. I'll take you school clothes shopping this week. We'll have a blast."

She doesn't answer but gives me a quivering thumbs down. Guess it's time to shut up.

Lark grabs my wrist with her tiny pale hand in a vice-like grasp. "St..." Whatever she was going to say is lost. Eyes closed, she flails a hand in the air, reaching for me.

No! The black tendrils of the MNP snake along her collarbones, up her throat.

"Run. We have to run," I whisper, and take off in a jog.

"Reinforcements are here!" Mai shouts.

I could sob. Lights bob up and down rapidly from the path ahead. We must be so close.

"Almost there. Look at all the lights on tonight." Mai tips her chin at the path ahead.

The upper entrance is bustling with activity.

"Lark, we're almost to the clinic. We've got you," I tell her, gripping her arm, but she's lost in a sea of agony and tears.

A familiar tall outline appears, running at a full sprint towards us. Ivan. The lights behind him show his hands are full.

In seconds, he's huffing at my side. "Scoot, baby, I can help her." He sticks an emergency assessment pod on the left side of her neck. "Hey Lark, we got you." He gives her a quick grin.

Aside from wails, she doesn't reply. His face hardens.

The assessment pod speaks, "Patient assessment complete." Glowing blue results hover in the darkness above Lark. "Patient is critical. Rapidly spreading MNP detected. Pain receptors overwhelmed. Widespread systemic inflammation. Recommendation: sedate patient to interrupt MNP cascade and do further evaluation."

It's happening again. Another coma.

"Love you so much, Lark," I choke.

She doesn't look up. I don't even know if she heard me. I crouch in front of her, smoothing her hair down and repeating "I love you" over and over.

Ivan tears the cap off a syringe with his teeth and injects something in her thigh. "See you soon, little one. We're all right here."

She reaches a hand up towards him. He catches it, giving it a comforting squeeze. Her arm goes limp. He gently tucks it by her.

"Arrrggghh!" His deep voice vents pure rage with that one syllable.

"Get her on her back, Mai."

Ivan yanks an auto-IV sleeve from his thigh pocket. Tubing runs from the sleeve to a small saline bag in his shirt pocket. He slides the clear sleeve on her arm. It flawlessly inserts the IV. Seconds later, saline and sedatives flow.

"Hold this, please." He hands the bag to me.

Ivan pulls a face mask in a sterile package from his cargo pocket on his pants. He tears it open before he firmly presses its rubbery edges on her face. He tips her chin up, rocking her head backwards and rips a tab off the side of the mask. An endotracheal tube is deployed into her throat. The whole mask suctions around the lower half of her face.

We're all silent as a whirring sound fills the air. Green numbers and vital sign monitoring waves bloom around the edges of her mask.

"Pulse ox is 99%. Heart rate is elevated at 158, but it'll come down now." Ivan blows out a sigh.

"Thank you," I say, tracing the corners of Lark's IV bag.

She's still here.

"Let's get her settled in the clinic," Ivan says.

"Lark!" Mom screams, dragging Dad behind her. Mom pins Lark's limp hand to her cheek. "It'll be okay. We're here now. We've got you." Mom flashes me a nasty look. "Story! She can't handle that much activity. You know better."

Her ALICE always says *activity as tolerated*. She was fine. Happy.

"Amelia! This is not Story's fault. At all," Dad says, not looking up from scrutinizing the vitals on her mask.

"No. She should've brought her back hours ago," Mom says tersely.

Dad pushes the button to cycle Lark's vital signs again.

"I've done much worse than ride horses with one of those. Her day of fun didn't cause this," Ivan says gently.

"You're not a nine-year-old girl with an AVM!" Mom screeches back.

"Sorry, you're right," Ivan says.

"Ivan was a nine-year-old boy with an AVM thrown into survival training!" I won't let Mom talk down to Ivan just because she's stressed.

He puts his hand on my back and whispers, "She's just upset."

I grit my teeth and step to his side. He's right, but I still hate it. Mom can't function when Lark's Agora swells and the MNP takes over. It's not new to me, but it sets my jaw on edge when anyone minimizes what Ivan's been through.

"Good work, Ivan. You got out here faster than an ALICE could have," Dad says. Though it's lying perfectly, he adjusts her IV tube and gives her mask the slightest wiggle. "Mai, take her to ICU room 217."

Dad doesn't look up again. Not at Mom. Not at me. He keeps fiddling with Lark's stretcher and equipment. The Helm could blow up right now and I genuinely don't think he'd notice.

Ivan wraps his arm around my shoulders, and I give him a tight smile. "Thank you, baby. Dad's right. You did a fantastic job."

"We should keep those supplies with her all the time until her Agora is out. I'll pack an emergency kit for her," he says. "We'll find a way to get her surgery approved as soon as possible. How are you feeling?" Ivan has me smushed tight against his side as we walk, and his words come as comforting rumbles into my left ear.

"Let's go see Lark's scans and I'll let you know."

"She'll be the life of the party in fourth grade before we know it."

She better be.

6

The next six days pass in a blur. Visit Lark in the ICU. Don't cry. Do two Agora removals, assisted by surgeons in training. Pretend to sleep. Pick at whatever food Ivan and Richelle try to make me eat. Repeat.

"You did it, Story!" Richelle draws a line through the last commander's name on my whiteboard.

I toss the cold container of veggie lasagna Ivan sent me hours ago in the trash.

"Eighty-seven more before we have data to present for Lark's surgery. Off to backwoods Australia in some ancient opal mine for the next batch," Richelle says. She's worked her butt off to learn and excel in her new role as my PA.

Eighty-seven. That number almost does me in.

A speaker in my lab booms, "Dr. Story Rhys, to the neuro-ICU. Dr. Story Rhys, to the neuro-ICU."

Lark! I leap from my desk and run for the hallway, Richelle hot on my heels. "You think she's worse?" I ask as we run.

"I haven't heard a peep, sorry."

In just over a minute, we're skidding around the corner into the main clinic's ICU. The staff at the desk stop chatting to give us a small wave, but I keep running. There's no flurry of activity or extra equipment parked outside her curtain. That's a good sign! I silently hope she's okay as I cover the short hallway.

I stop so hard at her door that my shoes squeak. *Please be okay.* I brace myself and peek in.

Lark is sitting up in bed, coloring. Mom stands at her side, holding a big cup of ice chips. Dad is perched on the edge of her bed, one hand on Lark's foot, the other swiping a tablet.

Richelle squeezes my arm. "You go in. I'll check back later."

My beautiful little sister sees me and grins. She's pale. Her hair is in the neat bun Mom and I made this morning. "Lark! You're up!" I wrap her in a gentle hug.

"Story! Did you make me bracelets?"

I should have made bracelets. I should have fixed her weeks ago. I'm a loser in the big sister department.

"Sorry, Lark." I force the words out around the lump in my throat. "I thought it would be fun to make them with you when you woke up."

Her glassy eyes light up. "Great idea! Mom, hand me a pen please, I want to draw some designs."

"Story, we have to chat in the hallway for a minute," Dad says, standing.

My shoulders drop. No, I don't want to. I know what he's going to say. I don't move from watching Lark sketching out a seed bead flower bracelet pattern.

"That's pretty, Lark." I smile, scooting her box of colored pencils closer.

Dad taps my shoulder and mouths "Out there."

"I'll be right back." I give her a kiss on top of the head and follow him.

He's a tall man. But right now, his slumped shoulders have taken at least two inches off his height. "ALICE sent me the report."

"Dad, can't I just be here for a little bit first, please?"

"No. You need to review the data as soon as it comes in."

"Is this helpful right *now*?"

"Her estimated death date is now January 2, 2056," he says.

I catch myself against the wall. "She lost a full year this time?!"

"Can you move the Agora removal training along any faster?" He pulls his glasses off and rubs his eyes.

"Yeahhhhh. I will." If it weren't for the babies, I don't think I'd see my bed again until her Agora is out. "I want to go back in with Lark. We'll talk more later."

He's so absorbed in her patient record he doesn't respond.

"Dad."

He nods, swiping across the tablet.

"Come on, she needs us," I say, but he's not listening. "Dad!"

With a jump, he locks the tablet. "I just wanted to look at a few more scans."

"Do that when she's asleep. She's here, awake, pain-free for now. We need to celebrate." I take a hesitant step forward, making sure my legs aren't jelly anymore. *Okay, we're good, twins. I won't fall.*

Back in her room, she shifts to make room for me on the bed. One of the volunteers brought us tea, hot chocolate, and snacks. The downy blanket from the warmer. The soothing tea. The no real sleep for days. Big mistake. I swear there's sand in my bleary eyes.

"Look at this pattern. Horse, flower, fern. Then it repeats. I also want to make some black sparkly Irontrace ones. These are going to look so cool! When do you think we can get the beads? Do you think Ivan and Francois will wear them too?"

"Knock, knock, Ross Fam!" Ivan strides in, jostling a tray of candy and a floppy stuffed horse. "What am I gonna wear?"

"Presents! Thanks, Ivan!" Lark squeals.

"What?" Ivan says, with a sweet, dumbfounded face. *Ah, my heart. He's perfect.* She giggles. He loses a battle to hold back a smile. "This is my lunch. My horse." He lays them on her drawing table and winks at me. "I guess she can have them though."

"Thank you!" She wraps the horse around her neck like a pillow, leaning back on it, then flips the lid off the box of assorted chocolates. "Mom, come help me pick candies."

Ivan pulls a chair over by me and kisses my cheek before sitting. "What have you been doing, my love?"

"Missing you." I lean my head on his shoulder.

"Sorry. I've been stuck in the control room. It's a very annoying job. Mostly managing people. Haven't blown anything up in four days!" He holds up four fingers for emphasis. "Oh. I went to see David again. He's doing great. Itching to get back to work. I told him if he steps foot in the control room, I'll blow dart him with sedatives myself as payback."

He flips a pen out of his pocket and throws it like a dart at the sharps disposal container. It hits the slot perfectly and disappears inside. Hope he didn't like that one. Definitely not getting it back.

"I knew you're still holding a grudge against him." I nuzzle my cheek on his shoulder. Maybe if I lean just right against him, I could sleep. Ten minutes and I'd feel much better.

"Story, come get candy. Your stomach's been growling like a bear." Lark holds out her box of chocolates, shaking it.

"Realllllllyyyyyy? Thanks for the intel, Lark," Ivan says, arching an eyebrow at me.

I grab two of his favorite milk chocolate truffles with raspberry filling. "Here, my love." I hand him one and take a bite of the other. Lark's a genius. This little candy hits me with a sugar rush right away. These need to be added to pregnancy survival kits somewhere. Maybe I should start an online shop for those.

"Story's been sipping tea. She said she was waiting to eat with you," Lark says.

"Tsk, tsk, tsk, my love," Ivan playfully scolds. He holds out a hand to pull me to my feet. "Lark, I need to go feed this lovely wife of mine. We'll bring you back whatever you want from Atlas Caverns."

"Ooooh...Beads!"

"That's it?" He leans in and whispers, "*Everything* is free here." Lark's blue eyes go wide. "The sky's the limit, kid."

She takes a deep breath like she's winding up.

"Cool. Then I guess a big salted soft pretzel. Do they have slushies? If yes, blue! This horse you brought is nice. Are there more colors, like a palomino? Peaches sound good. Can you find me some peaches, or a fruit salad? Red peppers and dip?"

Ivan laughs. "That's the spirit! I'm pretty sure we have slushies. If not, I'm ordering a machine later. Being Senior Commander has its perks after all." He recites her list back and she nods. "Phew, Lark. We may need at least a few hours to get all that." Ivan gives my hand a squeeze.

"Wait! Do they have peanut butter cup candies?" Lark asks, and we all crack up.

"We gotta get out of here before we need Obsidian to pull a wagon back with all this. We'll be back."

"Glad you're okay, Lark." I give her a hug and follow Ivan out.

In the hallway he folds me under his arm in a one-sided hug. "I missed you!"

"Missed you so much these last few days."

"What's wrong?"

A list of complaints as long as my arm flashes through my mind. Instead, I say, "Can we run, like *run,* run to the apartment? I need some Ivan time."

"Ivan time coming up."

I shriek in happy surprise when he scoops me up. "This isn't what I meant, Ivan! Put me down. I'll run with you."

"This is far more fun, wife. Admit it."

"Oh, it's infinitely better."

He doesn't show a hint of embarrassment at our growing group of spectators. The dozen or so staff at the desk turn our way. You-two-are-out-of-control grins break out among them. His backstory would break most people, but he went for what he wanted (me!), and we've built a happy life. He's not just a survivor. He's a living spark of happiness, turning something as simple as going home into a celebration.

At the apartment, he pauses so I can fling the door open. He rushes in, letting me kick the door shut. "You need a shower to get those nasty clinic germs-" He stops short when Richelle spins our way in his desk chair.

"You're back! I've been waiting ages. How's she doing?"

Sad Ivan groans come from his throat, making me stifle a laugh.

"Hey, Richelle," I say, as a deflated Ivan gently deposits me on the counter. "Lark's much better."

"I guess I'll start cooking," Ivan says, "Unless, you know how to cook?" He flashes a cheesy grin at Richelle.

"I make the best cheese and veggie sandwiches," she suggests.

"Cheese and vegetables after a three-hour tactical sim. Dream come true," he says.

Richelle throws a couch pillow at his head. "My bad, geez. We can't all be chefs like you!"

"Wait! You know what, can you run to Atlas Caverns for us?" She nods and Ivan dashes to his desk, whipping out a notebook. "I'm going to stay here and pamper Story, but Lark sent us with a whole laundry list of things to get." He rips out the paper, passing it to her.

"Yes, Sir. At your service," she says, giving him a goofy salute.

"Bye, thanks!" I sink onto the couch. Once the door shuts, I pop up, wagging a finger at him. "You are the smartest man in the world!"

He blows me a kiss. "Pathogen-free is the way to be. Shower. Now."

7

A few hours later, I'm rested, happy, fed, and chugging the water Ivan has been reminding me to drink. This is by far the best I've felt in weeks. Richelle, Ivan, and I are laughing down the hallway to visit Lark.

"Hey, Lark. They had palomiNOOOOO!" My voice gives out in her doorway.

Moulson sits with a couple of other council members at a table in the far corner, playing cards with Lark.

I lunge without thinking. Ivan flashes an arm out, catching me to his chest.

"The ICU has a no visitor's policy!" Ivan thunders. Heads turn our way. Cards freeze mid-air.

Mom gives Ivan a withering stare.

"Don't be grumpy, Ivan! They brought me cards and games." Lark points to a messy stack of shredded gift wrap on the table. "And. Look, new candy! I'll share with you since I stole yours." She jumps from her chair and crashes into Ivan with a hug around his waist.

Moulson twitches forward in his chair. What's he going to do, fight Ivan? That would end in about two seconds.

Ivan's eyes dissect Moulson. "Thanks, Lark." He passes her back towards me, making a barrier between her, me, and the members of The Bastion. "Guthrie. I've got something in the control room from Delac for you. Please follow me." Ivan waves for Moulson to follow him.

Good job, Ivan!

"I'm going to stay here and get to know my new friends, the Ross's." He settles back in his chair, picking up his cards. I nearly surge forward again when he crosses his feet at the ankles, settling in.

"The ICU doesn't allow non-family visitors. You need to leave."

Ivan plucks the cards from their hands and tosses them in a pile.

Moulson's face flushes. The council members murmur questions and apologies about why Ivan's so rude today.

Richelle bought a coffee that's more of a bucket than a beverage at Atlas Caverns. Ivan warned her that the seventy-nine-ounce coffee is supposed to be shared among a group of people. She grinned, filled it to the brim, and took a long slurp. She misses her brothers, so annoying him is her new favorite hobby.

I turn towards her and flick my eyes to the card players. "Dump the coffee."

She lights up like I just gave her a million-dollar check. "Target?"

"Old dude with blue eyes."

She saunters over, sitting on the edge of the table cross-legged. Moulson glares at her when she tosses her coffee lid like a frisbee, missing the trash can.

"What's this card game? Eleven spiders? What does that even mean? Do you want elevens? Or spiders?" Moulson's eyes nearly shoot fire at her. "Hi! I'm Richelle. Or do you really want eleven spiders? Like an I'll trade you mine, you trade me yours type of thing?"

She winks at Moulson, pretending to elbow him and then drops her coffee. I've never loved her more. Most goes on Moulson. Waves splash towards the rich leather briefcases and purses of the council members near their feet.

"What is wrong with you?" A woman jumps up, trying to save her purse from the steaming lake.

"I'm so sorry!" Richelle shrieks.

She grabs the sheets off Lark's bed and throws them at the council members, dragging them through coffee in the process. Her chaotic genius is on full display as she makes some kind of Jackson Pollock masterpiece using the sheet as her brush. The faster she mops, the faster coffee flings on their shoes, pant legs, and laptop bags.

"Yikes! Made it worse. It's a coffee apocalypse." They all glare at her while she laughs and cleans.

Ivan yanks open the paper towel dispenser, tossing the roll at

Moulson's gut. "Sorry. Richelle was trying to make you feel welcome." *Stop smiling, my love.* "Story, can you get her a new room, please?"

I hop over the creeping stream of coffee, scurrying to the central station.

"Hello!" The teen boy at the desk looks up. "Lark Ross needs a room on the stepdown unit. She'll be discharged tomorrow."

"Yes, Dr. Rhys. I'll run and prep her room." He grabs his tablet and jumps up. He left his computer unlocked. Can't have that. I reach over the desk and tap the lock key.

"She doesn't know who I am." Moulson speaks from inches behind me. His voice is thick with rage and grief.

Well, duh. "You shouldn't be here."

"She's mine but doesn't know me. What if your family was torn apart like this?" he snarls.

"You can't be in here," I say.

His eyes take on a faraway look. "It'll wipe the grins off their faces."

He's gone, mentally. I've been left standing with the shell of a person. I consider pressing my panic button, but I don't want to call the control room.

"Whose faces?" I ask.

"All of them." He grins and tries to grab my shoulder, but I duck to the side. "Thank you, partner."

"I'm not your partner. Never have been. Never will be. Never call me that again!" I snap.

He grabs me by the forearm and squeezes it so hard I almost scream. "What started as a war to get rid of The Bastion is now going to be a full-on familial purge. I got you out of The Bastion's headquarters. Made you famous for your surgical skills. You repaid me by helping me figure out my next move. I owe you, again. Tell me what you want, sweetie."

I shake my arm. He tightens his grip. "Get off me! Ivan will kill you."

"Dr. Rhys?" A hospital-gown clad Mai steps from her room.

He grips my arm tighter, yanking me his way.

"Let go of Dr. Rhys!" Mai yells, making him drop my arm.

Ivan bursts into the hallway. "What is going on?" he bellows, giving Moulson a withering stare.

I mouth "HELP!" at him.

Ivan's spine stiffens. "I need to give you something, Councilman Guthrie." He pulls out a small black box.

Moulson narrows his eyes and stares at Ivan.

Ivan extends it in his palm. "It's an access key, of sorts. You'll love it Senior Commander Delac had it made just for you. We wanted to make it easier for you to come and go from the control room whenever you want."

Moulson smiles. Ivan's got him.

Moulson reaches for it. Ivan flips it up, shooting arcs of electricity into Moulson's arm. He slumps forward, knocked out cold.

"Aww, what happened, pookie?" Ivan cracks up. He flops Moulson over his forearm. "Mai, open your bathroom door!"

"Ivan!" I hiss. "What'd you do that for?"

"SC Rhys! Why?" Mai blurts. "You can't abduct the council members!"

She rushes to open her door. Ivan hefts Moulson in. He lays him in an unconscious heap on the bathroom floor.

"He's just gonna take a nap for a bit. Need some camo to hide him under, please." Ivan arranges Moulson on his left side. Mai hands him the pillow and blanket from her bed. Ivan puts wrist and ankle cuffs on Moulson, then shoves the pillow under his cheek.

Ivan stands and washes his hands. "Mai. That..." He nods towards the white lump. "Is Anthony Moulson." She gasps. "I know, right? He made Guthrie up as a cover. He built some kind of biometric cloaking device that fooled everyone. One sec, gotta kiss my wife."

Mai laughs. "Of course you do."

He turns on SAM. A deep red welt in the shape of Moulson's hand encircles my forearm. Ivan's dark eyes see it then give Moulson a predatory stare. I better keep him close so Moulson doesn't wake up covered in bruises.

"You good, babe?" He gives a trail of kisses up my arm, shoulder, and neck to my lips.

"I'm worried you made him angrier." I can't take my eyes off Moulson. He's breathing but not moving. Will Ivan be arrested?

"Don't care if I made him mad. It's gone on too long." He squints at our bathroom prisoner then crouches in front of him. In a sudden burst of excitement, he twirls me in a fast circle. "SAM's the key! I can see he's Moulson. Not that I didn't believe you, but I was sweating there for a minute. It would've drowned me in paperwork if it was really some old dude named Guthrie. We really caught Moulson, baby!"

He aims his phone at Moulson and makes a recording, then shuts SAM off and zooms in on his slack face. After tucking his phone away, he shuts the bathroom door.

"Mai, call someone to take the council members to the control room. I'll be right there," Ivan says.

"Yes, SC." She dashes into Lark's room.

I drop my forehead on the counter of the empty central station. "We're okay, littles," I whisper.

What if Moulson tells AJA I'm his partner? They'll arrest me again. Ivan will have no wife. Holly and Huck will have no mom *if* I survive long enough for them to be born.

A tight feeling spreads to my neck. *I can breathe. I'm fine. There's no reason to feel like I'm choking. But am I choking? My throat feels too tight to get a full breath. Breathe, breathe, breathe.* It's not working. Now I'm lightheaded. I slide my right hand to my chest.

Calm down!

Huge hands slide over my shoulders, gently caging me in.

"What are we doing?" Ivan whispers.

I squeak out a sharp, "Celebrating."

"Breathe with me, my love. Ready?" He pulls my back tighter against him.

His broad, warm chest feels so safe. His left arm settles along mine, resting on my lower stomach. His right arm slides over my shoulder, pressing his hand on my heart. My breaths stay chaotic and shallow. My stupid heart pummels me. This is the worst! I can't calm down. He's trying to help me and I'm probably disappointing him.

"Shut everything out. It's only you and I. Focus. We're going to breathe in now. Feel me behind you. Match my rhythm," he says in an even voice.

After a few more wild breaths, my chest rises and falls in unison with his. I wish I could talk to tell him how much I appreciate his help.

"Think about holly plants in the snow. Picture them. Can you imagine how nice some freezing snow would feel on your neck right now? Breathe out." He exhales softly on the side of my neck. "You need to get out of the snow. It gave you goosebumps."

They're not from the snow, Ivan.

"Breathe in. Let's go to Australia. Imagine we're there. When you can, talk. Breathe out. Tell me five things you see."

We take several more perfectly in sync breaths. I rest my head back on his collarbone. My heart rate's back to baseline. Dizziness is gone.

"You. Me. A beach. A blanket. Cold drinks," I finally say.

"There's that voice I love." He reaches out to hold my hand, turning on SAM.

"He said I'm his partner."

"He's wrong. You're my wife. The mother of my babies. You're a brilliant surgeon. You're a whiz in the kitchen with making, uh, beverages." I scoff and bang my hips into him, making him laugh. "*That's* who you are."

My parents and Lark walk out of Lark's room. They greet digital Story and Ivan before walking off in a group. "Look! Your parents and Lark think they're us."

"They do. I love you, husband."

"I love you more, wife." He drops to his knees and hugs me around the waist before planting a kiss on my stomach. "Love you also, twins!"

"What are you going to do about Moulson's familial purge?"

"His what?"

I explain what Moulson told me.

"If this was anyone else, I'd say we have nothing to worry about since he's in custody. For him? I'm calling an emergency meeting."

8

"Do me a favor. Turn SAM off then on in quick succession. It'll bring our clones back."

"Will they disappear and freak my family out?"

"Oh, ye of little faith, wife! I gave them manners. They'll concoct an excuse to leave, then make a quick exit."

Oddly, Ivan's emergency meeting is held in David's hospital room. Didn't expect that. Ivan guides me between the press of bodies. Nearly every inch is taken up by Irontrace and Bastion members.

I glance at their faces. Seven council members from The Bastion. I don't know any of them.

As for the Irontrace in here, I've removed Agoras from most of them. They're A+ patients, sitting or reclining on extra furniture sprinkled in the room. Only three haven't reached commander yet—Ben Washington, Talia Gadot, and Travis Langston. Hopefully, The Bastion will approve them for the next Lancaster wave of surgeries. No idea when that will be, sadly.

"Got the door, Senior Commander," Cantone says. He puts some kind of doorstopper device along the bottom of the door. Steel legs shoot out of it into the floor.

A barricade?

"Story!" Richelle whisper yells. She waves for me to stand by her fold-up chair beside David and Dad.

I wind my way through the tight crowd to them.

"What's this about?" Dad whispers.

I offer a weak shrug.

"Dr. Rhys, thank you for not killing any of us," David says, sparking a ripple of laughs and thanks. "We're as anxious as you are for you to get more surgeries done."

"Looking forward to it," I say, smiling.

Ivan opens David's laptop, projecting a blank square on the far wall. "If you're here in this room, I'd like to extend a thank you for accepting my invitation," Ivan says. "Recent information has come to light that must be addressed immediately."

Two pictures appear. One of Moulson, and one of someone I don't recognize. "Please look to the left of the screen. There is Anthony Moulson. On the right, you see the newest council member of The Bastion, Mark Guthrie."

Ah, that's why I don't know who that is, he doesn't exist.

"We have been deceived in a most egregious way." Ivan hits a key and a program runs. Pixel-by-pixel, Guthrie fades away, replaced by Moulson.

Gasps and murmurs break out. David's eyes burn with pride.

"You let that man in Lark's hospital room?" Dad murmurs.

"No. *I* did not," Ivan answers. "I wrote a program to shield human brains from magnetic waves at the suggestion of our brilliant, beautiful Dr. Story Rhys."

He blows me a kiss. A smattering of applause breaks out. I turn crimson.

"Gollllllll-ly, girl, you struck gold," Richelle whispers. "I want one too."

"I ran this program on Mark Guthrie while investigating odd remarks he made today. My findings will shock you. Anthony Moulson has been using a weapon he built to interfere with the way human brains process information. His goal is to further de-stabilize The Bastion. I brought this to you as soon as I had concrete evidence. Please watch a clip I recorded about thirty minutes ago."

Ivan plays cell phone footage he made of cuffed, unconscious Moulson transitioning to Guthrie.

"Now watch this Helm security footage," Ivan says, playing the video on the left side of Moulson and I in the hallway. The right side shows Guthrie spouting the same evil nonsense at me.

If a feather dropped in here, you'd hear it hit the floor. Everyone is glued to the side-by-side videos playing on repeat.

David clears his throat and says, "Run your program on the Guthrie video so we can confirm, pixel by pixel, what you're saying."

"Yes, SC Delac."

Ivan plays the video, stripping Guthrie away into Moulson. Nobody moves. As the seconds tick by, Ivan grows visibly annoyed by their silence.

"Audio comparison as well. Look at the bottom sound waves. You'll see a perfect match," he says, crossing his arms.

David applauds, then everyone joins in. It's way too much sound for this tiny room, but Ivan has earned it.

"This is excellent!" David grins. "You've prevented further devastation. I can't imagine if Moulson was allowed continued access to the control room, votes on The Bastion, and ingress to The Helm."

"Do you have him in custody?" a council member asks.

"Sure do, Councilman Darrow," Ivan replies. He turns on a live feed of Mai's room. "He's wrapped up on a bathroom floor like the piece of human waste he is."

"SC Rhys, the world owes you." Darrow claps again.

I grip the back of Richelle's chair to hold me in place. It's the only thing stopping me from unleashing a fury of kisses on Ivan. He'd love it. David would have a fit.

"Woods, call in Air Titans to transport him to Columbus," Ivan orders.

"Yes, Sir." Young Travis nearly drops his phone. Mega props to Ivan for trusting him to handle this.

"I have a question." A striking Black woman pipes up. Her long braids are pulled back tight, but delicate gold cuffs in them catch the light when she stands. "I'm Architect Maseko. You're a doctor. A surgeon to be exact, Dr. Rhys?"

"Yes," I say. No idea who this lady is.

"Weaponized magnetic fields? That's an extremely specific thing to ask your husband to check for." Her eyes narrow. "Explain."

"Moulson freed me from Bastion custody with this weapon a few weeks ago," I admit.

A sudden rush of conversation breaks out. *Bye, Ivan.* I flick my eyes his way. He gives me the tiniest encouraging nod.

"You *knew* Moulson was Guthrie for weeks?" Maseko asks. "You better start talking."

It's my chance to be free! Ride this high that Ivan's got them on. I can't survive the stress and anxiety about Moulson anymore. That rat could try to get me in trouble for being his "partner."

"He told me who he was." Ugh, my mouth and throat are so dry. "At the time, I was extremely sick. I thought I was only gone for a couple of days, but it was weeks. The forest wardens poisoned me. I had to be revived multiple times." Dad puts a comforting hand on my shoulder. "That gave me a severe injury to my heart tissue in the process. I was in critical condition."

There are too many people staring at me. I wish I'd talked to her privately. "So. Yes. He told me who he was. If I was wrong or hallucinating and turned in an innocent man, he could've been killed. I couldn't handle that on my conscience. He somehow got The Bastion to say, 'Hey, Story, go be a surgeon, save the Irontrace.' That's what I've been doing. And I'm wiped out."

Steady your voice. You can do this.

"Actually, Ivan could only see Guthrie too. For all he knew, I had lost my mind. Until a little bit ago." I point to the video of Mai's bathroom. A team of Irontrace is loading still unconscious Moulson onto a stretcher. "Look. Ivan *proved* Moulson is Guthrie. He saved your butts from this embarrassment that The Bastion. Wait? Aren't you all like the original tech geniuses?" I stop to meet each of their eyes. "Sorry. I'm not trying to be mean. I'm a mess, my sister's been in the ICU. I don't know when I last slept more than a couple hours. Please don't execute me for being honest. Don't arrest me. Don't poison me. Let me save Irontrace, my sister, and live life happily married to my best friend."

Ivan's grinning like an absolute fool. If anything, he loves me more for this outburst.

The Irontrace are quietly conferring. The Bastion members speak fast among themselves. Maseko stands, putting her hands on her hips. As she takes slow steps towards me, a hush falls over the room. I shove my hands in my scrub pockets. Might as well give my babies one last comforting rub before I'm cuffed and thrown in a dungeon.

"Dr. Rhys. You've had quite a summer. Do you know why I'm here?" she asks.

"No," I say.

"The Bastion held an inner vote as a response to Moulson's wave of terror. I was appointed Lead Architect of The Bastion this morning in Columbus."

My eyes flick to Ivan's. I have no idea what she means. I've never heard that title. He gives an exaggerated grin, tipping his head side-to-side like a cartoon character.

I don't get it.

He points to his mouth, trying to get me to mimic him.

I pull my mouth into what I hope passes for a smile. He rolls his hand then mouths, "Say congrats," before going back to pointing to his huge grin.

I clear my throat and say, "Congratulations."

She snorts, looking between Ivan and me. "Clearly, you're delighted."

Perfect! I just confessed and had a near emotional breakdown in front of the most powerful person in the world.

"I mean it. Congrats. For real," I stammer.

"Thank you. I appreciate your honesty. Can I be honest too for a minute?" She leans even closer. I whisper, "Yeah."

"In Columbus this morning, my staff and I overheard several fights over which Helm Dr. Story Rhys will operate at next. Many other conversations had Ivan's name in them. His feats against Moulson. The fear he's inspired in council members by his treatment of Jordan. The Rhys name is on everyone's lips." She lays a hand on my arm, "I'm appointing you as head of ASTRA."

A panicked laugh flies out before I can stop it.

"No. I can't be the head of ASTRA. I'm struggling to keep my-" *twins and I fed and alive.* I look at Ivan. He runs a hand through his hair and grins. "Thank you. No. I'm sorry. My focus is on saving my sister."

My eyes find Dad's. "Give it to my dad!"

Dad shakes his head no.

"If you won't take it, you name the next in line. I won't drop this. Take some time. Think about it." She places a hand on my shoulder and gives it a reassuring squeeze. "In the meantime, no one is going to execute, arrest, or poison you. We need people with your candor in charge." She presses a business card in my hand then turns. "Senior Commander Rhys. You called this meeting. Get it back on track. Then take your wife home for dinner and a real night's sleep."

What if it's a trick? What if I'm for sure gonna be executed now? It wouldn't just be me. Ivan's whole family could be gone because I couldn't keep my mouth shut. Focus on the reasons to smile. There are several today. Moulson's arrested. The Bastion, at its highest level, knows I'm not his accomplice. Maybe if I'm head of ASTRA, I can ensure Lark's surgery doesn't get lost in forty levels of bureaucratic red tape.

Happy. Be happy.

Oops. I haven't heard a word of what Ivan's been saying. I should listen.

"As you can see, there's a ton of work ahead of us." He points to a list on his laptop. "We need to restore public trust in The Bastion and Kernel. Then show people the pandemonium is leveling out."

"Story, do you have any suggestions on how to do that?" Councilman Darrow asks.

Me? I look from Ivan to Richelle. An idea hits.

"Knowing about The Irontrace saved my life. The world needs to know you're here," I say. The council members shift in their seats. "It'll restore confidence faster if people see how many regions you're in, how closely you watch out for us. They'll feel better knowing someone is in their corner that's not a politician. Sorry, Bastion."

"Wise words. Looking forward to working with you, Dr. Rhys,"

Councilman Darrow says, reaching over to shake my hand.

"Thanks. Same."

"Do it. I want it on the news tomorrow," Maseko tells Ivan. "SC Rhys, I have to know. Why only invite a small group of Bastion members to this meeting?"

I've been wondering that too.

"I wrote a program to vet who's most trustworthy, has been integrally involved with Irontrace, and has no financial interest in The Kernel. From that list, you were the seven I chose. It worked out well you were visiting Columbus for the vote. Moulson infiltrated The Bastion. Councilman Jordan was a liar and murderer. Several council members refused to disclose ransom notes leading to thousands of deaths. The Bastion is bloated. It's sloppy. That ends now. With you all. If you want to help get the world back in order, stay. If you want out, then leave."

No one moves.

"Is this a rebellion against The Bastion?" Maseko asks.

"Does it come across as a rebellion?" Ivan blinks innocently.

A smile touches her lips. "This feels like an experienced group of professionals looking out for the best interests of the world."

"Welcome to Project Ilex." His eyes burn with a confident gleam that promises to move mountains to keep his family safe.

Ah, twins! Your dad just launched a covert op to make the world better for you.

9

My operating room is a full house.

Ivan posted Travis and Talia as guards in my lab with mobile workstations since he's swamped with Senior Commander duties. Dad and Richelle have turned it into more of a party atmosphere than a somber surgical suite.

I'm on our third simulation surgery of the day when the most horrific wave of nausea hits. How mortifying would it be to get sick in front of my colleagues? It would be a nightmare version of Richelle's coffee apocalypse.

Deep breathing doesn't help. "Dad, can you observe while Dr. Hunter removes the neural chip? I could use a break."

"I'd love to."

"Thanks." I shouldn't have pushed myself to help with three full sim surgeries.

The large monitor that connects my lab to the control room turns on. Ivan is sitting at his workstation. "Hello. Sorry to interrupt."

"Welcome, Senior Commander Rhys. This is the man who designed and built INES," Dad announces to the room.

Voices unmute with rapid fire commendations and questions.

Ivan speaks over them, "Actually, INES is based off Dr. Rhys's plans. Do you know what time the next group of guests will land in Columbus tomorrow? I'm coordinating their pickup."

I can't answer over my silent battle. Dad chats with him for a few minutes.

"Dr. Ross. Nice to see you're primary trainer in this one," Ivan says, clearly fishing for information.

"Story needed a break," Dad replies.

Ivan frowns. "Thank you for your time." His video feed goes black.

Twenty-seven minutes have passed. I know because I stared at the clock like it could help me while I was peppered with questions about what makes INES superior to ASTRA surgery bots. Every answer leads to more questions.

This is unbearable. I'm out. "Dad. I-"

The lab door opens. Ivan strides in, surveying the room. Seeing him always makes me feel better, but not this time. I want to scream for him to take me home. He stops about ten feet from the operating platform and crooks a finger, calling me closer. The platform rail squeaks in protest as he hoists over.

"Knight in shining armor reporting for duty," he whispers. "Are those two giving you a rough time?"

"Yes. I'm so nauseous."

"I'm gonna fix you. It'll feel weird though. You ready?" He smiles at my desperate nod. I almost screech when he swipes a near-freezing goop in the back collar of my shirt.

"Why?" I squeak. I fling my hand up in an ugly dance to wipe it away. Ivan's faster and catches my hand.

"Give it a second," he says.

Is the goal to annoy my nausea away? If so, he's doing a wonderful job. I stand like some kind of surgical attire mannequin with hunched shoulders. To my fresh horror, the icy goop splits. *It's alive and moving! Did he put leeches in my shirt?* The two sections of it slither across my shoulders and down the back of each arm. I shiver from the creeping, cold sensation.

Help. I look around for help.

Richelle covers her mouth to hide a fit of laughs. Talia and Travis whip to stare at their laptops when my furious eyes turn their way.

"What was that?" I ask in more of an exhale than words.

I'm done for the day. I reach back to tear my gown off but pause. The liquid stopped. It encircles each forearm like a soft cuff. On my right side, it clamps tighter than on the left, but after a second, the left clamps tighter and the right releases pressure, but stays in place.

Nausea is gone. I feel good.

"Better?" Ivan asks.

"Yes. How?"

"Pressure point pol-biometry resin bands."

A new Irontrace medical wonder to learn about.

"Amazing. It won't hurt them?" I whisper.

"I promise it won't. It's amplified pressure-point relief. Also stimulates hormones and neurotransmitters to keep you smiling."

"Thanks."

"Anytime."

He blows a series of kisses my way as he bounces down the steps. It would be so easy to leap over this rail and hop on his back. If only we could spend a day where our biggest responsibility is deciding which coffee creamer to use.

He looks at Talia and Travis, giving them a thumbs up then thumbs down as a check-in. They both give him a thumbs up. I laugh with them when he blows them a kiss too before jogging out of the lab. Forget TV. I could watch him goof off all day.

"INES, begin closure protocols," Dad says, then opens the floor for questions from our trainees.

He's explaining the reason for the polymer we paint on neural chip tendrils to Dr. Lehai.

A surgeon with an Australian accent interrupts, "Dr. Annette Figgs here. Gold Coast Medical Hub. Have you had any reports of mental health concerns spreading in the United States?"

"When?" I ask.

"Hospitals and pediatricians here in Australia are reporting a massive influx of patients with anxiety issues in the last couple of hours."

"Talia? Travis? Do you see anything on your monitoring?" I ask.

"Checking now," Travis says.

"Nothing showing in the U.S. Looking on the major Australian news stations," Talia adds.

"How many cases have been reported?" Dad asks.

"In the last hour, in the Gold Coast area, nineteen hundred and sky-rocketing."

"Talia, get ahold of Ivan, please," I request.

"Already on it, Dr. Rhys. Talia Gadot here in the INES lab. A surgeon from Australia needs to speak to SC Rhys."

Ivan appears on the monitor. "Go ahead."

Emergency room reports with redacted lines are reviewed for an hour between the control room and my lab.

"Dr. Rhys, Dr. Ross, please come to the control room to continue this conversation," Ivan requests.

The control room is dim and loud. Dad and I sit for hours as theories are thrown out on why previously healthy people are lashing out.

"Russia, Western Australia, India, China, are reporting the same issue. We're calling in as many additional support ALICE models as we can to interview and treat them," Dr. Marshall Nguyen says. He's an expert trainer for behavioral health ALICE models. "If you have any ALICE models we can use, we'd appreciate the access."

Ivan stands in the front of the control room, arms crossed, listening to the conversation flow between doctors and Helms all over the world.

"Yes, we'll notify hospitals to bring all standby models online," Dr. Bea Dawes, president of the Bastion Biomed Alliance, or BBA, says.

"How many patients can one ALICE realistically support in this capacity?" Ivan asks.

"For direct patient interviews, planning, and care, an ALICE can handle one patient every fifteen minutes," Dawes replies.

Ivan sighs sharply. "Fifteen minutes. There aren't enough ALICEs in the world."

A flurry of activity hits the control room when a flock of council members enter.

"Bring us up to speed, please, Senior Commander Rhys," Councilman Darrow says.

"Rapidly spreading mental health emergency. First cases reported in the Gold Coast Region of Australia six hours ago. No signs of illness or infection." Ivan gestures to the monitors in the front of the room. "Dr.

Dawes, how many confirmed patients?"

"Two point eight million?" she rattles off. "That can't be right. It was just two point four."

Darrow sinks into a chair. "What are their symptoms?"

"Panic. But that's putting it lightly. It's some kind of debilitating emotional response. Here's what we know. It's targeting primary care-givers. We have video assessments from ALICEs monitors. They're hard to watch," Ivan says, nodding towards someone in the back of the room.

Several monitors combine feeds, revealing one giant video clip of a woman. She's around age thirty, sitting in a hospital bed, playing with her phone.

Ivan cuts across the control room to his workstation. He spins his office chair I'm sitting in and says, "Go. Visit Lark, check on her, then head home. Your detail is going with you."

"No. I want to see this," I say, trying to spin to see the screen.

He locks the back of my chair in place. "It's awful."

"Then watch it with me."

He sighs, releasing my chair, then sits on the edge of his desk by me.

The woman sits peacefully in bed when a doctor in scrubs approaches her.

"Hi! Can I go home?" she asks.

"Gabby, are you ready to try again?" the doctor asks.

"I need to get home to my kids," Gabby says, face falling. The nurse waves her hand, and a man approaches the bed, holding a little girl. The woman's face crumbles into terror. She throws her phone down. "The kids! Where's *my* kids!?"

The little girl cries, reaching to embrace the woman. Gabby's cries turn to shrieks. She rips out her IV and tosses her blankets to the floor. She's fumbling, screaming, trying to climb over the bed rail to escape.

The doctor puts a hand on the man's back. "You should leave."

The little girl reaches for her mom. Gabby dives over the rail, cowering beside the bed.

"Out! Now!" the doctor yells.

"Mommy! Help my mommy!" the child screams.

An ORION rolls in, followed by hospital volunteers. The dad steps into the hallway. Gabby goes still.

"Ivan! Did she die?" I leap up. Ivan folds his arms around me.

"No," he whispers.

With no warning she begins violently seizing as her husband steps back in. Hospital volunteers drop to their knees, wedging pillows and blankets around Gabby.

"Gabby!" His screams turn to silent sobs as he watches the ORION arm dart out to sedate his wife.

A new clip begins, showing dozens of teen kids clustered in a hospital waiting room. Red caution tape surrounds the couches they sit on. Across the room, adults are gathered. Their mouths move, but you can't hear their conversations over shouting from the boys.

"Shut up!"

"Liars!"

"Mom! Answer your phone!"

"My dad works for AJA! He's coming for you!"

The panicked yells and conversations intensify until a woman tears the caution tape from the wall and sprints for the hospital exit. An ALICE speeds after her. An arm extends, injecting her with something. She falls onto the tile floor. The room turns into an uproar.

More adults make a break for the doors. Kids chase them. Everyone is screaming.

ALICE and AJA units take off in hot pursuit.

Dozens of people slump to the floor as a grey fog of AJA crowd control gases deploy.

People nearest the door kick and hit the ALICE units, tipping them over. One man sees an ALICE unit extend an arm towards a sprinting young woman. He grabs it, throwing the tall, slim robotic doctor through the glass windows on the front of the hospital.

Alarms blare. AJA darts that man with something. He crumples to the floor. The crowd charges the AJA. It tips over. Several people in hospital gowns see a clean way to the exit. They sprint through the doors, only to be met by a wave of new AJA units.

The video cuts out.

The assurance of safety in Ivan's arms gives me a pang of guilt. He wraps his hands across my lower stomach, as if he's shielding his family.

A fresh video plays of a youth soccer practice in India. Parents step out of their cars and walk to meet their kids. What should be a happy, tired reunion becomes pandemonium. Screaming breaks out. Not just screams. These are primal sounds, shredding the air around them. Children scatter from the soccer fields to the parking area, running for the terrified adults.

I can't explain it. My hands fly to my mouth. Parents run. Children chase them. The panic feeds in some kind of loop. Kids reaching for safety; parents recoiling in terror. It's horrific. The sports medicine ALICE footage zooms in on several adults. They have the same wild, unfocused stares, with panic etched on their faces.

Tiny arms and legs pump as kids run after them. What is wrong with these people? They're supposed to save and comfort their kids. Ivan holds me tighter. The parents run out of the parking lot. Coaches scream for them to stop. The video cuts out when a mom crosses the white line into the road.

"Ivan, what's happened to them?" Tears pour down my face.

"We don't know," he says. His thumbs gently trace my stomach, like he's assuring Holly and Huck they're safe.

On the screen we see a woman, maybe forty, sitting rigidly at a desk in a doctor's office. Across from her is a man in a suit and an ALICE unit. Her right hand shields her eyes as she angles her head away from a couch on the side wall. A man sits on it, with a teen girl on each side. Both of them have Em's hair, nose, and eyes.

"Em. I've known your family since we were in college," the man says, pointing to the softly crying girls. "Your family is *right there,* on the couch. They're ready to take you home."

She shakes her head so hard a hair clip falls to her lap.

"You're lying!" Her voice takes on a dangerous tone. "I have to get home to my kids. Now!"

"They're your kids." He gently holds a phone towards her. "Look. This is *you*, with them."

He stops, passing a box of tissues to her.

"Lies! This picture means nothing." She jabs a finger towards the people on the couch. "Their faces are missing."

"What does that mean?" the man asks.

"I have *no* memories of them. They're faceless monsters."

10

"Baby, go. Check on Lark. Then go home and rest." Ivan rises to his feet, gently shifting me with him.

"Is this coming here?"

"I don't know."

"Moulson?" I ask.

"I'd guess so."

"How? He's in custody."

"I'll find out."

I kiss his cheek. "If Moulson did this, he won't let it hurt Lark. I'm sure of that."

"I agree." Ivan leans over the desk to whisper to Travis. His clipped command gives me a chill. "Take Story home. Protect her, no matter what." He turns to me, smiling. "Gotta work, love you."

"Love you," I say. He hugs me so tightly I'm sure he left finger dents on my ribs, then turns slowly to go back to work.

I meander up the ramp, careful to maintain decorum. I'm the Senior Commander's wife, after all. But when I crash into the push bar to swing the door open, I hit it at a full sprint.

Travis and Talia step through the dim hallways on either side of me. Most of the time, I ignore the fact we live in an underground cavern. Tonight, with this new attack, lack of sleep, and general anxiety, I'm acutely aware of how spooky it is. I can't go home without Ivan tonight, even with my guards, they just don't know it yet.

The clinic is nearly empty in Lark's wing. I have yet to see a spider in the Helm. But tonight, it feels like I'm draped in the itchy sensation of spiderwebs. I run through the clinic until I'm in her cozy room and shut the door behind us.

Mom sleeps on a small grey couch, curled in a blanket. There's a perfectly cozy recliner in the corner and a blanket warmer cabinet. I type in my staff access code and pull it open, greeted by the smell of fresh lilac fabric softener.

"I'm going to sleep here for a bit." I pull a warm black blanket out.

Travis and Talia shoot loaded glances at each other. "Rhys said to take you home," he says.

I shuffle to the recliner in my blanket burrito.

"I miss Lark. Just for a bit?" I ask.

"You have to tell Ivan this was your idea," Talia says.

I snort. "I promise to take the heat. Here. You both sit, sleep." I point to the other two chairs.

"Nah, we'll sit out there and watch," Talia says. They duck out before I can ask what they're watching for.

Mom startles awake when my recliner footstool pops open.

"Hey, Mom. Gonna sleep here for a little bit."

She blinks her bleary eyes. "Why?"

"Nothing, just miss you two."

"Where's Ivan?" She sits bolt upright. "He's been working too hard lately. You're his wife, you need to take better care of him."

Didn't know I was going to get a lecture about my unworthiness as a newlywed tonight.

"He's going home in a bit. I'll go meet him in the morning."

"Oh good," Mom says. "Why don't you get some sleep? Give me your phone. I'll wake you if he calls or texts."

There's no way I can sleep. But if it'll make her leave me alone? I'll fake it. I toss my phone beside her. These blankets smell and feel fantastic. I tuck down in them like a cottony suit of armor.

"Night, Mom."

"Night, honey." Mom says, not looking up from her phone.

The families in those videos were so scared. I peek at Lark. Her white-blonde hair is splayed across her pillow. A horse from Ivan is tucked under each arm. Her tray table is covered with bead projects.

What if that happens to her and me? To her and mom? No. Moulson won't do anything to hurt Lark. I know it. Am I seriously placing hope in *Moulson*?

I am. He has to keep her safe. I'm tempted to test waking her. No, that's a bad idea. Let her rest. I need some rest too. There's no way I can sleep, but I don't want to talk to my mom.

I'll close my eyes and think of happy things. Lark's okay. Moulson's arrested. Ivan. The babies. I picture him holding our two little swaddled bundles. His biceps will make newborns look comically tiny. I can't wait. Against all odds, on this awful, horrible day, I smile. He'll make sure this is fixed by the time they're born.

The breeze hitting my face is warm and smells of real ocean brine, not the Baltimore Cove. Sea oats sway in the breeze on the dunes of Frisco, North Carolina.

David mans a huge grill in uncharacteristically cheerful green turtle sea trunks. Richelle dances beside him, laughing as she sips a green margarita.

Lark, Mom, and Dad splash in the waves with our (true to Irontrace) black lab at their heels. Mom throws a water float toy for the dog. Dad holds a happily squealing Holly. Her ebony black baby curls bounce in the sun as Dad twirls her, letting the waves tickle her feet.

"Hey, baby boy!" Ivan peeks from behind his hands at Huck, who shrieks with joy.

Ivan's reclining in a chaise lounge and I'm leaning against his sticky, sunburnt chest. Our chunky ten-month-old Huck stretches over my shoulder, his baby fingers making a soft smacking sound as he bangs on Ivan's lips.

"Ah! You're tough, little Commander." Ivan laughs.

Huck coos happy baby nonsense.

"Really?" Ivan replies. I laugh.

Ivan ruffles Huck's hair, making a curly wave with it on the right side of his little baby head, and Huck yells, "Da!"

That's it, my heart is going to explode. No one deserves to be this happy.

"Story!" Mom screams.

Tornado sirens crank up, then blare in deafening whoops. A freezing wind blasts from nowhere, whipping my hair around Huck, Ivan, and I.

"Get out of the water!" Ivan yells. The water recedes, sucking out to build a wave that looks like a mini tsunami. It captivates Lark, Mom, and Dad. Dad stands frozen, in the danger zone, holding Holly.

"Take him!" I gently pass Huck to Ivan and run for the beach access stairs.

"Story!" Ivan roars, but I keep running to get to Holly. "Story!" Ivan's scream is like a knife in my heart. I turn. A sandstorm has blown around him and Huck.

"Mama!" Huck cries before he evaporates into grains of sand. Ivan looks between his now empty hands, then drops to his knees, screaming.

"Huck! No!" My sobs for my red-haired baby boy are lost to the wind, disappearing with him and his yellow T-rex swim trunks.

I knew it. No one deserves to be that happy.

A hand shakes my shoulder, yanking me to a reality where sirens are still going off.

"Story!" Mom says, shaking me until I jerk fully awake.

Travis yanks off my blankets. "Story. Get up."

I stand but stumble forward on the twisted blanket pile. I grab my stomach. They're okay. Huck didn't evaporate. Holly isn't facing a tsunami.

"What happened?" I ask over the alarm.

"Story, this is awful!" Lark shouts, covering her ears.

"Lark! Look in my eyes. My eyes!" I snap my fingers for her attention. She blinks sleepily at me like I'm an idiot but complies. No fear. Thank the stars! She's okay.

Lark's door flings open and a volunteer sprints in, waving for me to follow. "Dr. Rhys, help us out here for a few minutes, please."

True to orders from Ivan, Travis is my living Irontrace shadow as I jog to the hallway.

"We have to override the patient door lockdowns since the fire isn't in this area," the volunteer says.

"Fire?" Travis snaps. "Where?"

"The residential hallway."

"How long will this take?" Travis asks the volunteer.

"Five minutes," she replies.

"You can have Dr. Rhys for two."

Before I can ask why he's got us on a clock, the volunteer stops.

"This is an emergency door lockdown panel. Find the other three in this hallway, sign in, override the security controls. Make sure you follow the manual staff override steps. Watch."

She quickly swipes through the options on the screen then locks it. "Next one is five doors down. Keep going. I'll do the other halls before the patients get locked in. Bye!"

"You do this one, I'll do the next one." Travis dashes past me.

The alarm sounds are dulled in this wing, but their echoes whisper down the hallway. How is there a fire? We live in an underground cave with stone walls and mostly tile floors, not exactly ideal conditions to fuel one.

After signing in, I go through the list of questions:

- What's the reason for the lockdown? *Fire.*
- Is the threat contained? *Yes.*
- Are all patients accounted for?

Crud, are they? I have to check.

I run down the hallway and stop at each doorway to peek in then pick back up at that question.

- Are all patients accounted for? *Yes.*
- Have emergency protocols been observed? *Yes.*
- Do the patients need to be evacuated? *No.*
- Is the control room aware of the emergency? *Yes.*
- Do you acknowledge you will be asked to participate in a follow up post incident interview as a result of this override? *Yes.*

A thank you message pops up. I swipe to sign out and run to Travis.

"I'll get the last one," I tell him.

"Wait! I can't see you if you go around that corner," he says, not taking his eyes off the screen.

"I thought you were in a hurry."

"In a hurry? Yes. Let you out of line of sight when Ivan told me to protect you? No. I'm not getting my head torn off."

"You all act like Ivan is so scary."

"Well...Ivan...he's uh, you're good for him. Stick around." He laughs.

I'll need the backstory on that someday. But for now, we sprint to get the last override done. He stands with his back to mine while I fly through the prompts. Back in Lark's room, the alarms are silent. She and Mom are gone.

"Come on, we gotta meet the group," Travis says and runs.

In the main hallway, a wave of arms clad in navy uniforms usher me away from him.

"What? Ah! What is all over the floor?" I ask. It feels like we're walking on a slip and slide. The tile floor is covered with a slippery blue substance. The men grip my arms, keeping me on my feet.

"Fire suppression foam. We've been looking for you," Air Titan Matthew Sullivan says. The sharp look he trains on Travis could start another fire. "Don't fall, Story."

I can't see much over the crush encircling me, but I recognize they're taking me home. The foam gets thicker as we go, soaking my shoes. The waterfalls outside this part of The Helm sound extra loud in the ambient speakers this morning.

Suspiciously loud.

Acrid air stings my nose and eyes. Is this air safe for the babies? We need some fresh air. A gust of fresh wind hits my face. This isn't the recirculated, purified air of our sandstone Helm dwelling. A humid August breeze brushes my skin, laced with a hint of mist from the falls.

Brilliant sunshine floods in the wall of windows I love to look out. The windows aren't open. They're gone.

The people in front of me part, revealing the last few feet to our home.

"Story." Ivan's muffled voice barks.

Our front door is obliterated. A fire destroyed the cozy little refuge where we fell in love. Blue fire suppression foam drips from the ceilings, the walls, making puddles on the floor.

I don't look in our apartment to see what's damaged. It doesn't matter what we lost. Who cares what's left in there?

I can't take my eyes off Ivan. He's *smoking* hot.

Literally.

11

My eyes are glued to the stretcher where Ivan sits, long legs dangling over the side. His cheeks are red from heat. The lower half of his face is covered by a mask with an inhaler-sized oxygen concentrator.

"Ivan!" I take off in a dangerous dash to him.

He tears off his mask, leaps up, and runs to me. Neither of us can get traction to stop in the slippery mess. We crash together in a frantic tangle of tears and kisses.

"Where were you?" He breathes into my neck. I run my hands over his face, neck, shoulders, arms, assessing him, checking the values on his pulse oximetry displayed on his mask. From his chest down seems okay except for small burns on his pants.

"Lark's hospital room. Are you hurt?"

"I told you to go home!" His wheezes turn into coughs.

"Breathe, Ivan." I hold his oxygen mask in place.

How close was I to losing my favorite person?

"I'm fine." He stifles a dry, violent cough, but then gives into a series of sharp, barking coughs.

"Someone get Senior Commander Rhys an AirMend breathing treatment right now!" I yell.

"I'm fine," he repeats. "Not hurt. Just a little crispy."

Oh, my love. More scars. Tattered pieces of shirt are stuck in small burns on his shoulders and arms. His watery, red eyes stay trained on mine. As his breathing slows, he lowers his left arm down my back, tracing carefully around until his knuckles rest on my lower stomach.

"I thought you were in the fire. I went in and tried to find you."

"I'm sorry! I'm not the most obedient wife." *I almost got him killed.*

"I'm painfully aware of that." His laugh turns to a wheeze.

"I'll let you know where I am next time, I swear!" I cling around his neck like I can press an apology into his skin.

Travis steps close. "Sorry, SC. I accept responsibility for her staying in the clinic."

Ivan wraps Travis in a crushing hug. Everyone gasps. I want to shout *"See! Ivan's the best, don't fear him."*

"Always listen to my wife," Ivan says through coughs.

Richelle runs up with the breathing treatment. I tear open the med mixture and pour it in the reservoir on his mask. He takes several slow breaths.

"Better, thanks," he finally says. "I sent Ben Washington to relieve Travis and Talia. He's got some bad burns, but he'll be fine. They've got him in the clinic."

Poor Ben! "He was in our apartment for the fire?" I ask.

He tips his chin up and down. Is our whole home gone? I lead Ivan to what used to be our blue front door.

"You can't go in. Just peek," Talia warns us.

The table that once held his *Welcome Home, Story* sign is burnt beyond recognition. The couch where we drew plans for INES is reduced to springs and a fire-blackened metal frame. Ivan's desk chair, where we sat when I realized he loved me, is charred. If I was here, yes, I probably could've helped Ben. But our bedroom is a complete loss. There's a good chance I would have died trying to get out. I shudder closer to Ivan.

"Don't worry about our stuff. We're okay. That's all that matters," he says.

David taps him on the shoulder. "Ivan, we need to talk."

"Why are you up?" Ivan blurts.

"Now. Let's go." David extends an arm to lead us away.

Ivan keeps an arm locked around my waist while we skate down the wet apartment hallway between floor maintenance robots. We make a quick stop in the central supply room. He fetches another breathing treatment. I slip some BurnMend kits in my pockets.

"Ivan, how do I know which ones are robots?" I whisper as we walk past the nurse's station.

"Clinic staff is all human. Anyone in the control room is a human. Everyone from Atlas Caverns or support staff that cleans, gardens, or does maintenance is a bot." I grimace at his words. That's a lot of people, well, robots. "It's in their eyes, I'll teach you. You doing okay?"

No! Fake it. I smile. "I had a dream we were at the beach with Huck." Not quite the full story, but close enough...

"Wish I could've seen it." He pulls me into Mai's room where the Project Ilex Irontrace are gathered.

"We have five minutes for a lightning debrief. Story, activate SAM," David says, shutting the door. "Talia, tell us what happened."

I tear open a BurnMend kit and make myself busy cleaning the few small burns on Ivan's left shoulder and bicep. Cool, medicated vapor from his breathing treatment swirls around us.

Talia stands, hands on hips. "We were posted outside Lark's room. Story, Amelia, and Lark were asleep. My monitoring picked up movement outside your apartment. Ben had gone in, but there was a signature for a lurking ALICE. Ben wasn't answering me when I asked him to go check out why it was there. I decided to run there."

She shakes her head, remembering. "But when I got there, it wasn't an ALICE. It was the strangest thing. I hit my panic alarm. Then it launched itself straight into your apartment door and exploded. Must've had some kind of fire accelerant in it. Took about three seconds to look like a wildfire had consumed your unit."

"If it wasn't an ALICE, what was it?" David asks.

"A baby stroller, wheeling in slow circles at their door."

Coughs tear through Ivan. I freeze. My swab of burn repair ointment hovering over his forearm.

David scoffs. "Well, that's about the creepiest thing imaginable. I would've pushed my alarm so hard it shattered."

Ivan and I stay silent, unmoving. Richelle ducks to catch my panicky eyes, opening her mouth in an O-shape. She raises her eyebrows and mouths, "You? Baby?" I give a tiny nod. She claps a hand over her grin.

"Look, here's the video feed from that time." Travis opens a laptop.

Everyone crowds to peek at a bassinet-type stroller wheeling down the empty hallway towards our apartment. Inside is a large sign that reads, *Congrats, Mom and Dad!* The stroller reaches the end of the hallway, then makes slow arcs outside our door.

Bright lights flash in the hallway, and the stroller disappears, leaving behind a smoldering area with flames on the walls and floor.

"Congrats, Mom and Dad!" David laughs, obviously thinking this was a stupid prank. "You guys have known each other for like..." He trails off. His eyebrows go up with calculations. "*Mom? And Dad!?*"

Ivan and I grin at each other.

Our Project Ilex confidantes burst into a happy uproar.

"Irontrace baby!" Talia bounces with excitement.

"Baby Rhys! Nice!" Henri grins.

"Congrats!" Cherise laughs.

"A baby? In The Helm?" Travis smiles.

David rubs his face, trying to swipe away the shocking news.

Richelle wraps Ivan and I in a crushing hug, squishing us together. She shrieks and dances in place, kissing my cheek. "A baby Rhys!" She tries to kiss his cheek too, but he dodges backwards, laughing.

Ivan kisses my hand and says, "It's actually Rhys *babies.*"

The room loses it again. David's lackluster response to our news disintegrates. He claps Ivan on the back, grinning. "Congrats!"

"The security concerns and implications for this. It's...a lot." Ivan shakes his head. "Get better, David. I need you to take your job back."

"Who else knows about the twins?" Henri asks.

"Just Ivan and I."

"INES ran labs under Story's name," Ivan says. "I hid them."

All the Irontrace freeze. Mouths drop.

"I'm sorry. I didn't think," I stammer.

It takes visible effort for David to pry his eyes from whatever silent, mental conversation he and Ivan are having. He does, then pats me on the shoulder. "Nope, it's fine. Don't worry."

The Irontrace trade glances for several seconds. Feels like Richelle and I are the only two with no idea what's happening.

"Super-*duper* seems like you should worry," Richelle says in the poorest excuse for a whisper I've ever heard.

"Five minutes are up," Talia says.

"I'm going home for the rest of my recovery. Baracu, set up a work-station in my apartment. Ivan, I'll track down what happened to Story's labs." David walks to the door. "Everybody else, to the control room. Get back to work under everyone's favorite Irontrace Dad."

"Tech Daddy! He's a Tech Daddy!" Richelle bursts.

The room erupts into loud chants of "Tech Daddy!"

"I will shoot you all." Ivan tries to look exasperated, but he can't stop laughing. "No! Just, no. Go work. That's an order. We're outta here." He leads me into the hallway. "Go spend some time with Lark before the Air Titans get here with your new round of trainees."

"When do you get off? You've been in the control room for. Wait. I lost count. Too long."

"No idea, sorry." He nods for Travis and Talia to join us. "Stick right beside Story. I want her in SAM as much as possible."

I open my mouth to protest. He curls his massive hand around my chin, gently shaking my head yes.

"Pleeeeeeeeeease," he coaxes until I relent.

"Fine. But Lark and I are bringing you new clothes and breakfast. Gotta keep these under wraps." I stick my hand in one of the burnt holes of his shirt and squeeze his bicep, making an appreciative face. He flexes, trapping my hand in the bend of his arm.

"Ha! Stuck now, love."

"Did you forget you need to go back to work?" I scold through laughs, glancing at poor Travis and Talia. They're trying their hardest to keep an eye on me without leering at Ivan's antics.

"Boo. I want to stay and play."

"Six more days. You'll be my regular old Commander Rhys again be-fore we know it."

12

I found Lark and Mom eating pancakes in Atlas Caverns. As soon as Lark sees me, she starts talking. "There you are! You disappeared in the hallway. I'm done. Want my leftovers?" She scoots most of a plate of pancakes covered with strawberries my way and hands me a fork.

"Is everything okay, honey?" Mom asks, brows drawn together. "Your shoes have blue stuff all over them."

"Oh. Yeah." I don't want to scare Lark. "There was a problem in our apartment and we had a small fire. Can you believe it? Ben Washington is in the clinic. He was in the apartment when it happened. Ivan said Ben will be okay."

Mom gasps, holding her chest. "Oh no!"

"It could have been much worse. Good thing Ivan and I weren't in there." I take a bite of pancakes and do a happy dance at Lark. The berries on top are near perfect. She mirrors my shoulder shimmy and steals a berry.

"Ivan's okay?" Mom is still clutching her chest.

"Yes. He ended up staying in the control room to work last night."

"Yay for Ivan! Thank goodness being SC is ruining his life, ha!" Lark giggles at her joke.

Mom blows a huge sigh. "Yes, I'm so glad Ivan is a workaholic. I thought for sure that was him in the apartment..." she mutters, shaken.

"Did Ivan lose his drawer of awards and medals?" Lark asks. "He let me borrow some of the gold ones. They're safe in my backpack. I was going to surprise my teacher tomorrow and tell her about all the cool things he does."

Ivan doesn't have drawers anymore. And wouldn't he just be thrilled if she had outed the whole Squadron to her class? "I'll check later. Let's talk about fun stuff. Like back-to-school shopping."

Her face lights up. "Can we go now? I'm already missing morning class and my friends. Let's go shop, then Mom can drop me off at school."

I can't tell her no. I'm too hormonal to handle her disappointed face. I'll blame the robots. "I have to talk to your ALICE and see if you're allowed."

She leans forward and whispers, "If you train the robots, doesn't that mean you really get to decide what I'm allowed to do?"

She's got me there. "Sometimes." Distract her! "I need to get Ivan a new shirt. Then do you want to take some of these pancakes to Ivan?"

"Yes!"

Off to Atlas Caverns. We've got to grab Ivan a new SC shirt.

Lark found an office supplies section and was in heaven. She said she could do all her school supply shopping here. She chose a black backpack and shoved it full of black notebooks, folders, pens, pencils, an engineering design kit with colored pencils and drawing paper, a black water bottle, and a small black cooler she swears will make the perfect lunchbox. The girl in all black will stand out among her sparkly, rainbow-clad friend group.

On the way to the control room, Lark happily skips between Mom and I, chattering. My heart hurts for all the families who are missing moments like this because of Moulson's purge.

"Wait here, I'll go give this to Ivan," I say as I loop my arm through the handle to open the door.

"Oh, can we come in too? I've never been in there," Mom says.

"I have to ask Ivan first."

Ivan stands sentinel down front. His arms are crossed as council members blast him with a barrage of questions. News articles and photos of families in turmoil are displayed on half the monitors. A huge screen stands with a list of bullet points outlining onset and progression of symptoms. The last bullet point nearly makes me puke.

Root cause: ??????

Ivan sees me coming and cuts across the room. His jaw is clenched too tight to return my smile.

"Am I reading that right? Six hundred million victims now?" I ask.

"And climbing." He kicks an office chair at a workstation so hard it doesn't roll. It flips over, leaving the wheels spinning.

"What have you found out?"

"It hit parents that dropped kids off at school. Now if they see their families, it gives them devastating panic attacks. They can see or talk to everyone else—doctors, me, you, each other, no problem. One glance at their kid? Their spouse? They're gone, trapped in a panic state."

"They don't recognize their family?"

"Nope. Patients can't see a face. Same story from everyone we've talked to. They see nothing. Just a dark void. Makes them absolutely flip out." He points to the screen, showing people frozen in panic. "Their poor kids are suffering nearly as bad. They want their moms and dads back."

"I'm sure."

"When we show patients pics or videos of their families, they're okay. But they don't recognize them. It's the actual people that make them panic."

"It's a panic disorder mixed with amnesia?" I ask. He nods. "What caused it?"

"Your guess is as good as mine."

"I brought you a shirt. And pancakes." I lay the bag on his desk. He rips off his old shirt and puts on the new one. I catch sight of several blistered areas from burns on his upper back. "I need to put meds on those burns too."

"Thanks for the shirt. I'm too frustrated to eat. Rain check?"

"Sure. *We* love you." The faintest smile finally touches his lips.

"I love you, baby." He kisses my cheek then stalks down the control room ramp, leaving me with his container of cold pancakes.

I step to throw them in his trash can, but the fast movement of the container wafts the pancake smell up to me. *More breakfast for the babies and me? Yes, please.* I pop the lid off and snack on them while we walk up the ramp.

"You're really going to eat those frigid trash pancakes?" Travis asks, cocking a brow.

"For sure. You want some?" I offer him a forkful.

"I'll leave them to you. And that whole situation you've got going on in there." He laughs, pointing to my stomach.

"Appreciate it."

Stepping into the hall, I'm hit with a mini panic attack of my own. Lark stares in the control room windows, a blank look on her face that I've never seen before. Travis dodges a pancake syrup shower when I smash the container into his chest.

"Hey, Lark! Lark! Is your AVM okay?" I throw myself on a knee and spin her to face me.

"I don't want to go to school this afternoon," she says, voice flat.

"Okay, no school. Mom can take you to do something fun while I work. What happened, Talia?"

"Nothing. We were watching you and Ivan." Talia looks as lost as I feel.

"Why don't you want to go to school, Lark?" Mom asks.

She points towards the control room. "The kids went to school yesterday. Now their families don't know them. Their moms are stuck in hospitals. I hate the hospital."

"Oh, Lark, school didn't cause this," Talia says. "The OWL AI teacher models are all fine."

Lark pushes back from me and snaps, "Talia. Tell Ivan not to chicken out. He has to keep hunting. This was something at school." I marvel that someone would imply Ivan chickened out of an investigation. "Those kids went to school. Something made their families forget them. Milk? Lunch? Crayons? Paper? Someone snuck tiny brain-eating robots in the milk? No way I'm letting milk robots turn me into something that scares Mom."

Mom laughs. "Lark, no one is putting brain-eating robots in milk."

"I mean, did they check for that?" I whisper to Travis and Talia. They shrug. "Lark, you wanna go ask Ivan?"

"Yes!" She yanks me towards the door for the control room.

"Wait, we can't just interrupt him." I peek in. Ivan stands with his back to us near the monitors down front. "Talia and Travis. Can you please take them in one of the side hallway meeting rooms? I'll meet you there."

"10-4, boss lady. Come this way, Lark, Mrs. Ross," Travis says.

They turn to follow him. I press the emerald to enter SAM. I carefully wind my way to stand directly in front of Ivan. He listens attentively to Dr. Dawes. Once she pauses, another doctor immediately cuts in.

"Dr. Charles Irving here. I have prepared a list of environmental factors that may have contributed to this." His "insights" drip with compliments to his own brilliance. He's presenting maybe an hour of research he fed into an AI model to make a slideshow. Ivan's face screams that this man is dead wrong.

Ivan holds his hand up to interrupt Irving, then glances my way. He lowers his hand.

I tug at the waist of his shirt. He barely moves, just shifts back a step. I do it again, tracing a finger along the top of his perfect iliac furrow. He nonchalantly tries to catch my hand. I move too fast and he doesn't make contact. I might start using SAM more often to cause some chaos in his day.

His eyes stay glued to the screen. I yank one of his belt loops. He steps a few inches closer. In a shocking turn of events, he drops his eyes, making perfect, burning eye contact with me. He arches a thick black eyebrow, and a restrained smile plays across his mouth.

That face! Goodness, my love. It's not fit for a boardroom. He narrows his eyes, sizing me up. I do it back, meeting his silent challenge. This won't end well. Direct eye contact with Ivan always leads to shenanigans. After about ten seconds of staring seemingly into each other's souls while the idiot doctor drones on, I'm the first to blink.

"How?" I whisper. Ivan quickly pretends to chew a fingernail to hide a smile. I know he finds nail biting revolting. Looks like I won our staring contest.

The speaker mercifully pauses. Ivan addresses the room. "I've been told there's a call I must take. Please continue exploring this riveting line of thought in my absence."

Ivan marches over to a doorway between the monitors and pushes a wall panel open, revealing a dark room. I rush in behind him.

"This is not what I had in mind when I asked you to hang out in SAM," Ivan fake-scolds. "Why, wife?"

"Lark has to talk to you," I say.

"Ah, well, this must be important." He crouches on a knee in front of her. "What's up, little Miss Lark?"

She rapidly repeats her thoughts on the familial purge. The rest of us can't hide our surprise when Lark and Ivan get into a serious discussion about her theory of milk robots.

He asks her a lengthy list of questions, his investigator eyes crinkling as he processes her answers.

"Did the parents get breakfast or lunch at school? I *HATE* school food. And the trays are so weird. You have to get a tray from the AI cafeteria people. It's always been freshly sterilized so even if you eat a cold peanut butter sandwich, the hot tray makes the bread warm. It's super gross. It's 2050, why do they do that to us?"

I snort. Kids and school food haven't made much progress.

"For breakfast I like yogurt and fruit, but I never get it. The hot trays make the yogurt runny. No thanks! That is disGUSting!" She speaks rapid-fire like usual, her thoughts building from each previous sentence. "You can't get the food until they scan your face. Then it cleans your tray and blows it dry to load it."

His eyes flick to mine. He goes still. I can tell he's using me as a silent sounding board. All at once, he grins, connecting some dots I've clearly missed. He rises in a flash, making Travis jump.

"Lark! You genius!" he says with a grin.

She beams. "Can I go to school now?"

He whips his head side to side. "Good Lord, no! You're all to stay in The Helm. I gotta go. Travis, Talia, get them out the back way." Without another word, he slips back into the control room.

13

"I brought you some friends," Matthew Sullivan, Ivan's Air Titan friend says.

"Always nice to see you, Sully," I say as Dad joins my side.

Dad turns to the group, launching into introductions.

"Dr. Benedict, I'm so glad you made it!" Dad says.

My whole body stiffens. Why wouldn't he have given me a heads up my former boss is on the invitation list? No. This guy shouldn't be here unsupervised.

"Talia. Benedict's a creep. Ivan ruined his marriage because he wouldn't quit touching me and every young woman within reach," I whisper.

"Gotcha. I'll tell Travis." She catches up to him, pulling on his hand. He turns to her with a soft smile. Are they a thing? News to me.

I never thought to ask what the Irontrace dating Irontrace policy is. Having seen the way eyes follow Ivan, I'm sure he's got a trail of old fans all over The Helm.

Dad's talking rapidly to the surgeons. There's not much for me to do or say at this point.

Dr. B. drifts backwards from the group to me. "Dr. Rhys. I'm looking forward to a long, productive working relationship with you." *Mmmhmm, sure ya are, Dr B.* "When I heard you built out the plan for INES while working full time for me, I was so proud of you. I took a massive chance to hire you. It seems my estimation of you was correct."

"INES wouldn't have been possible without my husband, Senior Commander Rhys. He's looking forward to meeting you after hearing all I had to say about you."

Ha! The color drains from his face. I love the power my scary husband has to make idiots wither.

"Looking forward to it." He tips his head and joins the group.

Richelle throws an arm across my shoulders. "Sorry I'm late! David bored me to tears with a lecture on computer file permits. Wait, maybe permissions? Something like that. Anyways, I fell asleep on his couch." She laughs. "How are you, mama?"

I start to protest, but no one appears to have heard her. "I'm good. How are you?"

"I'm fan-tas-tic! What's the plan for the day?"

She frowns as I explain the sim surgeries we'll be in for the next fifteen hours. In the lab, she and I fiddle at her Trusted Advisor station for a few minutes while Dad addresses our colleagues.

"Surgeons. There's a lot happening right now in the medical world that could captivate our attention. But we need to stay focused on our assignment. Using my daughter's Rhys Method, you'll be learning how to perform an innovative surgery. Let's get into it. Dr. Rhys, please assist Dr. Benedict as he works through his first sim surgery."

Well, isn't this a beautiful start to the day? Working elbow-to-elbow with one of the most annoying people I've ever met. Guess this is what I get for keeping my dad in the dark when I have problems.

The surgery is so full of questions and displays of INES technique that it seemed to fly past. Dr. B. is careful to keep a respectful distance for once.

We decided to take a lunch break before the next surgery. My dad is in his element, schmoozing and networking with the other doctors. That's the opposite of how I'd like to spend my time. Ivan probably hasn't had anything to eat or drink all day. My pancake breakfast wore off hours ago. I'll escape and go eat with him.

"Dr. Ross, I need to step out briefly," I tell Dad. He waves goodbye without looking my way.

What is going on with him lately? He and Ivan have disagreed on many things through the years. I'm wondering if being Ivan's wife means Dad is feeling at odds with me now too. It'll be interesting to see how he feels about being Grandpa to Ivan's kids.

Travis, Talia, Richelle, and I stop in Atlas Caverns to grab tacos. Richelle splits off to go eat at David's. The rest of us ride the elevators down and follow a short dark hallway that dumps us back in the tiny black room from earlier. Travis and Talia get comfy and tear into their tacos while I step into the control room in SAM.

Unbelievably, the situation has deteriorated further.

What used to be protests outside Bastion headquarters is nearly a civil war. Some monitors show crowds trying to break into headquarters and hospitals. Roving bands of people are fleeing their homes, looking for their 'missing' children. The purge's amnesia sure is effective. These people have no idea where they belong or to whom.

Screens with the local news show crowds outside of the twenty-seven story Lancaster Medical Hub. The hospital is beautiful. Windows gleaming in the sunshine. Most of the floral artwork has been repaired since Moulson's attack on the atmosphere models in May. A rainbow waterfall of flowers pours down the front of the massive building.

The lovely view can't hide the ugliness surrounding the hospital. Campsites for purge people's loved ones are contained in metal fences and razor wire. An army of AJA ground units encircle the area. AJA drone units soar above.

"For your safety, stop trying to interfere with the AJA units," the reporter warns. "Emergency rooms are busy caring for your loved ones. Field clinics have been set up to deal with hundreds of injuries protestors have sustained from AJA."

Footage shows several AJA drones nearly taken down when people stab sticks and metal poles upwards at them. Some hold signs demanding entrance to the hospital.

Ivan sits at the table in front of the room, surrounded by council members and Irontrace. They go silent when he stands to stretch.

"I'll be back momentarily. Take a lunch break, please," he announces to the control room then tips his chin at me. We cut into the little room. He locks the door. He shuts SAM off then turns it right back on, leaving Travis and Talia staring at our digital clones.

He drops to a chair, pulling me onto his lap. "Family purge? Yep.

That's what this is. Moulson sure is a man of his awful word."

"Dad's doing the next surgery. I've got time. Let's talk."

"Kids are terrified. The things the panic is doing to their moms and dads—Story, it's the worst thing I've ever seen. I know what it's like to be ripped away from your family. That was nothing like this. People are destroying, burning, breaking everything. I would too, honestly. Someone took you and stuck you in a hospital prison to keep you 'safe'? I'd burn the world to the ground to get you back. The Bastion has stuck their coward heads in the sand. ALICE has no idea how to do a press conference." He leans forward and rests his forehead on mine. "It's ALICE trainers and Irontrace scrambling for a solution."

Stress rolls off him in quiet, heavy waves. He always lightens the tension for me. Time to return the favor.

"The doctors don't even try to hide that they don't trust us." I plant a quick kiss on his forehead that makes his lips curve into a small smile. "They think Irontrace are criminals because of the whole Agora imprisonment thing." Left cheek kiss. His smile is getting bigger. "Alright, wife. Got any suggestions?"

Right cheek kiss. His eyes crinkle and his smile grows. Kiss on the tip of his nose. He catches my chin and gives me an expectant look. "Story?"

"Step one. Get us a new apartment," I say, doing a happy wiggle.

"Really? You'd be hopeless as Senior Commander!" He laughs.

My plan is working. The world keeps handing him tragedy after tragedy to fix. I can't stop any of it. But I *can* give him one steady thing untouched by the chaos. Me.

I tip his hand to look at his watch.

"You have ten hours left in there. Then you had better take me home. Have Richelle call Julianna Devareux, from LNN. I have her number. Go on the news like Maseko said. Tell the world about Irontrace. *Don't* be humble. Say how awesome you are."

I squish his cheeks in my hands, making his lips into something resembling a fish.

"Look at you. This is the face of a trustworthy, seasoned commander. You're doing battle for them. For their kids. You've spent your life guarding these people. You've lost friends and family to get to this point." I see he's coming around. "Plus, let's be honest, these babies deserve a celebrity Dad to match their famous Mom."

He breathes a happy sigh. "Thank you, baby. This was a perfect distraction."

"Anytime! One question though. How can you see me in SAM?"

He swipes his right eye and pulls off a clear disc. I gag. "Optic filter that works as a dampener for SAM. Allows me to see and touch you while you're in there. You'll never be invisible or out of reach to me, gorgeous."

He laughs as I fan my eyes. "Don't touch your eyes around me anymore. You're scaring the kids."

We had a wonderful six minutes to eat tacos until someone beat on the door for him to come back. I *hate* his new job.

14

Dad worked through the next surgery with a vascular surgeon named Dr. Wylie from the Cleveland Medical Hub.

A man named Dr. Ryland from the East Carolina Medical Hub asked an impressive number of intelligent, engaged questions from his seat. Every time I'd glance his way, his eyes were riveted to the monitor, his empty hands practicing the movements like a dance.

"Would you like to do the next sim surgery?" I ask him.

His face lights up. "Yes, Dr. Rhys. Thank you."

"No problem. I'll grab you in a few minutes." Lunch with my baby was too short. It might have made me miss him more.

I MISS YOU! Got our apartment lined up yet? One surgery left. -<3

I fold my hands into my black scrub shirt pockets. Time for my routine check-in with the twins. One hand on my stomach, I take several deep breaths.

They're okay. I can feel it. With all the problems in the world, my babies are safe, warm, and loved. How has it only been a few months since I was a lonely college student with no life? Now I'm a mom, a wife, surrounded by friends. ASTRA is mine for the taking.

My phone buzzes.

A team is setting it up now. They're making a whole candlelit dinner thing for us. -I

Haven't you had enough fire for one day? - <3

Have you seen yourself in candlelight?!?! This conversation is deeply unfair to my sanity. I better go. Have fun cutting necks open. See you soon, my love. -I

Dr. Ryland did an excellent job. But he's been keeping something from us. His secret is so blatantly obvious I couldn't stop smiling behind my scrub mask. *He's operated before!* From the looks of it, he's done many surgeries.

I'm going to ask Ivan to get a background check and add Ryland to Project Ilex. Another free thinker will be a welcome addition.

We're reviewing the procedures from today when every monitor in the clinic turns on. *STANDBY FOR EMERGENCY BROADCAST!* flashes on all screens except for the INES monitors.

Quiet questions fill the room. Travis, Talia, and Richelle look as lost as I feel. Travis tips his watch towards me. The time has been replaced by the same emergency message.

Richelle mouths a ghastly "What is this?" at me, holding up her phone to show the same thing.

Please let this be an Irontrace thing, not Moulson!

A blonde reporter appears, smoothing her hair. "Julianna Deveraux reporting live to a global audience. I'm here with some representatives of The Bastion with a public service announcement."

"My name is Senior Commander Ivan Rhys." I freeze at his deep, gravelly voice. "I'm *not* a representative of The Bastion. I speak for The Irontrace Squadron."

Oh, baby. Get 'em! His tan jawline is clenched tight, giving the impression he's already prepped for action. The lighting on his bearded, scarred face makes him look like the imposing, seasoned fighter he is.

Richelle squeals with joy and yells, "Ivan! There's our Tech-" *No, don't do it, Richelle!* "Man!"

I breathe a heavy sigh. Thank goodness she censored herself.

"My apologies. I was misinformed," Julianna says, blinking fast. Her frigid smile screams that someone is getting fired for this mix-up. "I'm going to ask the burning question we're all wondering, what is The Irontrace Squadron?"

"Let's get into it." He flashes a perfect Ivan grin.

She tries to casually lean back in her chair but misses the armrest and flaps her left elbow like a chicken wing to catch herself. We've all been there when he does that.

Ivan launches into an explanation of who Irontrace are and what they do. If the surgeons here are any indication of how people around the world are reacting, going public was the right call.

Dr. Ryland and Dr. Wylie appear at my elbow. "This can't be real, Dr. Rhys?" Ryland asks. "Isn't that your husband?"

I don't blame him for his disbelief. Suddenly finding out your whole world is run by a secret team your government has been holding captive is a lot to take in.

"Yes. That's my Ivan. The one who built INES."

"Extraordinary!" Dr. Ryland mutters.

Julianna presses for more. "If I understand you correctly, you're saying the Irontrace are the engineers who have kept The Kernel running all these years?"

"Correct. We are," he says.

"Well, what does The Bastion do then?"

He barks out a laugh then scrambles to cover it with a cough. *Chill, babe. You're gonna get us killed.*

"They do a lot of administrative duties to keep the Irontrace well-staffed and running. At my Helm, they frequently visit for status updates and to work remotely. Architect Maseko is heavily involved in our work to fix the familial purge."

"Why are you telling us about The Irontrace now?"

"Honestly, my wife. Hey there, beautiful." Every person in the room turns to stare at me. I nearly burst into flames. "She said knowing about the Irontrace made her feel safer. The Bastion agreed it's time to get to know us. So, from The Irontrace to all of you, hello world."

Her smile cracks, suddenly accusatory. "Why have you Irontrace been allowing the AI models to break every few weeks since May?"

"Julianna, have you ever been attacked?" he asks.

She wraps her sweater tighter, practically clutching invisible pearls. "I don't see how that's relevant, but no, I haven't."

"I have, obviously." He points to his face. "Many times, while defending The Kernel." Her jaw drops. "Take a second, travel with me back to April."

He weaves a spoken scrapbook of how well life was going under The Bastion. Granted, he leaves out the part about them executing people and buying kids to imprison.

"Schools were one hundred percent secure. Bullying was unheard of. Hunger was eliminated. The global food supply was completely balanced. No more natural disasters. Elderly citizens had more independence than ever due to homecare models. Anxiety and depression were at an all-time low."

Julianna is captivated. So is everyone around me. It's like he's talking directly to each one of us.

"2031 was the last recorded cancer death." He points emphatically. "*That's* what the world looks like when AI is running smoothly under Irontrace control. But The Kernel has come under attack in recent months. Your families are under attack." He drops his guard and lets the fire in his dark eyes burn. "That is unacceptable to the Irontrace! We love you. I swear on my life we'll fix this. As a start, I'm thrilled to announce we figured out how this attack was launched."

The room around me explodes into whispers. Lab coats rustle as everyone yanks phones from their pockets.

"Who was behind these attacks?" Julianna asks.

"Anthony Moulson. He's in AJA custody in Columbus." Ivan grins when sounds of a celebration break out from the newsroom around Julianna. "Moulson destroyed society as we know it. Happy to announce, his bank account has been liquidated. We'll disperse his billions to families affected by this familial purge."

Claps and cheers break out in the OR.

"What do you think of recent reports that The Bastion has plans to fully automate The Kernel and let it run without human interference?"

Their plans to what?

He lifts a hand, cutting her off. "I'd love to keep talking, but my time right now is far better spent working on how to help the purge victims. Thank you for your time." He jumps out of his chair and disappears. Gotta love this man. No time for nonsense.

The camera cuts to a flustered Julianna. "Tune into LNN for live updates. Visit the link below to learn more about the Irontrace Squadron, our hidden heroes."

The OR roars with questions about Irontrace. Dr. Ryland tries to keep us focused by asking a question about INES' angiogram machine.

The monitor behind the group turns on. A message pops up.

Apartment 417. Come home to me, my love. -I

That's why he ran from the chair. Well, there goes my train of thought. Why do we care about angiograms again?

"Sorry. Yes, notice the color overlays, they'll line up with um...my apologies." My brain is mush. Sixteen hours of technical demos and questions. I can't anymore.

Dad glances from me to Ivan's message. He sighs. "Dr. Rhys, thank you for your work today. You go for the night. We'll wrap up here."

"Thank you, Dr. Ross. See you all in the morning." The second the lab door clicks shut behind me, I activate SAM and bolt into an awkward, careful sprint.

15

Ivan put a SAM style of shield he calls a Fara-mar system around our new apartment's perimeter.

"Lark helped me figure it out. When kids are dropped off at school, license plate scanners log every car. Moulson hacked into them. Instead of reading plates, he unleashed some kind of EMP blast into each car *if* there was only one passenger in it. It's a horrific nod to his skills. Shame he only uses them to hurt people."

"No new cases since you shut those down?" I ask.

"None. Now we have to figure out how to fix this. I'm thrilled with this update. We stopped the purge from hitting anyone else. Senior Commander Max Darke in Perth is running the show tonight. He's excellent. I told them I needed to get some sleep."

I blow him a kiss and back away. "To bed with you then, SC. I'll go back to my lab so you can sleep."

"Dr. Rhys, get back here!" He dives over the back of the couch, trips, then falls, rolling toward my feet. He scrambles up, laughing. I screech, delighted, when he gathers me in his arms. "I've got burns! I require immediate medical attention."

The next morning we're up bright and early. Ivan lazes beside me in bed, holding my decaf iced coffee while I braid my hair.

"We need to get Lark's surgery done ASAP. I took time off for our honeymoon. Then those couple of days off after I got back from Bastion custody. I shouldn't have done that," I say. "Maybe Lark wouldn't have ended up with another Agora episode the other day if I'd have kept my research moving."

He scoots behind me in the bed, putting his legs out on either side of mine. "Here, let me help." He takes my halfway finished braid.

"Lark's episode wasn't your fault." He gently tugs my hair, weaving it with his nimble fingers, smoothing out each section as he works down my braid. "You can't work all the time. No one expected you to then. No one expects you to, especially now."

"I can't slow down."

"I'm not asking you to. I trust you to listen to your body and take care of yourself." He finishes my braid much faster than expected and crawls around to face me. "I've got some bad news though."

He flips the braid over my shoulder. The lower half is a twisted, definitely-not-braided, frizzy mess.

"Turns out, I have no idea how to braid hair. That really took a turn on me there at the end, sorry."

I crack up. "Are you kidding? This is perfect. I'm showing this to everyone. Richelle is going to want a matching one to surprise David with."

"David and Richelle? She's braver than I gave her credit for."

"She likes a challenge. Speaking of Irontrace couples, have you got some old fans in The Helm, Senior Commander?"

"Nope. Just the one girl I told you about. We spent all of our free time together for about five years."

Five years? Richelle jokes I've known Ivan for five minutes and we're already a whole life deep. I try to stay neutral, but my rotten voice betrays me. "That's a long time."

"Yep. Kristen. Agora took her out two years ago. I may be the worst person ever to say I never loved her. She was more of a loyal, constant friend to commiserate with. It was nothing like you and I. Kristen hated it here too, and having some*one* was better than hanging out with *every*one. When she died, I vowed to never put someone through that kind of loss. Everyone has looked at me since her death like I'm the unattainable one. Hence the googly eyes following me."

I kiss his hand. "I'm sorry you lost your friend."

"*Then* I met you. You were this seething, silent, mess of pine sap, knotted hair, and blood."

I burst out laughing, remembering how bad I looked that day.

"When you yelled at me and said I better not kidnap you or you'd fight me? Oh babe, I was absolutely feral for you right there on the spot! I'd never met someone like you. Everyone in my life until then knew me. No one had ever been wary, unsure, or doubted my intentions. It was so refreshing to meet someone who challenged me. It hit me that I'd have to actually prove myself worthy for once, to earn your trust and maybe a place in your life. I nearly screamed, 'this is the one, gonna shatter her heart in a billion pieces when my Agora blows!'" A crooked smile tugs on the left side of his mouth. I shoot a hair tie at his chest and grin. "Only you, my perfect Story."

"Let's make a deal. No shattering each other's hearts," I say. "We stay madly, screamingly in love no matter what happens."

"Deal." He pulls out a little velvet bag. "I had something made for you."

I loosen the drawstring and drop the contents in my hand. Two beautiful rose gold bracelet cuffs, each with decorative stamping and a smooth ball on each end. One has holly leaves and berries dancing along it. The other has a delicate huckleberry impression punched on it.

Ivan pulls off my resin bracelets. "I wanted you to have keepsake versions of your pressure point cuffs."

"They're beautiful! Thank you."

"You're welcome. We better get to work."

We were only fifteen minutes late to leave. I'm calling that a win. Outside my lab, I'm shocked to see Maseko waiting. This can't be good.

"Do you want me to stay?" he whispers.

"No thanks. Love you."

"Good. We're already late. Have a wonderful day. Love you too." He hands me my coffee, then spins, taking off for the elevators.

I turn and notice Maseko is watching. I wish he could've stayed. "Hello, Architect Maseko. How are you?" I ask.

"Good morning. I'm well. And you?"

"I'm staying busy, but that's good."

My lab is unlocked. Weird. When we enter, several guards in black suits are standing at attention. Ah. That's unexpected. Come back,

Ivan. Not a fan of this without you.

"Pardon the intrusion. They were checking to make sure I'd be safe," she says.

"Ivan's the same way for me," I say, plopping my bag, sweater, and coffee onto my desk. Travis and Talia walk in and look at our guests with concern. "How can I help you?"

Maseko smooths the back of her red satin dress and sits on my desk. "Why haven't you responded to my emails about ASTRA?"

I gesture to INES. "My sister, Lark. The surgeries and research I'm doing will give me what I need to get her fixed."

"That's it? Lark's the only reason you're refusing?"

"Excuse me, but that's a big reason. Leading ASTRA would slow me down."

"Or you could speed up the entire process. You'd be the top dog. You know the surgery works. Stamp it for approval. Just do it."

My shoulders slump. She doesn't understand.

"I've thought about it." I open my schedule app. "I could see myself in some big office, telling a surgeon to go for it, she's approved for surgery." I'm leading three sim surgeries today. Then Dad is doing three tonight. Who needs a turn leading a sim? I scan the list.

North? The guy from Georgia. I continue, "It wouldn't change the fact that we need data and case studies before her surgery. Yes, she has an Agora. But it's not like theirs. Hers is broken. We have to make sure we do it right. We need guard rails. To have the brightest mind, the most skilled hands."

She presses a hand on mine, holding my busy hands still.

"Take the job. I need someone like you. Humble. Data-driven. Passionate. One hundred percent committed."

I frown. I'm never going to be one hundred percent committed to leading ASTRA.

"Dr. Rhys. Is there another reason you're turning me down?" She crosses her arms.

"No."

"I'm not much of a marriage person. But if family is a concern, set your schedule." Her eyes flick to my stomach so fast I almost miss it. "It was brought to my attention that ASTRA's on the brink of a freeze. If it doesn't get a new leader, innovation will be gone." She snaps her fingers. "No new surgical procedures would be approved for upwards of a year or two. That includes Lark's surgery."

The room reels around me. "Why?"

"No new ASTRA models will be manufactured. The current ones will become stagnant. Stuck in the right now if that makes sense. By December, if the budgets and planning can't be hammered out, ASTRA is dead in the water as far as your sister is concerned."

"December?"

"Yes. Think about it." She stands. "I'm heading back to Pretoria in a couple of days. I have to know your final decision as soon as possible."

Decision? Doesn't feel like there's any decision to be made. I have to do it for Lark. But all the public speaking I'd have to do? The meetings I'll be trapped in with new people every day? Nah. My nervous system isn't built for that kind of wear and tear. I'm more of a hide in the OR and play with robots kind of gal.

"Thank you. Travel safe."

"Even if it's a no, I'd like to be friends," she says with a soft smile.

"I'd like that too. Bye."

I force my face to stay in a beauty pageant smile until she closes the lab door. *I'm barely surviving as is!*

I softly thump my forehead off my desk. What will the world think when the head of ASTRA goes on maternity leave in a few months? I'll lose their confidence. I wish I could be one of those heroic women who wants to be an inspiration, to proudly show how to manage it all.

That's not me. I'm not a manager. I'm way too young for this. Being in front of a crowd makes me want to crawl in a hole. I leave my forehead down on my desk, trying to manually pause the fast-growing list of reasons why I shouldn't do it.

"You good, Story?" Talia asks.

I ball up my fists. "Yep, thanks!"

The lab door opens and Richelle leads a crowd in.

"Morning! Let's get working Dr. Rhys." She bounces up the steps and points to a doctor from Dallas. "Dr. Keith, your turn. Come on up!"

Here we go.

16

Dad has had a weird, business-like demeanor lately. I miss him. We're on a rotating schedule of twelve-hour shifts. One of us is always in the lab, keeping trainees doing sims. I lurked at my desk until the day shift emptied out. Dad should be coming in soon.

Ivan managed to escape the control room a bit early. He immediately passed out on the lab couch. I threw a blanket over him and tried to arrange some pillows under his head. His torso and part of his legs fit on the couch. From mid-shin down is dangling.

Eighteen hour days in the control room are taking a toll on him. Not having cracked how to repair the purge victims has given him near-constant frown lines and bloodshot eyes.

"Dad! Hey. How's it going?" I ask when he carries his bags in.

"Good, you?"

"Good. Ivan and I leave for Australia in a week. I'm hoping we can get a couple other surgeons ready to do their own surgeries by then."

Ivan is over the moon to go on our adventure. We have to make sure the surgeons are set up and comfortable with the INES systems in new Helm locations. He and I are going to three locations in Australia. Seven in South America. Four in North America. Dad will head to Asia, Europe, and Africa for the other twenty-six Helm locations.

Even with bringing other surgeons on board, this project won't be done by the time the twins are born. Picturing myself standing swayback from the weight of twins in my third trimester makes my left eye twitch.

"If we can do that, it would mean less traveling," Dad says.

"That's what I'm thinking too. Have you picked anyone to do Lark's surgery?"

"I'd like to know your pick first. If we picked the same person, it will show me your ability to evaluate other surgeons objectively."

"Dr. Ryland."

He smiles. "That's my pick too."

"What do we need to get approval for Lark?"

"You're going off soon on your own, let's see how you'd approach this. Write up the considerations on the board."

After thirteen hours overseeing sims, all I want to do is drag Ivan back to our apartment. But for Lark, I'll keep working. I divide my whiteboard into several sections. *Approval. Risk Mitigation. Patient Education.* I add several list items under each section. What did I miss? There has to be something. I stand and review the items, hands on my hips.

"Thoughts?" I ask.

"You nailed it. Great job. One note. She and Francois have similar body compositions. It's safe to say we have the right size of pediatric stuff. This was a good exercise to demonstrate your critical thinking. You're ready for Australia." He raises an eyebrow. "Or even ASTRA, if you want it."

"Why does everyone think I'm ready for that?"

"Nothing has changed with it in nearly twenty years. You've turned the worldwide healthcare system on its head. You need to be in a position that will allow you to shake things up on an even bigger scale."

"It means a lot to hear you say that. Things have been weird lately."

"Ivan and I had a pretty big disagreement." He twists his lips.

"Really?"

"I'm surprised he didn't tell you. When The Bastion approved you to use INES for surgery, we knew we'd need a lot more manufactured. I told Ivan he should list himself as sole creator on the contracts since he drew all prototypes. He refused. He wanted to include the Irontrace who helped build your INES. Do you know how much money he lost?"

I grin. "A lot?"

"An astronomical amount. You can still retire immediately and buy several islands. I don't understand why he didn't accept a larger chunk to take care of you, my baby girl. He would only accept fifty-nine percent of the shares. The rest is divided between David, me, and nineteen engineers."

"They worked hard."

"Ugh! You're just like him. I told him I wished you had a husband that would put you first and let you live a life of leisure. Not a demanding Commander that will make you keep working because he's bad at managing money."

Those are fighting words. "I see why he's mad."

"He said if I feel that way, I'm a stranger to you. That I must have been so focused on The Helm and Lark that I'd never had a real conversation with you."

Those are also fighting words. "Have you two always been like this?"

He laughs. "Only since he hit those feisty teen years."

"Holly!" Ivan bellows in his sleep. It's more war cry than word. Dad and I jump. A chill traces my spine. Ivan leaps up, gasping for breath, trying to orient himself.

I run to his side and put my hands on his cheeks. "Hey, you good?"

"She was gone. Taken." He drops to his knees and hugs my waist.

I push the emerald to activate SAM. "No one took her. She's here, my love."

"What if I can't keep them safe?" His weary eyes nearly break me.

What if we can't? Ivan is always sure of everything. He's not sure anymore. Maybe I should freak out? Yes. Freak out!

No. Get it together. Only one of us can fall apart at a time, and it's not my turn. Deep breath. Be worthy of the title of his best friend.

"I'll help. We're not alone. We have Irontrace. What can I do?" I ask.

"See an OBGYN for a checkup. A human this time. Not another ALICE. I don't trust them. Can I do an ultrasound tonight? We can figure out how to read it. Please?"

He grabs my hands and kisses them desperately.

"Yes. Scan me." I made our excuses for the night with Dad. Who knows what our clones said to him. But seeing our rock-steady Ivan in distress has us spooked.

Ivan grabbed a small ultrasound device from the clinic. Back in the apartment, he laid me on the couch and must have told me he loved me a dozen times.

"You ready?" he asks, turning on his laptop monitor and connecting the ultrasound to it.

"I am. You?"

He nods, deciding where to place the transducer. I hear them before we see them. The sound of their tiny hearts gallop from the speakers.

Then we see them. *I love them. How can you love someone so much that you've never seen? Never talked to? But I do.*

Two tiny grey shapes are curled up in a black bubble. They're *really* there. Heartbeats flickering like sparks.

"The babies!" Ivan's voice breaks. "I love them! I love you!"

I wish they could see the wonderstruck look on his face. "They're perfect! I love you."

Watching them twitch and bounce captivates us. We speculate, trying to decide who is who, but can't tell.

"Hearts beating at a perfect rate. Growth measurements right on target for eight weeks, five days. Each in their own amniotic sac." He looks from the screen to my stomach then gives me a perfect kiss. It's a mix of sunshine and adrenaline. "Thank you, I needed to see this today."

He took a couple of pictures then we chose an obstetrician from his list of safe options. It was a nerve-wracking call to Dr. Julian Brown's office. Ivan introduced himself as Senior Commander Ivan Rhys of the Irontrace Squadron. I shrunk into a fit of giggles when he said, "you know, I'm the one from the news."

The office staff went wild and switched to a video call, passing the phone around. Good to know Ivan is using his celeb status for good. He buttered them up and convinced the receptionist to connect us to Dr. Brown's cell.

After a quick consultation, Dr. Brown agreed to see me for a checkup in a little over a week. I think he's more interested in seeing The Helm and Ivan. I still did a happy dance. I've got a real human physician to work with. We cuddled up in our happy little bubble and talked about future plans for most of the night. Ivan nearly had to drag my bleary-eyed self to my lab in the morning. I'll be maxing out my pregnancy caffeine ration in record time today.

Dr. Ryland and Dad are in the lab when I arrive. He passed Ivan's background check. Now's our chance.

"Dr. Ryland, I've noticed your skill level is years beyond other surgeons in the program," I say.

He smiles. "Yours are advanced too for your age."

"Thanks. I attribute that to my dad supporting my skills."

Dad clears his throat. "Guilty. I've let her play with ASTRA robots since she was a toddler. Did you have a mentor, Dr. Ryland?"

Ryland laughs. "Healthcare prodigies from Ocracoke, NC don't have many bots to play with."

Deny it all you want, Ryland. I know you've operated as primary.

"I'm sure you know the reason I started this Agora removal project?" I ask.

"To save your sister from a similar type of AVM," he says.

"Correct. We need to ask you for your utmost discretion before we continue this conversation," I warn.

Talia and Travis rise on either side of me. Even young Irontrace standing in formation is intimidating.

Ryland smiles coolly at them. "Consider my lips sealed."

"Lark's adopted. She had a malfunctioning Agora implanted when she was a baby as part of Bastion medical testing on orphans." Ryland's eyebrows shoot up. "She needs a complicated Agora removal. We've never found a satisfactory answer on what the difference is between hers and those you'll find in The Irontrace. My dad and I can't do her surgery."

He raises a hand. "Why? You're the expert. You've done Ivan and the others."

"If Dad or I are in there and something goes wrong, we'd...we just, we can't. Hers has to be by the book. And yes, I know, we're writing the book as we go." Suck it up. Don't cry. My words pour out too fast.

"She's a *child*. Ivan, David, and the rest of them are consenting adults. They knew what they were signing up for."

Dr. Ryland lays a hand on mine.

"We're looking for a surgeon with exceptional skills. You outshine the others," I say. He grins. "I want someone lined up, ready to do it the second her surgery gets the green light. Look at the trend of her Estimated Death Date." I hold out my tablet, but he doesn't look at it.

"We believe you're the best to do her surgery if you're willing to accept the challenge," Dad adds. "We just want to know how you learned to operate."

Rylan looks from the door, to Dad, to my guards before replying.

"On Ocracoke Island, in North Carolina, you're really on your own. Not in a bad way. In a…we can be creative and independent way. There's a small farm by a crumbling lighthouse. The farm's run by a resourceful group of retired Special Ops Surgical Team guys. They have an off the books surgery center. It's about as backwoods a setup as you can imagine. They took me under their wing. If you don't want ASTRA to touch you or your kid? Come to us. We can do just about anything. For a price, of course." He laughs. "Our methods are old school. Our equipment is ancient, but these hands have been repairing lives in a barn since 2047. You want someone to save your sister?"

I nod.

"Give me an INES. I'll be ready for whatever her Agora throws my way. Test me. Give me the sims you think will break anyone else."

"You're hired," Dad says, shaking Ryland's hand.

"Let's get to work," Ryland says.

17

The next several days flew. I barely saw Ivan.

Staying busy became my whole identity. I do my deep breathing check-ins with Huck and Holly. There's no improvement for the purge patients. I find myself calling or texting Mom all day to check on Lark. Sleep? I barely remember what that is.

I assist in sims, give lectures, and test new INES before they're shipped. On breaks, I hype myself to visit Ivan in the control room. I make sure I can only spare ten minutes at a time for him between meetings and surgeries. If he saw how badly I've been spiraling, it would add to his burden.

I just have to wait out his time as SC, then I'll tell him what's going on. When I take him meals in our meeting room, I grin, act bubbly, and hold his hand while he eats. Then I flee, even though he begs me to stay.

Since I keep running from him, he's resorted to texting me. A lot.

13 hours until I'm boring Commander Rhys again! How are you? How are the babies? Did you sleep well? -I

I drooled in my sleep on a lime green Sticky-Note on my desk last night. The very noticeable color transferred to my face! Darrow told me 15 minutes into a meeting with The Bastion. Super professional, right? -I

MISS YOU!!!! -I

12 hours until this job is over! -I

11.5 hours until I'm all yours. I sent coffee, a bagel, and fruit to your desk. Get in there and enjoy! I have to yell at more council members. Give the babies a pat hello from me. Love you! -I

I'm starting to think hiding my anxiety is giving him anxiety.

The babies say hello. Get out of there the second David's back! Do you know how hard it is to grow two people?? It's kicking my butt. Miss you.

Love you. -<3

I rush through two surgeries and skip to the elevator. His time as SC is up. He's all mine again! The down arrow lights up when I slap it.

Then I get a text.

Got tied up for a bit. Go do something that makes you happy. DO NOT DO anything responsible. Fun only. I'm sending Nathan to hang out with you. See you in an hour, my love. -I

No. No. No. The control room has to let him go. Be cool. Don't add to his stress. He does not need to know his text sent my heart racing and made my throat tight.

Sorry you're stuck. I'll go get into some nonsense. -<3

I know exactly what to do. I just have to get Lark. She flings open their apartment door right after I knock.

"Hey! Do you want to visit the horses?" I ask.

She jumps into the hallway and grabs my arm. "Yes! I'm done with tutoring for the day."

"Tutoring? By who?"

"She's the best! You've got to meet her." Lark yells back into their apartment. "Rosa! Come meet Story!"

Ivan's Rosa?

Yep. My robot mother-in-law peeks in the hallway, then rushes out to hug me.

"Story Rhys! How are you feeling?"

"Rosa Rhys. I'm doing well. How are you?"

"I'm always good, honey." She crinkles her face and grins.

Holy cannoli. Ivan makes the same face all the time. Did he learn it from her? Or teach it to her? I don't care. I hope Huck and Holly do it too.

"You wanna go see the horses with us?" Lark asks her.

"I can't right now, baby." Rosa frowns. "I have to clean up from our lessons, but I'll go next time, okay?"

"Okay, bye, Rosa!"

"Story, I want to hear all about how my boy is treating you

sometime. I raised him to be an extra good man."

"It worked. He's wonderful." I smile.

She leans close to whisper, "Those babies treating you okay?"

I suck in a sharp breath. "Talia, Trav. I need a minute."

"Lark! Race you to the stables." Travis tags her then takes off.

"I need more warning next time!" Lark squeals, chasing him.

"Ivan didn't spill the beans." Rosa holds a hand to my shoulder, locking me in place. "When he was twelve, he said I needed to be more like a human mom. To be able to look at my kid and see if he was unwell. He built me a body system analysis tool. I can see them." She giggles, pointing to my lower abdomen. "They're doing well. I knew in Lancaster Bastion HQ. It took you long enough to figure it out."

"Oh." I relax under her grip. A little warning would've been nice! Her skills could come in handy, especially for newborn twins. "How much do you charge for babysitting?"

Her eyes go soft. Misty, almost. Do robot eyes mist? "If my Ivan wants me to help, I'll be there in a flash."

"Thanks. That means a lot. I'll talk to him and let you know."

"Thank you. Have fun in the stables." She points a French manicured finger in my face. "No riding horses, mama."

"I promise. Bye."

I ponder the nice, but odd interaction on my way to the stables. She's not what I expected at all. But at the same time, she speaks and acts like Ivan. Her hug felt as real as any human body. Weird. Try as I might, I couldn't tell anything with her eyes that would signal she's a robot.

I grin when I see Obsidian's massive black head peering over his stall door.

"Hey, Sid. It's been too long. I miss you." I snatch a soft brush from the grooming cart and push his broad chest back to enter his stall.

He's a gentleman of a horse, and today, that's especially evident. I brush with long, smooth strokes. Starting on his withers, along his spine, down his sides. I know he can't understand me, but I talk the whole time.

"Project Ilex is incredible Sid. Ivan's building the world into a better place. He's so busy. I'm worried. He's not eating or drinking unless I make him. He sleeps a handful of hours at his desk. I miss him. And get this, stupid Bastion is pushing for The Irontrace to perfect The Kernel and step away from it. Can you believe it? That'll never work."

I switch to a small face brush. He lowers his head, bumping my shoulder with his neck.

"Sorry, bud, I didn't grab any treats." I tuck his forelock in a clip and work the brush down his face and cheeks in a lazy pattern.

"Ivan misses you too. I bet you're bored out of your mind. He's missing everything lately. In thirty-nine minutes, he'll be done as Senior Commander. He'll be ours again."

Obsidian tosses his head.

"Whatever you do, don't watch the news, bud." His ears flick at my voice. "Nearly all the purge people are living in hospitals, hotels, campgrounds, rental houses, and sad pop-up mini villages. Can you imagine if Ivan was gone like that suddenly?" I shudder at the thought. "You want to go on a little walk?"

"Story, what are you doing?" Talia asks, scrambling off her chair when Obsidian and I saunter out of his stall.

"He's going stir crazy. We're just walking."

"In your condition, you're going to hand-walk a nineteen-two-hand draft stallion for...?"

"For fun." I need this as much as he does.

Nathan steps out of the stall by her. "It's fine, Talia. I'll be shadowing Story. I won't let anything bad happen to her."

"I'm coming too, Story!" Lark bolts Storm's stall door shut.

I hadn't realized how cooped up I've been feeling until we step out of Ash Cave. Fresh air bursts with damp scents of moss, flowers, and trees. Warm September sun filters through the canopy. I close my eyes and soak it up.

"We're being happy, twins. Ivan would be proud," I murmur. I cluck to Obsidian, and he takes off in a fast walk.

"Faster, Story! This is so fun!" Lark runs ahead of us, arms stretching to the sky.

She stops and twirls in place, humming a happy song. This is a moment of perfection. I want to remember it forever. My sister, completely carefree. Ivan's beloved horse sticking close to me.

Nathan stands leaned against a huge tree, scanning the forest, but mostly keeping his eyes on Sid and me.

I grab my phone and start recording.

"Hey babe. This is too perfect not to," I pause to catch my breath. "Oof, Sid is fast. It's too perfect not to share this with you. Look at Lark! Oh, you can't hear her, hang on. It's the cutest thing. Stand, Sid."

I pull him to a stop and loop his rope around a log.

"Listen." I aim my phone at her and catch her song-filled antics.

The trees sway in the wind. Lark mimics them and hums like she's born of the forest itself.

"Wish you were here! I've got all your babies with me." I prop my phone on a rock. "Sid and I are on a mental health walk. I've been a little stressed from missing you."

That's not quite the truth. It feels like half my soul is gone without him. I rest my cheek against Sid's. He gently rubs his face on mine. His head is at least the size of my torso. He drops it to my stomach, huffing deep breaths.

"You know our little secrets, huh?" He stays in place, content. "Look how good he is. I could stay with him all day. But I'm too excited to bring these," I cup my stomach, "to see you."

Lark runs to my side. "We making a video for Ivan? Hi Ivan! Sid is so happy Story took him for a walk." She plants a kiss on Sid's velvety nose then runs off.

"Congrats on your demotion to Commander, baby," I say with a grin. Obsidian huffs, puffing a chunk of red curls over my forehead. I reach for him, and he lowers his mouth to graze. "Huck, Holly, and I love you. Muah!" I hit send.

Lark, Nathan, and I spend a few more minutes running around with Obsidian. Sid was unimpressed that I won't let him sample every patch of grass and flowers. Nathan was unimpressed that I wouldn't let him have the lead rope. He keeps looking at me like pregnant women belong in bubble wrap, not frolicking in the forest with a draft horse.

I see a flat white thing about the size of a football in a clump of tall grass by a log pile. "What's this?" I crouch beside it. "Talia! Lark! I found a little dog." The white lump is a tiny dog's body. "No, wait, it may be dead."

The chest barely rises, then falls. Then rises again.

"It's alive! Hey, pup." It blinks at me with honey brown eyes.

"There shouldn't be dogs in here. This could be a trap," Nathan tugs my arm to make me stand. I stay crouched.

"Story, don't touch it, you're gonna get a disease." Talia pulls at my shirt.

"We can't just leave it here," I say. Sid sniffs the grass around the little tan and white dog.

"We sure can," she retorts.

Lark unleashes a furious tirade. "I know you're a good person, Talia, but that's awful! It's a living thing. Look at its eyes. It needs our help. Let Story save it."

"Story, I *really* don't like this." Nathan lays a hand on my back. "Please, let's go. Now."

"Take Sid," I say, tossing the lead to Nathan. I grab a pair of gloves from my scrub shirt pocket then pull it off over my head. The athletic crop top I always wear on surgery days will have to do as a shirt for now. "Look. I'm wearing gloves."

Talia rolls her eyes as I swaddle the dog in my shirt.

"Come on, little pup. You weigh what, five pounds?" Its head flops to the side as I run for The Helm entrance. "Stay awake!" I kiss in the air until it opens its eyes. "Good girl, you're a good dog."

"It's got a brown spot like a heart on its forehead. It must be a good dog to have a love spot on it," Lark says.

"Don't touch it, Lark!" Talia snaps.

The bony, probably worm-ridden, terrier mutt is honestly kind of ugly. Its eyes protrude too much. Its forehead belongs on a dog three times its size. Something is structurally wrong with its jaw, and there's an odd tilt to it. Like a twisted Pug's mouth on a toy terrier body with an apple head Chihuahua face.

"Good girl! You're not much bigger than a bird, Birdy!" Lark says. The dog wags a short, curly tail. "What in the world kind of dog are you?"

She licks her dry, crusty nose. I wonder if she has fractures or nerve damage. She hasn't moved her legs.

"Don't let that dog lick you! Think of the babies." Nathan is staring at me like I'm one step away from disaster.

"Nathan, it's okay. It's *not* going to lick me."

"This is all just so stressful." He reaches to link an arm through my elbow as we approach wet rocks. "I won't let you fall. I've got you."

"The dog is stressful?" I ask.

"No. You. Pregnant. A baby...babies. It's a lot. I don't know how Ivan handles you." He shakes his head.

Handles me?! And I thought I was socially awkward... I laugh to diffuse my annoyance. Ivan would never treat me like this—as if being pregnant has turned me into a burden he has to carry. No. Ivan treats me like I'm something precious that he's honored to protect.

We step into the stables. I make a lot of space between Nathan and I. "We're back in now. I'm going to Ivan. I'll see you later, Cantone."

"Nah, I'm taking you to him. Get the dog to the vet clinic and let's go." He gestures for me to go first.

"Francois, help!" Lark yells from by Sid's stall. "We brought you a patient!"

Her little friend works here as an Irontrace vet in training. "A dog? Never had a dog patient before. Get it to my HEAL vet bot. This works on horses, let's see what it'll do for a dog."

He's a remarkable little boy. His left arm is in a biomend247 sleeve to repair nerve damage and muscle wasting from an Agora boundary injury. It doesn't slow him down though.

"What's your name, *petit chiot*?" he asks.

The dog keeps her weepy eyes trained on me. "Take good care of her, Francois. I'll check in later."

"I will."

I turn to leave. She lets out a pained whimper. "What happened?" I rush to the table. Her curly tail spins like a propeller.

"I think she wants you. Can you stay with her?" Francois asks.

"No. She's going to meet Ivan. He'll bring her back later," Nathan answers for me.

I like his answer though, so I just smile at Francois.

The HEAL bot announces initial assessment results. "Patient is dehydrated, malnourished, and needs medicated for systemic inflammation, anemia, and parasites."

Talia shoots me a look.

"You start her on meds. I'll be back." I lean in front of Birdy while he puts her leg in an IV machine. "Bye. You'll love *Commander* Rhys."

It's Ivan time!

18

The Lancaster Bastion members are in the control room, accompanied by their staff. You can spot the ones that are purge victims from yards away. Their eyes seem permanently bloodshot, with black puffy circles under them.

"Now AJA has let us down, on top of everything else! What is wrong with your AI models?" A middle-aged councilwoman named Eliza Dean stands inches from Ivan, screaming at him. "Unacceptable, Senior Commander!"

She points to a news story on the wall from Missouri. A staff member at a purge patient care village tried to abduct a woman.

"Why didn't AJA flag this person as a risk during background checks?" she shrieks.

"The-" Ivan begins a calm reply.

She starts yelling again, cutting him off. "Why can't you just fix them! One billion victims. You've done nothing for them."

"Excuse me, councilwoman, but it's not that easy." Dr. Chris Byrd pipes up from a monitor. "Their limbic systems controlling fear and emotions are compromised."

A delicate network of brain regions comes into focus on several monitors, to display one massive photo.

Dr. Byrd continues, "These areas of the brain translate our survival instincts into conscious thought then action. The amygdala you see up there in purple is an alarm system in our brain. It picks up on threats, fears, anger, and memories linked to strong emotion. The hypothalamus in green is like a regulator to help our bodies with emotions. Think of the cingulate gyrus there in blue as a bridge to help us process emotions. It assists with decision-making, emotional response, and our emotional aspect of pain."

Byrd pauses. The whole room leans in.

"From the scans and exams we've done, they're all malfunctioning at once. They're having episodes of intense, debilitating limbic hyperreactivity. It only activates around their immediate family members. What was once a beautiful, unbreakable bond is now severed."

"Thirty-minute break. Everyone go get refreshments." Dean interrupts him. Foolish woman. I want to hear more.

I approach Ivan slowly from behind in SAM.

He reaches across the desk and hands Dean a box of tissues. "Councilwoman Dean, I agree. It's unacceptable AJA put that young woman at risk. I assure you I'll personally tune AJA to compensate for this failure."

While she blows her nose, he pours a cup of water then hands it to her.

"Do you have any kids, Senior Commander?"

I freeze, scanning the room. *Where is David?*

"My wife and I hope to soon," he says.

"Do those kids a favor. Don't have them until the world is a much better place." She turns on her heel and leaves him sitting there.

He catches my eye with a hollow smile. I drop to the floor beside his chair and scoot until I'm mostly under the table.

"I know you heard that. Ignore her, baby," he whispers.

I lean my cheek on the side of his thigh.

"Why is she still calling you Senior Commander?" I ask.

He grumbles. "David said an emergency came up. I'm so sorry. Are you mad?"

"Nope."

Not mad. *Devastated.* That would be the correct word for it.

He slides his hand across my shoulders. I shiver closer. Good thing I'm in SAM. No one can see my white lace racerback crop top. David would have a fit to see me wearing this in the control room. He brushes his thumb under my shoulder strap, leaving his hand there to anchor us together.

"I like this look. But where did your shirt go?"

"I gave it to a dog with parasites."

"You what?"

If I answer, it'll open the floodgate of tears. I remain silent in my hiding spot, watching the monitors.

There's a muted interview happening with a Senior Commander at The Helm in Perth. I recognize the name of Ivan's "excellent" counterpart, Max Darke.

He's providing a grim-faced update on familial purge statistics in their region. Seven percent of patients in Australia are being treated for new onset of non-epileptic seizure activity. The man interviewing him is smiling too much. That's an unforeseen side effect of Irontrace going public. People are obsessed with them.

A report displayed from the U.K. contains global data on patients afflicted with transient aphonia and blindness as a stress response. Not only have these people lost their families and homes, but their speech and vision keep blipping out too.

"Thank you for the video. I loved it. You looked so happy," Ivan says, rubbing my neck and shoulders.

"I was." Guilt cuts sharp. How dare I be so happy with Lark and Obsidian while there's such misery in the world?

A story from Texas catches my attention. A pre-school with ninety-seven students aged three to five is pleading for parents from other regions to do background checks with AJA. They want people to join a 'parent share' program. If you apply to work with kids in Galveston, parents from Galveston will apply to work in your city and take care of your kids.

Those kids don't want rotating parents to care for them. They want hugs from their parents. To be tucked in by them after reading stories. To eat sandwiches cut in their favorite shapes by their real Mom and Dad.

Another news story with closed captions on is interviewing a group of victims living in a hotel in Washington. They're telling experiences with trying various anti-anxiety medicines to help them cope.

I'm glued to the scroll of words while a thirty-two-year-old father speaks about how badly the purge has torn his family apart. On a split screen is a picture of him, his wife, and three small kids having a cookout in their yard. They look so happy.

He's not happy anymore. His tears transition to sobs. He ducks off-screen. A deadpan little girl comes to sit in his spot. She's holding a floppy pink puppy and a sign with a rainbow of hearts on it.

Please remember me Mommy. I still love you. -Ladybug

Enough.

I give Ivan a quick kiss on the knee then stand. "I gotta go put my clothes in the incinerator and bleach my hands."

He shoots up from his chair to follow me. "That's extreme. Why?"

"The parasite dog."

"What parasite dog?"

Can't talk, I'll cry. Get away from him.

He slips in behind me as I escape into our meeting room.

"What dog, Story? Stop."

I dive for the door, but he puts a hand at the top, holding it shut. "Please, just talk to me."

I fling my arms around his neck. "What's wrong with those people?"

"The purge is twisting the way victims process things. They're fairly happy, seem okay. Until they see their family." He speaks into my curls, holding me tight. "Then they lose it."

A tornado of anxiety hits. Palpitations. Short of breath. Lark needs surgery so every day she can have forest dance parties. Congrats to me, I'm having twins in a world where families are ripped apart. I'm terribly sad for those people. Council members are screaming at my Ivan. How dare they? He's trapped as Senior Commander. He'll have to keep smiling, enduring their abuse.

The tornado is intensifying. I have to get out of here.

"I gotta go."

"Is Richelle staying with you?" Ivan asks.

"Mmhmm," I wiggle trying to back away from his hug. My struggle is useless. His grip tightens. He's proving how weak I am.

"Where's your detail?" he asks.

"With Birdy."

"Who's Birdy?"

"The dog."

Run. The heart thing is getting worse. My breathing is getting shaky. I push Ivan back, but it's like trying to move the walls of Ash Cave. His grip tightens.

Summon some words. He's the nicest person you know. He'll listen. "You're smashing the kids. Let go please."

He immediately drops his arms. "Was I really smashing them? Or are you trying to escape and hide another panic attack?"

Dang it, Ivan.

I spin, taking a desperate gulp for air. How can I get the invisible hand clamped firmly around my throat to relent? I tip my head back. No dice. Can't breathe.

Ivan's chest presses against my back. *Oh, I've missed this.* One of his hands rests on my heart. The other holds my stomach.

He shouldn't have to do this on top of everything else.

"Let go." I lurch forward.

His arms stiffen around me. I don't really want to escape. He must know it. I *need* him to hold all of me. Protect me from the world. Lock us away.

"Breathe with me, Story." He's so warm. So strong. I collapse back against him. "Like this." His chest expands. A strangled sound escapes when I mimic his movements. "You've been running away from me all week. No more of that, wife."

Maybe I can stay here and borrow some of his strength. We fall into rhythm while I catch my breath. He gently sways me, softly humming our favorite song against my neck. The relief of being in his arms is so intense it almost hurts.

I bet Kristen didn't have panic attacks. She was probably some brave Irontrace goddess that never needed help.

"I don't know what you're thinking about, but I'm thinking about doughnuts," he says after a few minutes.

Tears roll down my face, dripping onto his hands.

"You ever eat a doughnut covered in powdered sugar in all black Irontrace clothes? Keep breathing, my love. You're doing so good. White powdered doughnuts on a black desk? In the black control room? Over black carpet?"

He knows I haven't.

"My word. David and I had a twenty-hour shift one time when we were seventeen. We ate four dozen powdered sugar doughnuts on a dare. Keep breathing."

I'm barely using my legs at this point. I feel like I'm floating in some gentle river of peace made of his voice and touch. I'll drift wherever his calm leads me.

"Our SC at the time didn't think we could do it. He was a riot. Titus. He was always daring us to do stupid stuff. The sugar made it look like it snowed all over us. All over everything, really. I miss him."

He lays his chin on my shoulder. "You're doing such a good job, your heart rate is almost back to baseline. The janitor robots were squeaking and beeping, trying to get our sticky mess cleaned up. David and I tried to translate it to human language." He kisses my cheek. "Titus said it was too foul. He didn't want us to learn to string together that many curse words in a row. He always told us cussing demeans our position as Irontrace. He'd get furious if anyone used profanity in the control room. The punishments he'd think up for people that crossed him were always very public and incredibly funny."

He laughs softly in my ear. I love his laugh. It has some power over me I can't name. The world may be collapsing, but with Ivan? *My* world is going to be fine.

"The keyboards at several desks around us were a disaster too. Titus made us take all the keys off and clean them. The little ball inside the mouse somehow sucked up a bunch of sugar. David and I learned how to refurbish several accessories that day. Man, I wish I had a doughnut right now."

I take my first full breath since we came in the room.

"Better my love?" He smooths my curls in a pile on my left shoulder.

I turn to face him, too embarrassed to meet his eyes. "I've been avoiding you. I was hoping you wouldn't notice your lemon of a wife fell apart."

"Don't you ever talk about my wife like that." He gently taps a finger on my lips. "You know in the forest how everything grows, reaching for the sun? You're my sun, Story Rhys. Whether you're smiling. Crying. Panicking. Laughing that beautiful laugh that makes my heart race. Sleeping with my arm as a pillow until these fingers go dead." He traces his thumb along my lips. "I'll be reaching out, finding you through it all. Warm me up, baby. Glow on me. I'm here for every season. Don't run away from me anymore. Don't shut me out. I won't survive that. Without you, I wither. I'll cease to be."

There's his brutal, perfect honesty again. He's never been afraid to tell me exactly how he feels. He needs to know I've been a disaster without him.

"I'm sorry." I gently bite onto the side of his finger, shaking his hand playfully. He grins. "I can't live like this. With just bits and pieces of you. The world needs you. But I..." I push his hand onto my stomach. "*We need you.*"

"You need more Ivan time?" He gives me an expectant smile.

I nod so fast I blush. "I do. Sorry. I'm completely lost without you."

"Let's start with food. You and that litter in there could probably knock back your own four dozen soon."

The door behind us flings open. Irontrace members of Project Ilex file in.

David is the last to enter. He slams the door then speaks in a rush. "The chief of Columbus AJA facility called me an hour ago. Video surveillance of Moulson's cell was compromised. He's missing. Rhys, we need you back in the control room."

Ivan clears his throat and steps in front of me. "No."

"No?" David challenges. "You're Senior Commander!"

"The Helm needs one SC. As of today, I'm on medical leave for a private health issue," Ivan says.

My bad. I'm the issue.

"This Helm requires two SCs for the foreseeable future. Come talk to me privately," David says soberly.

Ivan squeezes my hand. "Be right back, baby."

He and David duck into the control room. Yelling breaks out. Why are those two fighting? I shift towards the door.

Henri blocks me. "No, Story."

No? Ivan will be mad someone kept me from him.

Voices clamor in a sudden wave. Ivan's voice is booming right outside the door.

Ivan opens the door and strides in. "Story, let's go home."

"Rhys. You're kidding!" Henri hisses.

David enters, closing the door to block out the cacophony in the control room. Council members are raging about how Moulson could have disappeared from AJA. "You better be online fourteen hours a day, Rhys."

"You know I will." Ivan gives a fast nod.

Their stare down ends when David turns to me. "The whole world needs him, Story."

A fist hammers the door. Nathan opens it a crack then yanks it open. A gawky young Irontrace girl with glasses gasps to catch her breath. She looks from David to Ivan.

"SCs! Travis and Talia were found dead outside Dr. Rhys's lab. We think it was an Agora emergency."

Ivan's arm clamps around my shoulders.

Breathing exercises won't fix this one.

19

"Black pants, black shirts, black shoes, black socks, black bras, black coats. These are quality fabrics, no complaints there." Richelle zips up the dress I'm trying on. "Has anyone ever told the Irontrace there's a whole color spectrum out there?" she complains.

Ivan sits on the floor of my dressing room. My faithful watchdog has followed us from store to store, working from his laptop for the last hour. He told David he's only working remotely for a few weeks.

Maseko said our trip comes with a strict dress code. She wants me to exude an experienced persona. Massive, tone-deaf embassy parties have been arranged in each country. We're expected to attend them all.

"Everything in my closet is covered with Birdy's hair. It looks like white sparkles on all the black," I say, turning to check my side view. The bright gold zipper on my ankle-length sheath dress feels like I'm breaking Irontrace dress code. I love it.

I'm not sure how much longer this will fit. It should at least get me through the funeral and Australia trip.

"Oooh, love it!" Richelle claps and bounces.

Ivan looks up at me and whistles. I do a little twirl. "Getting this one for sure. Unzip, please."

"Honey, don't buy such tight clothes," Mom says from the couch she and Lark are on outside the dressing room.

Richelle chokes back a giggle.

"Why?" I ask.

Lark answers for her. "Mom's always talking about you having a baby. She keeps saying 'When Story stops working because of babies.' Or 'You can do this or that with her kids, Lark.' Ivan, can you build the baby a helmet and vest like mine so it can ride horses?"

He keeps typing, deaf to our conversation.

Lark yells, "Ivan! The baby! It needs a helmet!"

He looks from me to Lark. "*The what* needs a helmet?"

"Your baby!" She laughs.

He tilts his head.

"Lark, let him work. He's not building a baby helmet," I say. He blinks at me owlishly. "Mom doesn't want me to buy a form-fitting dress because she wants us to get cracking on having kids."

Mom scolds her. "Lark! Don't spook the newlyweds!"

"Ah. Ha. I see." He leans to peek out the crack under the door. His eyes sweep over my mom with clinical precision. I can almost hear him making mental notes of her posture and tone. "Wear whatever you want, Story. You look gorgeous in everything."

"Awh, shoot." Mom snaps her fingers.

Ivan shakes his head and goes back to typing.

Richelle and I trade silent screams of excitement.

"Your turn!" I toss the dress at her.

Over the next couple of days, Ivan and I were inseparable. When I was assisting in sims, he brought his laptop to my lab. When he had to be in the control room, I conducted seminars and built INES training material in there. From what he says, he's close to creating some kind of band-aid for the purge.

I didn't realize how completely depleted I was until Ivan filled me back up. His love is constant, strong, and anchoring in a world that's broken. It hasn't erased the chaos we face, but we're reminding each other that we'll never face it alone.

Everyone has noticed. They say our names as one word now—"Ivan'N'Story."

The day before our Australia trip, David called a Project Ilex meeting. Ivan and Darrow are bringing Maseko up to speed.

"The BBA has no treatment plan yet. They're switching their focus now to mitigating the parental response. The top idea is to match kids with new families. Over my dead body. My wife and I will never agree to this stupid scheme," Councilman Darrow says. "My wife's confused from the purge. She'll be better soon. I'm not giving up my kids in the meantime."

"No one will agree to this." Dad practically spits his words out.

"What's the parental response been to this plan?" Maseko asks.

"Destruction. Fires. Rage," Ivan says. "Lancaster's Bastion HQ is gone. Darrow has had to work from here every day. Most of the Lancaster Bastion members have taken an extended leave of absence."

"They've just abandoned the people?" Maseko snarls.

Darrow nods. "Aside from these council members on Project Ilex, yes."

"Dude! That's super messed up! Can they do that?" Richelle asks.

"They're saying the Irontrace are responsible for the current version of The Kernel," Ivan continues. "The Bastion demands we force a fix to the ALICE models and deploy it. We need all the best minds in a room. If the docs can figure out how to regulate the busted limbic systems, we can use ALICE to fix them all in a matter of days."

"You're headed to Perth, right?" Darrow asks.

"Tomorrow," Ivan says.

"I'll assemble a conference. Force the leading ALICE trainers to sit and play nice. We'll figure this out," Darrow says.

"That'd be great, thanks." Ivan smiles.

"How many more surgeries do you have here?" David asks.

"None. Dad and I have been working round the clock to train others in sims."

"Will any of them be ready to do surgeries?" Darrow chimes in.

"Dr. Ryland is. He's going with Dad." I pause, curious to see how Ivan will react to the next part. "Dr. Benedict and Dr. Wylie are traveling with us to Perth. They're ready too."

Ivan bursts out shocked laughs. "Benedict!"

I twist my lips to hide a laugh. "Aside from Ryland, he's the fastest learner. Wylie is superb. Her skills may surpass Benedict's within days. They're all a bright group. I'm confident I can hand off more responsibility soon."

"Perth just got a lot more interesting," Ivan says.

"Darrow, work on getting the conference setup in Perth. Alan, Story, Ivan, please hang back for a minute. Everyone else, get to the control room," David orders. "Thank you for your time, Maseko."

David sits by Dad. "Dr. Ross, I need to ask you something. It's not meant to offend."

"I'll keep an open mind," Dad says.

"What did you do with Story's labs?" David asks.

My labs? My dad? No. The room tilts.

"Her what?" Dad asks.

"Her lab results. What did you do with them?" David repeats grimly.

"I'm not offended by your question. I have no idea what you're talking about." He looks at me, brows knit. "Story? What labs?"

I can't speak. I just look at Ivan.

Dad reaches his hand across the table. "Are you sick, honey?"

"Dad, I..." My voice cracks, raw. I reach for Dad but Ivan catches my hand and tucks it in his lap.

"No, Story," Ivan says softly. He glares at my dad the way he looks at Moulson. "David, what did you find?"

"A copy of Story's labs was delivered to Alan's computer. He opened them, renamed the files, made copies, destroyed the original, and put the copies in a hidden folder." David holds up his own laptop with a computer terminal history and file paths displayed.

"Alan! Why?" Ivan thunders.

Dad takes a ragged breath. "I don't even know how to do something like that."

Ivan speaks for us. "Story had some tests done. It generated an emergency alert on my laptop." Fear pricks the back of my neck. Dad's shoulders sag. Someone is framing him. "The labs should have been confidential. Then someone sent a bomb to our apartment with a message about the results. That's what caused the fire."

David takes over. "I've been investigating who accessed her labs in that brief gap of when they were ordered until Ivan could hide them. It led me to you. Only you. They weren't opened and manipulated by anyone else."

Dad shakes his head in disbelief. "Story. Are you sick? Why was there an emergency alert for your labs?"

Ivan answers firmly, "It's one of the many ways I keep her safe."

"Rhys, I haven't seen or read labs for Story. Why won't any of you tell me if she's sick?"

"David. My dad would never do this. He loves us. My parents are good people, he's-"

"This is an Irontrace matter now. You two can go," David interrupts. "I'm bringing an AJA to interview your dad."

"Seriously, David?" I ask. Every interrogation I've been subjected to led to a guilty verdict, earning me a Bastion-sanctioned death sentence.

"Let David take care of this." Ivan pulls me to my feet, wrapping his arm around me.

"Sweetie. Are you sick?" Dad pleads. "Please. David can interrogate me for days. Just tell me."

"I'm not sick. I promise."

Dad sucks in a sharp breath. "Delac, ask me anything. Have AJA ask me anything. I would never do something to endanger my family."

Ivan shuts the door.

I scrub a hand across my face, then push the emerald for SAM. "Why would David blindside us like that? Dad didn't do it. Ivan, I'm not just being sentimental. You know he's bad with computers."

"I don't think this was your dad. David has only ordered a few interrogations. He considers them a last resort. It'll be thorough."

"Can you set an alert to get the results?" The words feel like splinters in my throat.

"Of course, baby."

The question I want to ask most, *"Will he be executed for something like this?"* won't come out. "He'll pass the interrogation. I know it."

"Wanna lay on the couch with Birdy, and I'll make you breakfast?

Maybe she'll stop trying to bite me if I feed her bacon?" he asks, hope in his voice.

I could eat. And if Ivan's cooking? It'll be far beyond anything I would be able to make. "Doubtful."

Dad's results popped up in Ivan's phone right when David called for us to come to the control room. *I knew he didn't do this!*

David rushed to us, making an arc motion above us in the air, mouthing "Turn on the shield." I do, and he continues. "Good news! He passed. AJA flagged all his responses as truthful."

I sag against Ivan. Actually hearing it is even better than reading that he's not in trouble.

"What else did you find?" Ivan leans forward.

"Nothing. But an extremely skilled, dangerous person knows about Huck and Holly. I'll keep cracking away at it. Work for a few hours from the INES lab, then get back in here for a meeting with BBA."

Ivan nods, lost in thought. "I will. Thanks, David."

"Get to work," David dismisses us.

"I knew he wouldn't do this, Ivan," I say.

"I'm so happy he's cleared. However, we're back to square one. Someone in our Helm is a threat. I don't know how I feel about Australia now. It'll be good to have fresh safety protocols. But I don't want to give up my familiar ground when anyone could be behind this."

"Nathan, Mai, Henri, and Richelle are coming. We'll be okay."

"Do you want to tell your family about the babies?"

"No. I want to do it after Lark's surgery, so she won't feel like I've lost focus on her."

We got this, babies. Let's get Lark fixed and I'll tell the world about you.

20

Ivan's working from his desk in my lab. I'm walking Dr. James North through a complicated Agora removal sim. North works at a small Helm near Tallulah Falls, Georgia.

Dad came in near the end. I waved for him to join us on the platform. He hugged me like we just survived something unthinkable. Maybe it's the wrong call not to tell him about the twins. He passed the interrogation and he'd be so happy. I'll talk to Ivan about it tonight.

"That was incredible!" Dr. North gushes, relieved he passed the difficult sim. "How many more until I can operate on my Irontrace?"

"Get through as many practice surgeries as you can. Shoot for at least two a day until Dr. Wylie is back from Australia. Then she'll start working with you on their list of Commanders."

Ow! Why? A sudden sharp cramp on my right side makes me gasp. I take a deep breath. It fades away. I'm fine. I should take a drink break and sit. Probably need some extra hydration from 'growing the litter' as Ivan says.

Dr. North and I hoist up the bulky exam simulator torso. We need to drop it in the recycler to strip it down to components for re-use.

"You'll follow The Bastion's surgical planning document. Senior Commander, then Commanders, then any Irontrace over a certain age. They'll be at highest risk of rupture," I say.

Dr. North is watching me and not looking where we're going. He stumbles, losing his grip. Without thinking, I lunge to catch it. *Wrong move!* The forty or so pound jiggling mass of simulated human tissue and bone smashes onto my stomach. It immediately creates a fresh knifelike cramp in my side.

"Ooooch!" I choke back as much as I can of a screech.

The room turns into a mini storm of chaos. Ivan leaps up, tipping his chair over. He darts to the platform and dives through the rail. Richelle and Henri assume I'm under attack and fly up with him, scattering surgeons and supplies like leaves in the wind.

Henri takes a knee with his back to me, surveying the area.

Ivan hurls the torso off the side of the platform. "What's wrong?"

I stand straight and stretch. No consistent abdominal pain. Not dizzy. Not lightheaded. No nausea.

"I'm fine. I tried to catch the simulator and stepped wrong," I whisper. Everyone is staring.

"Mmm." Ivan narrows his eyes and grunts, tapping Henri on the shoulder, prompting him to rise to his feet.

"Sorry. Everyone knows I'm a klutz." Dr. North laughs. "Glad you caught it for us. Just call me Dr. Butterfingers."

Ivan crosses the platform to North in less than a second.

Oh no.

"Don't laugh about your inability to walk in a straight line, on a flat floor!" Ivan yells.

Dr. North shrinks.

"You could injure a patient. You could injure yourself. And the thing you should be by far the most concerned about is if you would have injured my wife. You're being entrusted with multi-million-dollar equipment. Do better or get out!" The room holds its breath. Ivan extends a hand to me. "David wants us in the control room for the afternoon, my love." His raised eyebrows and tight jaw read like a gentle warning. My time in the OR is done.

"Let's take a lunch break," Dad announces.

On the walk to the control room, Ivan asked me fifteen times if I'm really okay. The number of sideways glances he shoots my way to check on me would have given a lesser human vertigo.

"Dr. Brown will be here tonight at six. He'll give us all a clean bill of health. I know it, baby," I tell him quietly.

"Good. You caught that thing and made a sound like you were injured. I would've torn North's head off if that stunt hurt you."

"Well, I mean...in his defense, the first pain hit before he dropped it."

Ivan is fast. Both his thought processing speed and physically from years of tactical training. I barely see his hand flash out like a viper to turn on SAM.

"What first pain, baby?"

What is wrong with me? I shouldn't have scared him for something so simple. I put my hand on his cheek, my thumb carefully tracing his scar.

"I'm so sorry for scaring you. I had two painful cramps on my lower right side today." He puts a hand on my right hip, slowly rubbing towards the middle of my lower stomach. "One before I grabbed that sim torso and a second when I grabbed it. The second time it hurt more. I think it's because I was caught off guard. I'm fine, really."

"Wife, I don't like this."

"I know in my heart, we're all fine."

"Want Dr. Brown to come earlier? Sullivan can fly to Columbus and get him right now."

"No. Let's go see what David wants. Dad can take over for me in the lab. I'll sit and write training docs or something boring. Deal?"

He drums his fingers lightly against my stomach.

"As long as you're okay?" he asks, scrunching up his face like he's weighing options. "You're my sun Story. You have to be okay."

He just did it again. He made me love him even more. "I promise the three of us are fine."

"Let's go get you a comfy seat. Walk slow and easy, I'm right here with you." His eyes and hands stay locked on me like I'm the only thing in the world for our walk back.

David's control room is run in efficient silence. A few Bastion members sit quietly, working from the conference table. The only sound from Irontrace workstations is the rapid clatter of keys. Monitors tuned to dozens of news stations are muted. I cozy up at Ivan's workstation while he joins Darrow and David down front. Something's got them feeling sassy. Darrow's pointing angrily at videoconference monitors that are blinking to life one-by-one. A team from another Helm pops up on each screen.

The air conditioner in here is blasting. I wrap Ivan's fleece sweatshirt around me. That was a mistake. Now I'm warm in his cushy chair. A mostly sleepless night and another long day catch up with me. I'm too tired to write documentation right now.

What if I take a real break, just this once? The world won't fall apart. Well, it probably won't. I slouch to watch what's happening down front.

David paces, barking words I can't hear. His lean, muscled frame is topped by his buzzed blonde hair. Typical Delac. He's the picture of barely controlled anger. If a frown took on human form, it would be David Delac.

Darrow is half a foot shorter than Ivan. He's got brown hair that's greying in several spots and is always in a rotation of fancy tailored suits. Anyone could look at him and say, "yep, politician." Today his normally people-pleasing demeanor has been replaced by fiery eyes and tense shoulders.

And then there's Ivan. Even from across the control room, he mesmerizes me. His broad shoulders, thick arms, and massive six-and-a-half-foot frame scream that my wall of a man possesses brute force power that others simply lack.

Whatever they're discussing is ticking him off. He stalks around the table down front. He's alternating between talking to the members of The Bastion and gesturing to monitors. He looks back in my direction and points at me. Whatever clearly enthralled expression I'm wearing as I admire him makes him pause. He almost smiles but the group grabs his attention. His face darkens. He spins back around to talk to them, jabbing a finger towards the middle section of monitors.

"What's got you mad, baby?" I whisper. My eyes flick between screens in the general area he was pointing.

Ugh. They're expanding the parent share program to more states.

A new anti-anxiety medication trial has been approved. The only "working" regimen right now is to drug the purge victims until they're effectively a walking corpse. It works for about ten percent of them. Most can't or won't tolerate living like that. School sessions resume tomorrow. Those poor kids. Who will drop them off and pick them up?

On the bottom monitor, I see a small caption on a black screen. *Medical emergency at Tallulah Falls, GA Helm. Senior Commander Wes Darke- Agora rupture, 1407 EST.*

That's Dr. North's Helm. He's not ready to do surgeries yet. Especially not a complicated surgery where the patient has already ruptured. It's 1421. Depending on what emergency protocols they initiated, if Sullivan can get us there fast enough, I'll try to save him.

I rush down the ramp and blurt, "We're going to Georgia!"

The group turns to me.

Darrow speaks gently, "Story, he's probably a lost cause."

"I'd like to access his records and check for myself," I say.

"You need to focus on going to Australia so you can prevent this from happening to other, healthier Irontrace. Don't delay their care for him," Councilwoman Dean says.

"Wes Darke? Is he related to Darke from Perth?" I ask.

"Yes. His younger brother," David says quietly.

"Does Max know?" I ask. Darrow shakes his head sadly. "Max Darke is being interviewed right now, while his brother is dying, and no one is going to tell him. How can I go to Australia and face him tomorrow?"

Ivan lays a hand on my arm. "What do you need?"

"I need to see his ALICE assessments," I say. He turns a laptop towards me. I speak quietly to Ivan, David, and Darrow. "His clotting factors look good. Kidney and liver function are stable. His hemoglobin is low, which is a worrisome start for surgery like this. His lactate level is decent, so he's still getting adequate oxygen." I have to try. Australia can wait. "Can Sullivan have me there in less than an hour?"

"Yes." Darrow nods.

"Can Dr. Brown come with us on the flight to Georgia?" I whisper to Ivan.

Ivan grabs David, pulling him to the side.

"Dr. Rhys, no Irontrace has ever survived an Agora rupture," Architect Maseko says from a screen.

When did she get here? The council members at the table nod in agreement.

"Go to Australia instead. Stay focused," Dean says.

These people. They smile, act kind, act like they care. They've got us fooled until a moment like this. Darke has spent his life taking care of others. Now he needs someone to help him, or at least try, and it's a no?

"The Bastion supports me because of my skills and judgement as a surgeon. If I tell you that a dedicated, valued member of *your* team can be saved, I'm not wasting time. I'm NOT going to Australia until I try to help Darke."

Darrow leans back in his chair, watching me. The other council members wear frowns.

"Dr. Rhys, we do trust and support you, but you have to think of the larger good right now," Architect Maseko says. "There are purge people that need help."

"Sadly, I'm not the doctor to help them. I am the one to help Darke." I look at his chart. "Wes is an *eighteen-year-old*, is that right, Ivan?" He nods. "He's the youngest Senior Commander I've heard of. Who works the hardest in their control room? Who knows the problems in their region the best? My husband is an SC. I know what that job entails. They earn their rank, not just by their hard work, but by their sheer survival. SC Darke needs us."

"It's not our fault his Agora ruptured," a council member says.

"It's *very* much your fault he has an Agora in the first place! Darke has survived everything you've subjected him to. Tactical trainings. Having to outpower and outthink your brutal, murderous challenges you put them all through. Losing his home. His family."

Ivan's grinning at me which means I'm doing something right.

"My husband delicately glossed over that fact when he went public about the Irontrace. You let me try to save that young man, or I will tell this story to a world that already despises The Bastion."

Silence.

"Bravo, Dr. Rhys," Maseko says. "I've heard you give two impassioned speeches now. It's a shame we don't have an acting head of AS-TRA. This would be their decision. If you really believe in your ability to save Darke, that means you're ready to be head of ASTRA. Accept the job. You'll be the one to make the rules."

Ivan sits next to me. I shove my hands in my scrub shirt pockets. Trying to picture how it will work puts my brain in a mini tailspin. Too many cons. Not nearly as many pros.

"I'm still considering your offer," I say.

Max Darke is smiling from the TV. Why has no one told him about his brother? They're showing photos from a recent community event. A few buses of teens went to Perth Helm. He played soccer with them and gave away a ton of Irontrace shirts. They're beaming. He took away their pain of having parents affected by the purge for a day.

I can save him from the pain of losing Wes.

"Dr. Rhys. The Irontrace are working round the clock to fully automate ASTRA. I'm told within months it'll be running itself. Consider this a temporary yet necessary role to fill."

Under the table, Ivan slides his foot between mine, gently tapping my ankle. He's calm, not pressuring me either way.

"Okay," I say to Maseko. "I'll do it."

Ivan gives me wide, *look at you go, wife* eyes.

"Everyone. Meet the new head of ASTRA, Dr. Story Rhys."

Darrow grins. "Have fun in Georgia, kids."

David stomps over, squeezing my shoulder. He addresses dozens of faces staring down at me from screens. "Tell Dr. Rhys you hope her surgery goes well!" He bumps me with his shoulder and whispers. "Hurry. Save Wes. He's a good person."

"Thank you, Architect Maseko." I take off up the ramp.

A wave of well wishes for Darke breaks out behind me.

"Congrats, my love!" Ivan gathers his backpack and laptops from his workstation. "Sully left to get Brown. They'll be here in sixteen minutes."

"I can't believe we're really doing this."

"You were a force of nature. Freckled cheeks flushed with pregnancy glow, arguing to save your people. Absolutely stunning."

Dad, Mom, and Lark are lurking by the elevators.

"Congrats, honey! This is big!" Dad exclaims.

"You'll handle everything in the lab?" I confirm.

"Don't worry, go. Focus on Darke."

"Thanks, Dad."

"I thought we'd have another night together! This is too fast," Mom cries, hugging me. "Why do you have to go do his surgery right now?!"

Uhhhh, because he's DYING, Mom...

It's not a normal Mom hug. She's clinging to me like we're about to experience a death in the family. I can't understand why me getting the opportunity of a lifetime is so upsetting to her. My mom has always kind of been a mystery when it comes to Lark and I. Maybe once the twins are born it'll unlock some special motherly part of my brain that can understand why she cries so much when everyone else is happy.

"It's okay, Mom, we'll see each other in a month in Sao Paulo. Bye, Lark. I love you to the moon and back!" I drop to my knees and hug her.

Hug is an understatement. My grip is an attempt to tell her *see you later, I love you, do not die, stay out of the hospital, and I can't wait to see the look on your face when I tell you about the babies in a few months.* I breathe my quiet hopes over her shoulder.

Please be okay for a few more weeks until we can fix you, baby sis.

"Bye Story! Love, love, love you! See you soon. We'll have so many adventures to talk about. Take lots of pics. I will too." Lark chirps, bouncing with excitement.

"I will. Love you more, Lark! Call and text me every day."

We rush to our apartment and grab the bags we packed yesterday.

"Fly, Birdy!" I bend my knees a couple of inches and Birdy runs up my thighs like a plank, nestling against my neck. "Oh, good girl. I'm gonna miss you so much!"

Her tiny tail whirs like a propeller. "Lark will take good care of you, little pup. Keep taking your meds from Francois."

The five pound Rat Terrier-Chihuahua mix perked right up under Francois' treatments. She's not quite a year old and full of puppy energy. Ivan walks over to pet her. She pulls up a lip, snarling at him.

"I know, Birdy, you'll tear my arm off." He frowns. "Animals love me, what's wrong with this dog?"

She darts out to bite him. "Birdy, no!" I scold, spinning her away.

"Do we really need a vicious dog with twins on the way?"

"She'll know the babies are mine and love them. Right, Birdy, you'll love Holly and Huck?"

"We're in trouble when she realizes they're mine too." He laughs. "We gotta go. Kiss her bye."

She gives happy wiggles and kicks when I squeeze and kiss her before plopping her on the couch. "Stay, Birdy!" I throw her a couple of toys. She freezes, top lip stuck up on her front row of teeth. "Look, she's so good."

"She's something, that's for sure." Ivan laughs, shutting the door.

In the hallway, goodbyes are in progress.

"I'll call you from Georgia, okay?" Richelle gives David a hug and kisses his cheek.

His frosty exterior melts. He wraps her in a hug, gently lifting her off her feet. "Thirty-one days."

The sweetness of their farewell chokes me up. I made that possible. I saved David from the constant threat of Agora death. They have a future if they want because of what Ivan and I built in INES. Time to go give more futures, more lives back.

"Bye!" I call as I trot off with Ivan.

Mom's echoing sobs that I shouldn't go yet won't dampen my excitement.

21

"Two perfectly healthy babies." Dr. Brown smiles, showing us the ultrasound monitor in our little cabin on the flight. Ivan's grip on my fingers tightens. His stunned grin says more than words.

Dr. Brown is a nice, serious man in his late thirties. We chose him because of his pristine resume.

He went to college at an ancient Ivy League school in Boston. He flew through the ranks as a star in their women's health program. His ALICE model work has decreased maternal and fetal deaths worldwide. I'm not a fan of the thought of one of his ALICEs—or any other ALICE, really—delivering the twins. It seems like such an intrusion on a deeply human experience.

Maybe someday moms will have more control. But for now, I'm thrilled Ivan got him to work with us.

"Keep doing what you're doing, taking your vitamins, and they'll be here before you know it," Dr. Brown says. "You want some pictures printed off?"

"Yes!" We blurt loud enough to make him crack up laughing.

"That's what most parents say. I've got my own questions we need to cover. What you're expecting of me. Why you want a human doctor. How you're going to keep me on the right side of AJA for this."

Ivan launches into an explanation of our preference for human care. He tells of my unique situation where Moulson seems to have a grip on tech around me. Ivan's concern is at an all-time high because Moulson has been well-behaved in hiding since he escaped.

I'm not worried about what Moulson's up to. There has to be a threshold for how much evil one person can commit. He jumped so far beyond that with the purge. We've gotta be safe for at least a few months.

"Someone cared enough to steal her lab results and send a bomb," Ivan says. "We can't risk someone hacking an ALICE or ASTRA and hurting Story or the babies."

"I'm happy to take you on as patients. But I'll still have other cases to follow while I work with you."

I sit, staring at the ultrasound pictures while they hammer out the details of my continued care. Dr. Brown will be working remotely, traveling with us until I hit my third trimester. He said at that point, I'll need to slow down.

My favorite picture has the perfect outlines of Holly and Huck. It looks like they're waving. Dr. Brown typed a message along the top. *Can't wait to meet you! -Holly and Huck Rhys, ten weeks old.* I wish Dr. Brown could go so I could be with Ivan. They're talking about what Dr. Brown wants Ivan to build someday as a surgical OBGYN robot.

"What are you thinking about?" Ivan asks, leaning over to look at the pictures.

"I'm dying to see you hold them." Pure excitement takes over. I yank him down in a hug. He catches himself with his forearms, planting his shoulders over mine with a grin.

He's perfect. Everything is perfect. Before the end of the year is up, Dr. Ryland will fix Lark. I'm a real surgeon. I have a shot of fixing Darke. I'm safe here under Ivan.

"Can I stay here for the rest of the flight?" I ask, giving his back the lazy, affectionate scratches he loves.

He tips his head towards Dr. Brown. "May not be the best idea."

"Come on, Ivan. We'll step out. You clean up and get dressed, Story." Dr. Brown laughs.

"I'm so glad you and the babies are okay." Ivan kisses me then leaps up, following Dr. Brown into the tiny airplane hallway. I laugh when Ivan pokes his head back in and winks at me before shutting the little cabin door.

The jelly from the ultrasound and exam is everywhere. Like everywhere, everywhere. I wish this airplane had a shower, but oh well. I'll get one as soon as I'm done in surgery. For now, I get cleaned up the best I can in the little bathroom, then check my phone. Four minutes until we land.

Mom sent me several messages. They better not be an attempt to get me to join her sob fest.

Wanted to send you our flight info. Have a safe trip! Love you, honey!

There's a link to a FlyEU site. When I click the itinerary, it shows a slowly spinning QR code. Fancy. I've never seen one do this. It wobbles before disappearing. Their flight time pops up. They leave at 9:10 tomorrow morning.

Oof, I'm dizzy. I wish he'd stayed in here to help me. The exam table is covered with my crumpled sheet, towels, and the crinkly paper. I throw them on the floor and lean to get my bearings.

"Fasten seatbelts for descent," the speakers broadcast Sully's voice.

Time to get out of here. My honey is probably missing me. I scramble into the hallway and run to sit by my husband. He's in the back row. I throw myself down in the empty chair beside him.

"Hurry and get buckled in, Dr. Rhys," he says with a smile. I hold his hand. He yanks it away. "Story's buckled!" he yells.

A deep voice yells back, "Thanks!"

I pull his hand onto my lap. He rips away and gives me a face like I just kicked a puppy.

"What's wrong, baby?" I ask.

His blonde eyebrows shoot up. "Nothing. I just figured you'd want to sit up there with him." He points to the front of the plane. The other Irontrace and my cousin Richelle are scattered throughout, but as always, I want to be by my love.

"No. I want to sit by you." I lay my hand on his thigh. He jerks away.

Why is he cowering over there? Maybe he's realizing how quickly life will change once the twins are born. In the many years we've been together, I've never seen him so jumpy. Or grumpy.

Focus on doing Darke's surgery. There's a ruptured Agora to handle. It's game on. Don't spiral. You know he's crazy about you. And oh, his face in the ultrasound. I'll never forget the look in his green eyes to see our babies.

"Hey, come hold me. That goop was so cold, I swear it's still clinging all over me."

I loop his arm around my neck, sneaking a quick kiss on his cheek. He tucks his arm tight to his side.

"Listen, Story," he whispers in a near panic. "I don't know what this is about but keep your hands *and* your lips over there. Don't touch me anymore. You're making me uncomfortable."

I meet his green eyes, trying to guess what's wrong. He'd been so excited the rest of the flight.

Maybe landing is freaking him out. Something has him spooked. I rub my hand on his smooth freckled left cheek. He jerks back like I've slapped him.

The tires skim the landing strip. The plane gently bumps along, lurching to slow our fast skitter.

"My love, *what* is wrong?" I plead. "Come hold me."

He unbuckles and jumps out of his seat. As the unbuckled passenger alarm sounds, his slim frame weaves out of our row.

"Babe! Sit down!" I hiss.

I should unbuckle and go after him.

Knowing Nathan, he'll come back with some cute surprise for me.

22

"Something's wrong with Story!" he yells, grabbing the shoulder of someone in the front row.

What!? I'm fine. He's the one behaving oddly.

Chaos hits like he dropped a bomb. In a sudden wave, they all disobey the light to remain seated and leap up. My view of the backs of heads and shoulders turns to bodies running towards me.

Richelle gets to me first and throws herself down in my row.

"Story? What's wrong?" She frantically runs her hands over me.

"I'm fine. Nathan is being weird." I shrug.

Giant hands shove her out of the way. "Move!"

A huge frame drops to the ground in front of me. Huge tan hands caress my baby bump. I look at where a face should be.

But it's a black, distorted mess that keeps shifting like liquid. The more I try to focus on it, the faster it forms and collapses. There are no identifiable features. Something like a shadowy hook launches tendrils towards my face.

Maternal instincts kick in. *Save the babies!* I hit the dark void with a blow that nearly fractures my wrist. The sharp crack of my hand to this messed-up face echoes through the plane.

"Whoa! Ah, babe, what's wrong?" A deep voice comes from in front of me.

Why would this thing touch me? I push it backwards. It doesn't budge.

"NO!" I yell. The face swirls move closer.

What if they pull the twins and I in and we become part of this blackened swirl of tissue and pigment?

"Story, what's wrong?" the faceless void thunders.

"NO!" I scream. I have to get away from him. "Don't touch me!"

"Stop! Baby, it's okay. I'm here." The monster grabs me, pinning my arms to my sides in an attempt to hug me.

Use my legs! I get a foot free and kick him square in the chest. He catches that foot in his armpit.

"You're gonna hurt yourself, talk to us."

Why isn't Nathan helping me? Where is he? Where's Richelle?

I keep moving, trying to crawl away. Thankfully, he's so big he can't get his huge shoulders down in the row by me. There they are! Richelle and Nathan stand in the aisle useless, leaving me to fight. I get my other foot free and kick the black void. My tennis shoe connects hard with something.

There's a pained grunt. He leans closer, pinning me fully down. "Baby, what is happening?"

"Richelle!" I squeak out over his wall of a shoulder, but she just stares, wide-eyed. "Nathan!" I try to scream but can't get his name out.

"Get a med kit! She needs oxygen!" the monster orders.

Something has latched firmly around my throat. It has to be one of the spirals of this man's face choking the life out of me. He's going to kill me.

Babies, it's okay. I'll keep fighting.

"Story, are you hurt? You were fine. Stopstopstop. You're going to injure yourself or the babies!"

The man tilts me up into his arms, holding me inches from what should be a face. My chest burns for air. My heart hammers. This has to be what drowning feels like.

"Story! You have to breathe! Breathe, now."

I know I need to breathe! As hard as I'm fighting, he has my arms both held fast with one of his. I'm nothing against him.

Humans aren't this strong. Okay, so he's not human. What else could he be? Maybe that's why Nathan and Richelle won't help. They're scared of him too.

He lets go with his left hand and rubs my sternum. "Breathe!"

I finally get some air in.

"She's okay, right?" Richelle screams, choking on sobs.

This beast holding me captive must be tearing me apart if watching it makes her cry. She never cries. My OB, Dr. Brown, appears by me. He dumps the contents of an emergency med supply duffle in the aisle.

"Oxygen. Now." the monster yells, clinging to me still.

WHERE IS NATHAN??? I try to scream for my beloved husband, but I choke.

"Try through your nose. Like this." The monster touches my face.

No! He's going to get those black lava tendrils on me. I jerk my head back so fast my neck makes an unsettling crack.

"Don't do that, Story!" Dr. Brown yells.

I have to get to Nathan.

"Get off." My mouth moves, but there's no sound.

It's okay, Twinsies. Hang in there with me. This will be over soon.

"Let her go!" Richelle screams. "She wants up."

The faceless creature releases me. It's my chance to get to Nathan. I can't believe he isn't helping me. I jump to my feet, but I wobble.

"Story, what is it?" Richelle grabs me in a hug.

"What did you do to her?" the abomination roars at Dr. Brown. His huge arm lifts the doctor and tosses him backwards into a row of chairs. I knew he was dangerous! I'm getting tired, but it's so loud. Everyone is shouting.

Henri runs out from the hallway where I'd been. "I don't see anything in the room she was in. I'll check the plane for spy tech and malware."

There's a roaring sound in my ears. Is the plane engine on by me?

"We didn't do this!" the pilot challenges.

"Story! Breathe, baby!" The faceless monster comes back at me. The twisty, folding liquid-like shadows touch my cheek. Why is this thing calling me baby? "Breathe for Holly and Huck!" it says.

What does that mean? Who? I try more silent shrieks. The effort is too much. My vision flickers. I try to jump up, but it's too much. *I don't think we're gonna make it, twins. I'm sorry. I've loved you so much.*

It's so loud and hot. I'm exhausted. I'm supposed to be in surgery. *Sorry, Darke. We're all going to die today.* My lungs have a jagged, fiery pain in them.

My head is going to split open from the noise. No. My head hurts because my oxygen is depleted and carbon dioxide is building up. *Twins. I love you. I'm sorry. I've loved you from the second INES said you're coming.*

Richelle holds me by the ribs, keeping me in her lap. "Help! Ivan!" *Who?* She sobs. "She's dying. Ivan, she's getting floppy like a doll."

Why aren't the Irontrace saving me? They're just watching me suffocate. Matthew Sullivan and the other Air Titans stand behind the Irontrace, horrified faces watching me die. Richelle screams and sobs like life is being sucked from her too. A pang of jealousy hits. She can cry. If I could cry, it would mean I could breathe. She's right. I'm dying. I wrap both hands on my babies. This is the last time I'll hold them.

Dr. Brown's unmoving feet hang over the armrest. Is he dead? I bet he would've saved me if the beast called Ivan hadn't killed him. Why would this shadow man kill the person who could've saved me?

I'm too tired. Maybe if I pretend I died the man will leave us alone.

Someone snatches my nearly limp body from Richelle. Fresh terror hits when I realize it's the faceless man, pulling me back onto his chest, lowering both of us to the floor.

"Story, breathe with me, remember, we've done this. Breathe, like this." He puts his giant hand on my chest over my heart. It's intrusive. He has *no right* to touch me! Furious attempts to escape kick in. "Stop, breathe. You're going to hurt yourself. I love you."

Worthless Nathan is watching, hands cupping his face in horror.

The creeping shadows from the face are beside me. I duck to hide when they reach out, moving into what's left of my field of vision. He's got me by the elbows, but I'm desperate. The shadows are going to pull me in. Unsure if it's bravery, or compromised decision-making because of no oxygen, I reach my hand back and claw at the swirling mass.

Instead of the nothingness I expected, my fingers find a face.

I scratch and claw.

"Stop! Stop it! He's helping you!" Richelle wails, grabbing my hand.

"It's okay, you're okay. I'm right here," shadow man Ivan says. I swear he kisses the top of my head several times. I know you're right there. That's the problem! He's holding me by the ribs. My feet are free, so I anchor my feet on the floor and try to stand.

"Oh, baby, no. You're going to hurt yourself." His voice wavers. He must be some kind of law enforcement. His ankle effortlessly sweeps my feet flat. "I love you, baby." He wraps his leg over mine, immobilizing me.

Twins. I can't. I'm sorry. I'm the worst. I don't deserve you. I hope you don't feel any pain. Let's feel happy together. We're in the sun. At the beach.

I'm spent. My left cheek collapses against his neck. I can't move. Everything hurts. My head. My chest. My throat. It's getting dark.

"RespirMask. NOW! Hurry!" monster yells.

I'm so tired, I don't have any fight left in me. I fall back against him.

"Story, baby, here, breathe. I love you. I love you. I love you," the shadows whisper. Maybe the shadows are choking him to death too because his voice fades away.

A rubbery mask suctions on my face, filling my mouth with a horrible taste like plastic and sterile tools. The plane goes black around me. *I will not die today. Keep fighting.*

My fingers twitch to claw the mask off to get the babies and I fresh air, but my hands won't move.

Guarding My World

~ Ivan ~

"She's been having panic attacks for a couple of weeks. Nothing like this. She was going to talk to Dr. Brown about going on anti-anxiety treatment."

"I doubt he'll be her doctor now." Richelle glowers at me.

"She got sick after he saw her, what did you expect me to think?"

"How about you not knock him out, Ivan?"

We've been posted on either side of Story's bed for the last forty-five minutes waiting on the most recent round of meds to wear off. The AL-ICE has woken her up twice, but she goes right back into whatever nightmare state she's trapped in.

She's resting peacefully. Her heart rate is normal sinus rhythm at 72 beats per minute. Blood pressure is 106/68 which is fine for her. Respirations 14. Oxygen saturation is 99% on room air. No additional breathing support at this time. No fever. Her hands aren't cold anymore since I put the fresh blanket from the warmer on her.

I gently press her slender thumb's nail bed. The color blanches to white then comes back to a healthy light pink almost immediately.

"Stop poking at her. Let her sleep," Richelle says quietly.

I've considered kicking Richelle out many times. "Richelle, leave me alone." She doesn't need to be in here, especially if she doesn't understand simple medical tests like capillary refill.

I can't fault her for trying to protect my perfect Story. My whole family, my universe lays here in this bed. I'll take all the help I can get to keep them safe.

I'm pretty sure I know what's wrong with her, but if I say the words aloud, I'm terrified to make it real. *Come on, baby, prove me wrong.*

I lean my face down beside Story's pillow and plead again. "Please come back and be okay. If you're scared when you wake up, we can deal with that. Just don't panic until you choke."

Ah, shoot, my scabs busted open. It left blood streaks on her pillow.

"Now the right side of your face is torn up nearly as bad as the left side," Richelle says. "Why would she do that to you?"

I roll my right shoulder up to swipe the blood. My panicked wife clawing the flesh raw on my cheek doesn't even register as an injury. "She didn't mean to."

"Go get it cleaned up. I'll watch her. She's already going to feel bad when she sees what she did. At least wash the blood off." Richelle tosses a box of tissues at me.

What if she wakes up and I miss it? There's a bathroom right off her ICU room. It's got a supply cabinet by it. I could grab a wound cleaning kit and be back in less than a minute.

"Goooooooooo," Richelle quietly urges.

I lay my hand on Story's cheek and trace her chin with my thumb. Her face is tiny. She's so fragile. Why was she fighting me on the plane? What was she trying to tell us? Her red, then purple face, choking for air appears every time I close my eyes.

"I'll be right back, baby." *One more kiss. Maybe it's the one that will wake her, bring her back to me.* I lean down and give her a quick kiss on her chilly lips. Nothing. Not even a twitch.

"Don't fiddle with her. Leave her alone," I whisper to Richelle.

"Hurry." Richelle moves from the chair to sitting on the edge of Story's bed.

"'K." I rush out into the hallway and fling the supply cabinet door open. "Face kit, where are you?"

I grab the plastic lidded tray of supplies and run in the bathroom. My reflection makes me wince. The right side of my face looks like a sander hit me.

"Full strength, you'd have clawed this out, babe." The area around my right eye has bruising streaks. I dump the contents of the bottle of wound cleanser into the plastic tray, soaking the gauze towels. While they suck up the cleanser, I splash some warm water on my face then towel dry it.

"She should lead tactical classes on using fingernails in fights. Good job though, baby," I mumble. The wound care kit has thick white swabs. I swipe them across the abrasions, then fan it dry. I squint and crumple the right side of my face a few times to make sure it's not going to start bleeding again.

"Goopy stuff now." The lids on the two packets of quick heal antibiotic cream pop off when I give them a hard squeeze. Watching in the mirror, I try to shoot the contents of the tubes over the deepest scratches the best I can. She's gonna freak out when she sees me.

I hope these don't scar. They'll remind her everyday of...well I don't know yet what they'll remind her of. I throw the tray in the trash and jog out of the bathroom.

She's awake! I freeze to assess her. She looks exhausted but has the faintest glow to her face. I wonder if she remembers how bad her day has been. I hope she doesn't. Maybe it'll be like a nightmare. Where something awful has been vividly flashing in your brain, but waking up clears the fog.

"There you are!" I cover the tiled floor to her bedside in a flash. "How are you feeling?" I kiss her cheek then wrap her in a hug. Her shoulders stiffen then shake. "Story, what's? No," I groan.

We've lost her again. The chocolatey eyes that make my world go round are squeezed shut. Her arms fly up.

"Richelle! Get Nathan!" Her voice trembles between rage and terror.

Why does she keep screaming for him?

ALICE and ORION units whir into the room at dangerous speeds, nearly tipping over. I jump in front of her. They said the next time she does this she gets a forty-eight-hour sedation hold.

"Don't touch her!" I kick an ORION, sending it flying into two others. "You can't knock her out!"

Richelle sobs, pulling on my shoulder. "She was better!"

The ORIONs I kicked over have arms extended with syringes ready to go. We've kept it out of her official medical record that she's pregnant. I've been checking everything they give her to confirm it won't hurt the babies or her.

"Story, stop, please!" I beg.

She gets her ORION call light in her hand and swings it blindly, cracking me in the right cheek. I nearly see stars.

When she lashes it back to hit me again, I carefully catch her arm. "No! No more of that. I love you! You love me too. Stop!"

"Nathannnnnn!" her pitiful voice is so raspy.

"Ivan! Get Nathan!" Richelle has been pulling on my shirt with her freakish farm girl strength and the stitches tear at the seam. I can't hold the call light, fight Richelle off, and keep Story from falling off the far side of the bed. I rip the call light from the wall and kick it to the hallway.

"Get off me, Richelle!" I lurch free and reach over Story to yank her bed rail up. "Baby, it's okay. Stop, please." I catch Story's chin and kiss her nose. She loves when I do that.

That's the wrong move today.

Her screams fill the entire ICU. She spins away, and flips facedown, holding her stomach. I'll do anything for her, but I'm at a total loss.

"Nathan," she whispers. "Help, Nathan!"

More ALICE and ORIONs flood in. Med arms extended. I straddle her bed, making a wall between her and the bots. She lays behind me, sobbing.

"Page Dr. Alan Ross right now!" I yell. "ALICE! Emergency override! Irontrace number 391. ORION! Freeze!"

"SC Rhys, you are not authorized to do an emergency medical override at this Helm," an ALICE says, wheeling slowly towards the side of her bed.

Story pulls her pillow over her head, sobbing. These stupid robots. They're making her more upset. My hand twitches, flicking open my thigh holster.

"ALICE. Page Dr. Alan Ross," I order.

"Step away from our patient," an ALICE wall monitor says.

I draw my SurgePulse sidearm and fire. A pulse of electricity cracks across the room in an arc to fry the ALICE's hardware.

Story shrieks.

"Get out of my wife's room! Direct order. Emergency override!" I thunder. "Irontrace 391. Override!"

"Non-compliant family member." I hear the ORIONs hum at the same moment. Their tranquilizer arms click in place.

I lean, putting my back against my sobbing ball of a wife like a shield and raise my right hand. Nine more perfectly placed shots and her room is quiet. Safe. "Baby, it's okay, they're gone."

She's muttering under her pillow. "I won't let him get us, twins. I'll keep fighting. But his face...is gone. I'll be brave for us. I promise."

The thing that's been nagging me since the plane is true. *Moulson got her with the purge. He's using me to destroy her.*

23

The man with the black hair is back. I'm too scared to open my eyes, but I'd recognize that silhouette anywhere. I'll never get over the things I've seen him do. He's more monster than man. They said his name is Ivan Rhys. He says he's my husband.

He's lying.

...Right?

I roll away and curl around my stomach. I wish Nathan was here.

Ugh, my eyes won't stay open. Maybe I'll feel better after a bit more sleep.

When I blink my eyes open, hours have passed. Or has it been days? It should be illegal to be conscious with a headache like this. My dad, Richelle, and a few other voices float from behind the curtain that hangs between my hospital bed and the door.

Why am I in the hospital? Is it for this headache?

"Alan, there's no way I'm letting them give her a full dose, or even a partial dose of that," Ivan says.

"I'm her dad. I say she gets it."

"Again, I'm not trying to be mean, but that doesn't matter. She's *my wife.* What I say goes for her medically when she can't decide for herself."

"I don't get it. You're tying our hands with what we can try for her," my dad replies. His voice is nearly shaking with anger. "I know you love her. Just give me a reason why we can't proceed with that med therapy."

They're silent for too long.

Then Ivan speaks. "She's pregnant."

Dad gasps. "Ivan. No. You can't be serious. Not right now."

My dad knows I'm pregnant! Nathan and I made it into a whole cute thing to tell my family. Lark nearly shattered my eardrums screaming in excitement.

Ivan continues, "Twins. Due April fourth."

"Twins!? Twins!" Dad cuts out a sharp breath. "She's been working too hard for that! If I knew, I'd have made her slow down. *YOU* should've made her slow down!"

I'm not an idiot. I know what I can handle. And you did know, Dad!

"She wouldn't have wanted to. It would have stressed her out more if I pressed her to take it easy." Well. Ivan's right about that. "On the plane on the way down here, she saw her OB, Dr. Brown, for the first time. She was fine when I left her to change. I'm wondering if he gave her something topically that kicked in after I left?"

"When we get her toxicology reports back, we'll know," Dad says.

"You're *sure* she'd been fine?" Richelle asks.

"Yes," Ivan says. "It went great. We were so happy, looking at the ultrasound pictures." Cold fear pricks my neck. My dad and Richelle really are friends with Ivan. "Then she sat by Nathan, acting like a completely different person."

"Now we're here." Richelle sounds stuffy. I wonder if she's sick.

"Twins? In April? No, they'll probably be here in March if she's due that early in April." Dad's voice cracks with disbelief. He's being so dramatic. "Is this...um...good news? Is she happy?"

"It was surprising. That's for sure. But yes, it's very good news. This is what the labs were for that David asked you about. Someone is very upset about the babies. We're trying to keep it a secret since the bomb."

Dad's voice softens. "Ivan, congrats. You two will be excellent parents. I'm so worried for her though." I see his feet move towards Ivan under the curtain like he gave him a hug. "This wasn't the uh, reason for the elopement, right?"

Elopement? What is he talking about?

Ivan's boots retreat from Dad's feet. "*Absolutely not!* For crying out loud, do the math. You're a doctor."

"I'll help with her surgery schedule," Dad says.

Surgery! Darke is waiting on me! I jump from the bed and rifle through the cabinets for scrubs.

"She's up!" Richelle stumbles through the curtain. "Get back in bed!"

Her face is red and covered with tears.

Jackpot! The linen cabinet has fresh scrubs in my size.

"Whoa, Shells, are you okay?" I ask. I tear open a pack of gauze and remove my IV. "I gotta get to surgery, 'scuse me."

"Alan, get in here!" Richelle yells. She grabs my shoulders and tries to guide me to the bed.

I push her arms away. She pulls my hand. I fling it free.

"Richelle, stop it! I have to go help Darke. Get out of my way!"

She steps in front of me, getting more in the way.

Dad slides the curtain to the side and rushes to me. "Honey, you can't see patients like this." He gives me a gentle hug. "And you're pregnant? Really?"

"You knew! Everyone knows. Nathan and I told you all."

"Why on earth would Nathan tell me that?"

"Because he's my husband!" I shout. Dad's jaw drops. "You should be in Germany, Dad. Why are you here?"

"Ivan called me screaming that he was sending Air Titans for Ryland and me. That we needed to do Darke's surgery."

"Why? No! I'm doing it." I smooth a waterproof wound cover on my IV site. That should be fine when I scrub in.

"Story, sit down," Richelle orders.

I pull a pair of scrub pants on under my hospital gown. It's weird tying them with my growing baby bump. *Babies! Am I here because something happened to them?* I grab my stomach. "I'm in the hospital. Are the babies okay?"

"Yes. Holly and Huck are fine," Richelle says.

Holly? Huck? I swear I just heard those names somewhere. I sit on the edge of the bed, leaning forward to cradle my lower stomach. *I heard it on the plane.* "Who?" I ask.

Richelle's eyes go wide.

"Holly. Huck. You and Ivan's babies?" Richelle says.

My chest aches. I whisper to Richelle, "No. Can't be. He's not...I don't even think he's a human."

"He is! You stop this nonsense!" she whisper-shrieks at me.

Dad sits. "This is the first time you've really woken up. Let's see how alert and oriented you are. You know you're pregnant?"

I nod.

"What's your full name?" Dad asks.

"Story Caroline Cantone."

"It's not! I've been telling you that," Richelle squawks.

"Richelle, give her a minute," Dad says. "Who's your husband?"

"Nathan Cantone."

Dad makes a pained face. "Where are you?"

"Helm in Tallulah Falls, GA."

He nods. "Tell me about the last few days."

"I'm prepping for Australia to kick off the Southern Hemisphere of our Agora removals. We're starting with Commanders, then we'll work with surgeons we train to do the rest of them next."

"Good. Tell me a little bit about your family. Do you have siblings?"

I wrestle my scrub shirt over my gown. "Stop it, Dad. I don't feel good enough to play these games."

"I'd like to know how you're feeling. Tell me your physical symptoms," he says.

"My head hurts. Really bad. It's a sharp pain, not localized. It's everywhere." I weave my hospital gown up through the neck of my shirt. Finally, I've got real clothes on. "My body feels like I've been beaten with a stick. The whole thing hurts."

"Probably from fighting Ivan like a Jiujitsu queen," Richelle says.

I glare at her. What on earth is she talking about?

"Sorry you're hurting. I'll get you pain meds. Pregnancy-safe ones." Dad pushes a button on my ALICE monitor. "Tell me about your family."

"As you already know, I have one sister, Lark. She's in Ohio with Mom. We need to get to Darke's surgery."

"Ryland and I did his surgery two days ago. He's fine."

The room spins. "Two days ago? What?"

"We'll talk about that in a minute. Keep going. You're pregnant?" he asks and I nod. "Congrats. I'm so happy for you and Ivan, honey." *Ugh. Ivan.* "Have you picked out names for them?"

I smile. "Kristen and Josh."

He grimaces. "Those *certainly* are meaningful names to Ivan. What do you know about Ivan Rhys?"

I rack my brain for something, anything that will show them I'm not losing my mind. I'm drawing a blank. I don't think I hate Ivan, but I'm close to it. He's dangerous. He's not human. I don't believe aliens are real. He can't be something like that. Maybe he's some hybrid creature from a Bastion experiment? Those are real. Nathan told me about them. I shrug, silent.

Richelle's eyes nearly pop from her head. "I've told you multiple times who Ivan is," she says.

"Richelle? He's not...no. He tricked you." His black boots lurk under the curtain. I whisper, "He shot all the ALICEs and ORIONs that came to help me. He could've killed me."

Dad leans in. "Story, he was keeping those clinic bots from knocking you out again. He wanted to help you wake up so you could get better."

"He should have told me that."

"Would you have listened?" Dad settles back in his chair, chewing his lip. "What does Nathan look like?"

"My height. Blonde hair. Green eyes."

"Yes, that is what Nathan Cantone looks like. Tell me, as quickly as you can, how to do an Agora removal?"

I fly through the steps, throwing in as many technical details as I can to prove my brain is working perfectly.

"Are we about done here?" I ask, massaging my temples.

Dad taps his lips in thought. "Who brought you to Georgia?"

"Matthew Sullivan and the Air Titans."

"What happened on the plane?"

"My first pre-natal checkup."

"Tell me about your nightmare."

"How did you know I had a nightmare?"

Dad circles a hand to get on with it.

"A man with no face was coming for me. He's made of liquid and shadows. He punched Dr. Brown to death and smeared Brown's blood all over me. It wasn't a dream. The man is here. Ivan."

The ALICE monitor turns on by my bed. "Hello, Dr. Rhys."

"Why am I here?" I demand.

"Senior Commander Rhys had to use an assistive breathing device on you when the plane landed. It's standard procedure to admit you."

"Can I go home now?"

"Yes, you're stable for discharge," the ALICE says.

"Power down, ALICE," Dad says. "So, you know everything about your life except Ivan, and you're foggy on baby names?"

"I'm not foggy on anything," I retort.

"Story, I need you to listen. Moulson has somehow replaced your memories of Ivan with Nathan Cantone. Nathan is nothing to you. You're Ivan's wife. You two are crazy about each other. Work hard to re-orient yourself," Dad says. He stops and looks at Richelle. "You said they mentioned naming them Huck and Holly?"

"She told me Huck and Holly for sure. Look at her bracelets. Holly plants and huckleberries. Ivan had them made for her."

I lift my arms. Sure enough, beautiful, delicate imprints wind around each bracelet cuff. I frown. I didn't know these bracelets carried such a special meaning. My baby's names. And I forgot them? A sharp pang of unease hits.

What else am I wrong about?

"Coming in." Ivan swings the curtain out of the way. He's concealing his face in a matte black Irontrace helmet. "My face is covered, my love." His hopeful voice cuts out when I fold forwards. I smush the heels of my palms into my eyes until fireworks appear.

"She needs an MCDI scan to confirm she's a purge victim," Dad says.

"I don't want a scan. I want to go work!" I seethe.

"She doesn't have to get a scan." Ivan sits, his side touching mine. "I'm one hundred percent confident she's been purged. It's okay. Stay calm, baby. I'll keep my face hidden."

I twitch my shoulders away. "You want me calm? Leave."

"Let's have AJA interrogate her. We'll go from there." Dad swipes through the ALICE wall panel.

No. Shoot. No. I HATE interrogations. "No, please," I say.

"Yes. We have to find out what happened," Dad says.

I whisper to Ivan, "Do you have to be in here?"

"I'd like to. I love you. So much," he says softly.

I forget the disaster I'm in and turn, ready to tell him that's impossible. Shadowy tendrils snake out the bottom of his helmet. Panic is lurking, ready to suck me in. I lurch backwards, covering my eyes with one arm, grabbing the bed rail with the other.

"Get Nathan. I want my husband there if I have to talk to an AJA."

"Richelle, go get Nathan," Ivan says.

"You're joking?" She huffs.

"Go get him. We keep Story happy and calm."

I'm not happy! I'm not calm.

"Do you really want me to leave?" Ivan asks.

I turn in the bed, sitting cross-legged with my back to him. "What even are you? Really?"

"Ivan Rhys. Love of your life."

"Never heard of you."

He lets out a hollow laugh. "Dang it! I love you more than anything."

"Did you just laugh?"

"Would you be mad if I did?"

"Nope. You're proving my point. My husband would care if I suddenly forgot him. He'd be sad, scared. He wouldn't be laughing."

"Wife-" he starts.

"Don't call me that!" I hiss.

"Fine. Beautiful. There, is that better?" I shake my head. "I got you to fall in love with me once. I'll do it again."

Doubtful... "You're an Irontrace too?"

"Yes."

"Why haven't you fixed the purge yet?"

"Workin' on it." He presses some ultrasound pictures into my hand.

The top one has a message. *Can't wait to meet you! -Holly and Huck Rhys, ten weeks old.* The upper left corner has the name *Rhys, Story* and my birthday.

A terrifying tendril of shadow rolls down from his helmet. *Orient yourself! Those aren't real.* I swipe at the tendril. My hand swishes through the air. It's a trick of the light, an illusion. The tendril follows my hand. I fan my fingers back through it. I don't feel anything. It can't hurt me.

Ivan catches my hand. "You okay?"

"Don't touch me. I'm doing something."

My curtain slides open and Nathan steps in.

He came! I knew he would!

"Hey, what's up in here?" I leap out of the bed and run to bury my face in his neck. "Oh. We're still doing this? Hi, Story. Feeling better?"

I squeeze him, desperate for him to save me.

His arms stay at his sides.

"Nathan, tell them. Tell them you're my husband. I'm fine. Take me home. I have a splitting headache," I plead.

His lovely green eyes bear a sad weight. He pats a hand on my shoulder gently and says, "I'm sorry Moulson did this to you, but no." *No! Nathan, help.* "We'll fix you, don't worry," Nathan whispers, removing my hands from his neck.

"She needs to go have an AJA interrogation and doesn't want to go without her husband," Dad says.

"Story. That means you need Ivan. He's your husband."

This couldn't be going worse. Nathan doesn't believe me either. He was my last hope.

"No. You...Nathan." Tears burn my eyes. He shakes his head. "Right? You and me?"

His blonde hair looks like it got messed up in the chaos on the flight. I reach out to smooth it down, but he rests my hand by my side.

"Stop. Please." He twists his lips to the side. He only does that when he's overwhelmed. This must be as hard for him as it is for me.

Stupid purge! It stole my husband, my best friend. I need to show I'm still anchored in what's real. The interrogation can prove that.

"Bring in the AJA," I say.

"I need to talk to her for a minute. Everyone out," Ivan says.

My face must betray how I feel about that plan.

"You have to listen to him. He's the best. He loves you," Nathan says with a sad smile, then turns away.

I know what the purge is. What it can do. But when it comes for you, for your family? It takes away the beautiful things in life. A hollow, quiet grief settles behind my ribs. Nathan shuts the door behind him.

My love has left me.

24

"I want to talk to my brilliant, logical, Story. I know you're in there." Ivan speaks in a voice like he's scared to break me. "Do you think the AJA will approve you to go anywhere near an operating room if you keep this up?"

Keep what up? I'm not faking this. I glare at the floor.

"I'm your husband. Your emergency contact. Your medical power of attorney."

He's my power of attorney? I'll be signing in and confirming that in my chart later.

"Whether you remember me or not, I'll be with you for the interrogation. Fake that you can tolerate me. It'll lend credibility to your claim that you're okay." He offers me a hand. "Can you do that? Play nice for a bit? Then you can hate me again later."

I don't move.

"Story, I'm trying to help you. Remember, baby? We worked so hard to find a way to help Lark." He rests his hand between us. I do need to keep working and fix Lark. "Come on, we can do this. I'll stay behind you. I won't bother you. I know the rules of the purge. I've been studying it for a week straight."

Why is he studying the purge? Irontrace work on The Kernel, not healthcare issues.

"You're married to *me*. I love you." His voice is muffled by the helmet, but it's a decent voice. It makes my head feel the tiniest bit better. "I love you so much. I would never hurt you." I shuffle a step towards him. "That's it. Your brain is tricking you. This is not your fault."

He's right. This isn't my fault. It feels nice to try. It's good for the twins to keep a level head. And if I'm being honest? He does have a nice voice. A warm, rumbly murmur because it's so deep. He's coaxing me into some kind of stillness with it.

I take another small step towards him.

"Good job! You can do this. We'll do it together. You're not alone. I'm not going anywhere. I'm all yours, my beautiful wife."

I grab a pack of slipper socks from the bedside table and flop in the chair. "Stop calling me your wife!"

"*WIIIFFFFE.*" He draws it out in his vaguely Southern accent. His voice stays gentle, but now he's rushing. "I'm trying to help you. You're not married to Nathan. You have to get that in your brain before you talk to them. They know the truth. You can't fool AJA. You're so smart. Listen to what we're teaching you. Fight the purge. Nathan isn't your husband. I am. Remember that or you're going to fail this interview immediately."

I shove my feet in the soft, black clinic gripper socks and stand. He's sitting in my hospital bed.

"I should be there, get up." I tap his humungous boot with my foot. "Let's get this over with."

"I'll sit behind you. Let me be your support."

"Support me from ten feet away. I'm not even kidding right now."

He groans and leaps to his feet. AJA rolls in, parking in front of me.

"State your full name," the AJA says.

I stare at the *What's Your Pain Today* chart bouncing around on my ALICE wall monitor. Six. This headache is a solid six out of ten. Time to go convince them I'm happy to belong to a faceless monster named Ivan Rhys. This is going to be my ten.

"Story Caroline Rhys," I firmly say.

"State your full name," it repeats.

"Story Caroline Rhys."

"State your full name."

"Story Caroline Rhys."

"State your full name."

"Story Caroline Cantone."

"Let's begin," it says.

"Ha!" I exclaim at Ivan.

He whispers just loud enough for me to hear, "That's not a victory."

"Tell me about the last week of your life," the AJA says.

Several times, Ivan scoffs at things I say Nathan and I did. AJA quizzed me for an hour.

"Thank you for your time," the AJA says. "Interview complete."

"Display her results," Ivan says. My vital signs monitor switches to timestamps with green and red spikes. I walk to the screen and swipe through.

"Look! I was right." The AJA flagged several things as green *TRUE*. Ivan is an unknown monster. He's bent on hurting the babies and I. Nathan is my husband.

"My love, this is *bad*. This is really, really bad. It doesn't mean what you think it does," Ivan whispers.

"No. It means I...*I* know the truth."

"AJA," Ivan's voice is heavy with emotion. "Did Story pass this AJA interrogation?"

"No, Senior Commander Rhys," AJA says.

It feels like someone punched me in the throat. "Why?" I croak.

"Your reality is disconnected from fact," the AJA says. "You don't know your name or your spouse's name. You aren't aware of any details of your life with him. You state you're married to Nathan Cantone. We have already interviewed him. He has no romantic attachment to you, now or at any point in time."

Thanks, Nathan!

"Can I do surgery?" I ask.

"No," the AJA says.

"No. I have to-"

"Interview complete," it says.

"ALICE. Assessment results for Story Rhys." Ivan's voice changes. It takes on a low, dangerous quality.

"Story Rhys is a twenty-two-year-old female. G1P0 at ten weeks, one day gestation with di-di twin pregnancy. Their heart rates and growth are on track. Her limbic system shows critical dysregulation. Primary diagnosis? Familial purge."

"ALICE, what's your treatment recommendation?" Ivan asks.

"Immediately relocate Dr. Story Rhys into a purge care facility," it replies. "She's been matched with an inpatient room in Atlanta Medical Hub. They'll arrive to transport her in ninety minutes."

I gasp. ALICE wants to discard me like I'm an unwanted, pregnant cat. I pace around the bed. Time to get out of here. Should I hide? Run?

"ALICE," Ivan barks. "There are other options she can try before she's put in a facility."

"She has to learn to cope with her symptoms until the BBA finds a solution."

"Learn to cope?" Ivan snorts. He walks towards the door. "AJA. I'm taking my wife home."

"Story Rhys is now in AJA protective custody," it replies.

No. This is a nightmare. This can't be real. They want to take me away. Ivan is the worst thing I've ever seen. There's no safe refuge, no good option for me.

"AJA. Your audio output is malfunctioning. We can't hear you. Come on, Story, let's go." He reaches for me.

I wrap my arms through the bedrail. He's not taking me.

"Senior Commander Rhys." The AJA's volume has increased exponentially. "Story Rhys is in AJA protective custody."

"Story, I can't hear what that thing is saying," he says. "Let's go home."

The AJA darts out a sedative arm towards his thigh. He dodges to the side. It repeatedly booms commands through a loudspeaker. *It's going to attack him!* No one else believes me, but AJA can see how dangerous he is. I bet Dad can convince them I shouldn't be sent away. Yeah, the AJA can knock Ivan out and then I'll get help from Dad. I scramble to get my phone.

I message Dad quickly. *Help! Ivan's back. AJA wants to take me!*

"What? AJA, I can't hear you," Ivan says. He's grabbing chargers and bags with one hand like we're checking out of a hotel. The AJA speaker is so loud that my molars vibrate. It's yelling for him to stand down. "Baby, I'm going to make you such a welcome home feast. How does taco pizza sound?"

This isn't real. It can't be happening.

Two AJA arms dart towards his thighs. "Irontrace 391 taking reactive action," he says.

In the span of a breath, he shot the AJA and ALICE with some electricity weapon he pulled from a holster on his thigh. They tip over in a thundering crash.

The yelling, the robot speakers, the crash of them falling in a tangle. My head already hurts, he's gonna make me cry if he keeps this up.

"Stop shooting things!" I yell. Trying to put distance between him and I is nearly impossible with the robot bodies taking up much of the floor space. I crawl across my bed to cower beside it.

He's typing on my vital signs monitor. This is my chance to get help while he's distracted. I slide my hand across the bed toward the call light.

He moves like lightning, tossing it high out of my reach in a wall fixture. "Knock it off, wife. Stop being like that."

I shrink forwards to protect my stomach. "Don't hurt me. You know I'm pregnant."

"I would NEVER." He takes a shuddery breath. "I would never, ever hurt you...Sit down, please. I love you. I love our babies."

An ORION medcart wheels through the hallway.

"Help! There's-" I yell.

It stops. Ivan bursts into the hall, yanking the ORION into the room with us. Showing no pain, he punches it repeatedly, fracturing through its back panel. He shoves his fist in the components box and tears out a handful of wires.

"Just gotta, hang on," he grunts. There's some kind of plug connecting a rectangular silver box to the hard drive. He rips it apart then kicks the AJA, ALICE, and ORION into a messy pile before turning back to the computer. "Story, please. Would you give me five minutes and I'll answer any question you have? I love you. So much! I'll explain everything.”

Blood pours from his hand and wrist as he types. People don't act like this. We don't have power over AJA, or ALICE, or any of the AI models.

“Hello, my boy!” a woman's voice rings out from his phone.

“Hey, how are you?”

“I'm well. How are you, honey?” She sounds kind.

“Ready to come back to Ohio.” He chuckles, unaffected by his blood, my panicky panting, and the odd whirring from the robot's dying systems. “I emailed you a contract. There are instructions at the top.”

“One second,” she pauses. “No ambiguity. No termination traps. She'll have the safety net we want.”

“Thank you,” he says.

“Bye, baby! Thanks for the call. Tell our girl I say hello.”

Who is this triangle of people I assume I'm in? I don't know him. I don't know her. I forgot my whole life. And now I can't get a full breath.

“I will, bye.” He lays his phone on the table, shaking out the fingers on his right hand. “Oof. This stings.”

His phone rings. Panic is threatening to suck me in. I'm still short of breath and my heart is going wild. The room is starting to look wavy, like maybe it's spinning. Ivan unfurls an oxygen mask, pressing it gently to my face with his blood-free left hand.

“Here, my love. You're okay. I promise.” He tries to get the strap around my head but can't with one hand. “Two liters by mask.” His phone keeps ringing. I can't move. “Story, you're at ninety-one on room air. Put this on so I don't get blood all in your hair if I try to.”

That snaps me into action. I secure the mask on, sucking deep breaths.

He finally answers the phone. “Hello…Thanks for calling…Yeah…She signed them just now.”

He chats, unbothered by his blood loss. *What is he doing?* He flings his arm repeatedly at the robot pile. Their sleek metal becomes splattered with blood. It looks like a horrific crime scene.

"It's ironclad, right?" he asks. "Nothing will change your mind?"

"Correct! She's in. The press conference will…"

I creep to the supply cabinet and type my Irontrace clinic creds.

"A six-month contract is a great start…Okay, her copy is in my email…I appreciate you adding that disability clause. Never know what'll pop up in 2050." He laughs.

How can he stand there so nonchalantly?

"Yes…" I can't hear what the voice says, but they're talking fast.

"You're welcome. I've got my hands full right now. Have to go. We'll talk tomorrow." He tosses his bloody phone beside me. "You breathing better now, Story?"

He's trying to be nice. I'm a doctor, I have to help him. I grab a dressing kit and step towards him. "Let me see your hand, please," I say, snapping my gloves on.

"Thanks." He takes the dressing kit and dumps it on my bed, rotating his wrist to show the extent of it. "Check this out, ouch. That stupid ORION was harder than I expected to break into." He pours wound cleaner on his forearm, letting it trail down his hand. "You wanna stitch me up, baby? I just need a couple."

I picture where I'd put the neat, small stitches on his wrist. "No. You need to see an ALICE to make sure it's done right," I say. "Why did you punch it like that?"

"You told me to stop shooting things. I improvised."

He continues pouring the wound cleanser long after he needs to. It's flooding down onto the AJA and ALICE. Faint trails of smoke drift from their screens. SAM! Nathan built me a shield called SAM. I've never used it, but I'm going to try it today. I should've used this on the plane. I push the emeralds on my wedding band.

"Good idea, baby. Stay in SAM until we get out of here," Ivan says.

How? He shouldn't be able to see me! "You can't see me, right?" I ask.

"Of course I can. I made sure I'll always be able to see you in there. I turned off the digital clone feature. I don't know if my clone would make you panic."

"No. Nathan built SAM. He controls it."

He clicks his mouth, "Sorry, no. SAM is mine." Well, I'm not sitting around in something Ivan built. I shut SAM off. After he's poured all of the wound cleanser on the robots, he steps on their monitors, crushing them. "There. Made sure their brains are destroyed."

Even if he's not my husband, I don't want him to get an infection or be in pain. I pick up the wound cleaning swabs. This isn't so bad, I'm just working on injuries like I have for years. I add on an antibiotic gauze layer, tucking it gently. He stays quiet until I've put his hand in a padded dressing. That'll be okay until he gets to an ALICE.

"Thank you," he says. "Guess what? You're approved to do surgery."

"Don't lie to me."

He laughs. "I wouldn't dare lie to you."

My headache is getting worse. "When are they coming to take me?"

"They're not."

Dad and Richelle rush in. Dad's eyes jump between the robots. "Who's bleeding? What happened in here?"

"Check the logs. Those were faulty. They incorrectly evaluated Story. Said they were sending her to a purge care facility in Atlanta. Their audio output was busted," Ivan says. "Look, they injured my hand."

He's such a liar! "They didn't-"

"Yes. They. Did." Ivan's voice leaves no room for disagreement.

Dad shushes me. "Ivan saved you. The Bastion throws away interrogation results from faulty units. The last thing you need is to be trapped in one of those purge prisons. Let me look at your hand, Ivan."

"No, she fixed me up. Story, we need to talk," Ivan says.

"I'd rather you stay away," I say.

He doesn't listen. His feet step between mine, blocking me in. "Close your eyes, the helmet is coming off," he says.

"Don't!" I look down just in case. He tosses the helmet in my bed.

Infuriating man. I squeeze my eyes shut. He steps close enough that his chest is pressed to my shoulder. "I just gave you a fresh start," he whispers. "You can do this. Keep it together. Later, collapse at home with me. I'll keep that part of you shielded from the world."

He wants me to smile beside him. To let my life with Nathan disappear. "You want me to put on a mask? To pretend I'm fine?"

His lips are nearly on my ear. "You don't need a mask, my love. You're the strongest person I know. Let that strength shine. I'm right here if you need a safe place to fall apart."

I tilt my head towards his lips. "Get out of my face."

25

Not sure how one day can take approximately ninety hours, but this one did. Dad and Richelle said I'm too dumb and untrustworthy to be unsupervised, so they took me on a grand tour of the Tallulah Falls Helm.

We went to meet Wes Darke. He didn't have the tough Irontrace exterior I expected. He's the spitting image of Max. Sandy brown hair, square jaw, dark eyes. But Wes looked small, shaken. Hormones got the best of me, and I cried when he teared up, telling me how appreciative he is I started this project.

"My brother and I are so grateful," Wes said. His accent is a mix of Georgia and Australia. "I've lost friends to Agoras. I knew I was a goner. I thought I'd died when they woke me up in recovery. Your dad was there, telling everyone your plan saved me."

"Makes it all worth it," I smiled.

"I couldn't believe the head of ASTRA fought for me like that," he said with a grateful smile.

"Wow, that was nice of them," I said with a nod.

He gave me such a funny look.

"We'll let you get some rest, have a great day," Dad told him.

We attended a depressing midday funeral via videoconference. It was for Travis and Talia from Lancaster. I didn't catch their last names. They died from an Agora injury. I've never met them, but it's always sad when a life is gone. It makes me anxious to get Agora surgeries off the ground even faster.

For the whole funeral, I stared at Ivan's legs. I wanted to make sure he stayed in his seat, two chairs away. He got up once during the service and I almost cried, thinking he was coming to sit next to me.

But he went on the stage to speak about how much Travis and Talia meant to him and I. He spoke of how we'll never forget their vigilance, kindness, and love. Oops. I forgot.

Dad spent the rest of the day engaging me in chipper bursts of conversation. It was the worst. Turns out it's really news to him that I'm pregnant. "My baby girl is having babies of her own," he kept repeating, hugging me throughout the day. He talked about travel plans, Agora removals, asked me a ton of questions about my pregnancy, told me how I acted as a baby, and researched fun things to do in Georgia.

It was a one-sided conversation. I want to go home. To Nathan. He's the vibrant spot of sunshine that adds color to every moment. Today was all grey without him.

Richelle insisted on keeping me company in my apartment when they finally let me go home. I sat cross-legged in bed reading and re-reading Tallulah Falls patient charts until I'd memorized every name, date of birth, and medical history for my initial surgical group. After hours of reading, I couldn't get the sensation of sharp sand out of my eyes.

Richelle whispered, "Are you asleep?" at my back ten times before she dozed off. After the first couple of times, I stopped answering. Now I'm awake, processing the day.

"I miss you," I whisper to Nathan in the darkness.

If he was here, it would be like every other night. I'd have my head on his chest. One arm would be reaching up, running through his blonde hair. He's my best friend, and he's gone.

Think like a doctor. I'll write mental notes on myself.

Hey babies, you're alright, right? I put my hands on my stomach and lay, breathing. Nothing has changed when I do my check-in. I believe the twins are fine.

How does the purge work? Amnesia—check. Panic—check. But I'm different. None of them know *where* they belong. They just have a vague knowledge that they're missing someone. I want to be with Nathan. Mystery symptom of wanting to be with a specific person—check. Aren't I just special?

I retrace my known history with Nathan. There's no dates. No anniversaries. It's a flood of events over years. Our first meeting in the clinic at the Lancaster Helm when I was working with Dad a few years ago. Many romantic dates in the Helm and Hocking Forest. Him proposing in Atlas Caverns. Our huge wedding at The Helm with dozens of Irontrace. Richelle was my maid of honor. Lark was a junior bridesmaid. He was so happy when we found out about the twins.

Who do these memories really belong to? How did they get in my brain? They're vivid. They're real. And the fact that I'm the sole remember-er? It's too much.

My ultrasound picture is on the table beside me. I prop it up against the lamp and stare at it. Start with the ultrasound. It's the last memory I have before the plane nightmare. Nathan, Dr. Brown, and I were in a tiny room on the airplane. The time and date on my ultrasound picture confirm that it happened a few days ago.

But Story Rhys had that ultrasound for Holly and Huck. Nathan kissed me. I was happy. It was perfect. But it wasn't real. Nathan wasn't there. It was Ivan.

So, the emotions are real, but the people associated with them are wrong? Did I feel perfectly happy with Ivan in my ultrasound? Maybe Nathan wasn't put in my brain to hurt me. What if he was put in there to hurt Ivan? That does scream Moulson. To break me. And hey, let's put a knife in Ivan's heart too by making me fall in love with his friend.

My phone! Ivan must have texted me if we're married. I open my messaging app. No Ivan Rhys. I have a ton of messages from Nathan Cantone.

Love you more than anything, baby!
Race you home! Walking out of the control room now. (3,2,1, GO!)
Come home and drink margaritas while <> finish making dinner.
Me, you, coffee, couch, be there in 5 min!

It reads like a long-running, continual conversation between two best friends. It's full of love, flirting, and snippets of a shared life.

The swimsuit you ordered for the beach trip came! :-O
<>van time?

That's a weird one.

My favorite was something only a computer nerd would make. A harmless, madly in love nerd. Someone like Nathan, not that imposing wall, Ivan.

Drew you a map of where we'll be this evening:

```
+---------Our room-----------+
| _______our bed______    |
| | your side      my side| |
| | my arm  →_0__0 ||
| |           /|\ |\  ||
| |           /\ /\  ||
| |________________|  |
+----------------------------+
```

Apologies for looking like <> decapitated you in the pic. <> would never.

There's no my side of the bed anymore. Someone's side *is* my side. I know it in my heart. And what are the <>? Is that a code? It's sprinkled throughout the conversations. I think it's taken the place of the letter I. Why? That's an odd letter to replace with nonsense. I for Ivan? Strange.

When I see the last few messages, I nearly sob. In a panicky, tired migraine fog the other night, I'd been texting Nathan to help me. He didn't come, he just said it was killing him, then called me his wife and put an *-I* with it. Odd. Is he out there, missing me for real?

The last time I saw the clock was 3:01. I open my eyes at 5:15. A voice speaks in something like a prayer from a chair by my bed.

I dare to flutter an eyelid open. It's Ivan. I curl on my side away from him, imagining I'm curling around my babies (our babies?) to keep them safe. Dad and Richelle told me not to be afraid of him. They said he loves me very much and would never do anything to hurt or scare me.

Don't be afraid. That's a laugh. If they could see what I see, they'd have him removed from the Helm. Removed from society. I know it's a trick my brain is playing on me. But my word, it's awful.

If this is what the purge people have been going through, I'd run away too. But I know my priorities. Keep the twins safe. Fix enough Irontrace to get Lark's surgery approved. Leave Nathan alone, even though it hurts.

For such a hulk of a man, Ivan is very good at whispering. Whatever he's saying must be important if he felt he had to sneak in here.

"When I talked to your mom, she said your dad had just landed back in Lancaster. Thompkins will be flying them to Germany in the morning. She told me to tell you she loves you. I said I'd try."

He's telling me about his day.

"I wish you could talk to me without panicking or...." That part trailed off. I wish I could've heard it. "I hope you have sweet dreams, my love. You'd sleep better if I was wrapped around you. You're always so cold. I miss your icy feet between my calves in bed. I'd tug those soft red curls until you're dreaming in my arms."

Mmm, that sounds amazing. Just not with you. I roll back over to face him, keeping my eyes squeezed shut. This will be a good test. If he really loves me, he won't risk waking me.

A grief-filled sigh drifts in my direction. I lay for a small eternity, waiting to see if he'll reach out. He doesn't. Heavens, this man has impressive self-control. I don't. I miss holding hands with Nathan (Ivan?). I wiggle my fingers, careful to make sure it seems natural, like a sleepy twitch.

A warm, strong grip takes my hand. I lace my fingers through his. My brain may have forgotten him, but my hands sure remember. Great, now I'm hallucinating sensations. I swear there's a small blaze pressed between our palms. Chill, brain, this can't be real. There *is* something weird happening though. My skin is buzzing against his? I don't know. It's a mix of beautiful and dangerous. I can't let go. I'll add flaming hands to my list of symptoms.

"There you are baby. I knew you weren't gone. I've been telling them all you're still Story, even if you aren't feeling well." His lips brush my fingers. "Don't worry. I'm not going anywhere."

He continues his one-sided conversation. Telling me how frustrated he is. Thirty percent of Irontrace have been delegated to get The Kernel running without human intervention.

"They should fix the purge first. The Bastion's ready to move on. I won't. I refuse to abandon you and all the other purge victims. If people find out how many resources they're throwing at this? The world as we know it will be over."

His voice cuts through the static in my head. When he pauses, I crave more. He gasps with a hopeful breath when I follow the contour of his knuckles with my fingertips.

"I'm tired, my love. I followed you all day in my cloaking shield." He leans his torso lightly on the edge of the bed. His face rests near my arm. "Every step you took, I was right there so no one could hurt you." Really? "I've worked all night on the contacts to help purge victims. I don't think I've ever been this exhausted."

He can stay there for a few minutes. I may be scared, but I haven't lost compassion. And I have to say, his inexplicably hot hand seems to be the one I miss. My breathing syncs with his.

I wake with a start. *What is that?* There's something by my face, but I can't make it out. I gently touch it. A face. Ivan's swirly face! Terror seizes me, and I let out a panicked cry.

"What? What is it?" Richelle yells, flipping a light on.

The black swirls of Ivan's face are back, attached to his arm, leading to his hand I'm holding. I throw myself across the bed in a blind panic. Ow, ouch, shoot! Flinging hurt my side again. *You know it's Ivan, stop! Get control of yourself. Breathe!*

"Story, it's okay," Richelle says. "Don't start this back up, please."

"Baby, I'm in a shield. It's okay." I hear Ivan, but I can't see him.

"I can't stop..." I choke out. "How do we-stop...this?" My voice cuts out like a radio losing connection.

"IVAN! Get out!" Richelle shrieks, holding me against her chest. I slap her arms to free me, let me breathe.

"She needs to breathe!" Ivan barks. One glance at that shadowy void of his face set off some kind of explosion in my nervous system. I can't reverse it. "I'm not leaving until she breathes. Baby, breathe. Please!"

"Ivan, get Mai!" Richelle says.

The only sound coming from me are wheezy gasps and chokes. My lungs beg for air. I'm finally half free from Richelle's arms. She doesn't understand I'm trying to escape and grabs me harder. Panic rises. I might start puking. Can you puke if you can't breathe?

I don't want to know! I want air! I flail until she finally lets me fall on the far side of the bed. I'm crouched on all fours when I hear the apartment door slam.

"He's gone." Richelle says.

I smack the floor, arching my back. It finally works. Air stutters into my lungs, fracturing whatever invisible hand had been choking me.

"You're doing it, Story, good job!"

More air comes in. I'm okay. Crying is good. I can breathe. The babies have air. Ivan's gone. He better not come back.

Pushing My Wife's Buttons

~ Ivan ~

"I am competent!" Story insists. Again.

Mai reported the fresh round of panic to David.

David already spent twenty minutes chewing me out. Getting caught was my bad. Won't let it happen again.

"I get it. We know Ivan is the only missing spot in your memory." David nods at her from the large monitor. "Story, you're not going to Australia. I have already sent Benedict with a team in your place. The first few surgeries have gone well."

"David, those were my patients! I've studied their charts, I knew their histories," she hisses.

"It's not a competition. They need surgery. It doesn't matter who does it," he replies.

"Freakin' Ivan," she whispers.

She has no idea I'm sitting two feet from her. Close enough to see the red flush in her cheeks. It spreads up from the hollow of her neck, filling the ivory skin between her freckles. Oh no. She's quiet. It's bad, *very* bad when she doesn't answer. Story thinks out loud, but rages silently. Unless it's at The Bastion. She'll happily scream at them any day.

"You're not going. At least not right now," David says, breaking the silence.

"If you won't let me go to Australia, put me to work here. Let me prove I'm fine. I already familiarized myself with the patient records. I made a schedule." She takes a deep breath. "But tell Ivan to leave

Georgia, please."

David winces. "No."

Thanks, bud!

Story shoves her hands in her scrub pockets. I see the outlines of clenched fists. "Why?"

"You're in danger," David says.

"He's the biggest danger to me right now. I need him to leave."

David really, really hates it when people don't listen the first time. "Whether you remember him or not, that man's sole purpose in life is keeping you safe."

"If he knows as much about this familial purge as you claim, why does he keep pushing, trying to get close?"

You did that! You invited me closer. I know you, Story Rhys. You were wide awake, hanging from my every word.

"The purge affects people to varying degrees. We can't fix you if you won't let him study you. He's looking out for you as only Ivan will. Can you imagine my shock when I found out how many robotic units he had to destroy in your hospital room? That's as rare as eleven lightning strikes hitting the same postage stamp in the Pacific Ocean."

She doesn't reply.

"If Ivan determined those bots didn't have your best interests at heart? He was well within his rights as Senior Commander to act against them. Would another Irontrace have made that same call? Can't say."

"Why is he the only one who would do that for me?"

David leans forward and studies her. "Ivan would burn down the world for you. Don't ask him to."

My man! That's the spirit. I totally would. She doesn't have to ask.

"If I agree to let Ivan protect me, will you let me do surgery here?"

"Hold please." David mutes. His video flashes off, replaced with a black screen and an Irontrace logo. The words *Lancaster Helm* bounce from corner to corner.

My phone buzzes with a message from him. *Rhys! You going to obey this time and stay out of sight?*

Story's silent, invisible shadow, reporting for duty!

The Lancaster control room comes back into view. "If Ivan stays completely hidden, but is there at *all* times, is that an acceptable agreement?"

"I can't risk another episode. He has to hold up his end of the deal."

David's face takes on a hard look. "He will. Get to the INES lab and show everyone you're not as defective as we think you are."

If he heard that angry grumble she just made, she'd be in big trouble!

The monitor goes black. I hope she'll go take a nap. If I could talk to her, I know I could convince her. I follow her into the hallway. Richelle leans on the wall, playing with her phone.

I walk in perfect step behind Story's bouncing red curls. The scent of her lavender shampoo takes me back to the first time I was this close to her. I was a goner the second I saw her. How did we get so far from that?

Moulson. He took my best friend. He's full of malice towards The Bastion. I'm powered by the most honest force in the universe: her love. I won't fail. I'll bring her back.

Richelle grins at Story and hops to her side. "Morning, sunshine! You look better."

"I'm fantastic," Story snaps. She does not sound fantastic. "Did you schedule my patients?"

No, Story! Go lay down.

"Yes, I put the list in there." Richelle points to the INES lab. "Let's get you a hot tea to help that raspy voice of yours and then wait. What are we doing today?"

"We're going to work, Richelle," Story replies.

"Yaaaaaaay. Work. Was hoping you'd say that."

"Why are you saying it like that?" Story asks. "It's what we came here to do."

Wifey is TIRED! Richelle better feed or caffeinate her.

"Ivan is like tripping out, Story." Thanks, Richelle. "David's never seen him like this, even when Kristen died."

How is this helpful? If she takes Story down memory lane about Kristen right now, I'm arresting her. Sullivan will fly her back to Lancaster. I almost chew my lip off waiting to hear what gem Richelle will throw out next.

"You guys are the cutest. He worships you. It's kind of disgusting." Richelle laughs.

She's not wrong there. I do.

Story finally answers Richelle. "Well, then help me. I'm begging you. Nathan hates me. I need to fix things. I miss my husband."

Richelle grabs her arm. "You have to knock that off! Nathan is not your husband."

"I didn't say he was that time. I just meant I need to fix things with Nathan and my husband."

"As in Ivan, your husband?"

Story nods a very unconvincing yes and walks into the coffee shop. Richelle, the worst bodyguard I've ever seen, pulls out her phone and scrolls, staying in the hallway. I stick close behind Story as she orders her breakfast and coffee. I'll have Richelle get me something later. I don't want to spook Story by telling her I'm here.

I'm going to dig up some monitoring from the Lancaster Helm and make her a memory video or photo album. I know she won't recognize me, but the purge people don't panic at pictures of their families. It's seeing us in person that nearly kills them.

By the afternoon, Sullivan had delivered Dr. North and Dr. Wylie, along with a few other less experienced surgeons. They're getting settled in their rooms while Story preps the training area in the INES lab.

Breakfast passed.

Lunch passed.

It would be nice if my workaholic wife remembers how much food I need to keep these muscles she loves thriving. I'll be adding food and drinks to my backpack tomorrow.

My brain is firing on all synapses from stress and hunger. I've made a huge list of things I've learned about the purge.

When we open a computer file and repair it, it's rewritten at that location. A brain recalls a memory, that memory is rewritten, reinforcing it in our minds. Moulson has found a way to introduce errors to the previously written memories. I've gotta find a way to restore the originals somehow.

I'm wondering if we should lean on neuroplasticity, memory reconsolidation, or—my favorite so far—neuromod resets. I've got it written up in its most basic form. I like it so far. I prep an update for David.

Senior Commander Delac,

*Due to recent personal events, I have undertaken research on the familial purge independently through The Ilex Corporation ("IC"), **<u>with no use of Bastion or Irontrace resources.</u>***

This work structure avoids real or potential conflicts of interest, given the involvement of a closely related patient. We need to schedule meetings to review requirements with general practice & OB ALICE trainers, the BBA, and Architect Maseko.

*Not only do my plans approach what we need to fix from a neuro standpoint, I'm also addressing the emotional aspect for affected patients and families. The purge must be **<u>fully</u>** repaired.*

<u>Note:</u> Attached you'll find contracts governing IC. All intellectual property conceived, developed, or derived under this agreement shall remain the sole and exclusive property of IC in perpetuity. No ownership rights shall be conveyed to The Bastion under any circumstances.

Please review and respond ASAP.

- *Respectfully,*
  Ivan Rhys
  Senior Commander, Lancaster, Ohio Irontrace Squadron
  Founder & CEO of The Ilex Corporation

"We'll see if I'm fired in the next ten minutes," I mutter, hitting send.

Fixing the purge is *mine*. The Bastion can't touch it. Knowing those monsters, they'd twist it into something hurtful.

Alan built a corporate ops dream team for IC. He and I went 50/50 to pay for a Swiss legal-finance task force. A couple of his old law prodigy friends specifically curated a team of sharks, hungry to prove they could outsmart AJA lawyer models.

They took my back of the napkin idea for IC and turned it into an untouchable, elite entity. As proof of concept to flex their skills, they freed Rosa from The Bastion's ownership.

I stand and stretch, hearing things that don't normally pop on me crack and crunch. This hiding in the shield gig is going to wreck my body. I set a watch timer for ten minutes. I'll do silent jumping jacks, watching Story work.

Ah, headphones, my love, really? How is she going to hear murderers sneaking in? Or bots whirring up behind her?

Good thing I'm here. She must be listening to her favorites. It's making her steps light as she bounces between the platform, her desk, and the whiteboard. No one is in here, so she tossed off her black scrub shirt. Her tiny baby bump peeks out of the gap between her pastel blue lacey running top and the neat bow she tied in her scrub pants.

"Don't do it, Rhys." I sigh. "Just keep jumping."

Gracious. She's perfect. I can't believe that's my wife. I don't know when I stopped jumping. When my watch timer buzzes, I'm standing still, watching her like some drooling fool. Get it together, man!

Where did Richelle disappear to? Story needs someone to keep her company.

She draws lines across the whiteboard to make three rows. Then six columns, printing a name in each box. She steps back and smiles. That smile could power a Helm for weeks.

"Once I get Wylie and North up to speed? Bet we can do four a day," Story whispers.

I have to be the voice of reason. That's too many surgeries. Last time she fell in love with me, it was from my messages, calls, and general Ivan charms. I'll do it again. I grab a marker from the whiteboard tray and write.

Three a day is too many! Don't even think about four, wife! -I

She stares at the letters.

"I? Wife? Ivan, have you been in here watching me?" She turns, surveying the room.

David said I have to guard you. -I

"Have you been in here the whole seven hours?!"

I've missed you too! -I

"You gonna be there all the time, no matter what?" She grabs her scrub shirt and pulls it on.

Sure am. You look beautiful today. -I

She makes a grumpy growl. "When they said you'd guard me, I didn't imagine this."

Would you prefer I sit and hold your hand, wife? -I

"I'm not your wife. I can't be." She rubs her eyes. My poor baby. Her eyes have dark circles around them. I shouldn't tease her. "Only an awful person could forget their husband."

You're the best person in the world, <3. -I

"Just talk to me, please," she says.

I sit on the edge of her desk. "You're not awful." She flinches at my voice. "I was taken from you. From your memories. Replaced with something terrible by Moulson."

"He replaced you with Nathan. He isn't terrible. Don't talk like that about him."

Holding onto him must be a lifeline right now. He's too emotionally inept to give her a decent hug. Granted, I'm not rooting for him to get his paws on her. But good grief, he could've at least given her a friendly embrace.

She seemed to like holding my hand last night. I'm gonna see if my adventurous Story is ready to try fighting the purge. "Nathan is a good person. I'll give you that. Would you like a hug? Might make you feel better."

She shrinks away from my voice. "No. Please. Don't touch me."

"Don't come at me with a bone saw. I'll behave," I tease.

Adorable little thought lines appear on her forehead. "You must hate me. I love Nathan Cantone. I know I shouldn't. I have *years* of happy memories with him on replay."

Curse you, Moulson! "A+ for effort, my loyal lady. You're being faithful to the wrong person, though. I'll keep watching to make sure he fends off your grabby little hands."

"I think he actually hates me. You don't have to watch him."

"Is that an invitation to watch you even closer? If so, I eagerly, whole-heartedly, accept."

Her lips press in a line. The tiny smile lines around her eyes mean she's not hating my jokes. "Stop!"

"I'll get you to crack. I know all the buttons to bring you back."

"You're not very humble."

"Not the first time you've told me that. Guarantee it won't be the last."

She snorts. Goodness, I've missed that sound. It takes every ounce of self-command I can muster not to cross the few feet separating us to show her how much I love her. How much I miss her. At least she's talking to me without spewing venom my way. Baby steps.

"I can't figure you out," she says. "One minute you terrify me. The next you're so careful and sweet."

"I'm only scary when I need to be. The rest of the time? I'll be whatever you want."

"Are you in a SAM?"

"Nope. Just a plain old cloaking shield. Useless in a fight. Learned that the hard way."

"If you've been in there all day, you need to eat and drink something." She opens the top drawer of the desk.

I could cry. Food! Jerky, protein bars, trail mix, dried fruit, electrolyte drinks, water bottles, mini packs of doughnuts. "Story Caroline Rhys. You've made me the happiest man in the world." I tuck several items against my chest.

"I would have gotten you food if I knew you were here. Sorry."

"I know." I advance dangerously close to her and say, "Because you really are the best person in the world."

Richelle bursts in with Story's seventeen Irontrace Commander patients. She sees my messages scrawled around the whiteboard and grabs an eraser. "I'll just get rid of these. Trying to look semi-professional,"

Richelle says.

Story winces and wiggles to the right. I hope her side isn't hurting. Dr. Brown said it was okay. She'd be feeling tissues growing, stretching, and not to worry since the twins look great.

She turns her gorgeous grin to the crowd. "Welcome! Thank you for coming. Let's discuss the Rhys...Rhys method." She stops, and her eyebrows go up.

That's right, baby! We built this whole thing together. Richelle circles her finger as if to say get moving.

She clears her throat and starts again. "Let's discuss the Rhys method for Agora removals."

The Irontrace sit, riveted. Story, North, and Wiley cover the surgical plan, recovery, and schedule over the next couple of hours. My ravenous stomach thanks Story as I quietly tear open snack after snack.

"We've got a team of Commanders from the Lancaster Helm to run your control room," Story says. Questions trickle in about how this Helm will run during their recovery period.

Sure would be handy to have an experienced Commander here to chime in.

"Commander Luke Buford here. What will your team do with our high priority projects?"

"What projects do you have in mind?" Story asks.

I cast a notepad session from my laptop to a monitor behind the group. They can't see my rapid-fire typed answers for Story.

Tell them this:

All currently in progress projects need handed to Nathan Cantone. (No, this is not a retaliation to keep him away from you!)

Any new projects that aren't Priority 1 or 2 need a delayed start date for at least a two-week sprint. If a new project is a P1/2 discuss it with Nathan.

This Helm's primary focus should be on normal Kernel maintenance, letting Story Rhys know what a stunning genius she is, and monitoring for Moulson. I love you! -I

She reviews my information with the group and then asks if they have anything else to discuss. Commander Robert Field launches into a long-winded backstory on a project related to local water filtration models. Story's tired eyes glaze over. I make hearts bounce around on the screen to wake her up. She frowns.

Tell him to give it to Cantone! -I

She opens her mouth to speak several times, but Fields won't let her get a word in. He's holding us hostage for a water filtration seminar none of us signed up for.

I broadcast a typed message through the room's speakers. "We've arranged for a reception with hors d'oeuvres in the lounge area of the lab. Take an immediate twenty-minute break."

Fields continues to talk. These Irontrace sorely lack discipline.

I broadcast a new message. "Break time. Now."

That shuts him up. A burly Irontrace books it towards Story. I silently sprint to her.

"Dr. Rhys! I've been dyin' to meet ya'!" Commander Buford bellows in a deep Southern drawl. He shakes her right hand so hard sweet tea sloshes from her cup.

"No, call me-" Story starts, but Richelle grabs her shoulder.

"Story. He said *Dr. Reeesssse.* He pronounced your name right." Richelle cackles. "Sorry, Commander! She struggles with these Georgia accents."

"I was going to tell him he could call me Story." She shoots Richelle a dagger-laced smile. "Can you excuse us?"

I follow them in the hall.

"Richelle! Really?" Story blurts.

She gives Story a blank stare. "Really what?"

They're gonna need a palm on each of their foreheads to keep them separate. Not sure if my right hand is up for that. I could tuck Story under that arm. She may bite me today though.

"People already think my brain's busted," Story hisses. "Don't make it worse!"

"I thought you were gonna tell him to call you Dr. Cantone."

"Dr. Rhys? Puh, no," Story spits back. "They can call me Story."

Richelle snatches Story's left hand, putting her engagement and wedding rings between their faces. "I'm trying to help you remember, this is from Ivan! The secret man? You tried to hide him from me, but this rock and your beaming smile gave you away. Listen here. David said you're on very thin ice." Richelle pauses, looking my way. "See, dude, I'm helping her find the way back to you."

"Did Nathan give you a contact lens so you can see Ivan?" Story asks.

"No!" She grabs Story by the shoulders. "Nathan didn't build any of this!" Richelle's blonde hair bounces. "Oh look, a cool shield? *Ivan built it!* You like my contact that lets me see invisible people? *Ivan built it!* Fancy surgical robots? *Ivan!* Are you enjoying not puking from being pregnant? *Ivan made you these bracelets!* Those babies? *IVAN's!*"

Story sighs towards the ceiling. "Invisible Ivan, you there?"

It takes a heroic feat of strength to keep my hands to myself. "Yes. Right here, baby."

"Come on then, husband."

"After you, gorgeous."

She turns in the direction of my voice. "Are you always like this?"

"All day, every day," I say.

"He really is," Richelle agrees, nodding.

"Good grief," Story whispers.

26

Richelle invited all off-shift Irontrace and turned the happy hour into a party. My favorite part was the "Where's your first vacation going to be?" panel. The responses were so sad and similar. Many Irontrace spoke of wanting to see their original home again. It's like the child inside froze in time, longing for what they knew before. I wonder where Ivan is from. Where he'd want to go.

Councilman King from the Atlanta Bastion said he had a special presentation for us. "Due to Dr. Story Rhys's dedication, we have someone here who would like to talk to you."

The room cheers when Senior Commander Darke walks in.

Henri sits beside me. His always-smiling face darkens when monitors around us turn on. A reporter is gleefully covering the headline: *Human surgeons do first emergency surgery in twenty-four years.*

"Please welcome Dr. Story Rhys. Live from the Tallulah Falls, Georgia Helm!" Councilman King says.

"Do not go up there!" Henri lays a hand on my arm. He pops out of his chair and walks, hands in pockets towards the front of the room.

My nightmares are made of this. Everyone stares. Clapping breaks out, encouraging me to walk to the microphone.

Run away! I'm close to the exit, I could duck out. If all the eyes weren't glued to me, I might. The applause has been going on for too long. Now people are starting to chant my name. Nathan meets my eyes, and he gives the slightest shake no. No? If he and Henri don't want me up there, there's a reason.

Yep, I'm outta here. I'll hide in the hallway. I try to stand but my legs are jelly. Great. Now I have generalized anxiety disorder, Ivan the shadow monster anxiety disorder, and I have no ability to do public speaking. David is gonna pull me out of the OR when he hears about this.

An unseen hand grabs mine. Not just any hand. Ivan. He's a life preserver in the sea of stupidity my life has turned into. He turns on SAM.

"Let's go. Right now," he orders in a rough whisper. He tugs for me to follow him into the hall. "You okay to walk?"

His familiar hand fixes something in me and I jump to his side, legs steady. "Yes."

He gently leans me against the wall. "Stay right here where I can see you. I'll be back."

I catch the door behind him with my foot so I can hear what happens.

"Where have you been hiding, Senior Commander Rhys?" Councilman King says. A round of excited whooping and conversations break out.

"Hello, Councilman, Senior Commander Darke. Wonderful to see you all. Apologies. My wife got an emergency call."

"I'm sure you'll be happy to give this to her on behalf of the Tallulah Falls Helm," Councilman King says.

"Thanks! This is wow. Definitely the first one of these she's gotten." Ivan's voice betrays the small item they've handed him must be garish.

"We were hoping to interview her about the history-making work she's doing," King says.

"You're right about that. She's doing exceptional work. The world needs to know about it." Ivan goes on to expound on my valedictorian-earning academic record, my surgical skills, and my passion to save people. He wraps it up by emphasizing the surgery on Darke was considered hopeless, but I pushed to get it approved. "The world is a better place because of Story. I'm so proud of her."

He knows my whole history. I feel robbed not knowing his. I'm mad, and I'm sad, and homesick? A hole has been blown in my life, taking something important with it. Maybe it's him. I don't know, but I'm grateful to him for saving me from the interview.

The glass lab door flings open. "Story, go sit down by the stairs."

Richelle blurts, pointing to a small alcove about twenty feet away. "Hurry! Here he comes."

I plop on the third step down, leaning with my head resting on my arms. The tiles laid over sandstone are cold, but at least I'm out of the crowd. This isn't too bad. Bed has been screaming my name for hours. I'm ready to crash for the night, even if it's on these freezing stairs.

Ivan speaks from beside me. "Richelle, get everyone out of the lab except the Tallulah Falls Irontrace. Time for an emergency meeting."

"Will do, boss." She doesn't move from beside me. I wish I could see what he did to get her moving because she sputters, "Oh, you mean like, right now, right now?"

"That's what *emergency* means," he says.

Richelle jumps up, leaving me staring at his boots.

"Thank you, Ivan. I hate talking in front of people."

"I know. You also hate going on the news."

I don't think I've ever been on the news. I'll take his word for it.

"How are you feeling?" He sits beside me.

You got twelve hours to listen to me complain?

"I'll rephrase. Is there anything I can do to make your life better, even if it's just for tonight?" he asks, quieter.

"Got any contact lenses to remove your face and neck? The rest of your body doesn't bother me."

"It sure used to!" His happy laugh makes me smile. I burrow my face tighter into my arms. "Yes, I'm working on them. Are those kids of mine being nice to you?" I nod. "Progress. You didn't yell at me and say they're Nathan's."

I bite my lip to hold back telling him that I'm not dumb. I can accept it when I'm wrong. Fighting with him would take effort. I settle for giving him a thumbs up.

"Are you tired, my love? I'm worried you're not getting enough rest."

"I'm feeling good." I'm feeling awful.

"I'm going to do something. I promise you'll love it. Don't get mad."

"Please tell me it's handing me a cup of hot tea?"

"No. Much better. I will make you tea after, though."

I yelp, surprised, when his hand twines into a handful of curls at the base of my neck. He tugs on them gently. His hand doesn't stay there; it trails over my neck and skull like he holds a map of where to go under my mass of hair. Each time he releases my curls, he grabs just the right handful next. Tears spring to my eyes.

This feels familiar.

"You may not know me," he says. "But I know you. You're not good. You're exhausted. And cold." My head rolls to the side, anticipating the calming path carved by his thumb. I lean just a bit closer. We sit quietly.

"Buttons, wife. Told you I know them," he whispers close enough to my ear that it puffs my curls. "Now, sit up. I'll leave you alone."

No! Don't leave me. "Where are you from? Where do you want to go on vacation?" I mumble into my arms. He may not have heard me.

"I was born on Padre Island, in Texas. I moved to a ranch outside Billings, Montana when I was seven. Sent to the Lancaster Helm at age nine. Vacation? I don't need one. You're my place of peace. The bright rays to warm my life come from your love. Where you are is where my soul can rest."

That's the nicest thing anyone has ever said to me. I lay my hand out, palm up. My breath catches when his hand engulfs mine, pulling me into a sitting position. I squint one eye open to make sure he's shielded.

"Sorry I'm not that person anymore," I say, opening my eyes.

"You are. I promise. Come on, baby, we need to get to the meeting."

Richelle has cleared the INES lab of everyone except Irontrace. The monitors turn on and a sea of familiar faces, including my dad, join the lab.

"Status update. Moulson, still missing. Familial purge, no change," David says. "New anti-anxiety med trials are failing. They've been trying to put some patients back in their homes. Kind of how Story can be around Ivan. Overall, that's going badly. Family members don't respect the purge like Ivan does. They keep testing its limits. If people could just follow basic directions, they could save themselves grief. But common sense is lacking, and their loved ones are paying for it."

David goes on to list two highlights followed by a depressing number of lowlights in reports from the BBA. "Some previously healthy people are having heart issues. From what we can tell, it's caused by the purge's chronic stress. It's affecting the youngest age groups. I'm talking perfectly fit twenty-something people. We've equipped the AJA models guarding their residences with cardiac monitors."

Tickticktick. My wedding and engagement rings make a tiny metronome of nervous energy on my armrest.

"We have to assume that the youngest purge victims are at highest risk for developing severe complications. They're the immediate patient population to fix before the damage becomes irreversible."

He's talking about me without directly mentioning my name. I saunter to the back of the lab, disappearing behind a massive row of bookcases. There's a dusty stack of autoclave manuals I drop my forehead onto. Their worn leather covers are soft on my forehead. I could use some softness right now.

Hey babies. We need to keep it together and get through this. It's you and me, okay? I'm learning how to stay calm, to breathe for you.

Ivan speaks from behind me, "Can I help?"

"No."

Ground yourself. Five senses. That's one way to help anxiety. Smell. The books smell old and dusty. Sight. Their colors are tan, white, grey, black. There are eleven books on the second shelf down. I don't recognize any of the doctor's names who wrote them. Taste. I'm not gonna lick a book. But my mouth tastes dry.

"Are you feeling panicky?" he asks.

"No. Trying to ground myself."

"Do you need a hug? I could use one after hearing that report."

Yes, I need a hug. I want to collapse against someone who can fix me. What if I hug you and panic and can't breathe again? It doesn't matter what I need, or what you need.

"Sorry, no."

"Well, I'm here if you change your mind. I gotta come out of my shield. Eyes closed."

His unshielded right hand offers me a ceramic mug with tea. The scent drifts to me. It's my favorite. The caramel vanilla tea with honey I drink a few nights a week.

He has two stitches covered by a see-through bandage. I let my eyes drift up his heavily muscled arm. It's connected to a massive set of shoulders. He's wearing a black button-up SC shirt and black cargo pants with boots that lace up. His arms are a rich olive skin tone. I drop my eyes to his knees. I'm scared to look any higher.

But from what I could see? Looking at Ivan is not a bad view at all. He'll make an imposing Dad for the twins.

I trail behind him, eyes glued to his back, before taking my seat next to Richelle. I don't want to sit for a whole meeting with my eyes closed. It's disorienting. I hold up a stack of papers, blocking anything above his hips from view.

Richelle leans over to see what I'm looking at. "Not a bad way to attend a meeting." She laughs.

"Ivan, we read your proposal and decided you're taking point on the familial purge," David says.

"What do you need me to do?" Ivan asks.

David shifts in his seat, "Work through IC or however you're doing it and find a way to fix the purge victims."

"Yes, Sir," Ivan says.

He must make tea for me a lot. It's the perfect ratio of tea with a hint of honey. Most people can't get it right.

"Would you like to lead the security update, or am I?" David asks.

"This one is mine," Ivan says, pacing. "I'd like to know which one of you embarrassments to The Irontrace decided to tell the news, and thus the whole world, my wife's location?"

Eyes dart among the Irontrace.

"Ah. Too bad. I do love honesty." Ivan must be a mobile speaker; he's striding back and forth in front of the room. It's hard to keep my papers following him so I can keep my eyes safely on his belt buckle. "Tallulah is a small Helm. Many of you here are older than SC Darke. Yet he's promoted faster than all of you. Henri, Mai, and I have seen several instances of you blatantly ignoring protocols. We believe you're intentionally taking advantage of his age. Piling the SC work on him so you can stay slothful and undisciplined." The Tallulah Irontrace shift in their seats, looking at each other. "In Lancaster, we're accountable to each other. What I do in the control room is visible to fellow Irontrace."

"Correct. We keep an audit trail," David says.

Ivan stops pacing. "I'm going to ask again. Who came up with the foolish plan to tell the world my wife's location?"

A man stands. "I thought it would be a nice surprise for her."

Ivan snorts. "A surprise, Commander Nitwit? Ah, my bad, Commander *Nichols*? Surprise, you've been demoted. You're now the lowest ranked Tallulah Irontrace. Two ten-year-olds rank higher than you."

Murmurs and conversations break out. Darke stands to protest. "Now, Commander Rhys-"

Ivan stops and leans forward. "Hey Darke, how's that surgical site working out? Did you think it was nice of her to scream at The Bastion that you were worth saving? They told her she wasn't authorized to come here. To let you die and go on her way to Australia. She *raged* at them, fighting for you." Darke is silent. "Do you know how she's alive to do surgeries on you people? Do you know how many times people have tried to abduct or kill her because of her work to fix Agoras?" I yank to move the papers with him as he cuts across the room towards the man who called the news. "Any of you put my wife in danger like that again, and I'll put it to a worldwide Helm vote that this facility be shut down. The world needs Story. We could lose a few Helms."

No one speaks.

"We want confirmation that you understand what we're saying, Tallulah Helm," SC Max Darke chimes in from Perth.

"Acknowledged. No more surprises," Commander Nichols says with a grin.

27

"I outrank you. Request denied," Invisible Ivan says.

I wasn't aware someone you can't see can be so annoying, yet here we are. "You can't sleep in here. Last night almost killed me," I argue.

My message notification keeps dinging. Lark has Mom's phone and is sending me picture after picture of their new apartment and the view from the balcony. *Send me a pic of your view in Georgia!*

She has to know being at a Helm means I'm in a new cave. *No view here. Underground again, sorry! I'll send pics when I can of their horses. Go to bed, Lark! Love you lots.*

My phone dings almost immediately. *Underground again?!? What apartment number? At home you're 417.*

I have no idea. We've been taking the elevator to the seventh floor down, so I send her a quick, *We're seven levels down!* "Ivan, what's the unit number we're in?"

"Why?"

"Lark was asking."

"Oh, tell her hey from me."

Won't be doing that. She probably couldn't care less about talking to him. "What unit are we in?" I ask again. "I didn't look."

"Story, this is what I'm talking about. You shouldn't text info like that."

I grunt in frustration. "To a nine-year-old? I can't tell Lark?"

"No. You shouldn't."

What a dramatic man. Lark is not going to leak secret info about our location to someone. I'll wait until he's asleep and text it to her. I send her one final message for the night *I love you! Call you tomorrow.*

"Ivan, go. Sleep out there. I'll leave the bedroom door open all night. I don't want you in here. It's too weird."

"No. I'll stay in my shield."

"You're shielded out there." I point to the living room.

"Call David if you want. I'm not trying to be mean or stress you out. But I will be doing what I say is needed to protect you. And that means I'm keeping an eye on you tonight."

This bed is a disaster from me tearing it up in my panic last night. I throw a couple of the pillows in the chair for him and put the other two along the headboard.

"Kids are his." I've heard that all day from everyone.

"You're his wife." That's also played on repeat all day.

Surgery is the only thing that makes sense in my life right now. I'm really enjoying the constant threats to be pulled from it if I express any concerns that Ivan is a stranger. As ridiculous as it is, I'm still mourning Nathan. It might not be their reality, but it's mine. I need time to adapt.

"I don't technically have to tell you I'm here. David ordered me to guard you. I could lurk, without you knowing. My covert infiltration training was top notch. You have to appreciate the fact that I respect you enough to make my presence known."

The corner of the sheets has popped off the far side of the bed again. I crawl across it to tuck it down again. The sheet on the opposite side pops off. Stupid sheets! In this strange bed. In this strange new room that's a million miles from home.

Maybe my annoyed growl as I crawl back across the bed will scare him away. Before I can get there, the sheet is smoothed out and tucked under the mattress corner by a hand I can't see. I sit on my heels in the middle of the bed. "I'll sleep in the chair. You can have the bed."

"Absolutely not, wife. I'll sleep in the chair."

If I see his face, maybe it will fix me and bring it all back. "How long until the contact lenses are ready?"

"Maybe three days? I have to account for keeping Holly and Huck safe. I'm thinking of seeing if I can add in some kind of monitoring for them as well."

"Through a contact lens... on my eye?"

"Yeah."

"Impossible."

He softly laughs. "I've heard that before. I worked on it most of the day. Look in my notebook in the kitchen tomorrow."

My tired, pregnant self just got wrapped up. I fling the blankets back. No way I can wait until tomorrow. "I'll sleep better if I take a peek."

I find his black notebook on the counter and spin it towards me. It's open to a page with *OPERATION: Bring her back* written in small block letters. I meander back in the bedroom, analyzing the information. Page after page of project goals, safety considerations, risks, and incredible prototype sketches. What if I put in the contacts and see his face and everything floods back? It would be like he brought me back from the dead.

Crud! My traitorous hormonal eyes dripped a couple tears on the last page. I try to swipe them, but it smears his drawings. "I'm really sorry, I messed this one up." I lay it by the chair.

"Crying is not very surgeon-y." He laughs. That's a terribly odd thing to say. I frown. "Oh, sorry. You probably don't remember that."

I turn off the light so he won't be able to see me. "Remember what?"

He blows a big sigh. "Our whole life."

Of course I don't remember our life! He should know that.

"To me, our life starts with awful things. Where is Dr. Brown? Dead? I haven't seen him since you knocked him out and smeared his blood all over me. Then you pulled that give her whatever she wants nice guy stuff and had Cantone come in my hospital room! You let me act like an idiot. I *like* working with The Irontrace. I'd appreciate you not making me look stupid in front of them."

He's silent. I shouldn't have yelled at him. He seems nice. And he's crazy about the babies and me. His notebook is evidence of that. I'm hormonal, exhausted, and positively heartsick for my husband to come and be my husband. This is a wonderful time for a hormone fit to make me seem completely unhinged. I put my hands over my face and burrow into my pillow. I have to stay calm. No more of this. No more of him. Is he just standing there, staring at me?

"If you're staring at me, stop."

"Would you like a hug?"

YES! "No. What I want is to go home. But I have to stay here so I can fix Lark. I hate it here."

"I'm sorry you don't feel well."

I can't answer him. I'm barely keeping it together.

"Good night, baby." His voice comes from near the doorway. Finally, he's going to leave me alone.

Neck Snappin' List

~ Ivan ~

We turned the INES lab into our substitute control room for a somber emergency meeting before dawn.

"The first nine deaths from the familial purge hit last night. A group of husbands in Ireland were trying to deliver a message to their wives in a purge camp," Councilman Darrow says. "The AJA guards thought they were attempting to break in. They threw the care packages from their families over the fence line and were attacked while they were on their way to the parking area."

The monitor shows a breathtaking lush field near a cliffside overlooking the ocean. A red brick hospital stands out, bright and cheery, surrounded by a drab sea of temporary grey trailers.

My focus is on the smattering of white sheets clustered on the ground. Their edges gently whip in the wind. AJA drones and ATV models bustle between them. Tent poles are being staked in the ground around each body by CLEANR maintenance bots. It makes my blood boil. Since they were executed for criminal activity, they'll be incinerated in place. Then the CLEANRs will till the soil, lay sod, and pretend nothing happened.

Guys trying to cheer up their wives were murdered by robots who don't understand human nature. There will be no joyful reunion for them when this is over. Just devastation. I've spent my life working with The Kernel. When I see things like this, I'm sure the best solution is to destroy it entirely.

"The news in the area has been blacked out by The Bastion."

A metallic clang rings out in the room. I ripped the armrest off my chair. It hit the ground before I could catch it. *Shoot!* Probably scared Story. It won't go back on. I really fractured this stupid thing. I blame the maintenance bots for missing a weak weld.

We've told those blundering fools in The Bastion that media blackouts will only intensify their problems. They're going to make things worse if that's even possible at this point.

"I'd like to go over another reason we're becoming increasingly concerned with the purge," David says, then pauses. "In addition to families getting angrier, we now have seventy-four patients in cardiovascular intensive care units for stress-related arrhythmias. These patients are in their twenties. Safe to say our theory on the youngest patients having most extreme symptoms is correct."

Thank heavens I'm in my shield. If Story could see my face right now, it would make her panic on a normal day. Story is one of the youngest patients. She's only twenty-two. And if it's affecting the youngest patients the worst, what's the prolonged stress doing to Huck and Holly?

Forget sleeping. I'll work nights too from now on. No one will notice. Moulson is on my list. I'm gonna make sure he's held accountable this time.

"Rhys! Anyone know if he's still in here?" Councilman Darrow yells.

People shift in their seats as they sweep the room. If I'm growing more invisible to people around here, that's a good thing. I've got some plans coming together that I'd rather go unnoticed. I'm only looking at Story. She sits two rows in front of me. I chose my seat a bit off to her side so I can see part of her face and read how she's doing by the set of her shoulders.

Right now, her back is straight but not locked in place. Her shoulders are tight but not hunched up in panic. The fragile tilt of her neck gives away that she's bracing herself. She keeps her eyes glued to the monitor, ignoring the ripple of people looking for me.

"I'm here," I call out.

There go her shoulders. Higher, tighter, making her scrub shirt fabric strain slightly across them. In a few minutes, I'm kicking everyone out so she can drink coffee and prep for surgery.

"Ivan, IC has Bastion's full support. Use whatever resources you need," Darrow says. "Odd approach, but whatever gets it done."

"Thanks," I say. If they'd have pulled me away from it, I'd have taken a sick day, or month if needed, to keep working on it. "Who's been working on it aside from me?"

"ALICE trainers," David says.

I groan. "They're way out of their league."

Story scoffs so hard it sounds like she choked.

"Do you not like that plan, Dr. Rhys?" Darrow calls out to her.

"Ivan's an Irontrace, not a doctor," she says, prompting several laughs.

"Ivan is a highly respected biomedical engineer, known around the world," David starts harshly, then reels it back. "He doesn't have to be a doctor to help get us to a solution for the purge."

Hopefully, that'll get me bonus points with her. David isn't bad for a wing man. He keeps at it and I might be back in our bed by the time the twins are in kindergarten.

"Cantone, Baracu, figure out a schedule for the control room down there. Keep it as fully staffed as you can."

"Yes, Sir," they reply.

"The rest of you, find Moulson. Dismissed." David stops to confer with Darrow as everyone files out, leaving Richelle, Story, and I. "Story, do you feel up to doing surgery?"

"I do."

"Come close to the camera please," David orders. She sneaks a look at Richelle, who waves her on towards the front. "What's your name?" He asks, keen eyes peering into the camera.

"Story Rhys." Her subdued voice makes me wince. *Love you too...*

"Good enough for me." David smiles. "Love the enthusiasm. About time someone knocked Ivan down a few pegs."

"Told you two she's fixed!" Richelle shouts.

"Glad to see it for myself. Ivan, keep Story safe and focus on the purge," Darrow says. "See you tonight."

The monitor powers off.

"I'm going to get breakfast. Want anything?" Richelle asks Story.

"Coffee, please, and a bagel."

"What kind?"

I answer from inside my shield on the couch. "May I suggest her favorite pregnancy breakfast? Decaf caramel coconut iced coffee with whipped cream. A toasted until it's burnt everything bagel with veggie cream cheese spread. Bring her a fruit and yogurt parfait too with extra strawberries. She never wants one until she sees mine."

Richelle looks at Story to confirm and she nods.

"Get him something too please," Story says, "I don't know what you like to eat, Ivan."

Well, knock me over with a feather, she's trying to keep me alive.

"Black coffee. Lots of it." My backpack is loaded with yummy things. I learned my lesson the other day. I'll hide in here and stress snack while I work. Knowing Story, it may be a sixteen-hour day.

"Got it, I'll be back." Richelle waves and rushes out the lab door.

Story pushes the blue button on the rail to kick off the operating platform sterilization process. I watch her for several minutes while she does surgery prep. First up, she turns on her playlist of classical music. Then braids her hair, tucking it in her surgical cap of the day (today it's dancing flamingos and tiny shrimp). She saunters around the room, sipping ice water, searching.

"Ivan?"

Be cool! "Yes."

"You're quiet today."

"Sorry, I was thinking about purge stuff. Do you need something?"

"Oh...sorry. No. I'll talk to you later."

"It's fine. I'd always rather talk to you." I throw my notebook on the cushion beside me and jog to her. "How are you baby?"

She squints toward my voice. I think she's trying to get her bearings and find me. "Good. How was your night?"

"It was awful. Barely slept," I say.

She smiles. Ah, that smile. "I had this picture in my head you'd be heroic and say it was great. That you loved the chair."

"Can you not tell I'm a giant?" I laugh. "I alternated between the fetal position and propping my feet up on the bed to stretch out." Uh oh, the smile is gone. Maybe this was a test to see if I slept in the chair or obeyed and went to the living room. "How are those babies treating you?"

"Good."

How can I stand here and pretend we're nothing to each other? She's stunning. Her hair is up in her cap. Those red curls are as wild and strong as she is. Flyaways have escaped around her neck. A faint flush tints her freckled cheeks. Her eyes look tired but have a spark of excitement, probably at the thought of spending all day in surgery. They stay busy, looking for me.

"I really don't like not being able to see you." She frowns.

"I really don't like watching you pass out from hypoxia."

"Sorry I'm scared of you."

"It's okay to be scared of what the purge makes you see. Just never fear *me*." She looks adrift in uncertainty. Time to take a risk. "No panicking. I'm going to touch your face."

She flinches. Wrong move. Maybe I should've just kept talking to her for today. Then she steps forward.

There she is.

Her shoulders jerk when I settle my palm on her cheek. My thumb moves carefully along the curve of her jaw and neck. I fully expect her to slap me and dive backwards after how mad she was last night. Instead, she grabs my forearm and tugs me closer like she's starving for contact.

I know I am.

"Tell me something about what's missing, Ivan. Tell me something real." Her eyes are bright with tears.

I'm a moron. She isn't simply scared of what the purge makes her see. I'm a whole new person to her. I'm a stranger. The despair she's feeling fairly smacks me in the face. My darling wife is grieving the loss of her husband, Nathan. She needs a friend.

I can work with that. I'm *very* friendly with Story. "We race to get each other drinks."

Her lips press in a puzzled line. "What?"

"Okay, picture this." I keep my thumb on her cheek while I talk, slowly inching my hand around to the back of her neck. *Gently, slowly. Don't scare her.* "We're cuddled up in bed, on the couch, wherever. Well, wait. You need to keep in mind, I'm not usually this well-mannered, keeping to myself on a couch across the room from you. And if I'm more than an arm's reach away? You fix that real quick."

That faint glow on her cheeks gets brighter.

"Anyways, you'll say, 'Hey, handsome, wonderful husband, light of my life and center of my universe.'" She shakes her head at that. "'I'm going to get a water, coffee, tea, fill-in-the-blank, do you want one?'" She relaxes her neck into my hand. It's working! My fingers draw lazy strokes along the base of her skull. "Then I'll be like, 'Sure, I'll take a...whatever,' but then I cast you to the side off my impressively buff chest and sprint to the kitchen to make whatever drink you wanted and get it back to you with minimal spillage."

She laughs. The glint in her chocolate brown eyes lights me up. Don't spook her. Keep behaving.

"And you do the same. You hear I want a drink, and you fly to get it. So, we've turned it into a race. You fight *dirty*, you dart in front of me, I have to dodge so I don't bump you. I've crashed into more than a few doorways to protect you from playing human bumper cars. I had a bruise on my side that perfectly matched our bedroom doorknob from you accidentally hip checking me to make me a margarita three weeks ago."

Now she's really laughing, but she tilts her head away, maybe feeling self-conscious.

"No way, Story, you've never been shy with me. Don't start now."

I gently steady her with my hand, holding her right in front of me. She doesn't try to escape. I about bite a hole through my lip when she lays her face against my forearm.

"Can it not be contacts?" she asks softly.

That came out of left field. "I'm sorry, what?"

"I know you're making contact lenses for me, but the thought of touching my eyes grosses me out. Can it be glasses?"

"That's something I didn't know about you. We're both learning today." She just gave me this gift, a little gem of knowledge about her. "When you said I was scaring the kids with my optic filter, I thought you meant pregnancy was making you nauseous. I didn't know you were serious."

"I don't know what that means. Do you wear contacts or glasses?"

"No. You were talking about the one I wear so I can see and touch you when you're in SAM. Yes, I'll make you glasses." I want Story to feel safe, not like I'm going to be pushy. "You go read charts. I'm going to work on writing up the files to print your glasses. You and those charts. You used to read them in bed while holding my hand. I'd sleep. You'd read."

"Can you tell me about that later?"

"Depends on if I'm still banned to a chair."

She snorts. "Go work."

"Yes, Doc." She makes a face like something tastes bad. "What's wrong?"

"Did you used to call me Doc?"

Doc and I would be having a VERY different time here in Georgia, that's for sure... "Yes. From the first day we met."

"Nathan would call me Doc. That's wrong? It was you? Sorry."

"It's not your fault. I'm gonna go work on your glasses. One peek at me and," I lean down to whisper, "you'll see I'm far better suited for you than Nathan could ever be."

She looks down and smiles. "Get working then."

I wish I could stay by her and talk for days. I'd be okay being the only one holding onto memories of our old life, making new ones with her until we're a hundred years old. She's still guarded though. I need to stick with the slow drip of love and support.

Richelle bustled back in and set up breakfast on the coffee table. Story sat about a foot away from me on a different cushion. I scooted closer to her. We talked about purge news. When she handed me half of her bagel she scooted until her side was against mine.

She's probably just cold. I'm more than happy to warm her up. Good thing she can't see my face. It keeps her from seeing me grinning every time she passes her yogurt to me for a bite.

Richelle played with her phone the whole time. Several times, I caught her pretending to look down but sneaking glances at us. When Richelle crossed the lab to throw away our trash Story leaned closer.

"I am so sorry I was mean to you last night. I never want to be mean now that I know you're for sure a human," Story says. I laugh. "I really didn't think you were there for a bit. I'm sorry. You're a really good person. Thank you for helping me."

She clumsily trails her hand up my arm to the back of my neck and gives me a terrified, shaky half hug. I try to pull her closer, but she jumps away like I electrocuted her.

Don't leave her hanging, do something! I dive to catch her hand.

"No. You weren't mean. Listen," I say. "I'm really proud of you. Your world has been blown apart, but you're so brave. I can see how hard you're trying."

Her lips curve into a warm smile. Those words were what she needed. Everyone else keeps telling her how broken she is. They're wrong. She's still Story.

"Can I give you a real hug?" I ask. "Tales have been told about my epic hugging skills."

"Shoo. Go work, SC Rhys."

"Understood, Dr. Rhys. Focus now. Fun later."

She opens her mouth to protest but only lets out a small squeak. I've got her. I drop her hand and back away. If I know Story (and I do...), she won't be able to shake that smile for hours.

28

Life is a nonstop mess of anxiety and blood. Especially blood. Saving every drop of it in surgery has taken over as an obsession.

I'm in the operating room for the better part of the next eight hours. Wylie and North assist while I work through the first surgery on Commander Long. It went well. There was minimal blood loss, his Agora came out easily, skin graft applied, bandage on, and we shipped him off to the ICU for recovery. We moved right on to Cici Hernandez. Her surgery went great too.

I smile, making a checkmark by their names on the whiteboard. Two closer to proving the Rhys Method is safe enough for Lark. I need to go take pictures of the horses here for her later. Richelle and Ivan had Wylie and North go out to tour the clinic. They talked me into sitting on the couch with my feet up for about forty minutes during our late lunch.

"How's it going?" Henri asks, dropping into a chair across from me.

"Good," I say, sipping my coffee. "We'll be done at least two hours early. How are things in the control room?"

He props his feet on a cabinet, pulling a sad face. "Same. The Kernel's fine. Moulson's a phantom. Brains are broken. People are losing it. Go do what you gotta do, Ivan. I'll make myself cozy in here."

"Thanks, I'll only be like an hour." Ivan gives my knee a squeeze. "Be back soon, baby."

No. He can't just leave me, after making such a big deal about guarding me 24/7. This has to be a joke.

The lab door opens and closes. I jump off the couch and jog through the lab towards the door to ask where he's going, but Henri leaps up and follows. "Story, if you go out there, I'm coming too."

Gah! These Irontrace. "Why?"

"Orders." He shrugs.

I stop. I'd like to be the kind of wife that tells her husband goodbye, even if it's for a brief time. "David needs to settle down."

"He has. Those are Ivan's orders. I have to have both eyes on you *and* all electronics around you."

Don't get weird and clingy, it might make him hate me. If he starts pulling away, I'd be sad. "Oh. Why electronics?"

"Moulson used the plate scanner to do some kind of limbic system alteration. We're trying to figure out how he might have done something like that to you with Dr. Brown's equipment."

"Dr. Brown didn't do this?"

"No, he's been fully cleared."

"Is he going to report Ivan to AJA for beating him like that?"

Henri laughs. "Like what? He punched the guy once. It knocked him out cold. Ivan apologized. Brown's fine. Brown said he'd have panicked and done the same."

One punch and it covered Ivan's hands with blood? I suppose there's a chance I imagined the blood the same way I made up a whole life with Nathan. "Why were his hands so bloody when he put the mask on me on the airplane?"

"Because you-" Henri starts, but Richelle cuts him off with, "Who knows, Dr. Brown must have what they call thin skin or something? I don't know the doctor words for it."

Did I hurt someone on the airplane?

"Richelle, why were Ivan's hands bloody? He smeared it all over my hands and arms." My heart starts to race, pulling me back into the moment. *Stop it, Story.* It's just the purge messing with you. "It's part of the reason I couldn't calm down. The blood, his shadowy face, he was squeezing me, crushing my ribs."

The lab door flings open. North and Wylie spill in, breaking the moment with laughter.

"We ran into the third case of the day, they're ready out there when you are, Dr. Rhys," North announces.

"Out! Get out of here right now!" Richelle yells. They freeze.

"No. We'll talk later," I say, shooting Richelle a fake grin.

Dr. Wylie and Dr. North already seem to have concerns about my mental status. Don't want to make it worse.

Richelle puts her hands on her hips and stares me down. I've seen her do this with goats, cows, sheep, to scare them away from fences she's mending. *Great, I'm just another cloven-hoofed animal for her to manage.*

I turn to my surgical team. "Let's kick off the sterilization process and get prepped. You ready to take the lead on this one, Dr. Wiley?"

"I am!" She slaps the blue button to sterilize the operating platform.

After we get Commander Platz on the table, North stands directly beside her as an assistant. I stand on her other side, a sterile towel wrapped around my gloves, watching.

I'm staying focused on the surgery, but *where* is Ivan? It's been almost an hour. I look to the couch by Henri and Richelle. They had been on it, but now they've moved to desks, focused on their laptops. I'm sure he snuck back in at some point and kicked them out of his spot; I just can't see him because he's in his shield.

A blaring sound wails in the distance. I whip to look at the monitors. The screech of alarms is muffled by the rocky walls, making haunting echoes down our hallway.

"Patient is stable, you're doing a great job, continue," I tell Dr. Wylie.

"What is that?" Richelle whispers sharply at Henri.

"Dr. Rhys. What's going on?" Dr. Wylie asks, staying frozen with her hands above the open incision.

I have no idea! I'm just as clueless as you.

"I'll find out. Would you like me to take over?" I ask.

She draws a shuddering breath. I know that breath. I've taken one like it many times myself. She's weighing her options, deciding if she has the strength to keep going.

"I'm almost done," she says, lowering her needle driver to keep working. "This is my first full surgery as primary. Please let me focus."

That's it, *that's* why I chose her to be the next doctor to do this. "That's great, carry on."

Richelle and Henri are whispering up a storm at my desk. The alarms haven't gotten any louder, but they're still blaring. I wrap the sterile towel tighter around my hands and step to the edge of the operating platform.

"Ivan! What's going on?" I whisper.

Richelle does a double take. "Story, he's not in here."

"Where is he?" I ask. My heart takes off at a choking gallop.

She knees Henri, hard. He smiles, one of those 'don't freak out and turn into a hysterical woman' smiles. "We're getting more info now."

Mai opens the lab door a few inches, flooding the room with emergency alert sirens. She squeezes in, then slams the door behind her and locks it. "Hi! You having a good day in here?" She smiles broadly.

"We are," I say.

She turns, and her grin drops just a second too early. I catch the fleeting look of terror? No, maybe anger that takes over her face. She shakes her head at Henri. I have to plant my feet in place so I don't run to wring the truth out of them.

He leaps from his chair and cuts across the lab to confer with her. I lean as close to the edge as I can while maintaining sterility, trying to hear what they're whispering. It's impossible. Henri jumps up and grabs the strap to lower the steel security door. I flinch when he and Mai crash it into its grooves on the floor, placing a stopper bar along the bottom to lock it in place. Oh, that's cute, we're gonna die in here.

Ivan's out there. *My* Ivan is out there.

"Henri, how will Ivan get in?" I ask, a knot of anxiety blooming in my stomach.

Why bother asking? If that door's shut, it means he's not coming back until the emergency has passed.

"He'll be back soon." Henri smiles at me and pulls a chair over to sit by the door. "Bring my laptop over, please, Richelle."

"How much longer will the surgery take?" Mai asks.

"Dr. Wylie?" I throw the question to her.

I know she's got less than thirty minutes left until she closes the incision. Then the patient will be bandaged, flipped back over, and out of here within forty-five minutes. If she's going to be primary surgeon without me, she needs to be able to answer questions like this.

She holds the neural chip up in her forceps and inspects it. "We'll be out of here in less than an hour."

"Excellent, thanks," I tell her, nodding in agreement.

The distant sound of alarms shuts off and Henri slaps his thighs. "Perfect. Everything is under control. Everybody can get back to chillin' now. Richelle, crank up the music."

"Does this happen often during surgery? Alarms? Emergency doors?" Wylie asks.

"Not just during surgery. That's a normal Tuesday morning at the Helm," North says, laughing. "Never know what to expect around here."

"They can't leave the boundary, so all the surgeries have to be done in Helms?" Wylie asks.

"Correct," I reply.

"Dr. North, would you like to close the incision?" She tilts her hands up towards her shoulders and takes half a step back.

"Of course." He eagerly steps forward, selecting a fresh needle driver, loaded with absorbable suture material and a pair of tissue forceps.

Talk to North. Don't think about Ivan being trapped. You don't even know what he looks like. Stop picturing those tan arms bleeding. Or worse. He's not dead. He can't be. Helms come under attack. It's life for The Irontrace. Move on. No tears. Deep breaths. Yes. Keep breathing. Somewhere in the Helm, he's fine.

Richelle is back on her phone, thumb skating across the screen, looking bored. Her left foot catches my eye under the desk. It's tapping on the floor like a silent jackhammer.

Dr. North asks me questions for the rest of the surgery. Wylie watches, still as a statue.

"You wanna add on another surgery today? I'd love to do a full one," Dr. North says. He's kind of a goofball, but he's unflappable. You can't stress the man out. Gotta say, I'm a bit jealous of him.

"Maybe we can get four done tomorrow? I'd like to get more

information on what triggered the alarms," I say. He and Wylie don't know I'm pregnant. Now is not the time to tell them I need to rest.

"You think we can do five?" Wylie asks in a clipped voice.

"Five?" I blurt. "Let's try four. Love your ambition though."

Invisible Ivan would never allow five. He's mad about three a day. He'll blow a gasket when he hears I'm gonna try four. Maybe he'll blow a gasket. Or am I a spoiled wife that can get away with anything? I dunno.

"Let's get this week over with as soon as possible. Then I'm going back to Miami. I miss the sunshine and..." Wylie stops to look around like the INES lab makes her skin crawl. "And a better working atmosphere."

"We've had a long day. Let's talk about it in the morning. Thank you for your help so far." I unleash some kind of sad surgeon puppy dog eyes at her. She has to see that I'm begging her to stay and help.

Where's Ivan? He should be back.

"Henri, can we send the patient to the ICU?" I ask.

He grimaces, looking at his laptop. "Meh, let's give it fifteen more minutes before we open the door."

I groan. Wylie, North, and I fuss over Platz until Mai and Henri release the door.

"Rhys is stuck in the biomed lab. He'll meet us later," Henri says in more of a grunt than words. "I ordered food. I'll lock us back in so we can eat."

North pushes our patient towards the door. I'm an adult, they can't keep me here against my will. I follow Platz's bed and stand, just over the threshold in the hallway. "Henri, how about you tell me for real what's going on? I won't hesitate to make your life a lot harder by running away."

He laughs a deep belly laugh. "Sit, Story. We'll fill you in."

Richelle launched into an explanation while Mai gathered our food from the delivery cart. The alarms had gone off because an ALICE had malfunctioned. They put a few hallways in lockdown temporarily. There was no threat to the rest of The Helm. That's an underwhelming story. Wiley will feel much better about being here once she hears it. That doesn't explain where Ivan is though.

I blurt the question I've been mulling over for hours, "Why were Ivan's hands so bloody?"

The conversation they'd been having about whether gators live in the lakes by us or not goes silent, broken only by the *pft!* sound of Richelle twisting the lid off a bottle of soda.

Richelle, Mai, and Henri look between each other.

Henri taps a finger on his lips before speaking, "You didn't mean to." My heart drops. The purge broke my brain and I hurt someone, then placed the blame on Ivan. "He's helped you with panic attacks in the past. He was trying to get you to work through a breathing technique you've done before."

On the plane, Ivan had me laid back against his chest, telling me to *"Breathe with him."* His arms were so tight that something was making it hard to fill my lungs. In hindsight, it was anxiety choking me, not him.

"The purge made you desperate to defend yourself," Henri says. "When Ivan had his face by yours, you showed really impressive tactical skills using your fingernails to defend yourself. Must've hit a little blood vessel on his forehead, and one on his nose. He bled like a stuck pig on both of you."

"Oh, no. I scratched him? I hurt him," I say.

Richelle laughs. "If we're gonna be honest, let's be honest. It wasn't so much a scratch, you kind of shredded him. Henri's being nice."

Last night I yelled at him for beating Dr. Brown until he was a bloody pulp. I'm the real monster.

"When will Ivan be back?" I ask.

"Couple hours," Mai answers. She takes a long drink of lemonade, avoiding my eyes.

"He said it would be an hour, but that was hours ago. What's wrong?" I'm not even sure why I asked, there's no way they'll tell me.

Mai and Henri give noncommittal shrugs. Richelle silently plays with her phone. Whatever. I'm tired and want to go home. Maybe he'll be there soon.

I force myself to eat some salad. I ignored it for too long, and now it's room temperature. Warm lettuce is disgusting. Croutons dipped in ranch? Sounds like a balanced meal. I'll eat a few carrot chunks and some cherry tomatoes just for the twins.

"Hey, I'm gonna walk to the stables and take pictures of some of the horses for Lark." I grab my paper food containers to throw away.

"Wait! We're coming." Richelle jumps up, scooping her dinner and drink items into the trash.

Henri stands, shoving way too many inches of the rest of his meatball sub in his mouth and tucking his water bottle in a pocket on his pants.

"Okay, we're ready," Henri says around his huge bite of sub.

"Oh, we're going as a group. Cool," I grumble.

"You only go places in a group for now." Richelle laughs, elbowing me in the ribs. "It's your dream come true, my little recluse!"

Yay...

29

After the stables, Henri and Mai handed their babysitting gig off to Nathan. I protested in my harshest whispers, but they wouldn't relent. I've been trying to avoid him as much as possible. I spent a long time in the shower and then got in bed to read patient charts.

Lark texted me again. *Thanks for the horse pics! We're in apartment number 24. What about you?*

My bad. I forgot to check last night. I will now. In the living room, Nathan sits on the couch, working on his laptop. "Hey, what's up?"

"Nothing. Just checking something for Lark," I say, cracking the door open to see what apartment number we're in.

Nathan jumps off the couch when he hears the door open. "No. No! Wait. Where are you going?"

Ugh. This is fun. Where is Richelle?

"Lark wants to know what apartment we're in. She loves comparing what floor we get put on."

"No. Stop." He reaches for my phone. I take a step back.

"Why? She's a child." I lock my phone and slide it in my pocket.

"Because you shouldn't take a risk like that for anyone, even her. Moulson knows you're at this Helm. Don't make yourself an easier target with your precise location going out on a text message."

The look in his eyes is so honest. Those kind green eyes say more than his words do. Ivan said the same thing. If I could look in Ivan's eyes too, maybe it would be easier to believe him.

"Okay." This is the most awkward moment of my life. If my memories could be trusted, Nathan's favorite way to spend an evening is wrapped up with me on our couch, reading, talking about our day, and sipping drinks. Years of our life flood me as I stare in his green eyes. It's all a lie. None of those years were spent with Nathan. Those seasons, those years that passed were with Ivan. He's where my story lives.

"I'm sorry for making you uncomfortable the other day." I turn to make tea. "Do you want some tea, Commander Cantone?"

"Call me Nathan. And no. I appreciate it though. Ivan messaged me. He'll be here any second." He walks to the couch and gathers his stuff.

"It's nice seeing a human in here. I never have any idea where Ivan is." I shake my head at the ridiculousness of my current life. The apartment door opens. I don't see or hear anyone, but the door swings shut and locks. "See?" I give a soft, exasperated laugh.

"How's married life you two?" Ivan asks. His voice sounds off.

Nathan puffs his cheeks into a sigh. "We've come to a divorce agreement. Treat her well, or I'm coming for you, Rhys." He slings his backpack over his shoulder and heads into the kitchen by me. "Later."

Nathan pulls me into a hug. I drop my teabag and spoon. It happens so fast I don't have time to tell him I'm over the must hug Nathan phase.

"It's not so bad having a wife. I think you're onto something with this marriage thing, Ivan," Nathan says, then winks.

Ivan's deep voice booms from the living room. "Nathan, you've got five seconds to be out that door."

Nathan gives me a kiss on the cheek. I gasp and duck away. It's all wrong. Turns out, I do *not* feel anything for Nathan. Real effort is involved in not making a face that would definitely hurt his feelings. I look for Ivan to help but can't find him.

"Cantone!" I hear angry boot stomps coming for us.

Nathan flashes a look of sudden, genuine terror. He sprints to the door, yelling, "Later, Rhys's!"

"He might actually be in love with you now," Ivan huffs.

"Happy to report, I don't love him anymore." I pour a second cup and set them on the counter. "I made you tea. Not sure if you like it the way I do. I got a delivery with foods and snacks Henri said you eat."

"Thanks. That was nice. I'm pretty beat tonight. How about you?"

"Where were you today?" I reach out my hands to feel for him.

"You miss me? Or simply curious?" he asks.

"I'm getting used to having you around." I must be close to him. I smell a person who just had a shower, like fresh soap and shampoo. Is he going to stay in another apartment without me? "Marco."

He responds from directly in front of me. "Polo."

I swipe my hand up to find his injured cheek. "I'm so, so, so sorry I hurt you on the plane." I trace it with my fingertips. There are definitely injuries there I can't see. "Aww, I'm *so* sorry for this. Really."

"It was literally just a scratch. Who told you? Gosh, you're cold, baby." He pulls my hands to lips I can't see and blows warm breath on them. It gives me a happy shiver.

"When I was panicking, I was sure you weren't a person. I was fighting some terrible creature to save me and the babies. I mentioned to Richelle and Henri that you had beaten Dr. Brown until he was bloody and they defended you. Turns out I'm the monster this time."

"You're not a monster. I'm not a monster. Moulson's the monster." More warm breath on my hands. He rubs them between his. That same not a fire, fiery feeling passes from his hands to mine.

Shouldn't have added the monster comment. I've said hurtful things two nights in a row. I should pretend I'm asleep and try to think of a way to not ruin his evening tomorrow.

"I'm sorry." I walk to the bedroom. "I keep messing things up. I don't know how to read your voice. And of course I can't see you."

"I'm figuring out you really don't remember anything since May."

"What happened in May?" I ask, snuggling down in bed.

"We met in May."

"Hmm, May. What year?"

"May 2050."

I bark a laugh. "No. We can't have met four months ago."

"Why is that my love?"

Oh, dear heavens. He's not joking. I'm the least impulsive person in the world. There must be a very good reason I'm here with him now.

"I'm a planner. You'd know that if you're my husband, right? I would never have time to get to know someone, date, be engaged, throw a wedding, and prep our life and home to have twins in four months."

"You *begged* me to marry you at the top of a waterfall after you'd known me for three weeks. It was perfect."

"You're lying." I try to hide nervous laughs.

"I swear."

I'm too embarrassed to respond. He was right earlier; I must not be shy around him. The silence grows. It settles around us, and I'm okay in it. It's a comfy silence. The kind you feel safe in.

"Ivan?"

"Mmmm?" He sounds groggy.

"Why did you never text or call? I checked my phone."

"I did. Constantly."

I dial the number for Nathan Cantone in my phone. Ivan's phone rings. I hold my phone out. "Look, they did this to trick me. I laid and read these that first night out of the hospital."

"May I?" He swaps phones with me and scrolls. "Look. They got rid of all the I's."

"The what?"

Each message is signed '*-I*' in his phone. "It began as a joke. I signed everything to you with an I. After about a week, you started signing everything to me with a heart. Someone removed all capital I's from our texts. Once we got here, see, the *-I* is back from when you were texting me in the clinic. I thought you were asleep with your back to me. Guess you'd snuck your phone out of Richelle's purse. She'd been keeping track of it for you."

He navigates to my phone's *Settings* menu. "Watch. I'll fix it." After typing something about restoring original message data, my phone replaces all the capital I's that were missing.

"Thank you. This really helped." I could cry. He's the author of all those beautiful messages.

"Sleep good, baby." He lays my phone down. He must be sick. He's much more subdued than normal. I wish I could see him.

"Are you okay?"

"Yep. Just had a long evening in the biomed lab."

Maybe things went badly with the purge stuff he's working on. "Problems with making my glasses?"

"No. I'm happy to say that's going well."

"Can I see a picture of you? My phone doesn't have any."

He makes a thoughtful grumble. "I'm scared you'll panic."

"Please? None of the other purge people are bothered by pics."

"Okay. A quick glance. I don't want the babies all riled up after the long day in surgery."

I laugh. "Can eleven-week-old fetuses even get riled up?"

"As an amateur OBGYN, I vote we not mess around and find out."

"A what?"

"It's...nah, it's an old joke." His laptop lights up, and he lays it on the bed, facing away from me. "Here you go. Listen to your body. If you feel panicky, slam it shut and tell me right away."

"I will." I squint an eye at the screen. The background image is a picture of me in my old Lancaster bedroom. There's a bright, full moon shining in my window. My face is lit up with pure joy in the split screen picture. The other half of the screen makes me gasp.

Both eyes fly open. Ouch, the screen is too bright, but this is worth it. My jaw drops at the man in a Helm apartment. No way. This cannot be my husband. I'm horrified by the way I've been acting. This nerdy girl from rural-ish Ohio and him? Impossible. A quick peek turns into me staring at this picture for too long. Uncomfortably long.

Close your mouth, he can see you!

Well, he is my husband, he probably isn't hating that I'm half a degree away from bursting into flames. A man with deep brown, almost black eyes that are crinkled at the edges in a happy, one-sided grin stares back at me. A jagged lightning bolt of dozens of stitches trails from his hairline down onto his neck. It doesn't take away from his features. It adds to them. He's a person who has been through disasters. A survivor.

"*That's* your face! Seriously?!" If only the floor could swallow me whole until my brain is better.

"It is."

He looks kind, like he'd wear a smile easily. He has thick black hair with a swoop of waves in the front. My fingers practically twitch. I could see myself running my hands through it. Either tucking it back stylishly or ruffling it playfully. Oh my, that hair. This picture is of two people who are *very* much in love. I want to be that woman again, with him.

Try as I might, I'm unable to catch even a fleeting memory related to this man or picture. "Why did we take this picture?"

"That was on, hmm, day eight of us. You told me that on days it felt impossible to be apart, it was okay because we're under the same moon. The next time you came to The Helm I proposed and we eloped."

Phone! Where's my phone? I want to put his picture everywhere. I'm going to memorize his face. I fumble to unlock it.

"Hey, uh, whatcha doin'?" Ivan sounds hesitant. "You calling a divorce lawyer?"

I take a picture of his laptop screen. I make a copy of the picture and crop it to show just his face, setting it as my home and lock screen background.

"Do you recognize me at all?" His voice is bright with hope.

If I tell him no, I'll cry. If I cry, I'll sob. If I sob, I'll need him to hold me. And if he gets ahold of me? I won't be pulling away.

"You're like...really..." I pause to compose myself. I'm not sure if I'm on the verge of breaking down in tears or doing that thing dogs do when they're overjoyed to see their owner, and they fling their whole body into you, smashing you with a wave of love and affection. I really can't trust my hormonal self. "You are a very, *very* attractive man."

He bursts into laughter. "And you are the most beautiful woman ever, even though you clearly couldn't pick me out of a two-man line up."

I snap his laptop shut and lock my phone so he can't see me smiling like a fool. "Correct. Never seen you before."

The dog thing. Yep, I'd go the dog route on him. So much for the remnants of loyalty lurking for poor Nathan. I'm feeling very divorced from him right now.

"Can I give you a hug good night?" he asks.

"I don't think that's a good idea. Sorry. I'm still terrified of you." I mean, I am scared to panic. But here in the dark where I couldn't see him if he was right in front of me? I'm more scared if he hugs me, I won't let him go. "Can you please stay over there so I don't go into cardiac arrest?"

"Thank goodness Nathan can hug you in the meantime." There's not an edge of jealousy or anger in his voice. He's trying to tease me without forcing the hug issue. "When I found you under a pine tree you nearly put me in cardiac arrest."

"Tell me about it."

"Nope. Not from this chair. It's cold. And lonely." He's playful.

I ball up the comforter and throw it at his chair. "There. You're warm. Now tell me a story."

"Nope. Still lonely."

"You're really going to hold my memories hostage until I let you back in my bed?"

"Yup."

I crack up laughing. "You suck!" He gives a big, happy laugh.

"For real though. Our story is more than words. It's something you have to feel to believe. You're not ready for it yet."

Try me, Ivan. "Go to sleep."

His laugh cuts through the darkness, but he doesn't respond.

"What?" *Come on, tell me something!*

"Nothing. It's just...you told me that another night not too long ago when we were strangers in a bedroom. Love you, baby."

I know how sad I was to realize Nathan didn't love me. Ivan's nice. "Love you, uh, Ivan." Gah, that sounded like a robotic recording.

"You are *such* a faker!" We crack up.

What is it about him that made me throw caution to the wind and marry him? Why did I feel like I had to rush into it? It's alarming how easy I'm finding it to be hooked on him all over again.

Sniffing DNA

~ Ivan ~

The good news is, having a real conversation helped Story go to sleep. The sad news is, she's asleep. I'm bored. I had every intention of coming back here and crashing once they let me out of recovery, but then Story wanted to talk.

Not her fault. I told everyone if they breathed a word to Story about what happened, I'd send them to work in the maintenance facility cleaning the sewage processors for a month.

I was practically floating through the clinic hallway earlier. My first print of the contacts was perfect! They passed every test I threw at them. I set them up for their final round of testing in the biomed lab.

I was passing SC Darke's room on my way back to the INES lab. There was a weird noise, something like a struggle happening. An AL-ICE had him backed into a corner with four scalpel arms out.

I rushed in and disabled three of its arms. The fourth one snaked around and got me under the ribs on my left. It pulled out then came right at me again. I ducked to dodge it and snapped that arm off, but the damage was already done. I swear this Helm's tech is cursed, something is up here. Yet another reason to stick close to Story.

I'm being obedient, sitting in my chair in the corner. If she knew what I'd been through today, she'd have insisted on taking care of me. Even though she's sick right now, she's *Story*. She'd want to take care of me. I won't tell her until she realizes what we mean to each other.

"I had surgery today. Anesthesia counts as sleep, sort of. Time to work," I whisper. I creep over and watch her for a minute. Red curls tangle around her on the pillow. Her breathing is slow and even. "Sweet dreams, my love."

Time to get cracking on step two of the purge fix. I open my biomed programming laptop and wait for it to get its many bells and whistles running.

"Hey, Burt," I say as it turns on. Burt's not an acronym. It's a random name I gave it years ago. Burt is a computational beast, in all the best ways. It's run by an AI system I wrote in my free time. It's amazing if I do say so myself. I miniaturized a supercomputer and turned it into something portable. The AI program for Burt is similar to Rosa, but it's more of an employee than a parent-child relationship.

AI can do a multitude of tasks for us. It's the "for us" that's key. A lot of genuinely stupid people have written programs to give it autonomy that grows without intervention. They're happy they can be lazy. Then they panic when it becomes more than they can handle. Duh, Sherlock, you taught it to make increasingly complex decisions without you.

When I was taken to The Helm, they gave me a basic design document to build Rosa. The AI moms were supposed to follow the same workflow. Do childcare tasks (feed us, make sure we brush our teeth, read us a tech manual as a snooze-inducing bedtime story), validate they completed their childcare duties, then charge for the night. Their task was keeping us alive in the most basic way possible. Boring! I wanted more.

I followed the requirements from her design doc, then added pizzazz of my own over the years. I made her into what I never had in a mom. I gave Rosa kind, upbuilding speech patterns. She generously gives hugs to release oxytocin and lower cortisol. My sense of safety was obliterated when The Bastion took me. In the limited way a robot could, she helped give a semblance of family back.

Food was my favorite thing before Story. I programmed as many chef models as I could fit into Rosa. She made sure my friends and I had a steady, black-market like supply of baked goods that would've made our SC furious. She swears all the extra milk I washed down her cookies with is the reason I'm a giant. I think it's because my dad was tall too, but we never talked about my family. I gave her a bio-analysis tool to check my health. Yes, even kids at The Helm get sick.

But my favorite thing I did to make Rosa stand out from all the AI moms? I wrote a values optimization program. She recognizes human vulnerability, then responds with kindness, patience, and respect. The more I taught those values to her, the more she made sure I adhered to them myself. We were our own little check and balance system of "how good of a human were you today?" Honestly, I've failed at that question more than she has over the years.

As my skills grew and I wanted to build things for myself, I took bits and pieces of her logic and put them into Burt. Whatever I build through Burt has the same priority as me—helping humans. Do no harm, ever.

I feed my requirements for Story's glasses into Burt's bio-code engine. It'll take my ideas and generate several alpha prototypes I can run through tests for Story.

"Calm down, Burt, geez." The laptop fans whir to life when it gets to work. "You're gonna burn a hole in my thighs."

I sneak back out to the kitchen and put Burt on the counter. Thankfully, I brought my personal laptop on the trip. I'd debated but decided it could come in handy. This one is completely cordoned off from The Bastion, Irontrace, everyone. Usually, I just talk to Story and Alan on it. Not today. I'm about to write a program that has to stay off the radar. Rosa would not approve of what I'm about to do. This one will cause some harm.

"Thanks for the idea, Birdy," I whisper as I open my code editor. It was unacceptable to Lark to not know what breed of mutt Birdy is. From the way she treats me, I'd have guessed she's a mix of crocodile and hyena.

The day after we brought Birdy home from Francois' quarantine, Lark cornered me. "Ivan, can you run her DNA and find out?"

Free time for dog DNA tests was sparse that day, so I hesitated.

"Pleeeeeassssseeeeeee, Uncle Ivan, I really want to know," she begged.

"I'm not your uncle; we've been through this." I laughed.

"I'm not calling you Brother-In-Law Ivan. I've decided you're my uncle no matter what you say." She shrugged, then a sly grin lit her face up. "And as a kid with an Agora, it would help me feel better to know her dog breed percentages. Sometimes, the pain is just so bad…"

She pretended to do one of those damsels in distress faints. Laying an arm across her forehead, she slowly collapsed over like she's dying. Then she popped back up and grinned to see if her performance worked.

I wagged a finger at her. "Well-played, kid. I'll do it, but you have to help. You gotta learn with me about DNA, dog breeds, and how to code it with PyJav."

In hindsight, maybe I shouldn't have taken on training computer science to the daughter of an evil computer genius. My only defense is I was dog tired when she asked. She and I sat for a couple of hours while Story worked. We wrote our *what_is_birdy.ir* program for Burt. Lark did a buccal swab on Birdy, then we ran it.

While we waited, she mentioned something everyone else had only danced around with her. "I've been wondering. If only the Irontrace have Agoras, and I have an Agora, does that mean I was born an Irontrace?"

Her face. It was a knife to the heart. She was begging me to tell her she's in the club. She's one of us. What else could explain how it got in her neck? Story was oblivious. She had earbuds in, working from the couch.

"Lark, however your Agora got there, I'm sorry." Her face fell. "Do you want to be an Irontrace?"

She nodded so fast she almost shook her loose tooth out.

"One sec." I walked to my dresser and grabbed one of Story's Irontrace T-shirts. "Here, this is yours now. Raise your right hand."

She put on a face so stern it could have frightened David Delac and raised her hand. There's no such thing as an Irontrace-swearing in. But this is much cuter for a kid than the typical Helm welcome. The rest of us were dropped into a deadly sim and if we made it out, they handed us an Irontrace outfit and laptop.

"Lark Ross, do you promise to only ever do good for the world with technology?"

"I do." She nodded gravely.

"Good enough for me. As Senior Commander of this Helm. You're hired. You'll work to be a…" I gestured for her to fill in the blank.

"Senior Commander's PyJav assistant coder and jewelry maker," she said.

"Okay, let me type that in…Done. In about an hour, Story and I will take you to get your badge," I told her. "Welcome to the Irontrace Squadron!"

Lark turned to check on Story then turned back to me. "Answer me. None of them will say. Am I gonna die?"

I was tempted to stage a distraction and run away. "Lark-" Not really sure where I was gonna go with it, but she cut me off.

"Sometimes I pretend I'm asleep in the hospital. I've heard them talk about my death date. When is it? Tell me. I have stuff I want to do before I die. I need to see how much I can get done."

She didn't look sad. Her little blonde eyebrows were raised, head tilted to the side like an actual tiny lark.

"I had a death date too once. Did you know that?"

"Really?"

"I had less than a year left. Story saved me. Death dates don't matter around her. Your sister's love is *literally* stronger than death. It's her superpower. Few people can say that. So don't worry about what some dumb ALICE says. Believe in her. I did. I do. She saved me."

Story cleared her throat lightly from beside me. She dropped to sit on my knee and kissed my cheek.

Lark announced, "Oh, she's fifty percent Toy Rat Terrier, fifty percent Chihuahua."

I threw up my hands. Story dissolved into laughs. *Kids!* "Birdy is also one hundred percent terror," I added.

"You're just jealous cuz she hates you!" Lark laughed.

"That's it, for sure," I said, rubbing my left index finger that Birdy had nipped the night before.

Back to DNA. It's one of the easiest ways to confirm identity. Even in 2050, hunting people by their DNA is a red line no one will cross. The way I see it, ripping families apart, making my wife choke in panic—those are some of *my* redlines. They've been crossed.

I copy and paste *what_is_birdy.ir* into *pay_moulson_a_visit.ir*. I'm gonna build DNA sniffers and hunt this human piece of trash at a molecular level. It's never been attempted. Doesn't mean it can't be done. Also, this probably shouldn't be done, but I don't care. I lose myself in the flow of coding until Burt buzzes in the kitchen.

"I'm coming, hang on." I jog on my tiptoes to the kitchen. "Seven!" I do a stupid little robot dance. "Amazing! Let's set it to print these baddies and see how it goes."

Usually, I get three or four testable proofs of concepts. I'm floored to have this many to work from. These won't fix the purge. They'll make it survivable. I can't wait to pick them up in the morning. Story will be looking in my eyes again soon!

Gotta keep working on the DNA thing. I walk past Story's bed. Her face is taut. She's wiggling like she's in a bad dream. Easy fix. Gently as I can, I lay my hand on her cheek.

"Shhhh," I whisper. "Good dreams only. You're too precious for anything else." After a few seconds, she relaxes and pulls my hand under her cheek. Not close enough, she rolls, pulling my forearm under her. She must be missing me more than she realizes. I sit, watching. She's out.

Maybe I should lay down and sleep. An hour, tops. She wouldn't even notice. Her lips twitch into a smile. She deserves all the smiles. The only way to replace her panic with smiles is to keep working. I remove my arm and hand, an inch at a time, then tuck the blankets tight around her. Perfect. Didn't wake her up. I'll be a professional swaddler by the time the twins are here if I keep bundling her up at night.

pay_moulson_a_visit.ir will be the most invasive surveillance program ever written. Tracking his genetic signature won't take much effort. The rewards will be worth it. As I work through the steps of my program, I can't help but grin. Sorry, Mom.

30

Ow!

My right side woke me up with a stabbing pain. What is going on with the muscles over there? My left side is handling pregnancy like a champ. It always seems fine.

I probably just need to reposition. Not sure what happened, but I'm wrapped like a human burrito in the blankets. I struggle free, then roll over on my back. Rubbing my stomach takes the cramp away. Yeah. That's better now.

Today I'm feeling like something has popped out or changed with my baby bump. Nathan would love this milestone. My eyes fly open. No! Not Nathan. Ivan. A pang of guilt hits. Please, be asleep in your shield, Ivan. I don't want to catch a glimpse of him when I check the time. I turn away from his chair and click the unlock button on my phone. 5:01.

"Surgery day!" I silently sing. Today's procedures should be easy. I'll have four more positive outcomes to add to my growing research file for Lark's surgery.

"Let's go, babies," I whisper, giving my stomach a rub. I'm kind of worried that Ivan isn't talking or rustling when I get up. He must be a sound sleeper. I'll leave him. I sneak out, closing the bedroom door.

Teeth brushed, hair done, makeup on, wearing fresh scrubs and hot pink running shoes, I pour two coffees. Richelle said Ivan likes these egg bite muffin things with bacon and peppers in them. If I can't make him breakfast in bed, maybe breakfast in chair can make up for what I've been putting him through.

I microwave a few of them for him, careful to stop it before it beeps. This is too much stuff to carry. I should have thought this through, but

I was excited to try and be his wife. I balance his little plate of muffin-shaped egg things in my left hand and grab the handles of both our coffee mugs in my right hand.

I know we'd drink coffee together every morning. This feels right. Look at me, I'm doing the hard work to be normal again. I bump my butt against the door to open it. Light spills in from the living room.

Something metallic catches my eye. There's a silver cable of some kind coming down from the vent on the wall by Ivan's chair.

"Ivan!" I shout, dropping our breakfast on the tile floor. The cable recedes into the ceiling. "Ivan?" No answer. I can't see him. No movement. "Are you here? Answer me." I hiss. The room smells weird, almost like bleach, mixed with the scent of coffee I spilled. This is all wrong.

I don't know what will happen if I press the panic button on my ring. I do it anyways. Ignoring the fact that I'm crushing ceramic shards from our now broken coffee mugs into the floor, I rush over to Ivan's chair, stopping when my feet get tangled up in his.

"Ivan, I can feel you!" I run my hands up his knees, thighs, stomach, chest, to his shoulders and shake his chin gently. "I can't see you. Be visible!" I shout. His head feels floppy. He's unconscious. "How do I see you?" I feel around on his wedding ring for a button. This isn't like mine; his ring is smooth.

"No button, why is there no button? How does your shield work?" I put my ear on his lips and hold my breath, listening. A faint breath puffs out of his pillowy lips onto my ear.

"You're breathing. That's great!" My fingers fly to his neck, finding his carotid pulse. It's there, but fast and thready. "Wake up, Ivan!" I put my ear on his chest, lungs are clear on both sides, respirations are slower than I'd like. My phone rings.

"Please, wake up!" He's so limp. I'm worried he'll fall if I step away. But we need help. I dive to answer my phone.

"Story?" David asks.

"Help! Someone poisoned Ivan." I'm keeping my fingers on his pulse, but this stupid room smells bad. I've got to get him out of here.

"Where are you?" David barks.

"My bedroom. I think the room had a poisonous gas tube that piped something in to kill him when I got up."

"Sending help now. Wait…"

"No! Don't wait! We need it right now."

"Hold please," he says.

They're not supposed to put us on hold! This has to be an illegal breach of Irontrace behavior. "David! Get back here! I can't drag him out. I'm worried about being in here with the babies!"

How can I get us out of here? If we weren't always in caves, I could open a window to help him get fresh air. The next Helm we go to better have windows and sunshine!

"Blast it!" I drop to my knees on the ceramic mug bits I've kicked everywhere. I need to see how the chair is made that Ivan's sitting in. Maybe it has wheels. Nope, no wheels, just legs. His bag! He's got a backpack in the living room. Maybe there's something in there that can help.

"I'll be right back." I leave my phone on the floor by him and run to the living room. I flip his bag upside down. Pens, notebooks, chargers, protein bars, a little wooden frame, and a first aid kit fall out.

"Yes!" He's got three RO2100 Irontrace masks. They'll maintain his oxygen levels, prevent any new gases from getting in, and get rid of toxins. Then he'll wake up. *Right?* I tear one open and run back in with him.

"Got you a mask." My feet crash into something near the foot of the bed. "Aww, you fell! I can't see if you're okay. Ribs, chest, shoulder, neck, here, get your head in my lap." I throw myself down and scoot his head up onto my thighs, trying to orient myself to his body by touch. Once his mask is strapped on, I feel the pulse in his neck. It's weak, but still there. "Ivan, please, wake up. David! What are you doing?"

"I'm here," David says.

"Get someone, anyone!"

"All the comms are down in the Tallulah Helm. Air Titans are on their way. Stay with Ivan," David orders.

"Why?" Did Richelle die? Nathan? Mai? Henri? Cherise?

"Help will be there in seven minutes."

My mind races, weighing my options. I could make it out of here and check on everyone in far less than seven minutes. I'm fast. The others could be dead if we wait. "David, can you split SAM and pull Ivan in?"

"SAM *would* keep toxins out. One sec," David says.

I keep holding Ivan's head. "Ivan, I'm right here, you're fine, we're all good." My fingers absentmindedly stroke his face. I wish I could see him. That familiar awful feeling creeps in that I'm disappointing Nathan. My hands fly up into fists. *No! Take care of your husband, Ivan.* When I reach out to feel his pulse again, my hands aren't shaking.

I'm gonna get through this. I'm back in my familiar emergency mode. I won't cry. I won't panic. I'm in control. It feels great. "David, can you pull Ivan's vitals once he's in SAM?"

"He's in. Pulse 56. Respirations 9, clear. Pulse ox 89% but climbing. It's 91% now. It won't do blood pressure. 92% now. Resp rate 12."

"Ivan, wake up, please. I gotta go help our friends. I'm sorry to leave you. I'll be back," I whisper into his ear. "I'm going to find the others."

"No! Story. Stay." David sounds gutted. "I'm not getting any signs of life aside from you two."

They can't be dead. "Your data is lying, David. I'm going to find Richelle and the others, with or without your help."

I grab the edge of the sheets, pulling the blankets and pillows down on us. I tuck the pillow under Ivan's head the best I can then arrange the blanket like a halo to stop anyone from running into him.

"Ivan, I'll be back. I have to go."

"Story! Stop," David bellows.

"David, help me try to save them." With a final glance at the vents to make sure the poison cable didn't come back, I leave the bedroom. "Where am I going, David?" I whisper, but I'm not sure why. It just seems like a whisper-y time.

"You cannot disobey my direct order!"

Whatever, David. I'm a doctor, not an Irontrace.

"Turn on some lights!" I hiss, fumbling with my phone. "Or do something with the HVAC system. Flood their rooms with clean air.

Can you do that? Help get the gases out?"

"You're infuriating, Story!" I hear a hopeful twist in David's voice.

"Shut it. You love Richelle too," I mumble.

"Every room on your side of the hallway for the next several doors are the Lancaster Irontrace. Put your hand on the wall and follow it until we get the lights on. What did it smell like in your bedroom?"

After several tentative steps, clinging to the wall like three lives depend on it, my fingers brush into a doorframe. "Yes! Door one!" I beat on the door, but no one answers. An icky feeling hits. The only sound in the hallway is my breathing and occasional background comments from Lancaster. "David, can you unlock it? It's pretty scary in here. Terrifying, honestly."

"Hang on, Schmidt's accessing the doors now to unlock them all at once," he says. "What did it smell like in your bedroom, Story?"

"Kinda like bleach. Can you pull data from SAM for an air sample?" I snap my lips shut, holding my breath. Metal casters wheel along on the tiles in front of me. They're out of the reach of my light. "Hello! Who's there?!" I yell. "Woods, hurry. I'm freaking out."

My voice trails off. I want to keep listening.

"Story, you're in SAM. Whatever is in the hall can't hear you yelling at it. You're okay," David replies in an even voice.

SAM! Ivan built SAM. Wait. I don't know Ivan. What if he's actually an idiot and SAM doesn't work? I creep forward a few inches, propping my shoe into the bottom edge of the door. Something snaps to my right as a wheel crunches. I fling my hand up to cover my mouth.

"David! What's by me in the hallway?" I whisper.

"Focus! Get in their rooms. Under every bathroom sink will be a first aid kit with RO2100 masks. Get the mask on them. Run to the next room. That's all you gotta do."

Hmpf. All I gotta do?

I alternate between beating on the door and twisting the handle. "Whose room is this, David?"

"Nathan's."

"I'm activating a unit of emergency medical service ALICE models from their clinic," Woods blurts.

"Please tell me those are the wheels I hear?" I lay my forehead on the door. *Open, please open.* I'm about to run back to Ivan. This was dumb. I can't do it. What if the wheeled things get to him?

"You hear wheels...already?" Woods asks.

"This was so stupid, why did I come out here?"

"Go back to Ivan!" Woods says.

I made the decision to come out here. Suck it up and be brave. "Can you split SAM again to get around all the Lancaster Irontrace?"

"No. But we can try some other protocols. You, focus! Mask on them. Sprint to the next. Trust SAM," David orders.

The Helm alarm sirens shriek and emergency lights flood the hallway. All the Lancaster Irontrace doors fling open at once. "AHHHHH, yes!" I run into the first apartment.

"Put your phone in your pocket," David says in a weird splintery voice. "We can see what you see from SAM."

After grabbing the first aid kit from his bathroom, I slap my hand on his bedroom door once. "Nathan! I'm coming in!" His face is turned away. He doesn't twitch or move at the sound of his door slamming into the wall. I drop on my knees in bed beside him and grab his slack jaw, opening his airway. "Nathan! I've got a mask for you, here!"

I roll him on his back. He flops over, arms at an awful angle. "Ah, move." I try to get him positioned a bit better as his mask flickers to life, confirming he's at least got vitals.

An industrial filtration system roars on suddenly, bursting fresh air in from above like a chilly shower of wind. The floor vents whir open, curling the dangling sheets towards them. Nathan's blonde hair dances in the jets of air.

"David! You see this?" I ask while I fight to put the RO2100 on his face with my right hand. My left hand feels for his pulse.

"We see. Vitals coming in. Get to the next one," David says.

I sprint out of Nathan's room and grab the doorway, slingshotting myself into the adjacent room. "Help is here! I'm coming!" Same routine. Bathroom. First aid kit. Mask. "Whose room am I in?" I tear the mask out of its sterile packaging.

"Richelle," David mutters.

Air vents are already gusting wind in this room. Her mass of long blonde hair spills across the pillow.

"Wake up, Richelle!" I roll her on her back. Oh no, my sweet friend. She trusted me and came here. Now she's been hit by this gas or whatever is happening. It's not good whatever it is. Her left arm lays unmoving, draped across her forehead. Mask on. Vitals look good. I rub my knuckles on her sternum, trying to get some response. A soft, barely-there groan escapes her parted lips. "Did you hear that, David? She's here!"

"Get to the next room, Story. They don't have time for you to fiddle around!" It's probably easier for him to yell at me than look emotional as SC.

I sprint for her doorway. Henri and Mai done next. Only Cherise left, then I'll go check on Ivan. I'm crouched, pulling the mask from under her bathroom sink when the emergency lights turn off. The sirens go silent. The darkness is so intense, I can't see the mask in my hands.

"David, is this a good or bad sign? David?" No answer. I snatch my phone from my pocket. No cell service. Helms always have cell service. SAM, don't fail me now. I reach out and feel the bouncy membrane of its shield. My fingers meet faint iridescence. I slide my hand up the wall and flip the bathroom light. Nothing. I don't know Helm emergency protocols like Irontrace would. I do know them well enough to confidently say, this situation's getting worse.

Stay calm for the babies. Cherise is the last one of the Lancaster Irontrace. I'm too scared to talk to myself or the twins.

What would I say anyways? *Hey babies! Daddy got poisoned and might be dead, I don't know. I had to leave them to save the other guy I thought was your daddy. He may be dead too. Oh, the rest of our friends might be dead. Now I've lost comms with the people who could help us in Lancaster. Don't worry, babies, let's do grounding techniques to slow our heart rates. Way to not spiral, Story!*

I function best in emergency mode. Get back in it. Think about these apartments. Visualize the setup. Get in her room and secure the mask on her. You can do this blind. You did it on Invisible Ivan.

Oh, Ivan. Please, please be okay. I want to hear more about us.

I stay frozen, listening. The turbulent flow of fresh air surges into every vent. "SAM, I wish you had lights!" I pull out my phone and swipe down the lock screen menu.

Turn it off! Cherise has to get her resp-repair mask on. Okay, I'll turn on the flashlight, count to three, and turn it off. Nothing should be able to see my flashlight, right? I should've asked more questions about SAM. I don't understand how it works. I wish I'd read a manual or watched a tutorial.

Flashlight on.

"One." I lurch towards the bathroom door.

"Two." I step into the living room.

"Three." I just have to follow the wall to her room.

Once I'm in there, I'll shut the door, shove the comforter down by it, and leave my flashlight on. Swallow the lump in your throat. Get to it. I press my left hand on the wall, firmly gripping the mask.

Talk to the twins. Teach them something, anything, just talk to them and distract yourself. No one can hear you. SAM will keep us safe. I think?

"Hey, Mom again here. Sorry for the stress lately. I want to disappear with you both and your daddy to a warm island. We'll float and do nothing. No worries for us. It'll be great, my little loves."

I should be close to the bedroom. Probably two feet left.

Every muscle snaps to a stop.

What was that?

My left foot kicked a wheel. Shoot. Maybe there's something along her wall the other apartments didn't have.

I'm scared to kick it again. What if it's an AJA or ALICE and it sedates me? What if it's something scarier, lurking in the dark? You're a mom now, be brave!

Nahhhh. I'll be brave once some Irontrace are here with me. For now, I choose the chicken life. I press my engagement ring panic button several times. An ominous hiss from a robotic piston arm nearly makes me scream. It's got to be six inches from my face.

"We're fine, babies. On a walk to help a friend. In SAM."

ZZZZZZZZttttttttt! That's the sound of a robot arm, loading for spring action. I drop to the floor, curling in a tiny ball and turning on my phone flashlight. My knees! My shins! Yikes. It's not terrible pain from the chunks of cup in my legs, but it feels like I've got about a hundred glass splinters digging in from knee to ankle.

Directly above my head, the arm hammers into the wall. Crumbles of drywall crash to the floor, illuminated by my phone's light. That would've gone clear through me!

"It's okay, Huck and Holly. It doesn't know we're here. Your daddy built SAM, we're safe!"

SAM better work, Ivan. I'm sitting on my ankles like some kind of bird on a nest. *Brain, get working.* Plan how to get outta here, and fast. I thought my baby bump was adorable when I woke up. In this position? It's kinda awful. Crouching like this feels like some kind of hard water balloon being smashed into my lower abdomen.

"You two are in the dark, I am too now. I'm gonna see if we can crawl and not crash into the robots. I think they're AJAs. Ready? One, two, three." I immediately lose my balance. Quickly tenting my fingers out on the floor holds me in place so I can get my bearings.

"Ooh, Double H, I about sunk our battleship. I'm good now."

I've got to be so close to her room! Keep going. Keep crawling. It's working. It's slow, but it's getting me there without having my torso obliterated by an AJA battle arm.

"Uh, oh, babies. What's that?" My forehead bounces off SAM's shield. I should be inches from Cherise's door. "No, move SAM." I stretch my arms. SAM won't move with me. It's caging me in. "SAM? Go."

A new, fresh horror. I'm going to die in this shield, trapped in a ball on the floor. SAM should move *with* me. Not become an impenetrable wall that holds me in place. I hold my light up to see how much farther we've got. Maybe a foot left to her door.

AJA wheels! These huge black wheels blocking my way are meant for cruising through crowds or over any terrain. Or driving over pregnant girls crawling along in the dark.

Why is it here? Woods called ALICEs, not AJAs. I know these things speak. Eerie beeps and whirs send up a sickening cacophony around me. Their mechanical systems are booting up for action. I press my hand on my mouth to suppress a shriek. I'm gonna die today if SAM doesn't work.

I try crawling towards her room again, but SAM is an unyielding barrier. I'm stuck. "SAM? Move!"

SAM sends something like rippling, liquid color up over me from the back. The iridescence flares blue, green, and violet.

"What in the..." Something is crashing into SAM! A white impact point makes a flash on my right. It fades out to molten light shimmering over the shield's surface.

An AJA talks in a booming law enforcement voice. "Make yourself known! We're officers from AJA. You are in danger if you refuse to comply!"

I know I'm in danger. From you! There is no chance I'm shutting SAM off to reply. I crouch into a smaller ball, curling over my stomach. A full barrage of something is launched against SAM.

"What is happening!?" I grit my teeth and tuck tighter.

Constant impacts spark flashes of light, illuminating the silhouettes of AJA arms. They draw back, then strike us again and again.

"SAM, can you call David?"

SAM is going through some kind of awakening. I rock back on my heels and watch a rainbow bubble of shield inflate around me. The iridescence is intensifying. I fan out my fingers to test the edges. I can't feel them and can't see the familiar flash of color from touching SAM's boundary.

We're under constant barrage from I honestly don't know what. Safe to say, bad guys? Not sure. The rainbow shimmers shift to a lingering lightning pattern. Fractals blend and blur together until the air seems to hum.

"Are we winning, SAM? I really need you to win!"

The hairs on my arms stand, caught in some kind of static electricity. An incandescent white and gold glow envelops me. I can't see anything. No more friendly rainbow colors. No AJA arms coming in a relentless hunt for me. I see the white glow and...pictures? They flash around on the inside of SAM's walls, then transition up to SAM's ceiling, now several feet above my head.

It's a slideshow. Ivan's voice speaks from inside SAM. "Emergency protocol has been activated. Smile, beautiful, you're safe. Love you more than life itself." His recorded message repeats several more times.

I try to look at every picture, but there's too many. Each lingers for a couple of seconds, then swipes up, replaced with a new one.

Did he make this for me to watch while I die?

Photos of Ivan and I riding a black horse. Him sitting on a couch holding me while we both laugh. Dancing in a kitchen. Hiking with Lark. Several pictures of us lying in bed. A few in Atlas Caverns with our friends. Sometimes, a short video clip plays a moment I can't remember.

Look how happy we were. My shoulders drop. I don't wanna die in this stupid dark apartment! SAM's vibration has grown so loud I can't tell what the AJAs are doing. The bright light inside SAM suddenly dims, taking my life in pictures with it. To be cast back into this silent, dark room is almost cruel.

Another recorded message from Ivan plays, "No threat detected. Now get your butt home to me!"

My fingers glow when I test SAM's boundary. The iridescence signaling the edge of the shield is back. I pan my phone flashlight around the room. SAM fought a whole battle in this apartment.

SAM isn't a shield. It's a weapon! A highly effective one at that. At least a dozen AJAs have faint tendrils of smoke swirling up. Their metal components are white-hot, untouchable.

"Your dad did it, babies! Let's go save Cherise."

It's a terrifying ten-inch walk to her room. Each AJA unit has many arms, with various tools and weapons. Every arm is engaged, extended. Syringes with crowd control drugs, terrifying scythe stabby things, claw arms that look more like toothed guillotines, and metal chains with dangling cuffs that have a voltage symbol on them.

I was their target. Ivan saved me with his SAM.

"Palpitations, palpitations," I sing to the darkness, stepping gingerly. The glinting metal is a dangerous warning. Without Irontrace like Ivan, our lives are at the whim of these AI models. I wouldn't have stood a chance.

"Cherise! I'm here." I duck in her room, locking the door. I rip her comforter off the bed and tuck it at the bottom of the door. Why am I doing this? Is a cotton comforter an effective barrier from all the dead robots? Maybe. It can't hurt, I guess. I flip the light switch. No power in here either. "Seriously!" I frantically flip the dead switch several times.

"Phone light it is," I mutter, aiming my light at her face. "Oh no, Cherise." She's as floppy as the rest of them. Thankfully her room has the same fresh air forcing its way in the vents. "It's Story." She's out, but I want her to know she's not alone. "I'm here to help." Never mind. She can't hear me from in SAM. I push the panic button on my engagement ring again and stare at my phone.

It'll ring. It has to ring. They always call me back. Her pulse is fast and weak. Her respirations are rapid, crackly, and shallow. I push the panic button a few more times and take a deep breath. They'll call.

Several minutes pass. I check her vitals way too many times. I braid her short hair into a cute headband. No cell service. No phone call.

"I'm going to go check on Ivan. Be right back." I need someone to give me a pep talk. I pull the comforter away from the bottom edge of the door, squinting under it to see if there's light out there. Still dark. This is the worst. I hate this Helm! I want to go home.

Get out there. I've gotten this far. I pull the door open a tiny crack. Smoldering AJA units clutter the floor under my flashlight beam. Please don't let me get trapped by an apartment fire now.

None of them move. SAM did a thorough job dispatching them. I swing the door open several more inches and shine my light from floor to ceiling. I'm alone. It's a terrifying relief.

"All the bots are shutdown babies, we got this."

Light floods the apartment. I nearly shriek. Light is good, it means things are getting better, maybe. But this burst of sudden brightness came as a shock to my frazzled nervous system.

"Hello? Anyone?" I call. Why bother? They can't hear me in SAM. "Come on, someone! This Helm is small, but I know there's people."

My path out of here is littered with downed AJA arrest bots. They never freaked me out much until this morning. They're far different than the interrogation models I'm familiar with. Those ones are nothing more than a face on a screen.

Arrest bots are about six feet tall. They're the least humanoid of all the bots. Blank, mirrored face monitors meet their bulletproof silver chest panels, trailing down to their odd silver legs with wheels they skate on. They have too many joints per limb, and they bend at unnatural angles to gain a speed and strength advantage. The effect is chilling.

"It's so quiet in here, babies. I'll talk to you. Let's chat about how bad Ivan hates robots! He likes to use them for target practice."

I cringe at every brush of my shoe or ankle into an AJA. Each time a wheel spins or a wire buzzes, I'm sure it's being amplified through some alarm system to summon more.

Finally! I stumble into the hallway. "We did it, I made it out!" I cheer for myself. The hallway is bright, but empty and quiet. I collapse against the wall, forehead on arms to catch my breath.

The harsh slam of boots running on stone rings out, sprinting my way. Ivan yells, "Close your eyes!" Happiness bubbles up in my chest. He presses my forehead to his lips, holding me. "Please say you're okay?"

"I am. Are you? I didn't want to leave you, but I had to try to save them. I'm sorry. I made you breakfast. Kind of. I microwaved. I can't cook." He laughs, then kisses my cheek. "I dropped your breakfast and I ruined our morning and my knees have like a million bits of ceramic in them. Please don't be mad I left you. I was so worried about you the whole time. I was on my way back to check on you."

"I'm okay. I promise. Thank you for saving them," he says, giving my forehead a kiss. "Go in Mai's bathroom. Wait for me. I have to talk to them for a sec." He points to the Air Titans, ALICE, and AJA units speeding toward us from both ends of the hallway.

"No! Don't send me away."

"Plan B. C'mere. Stay in SAM." He turns his back to me, all quiet authority. To anyone watching, he looks like he's waiting to command his people. Only I know his secret. His hands are locked around mine, low on his back.

The adrenaline rush crashes. My wobbly legs are screaming lies. According to them, I've run a marathon while being beat like a pinata. I scoot closer until my cheek and chest rest on Ivan's back. "Cherise needs help first," I whisper.

"Sullivan! What are you doing here?" Ivan's voice booms.

"Heard you got yourself in a hot mess *again*."

"Start in there with Cherise. Get everyone else to the clinic." Ivan flings a hand at the AJA and ALICE units gathering around us. "Get out of here, robots." They roll away. Ivan drops his voice to a whisper. "Sully, start an investigation into this Helm. Call Lancaster and Perth. It's not a random hack. Someone here did this."

Sullivan leans back and nods gravely. "I'll start a comm channel."

"I'll be at least an hour late, maybe two. I have cleanup to do here." Ivan gives my hip a too-familiar squeeze, catching me by surprise.

The Air Titans walk away in perfect lock step.

"I was terrified when I woke up and you were gone!" Ivan gently lays an arm on my shoulders, leading me down a hallway.

"Where are we going?"

"I'm going to hug my wife."

31

"Wait!" I step from under his arm to the opposite side of the hallway. "I have patients. I want to check on Richelle, and Mai, and Henri, and-"

He blows out a heavy breath. "If you insist, we'll go check on them. Then I get to spend time with Story *Rhys,* not Story Cantone."

"Oh. Okay. Yes." *What did I just agree to?*

We visited our friends in the clinic and confirmed they're okay. There was an aerosolized compound pumped into the Lancaster Iron-trace rooms. The Air Titans are evaluating air samples to see what it was. The compound was released after I was in SAM, so the twins and I aren't in danger.

"Story, come with me for a minute, please." Ivan led me to a clinic with an empty bed and slid the door and curtain shut behind us.

The initial wave of anxiety about Ivan hugging me has faded. I thought about it while we visited our friends. Now that we're in this dim room, away from everyone, I'm ready, maybe even a little excited.

"Have a seat, please. You want me in or out of my shield?" he asks.

He turns on all the lights and aims an exam light at the bed. So much for the dim romantic atmosphere. "Out."

His back comes into view a few feet from me. He's digging through supply cabinets. Then he stops to wash his hands. Am I supposed to wash my hands too? What's happening? I sit on the bed, waiting.

"This won't take long, don't worry," he says. "Eyes closed, baby."

I laugh from nerves. "I figured. A hug takes like five seconds."

"This isn't hug time. It's prep for it."

"What kind of hugs do you give that I'll need to be medically prepared for it?"

He snorts. "You said you've got ceramic cup pieces in your knees. We can't have that."

"I forgot about the ceramic."

"I didn't."

He scoots on a little wheely chair beside my bed. I've got a hand up so I can't see his face. Without a word, he pulls my legs across his lap. They were fine on the bed, but I'm not complaining. The knees of my scrub pants have dozens of tiny holes cut into them. I slide my scrub pant legs up to my thighs. Jagged white cup confetti is embedded in my bloodied knees and shins. It will take ages to get this all out.

He works quickly to do an initial cleaning of the area and spray it with a numbing mist. He's more efficient and gentler with wound care than many doctors I know. I should stop laying here like a potato while his fiery hands work on me. "I can do it. Let me help."

"No. Lay back. I'm taking care of my wife." His voice is happy. He pulls out a small brown paintbrush-looking device and hovers it over my knee. "This is a pretty cool extractor. It uses a charge to draw non-skin particles from wounds."

The white and blue shards tremble slowly before sliding up and disappearing into the bristles.

He rests his elbow on my thighs, leaning forward to inspect my knees. "Looks good. Do you think I got them all out, baby?"

He's so close, but so far away. It's too much on my busted brain. "Yes. But can you please go back in your shield?"

"Why? You panicky?"

"I can't do this anymore. I want to see you. To look in your eyes. Sorry. Don't trust myself not to look."

"There's a little toolkit attached to my belt on my right hip. See it?"

"Yes."

"I can't touch it because of my sterile gloves. There's a button on the part towards the front. Push it for me, please."

"I will. This is so dumb. Sorry. I can't believe I'm asking this. Can I hold onto you if you go in it?" I mumble. "Yesterday you were in your shield and went away. It scared me."

He makes a happy grunt. "Yes. Definitely hold onto me. I've missed you like crazy."

My shaky fingers rebel. They don't want to push the button that will send him away. I know I'm not really sending him away, but it feels like it. I work four fingers between his belt and hip then push the button.

He keeps working quietly. If it weren't for the wound care supplies silently floating around and the comforting heat of his hip on my fingers, I'd think he left me alone.

"All done."

"Thank you. You did a really good job."

"Thanks. I need to tell David something. Wanna come with me?"

He tries to scoot his chair back. I don't let go of him, and he jerks to a stop. "Sorry. My hand is stuck."

Please react how I think you will.

"We've had this problem before. I used to call you my octopus wife. Feel free to wrap around me anytime."

"Octopus wife reporting for duty." We laugh.

Wait...I really like joking around with him. Actual bubbles of happiness rise in my chest every time he laughs. And judging by the way he pulls me even closer when he helps me stand, he's enjoying this just as much as I am.

We went to my lab for a mini control room chat. David nearly burst blood vessels in his eye from yelling when Ivan said he was taking a couple hours off to recover. I think they're best frenemies? Unsure. Old Story would know if they actually hate each other. While Ivan yelled back, I reviewed my schedule. Wylie and North will start the first patient without me.

Ivan was practically skipping when we left the lab. "Work and emergencies will always be there. My time with you is precious. I want you to see what kind of husband you've got."

"I'd like to know that too."

He pulls me to a stop at an emergency exit. "Close your eyes." A cool mist hits my face when he guides me through a doorway. "Open your eyes," he says. "I want to show you the Hurricane Falls."

We're on a screened-in maintenance balcony at the top of a cascading waterfall. There's a comfy lounge area with an outdoor couch, chaise lounges, and stained wooden Adirondack chairs. The sun hasn't yet risen in the September sky, but a rose gold light spills over the ridge of trees. Morning fog nearly hides the gurgling water below. Crisp air carries the earthy scent of fallen leaves and damp soil.

I sigh and take a deep breath. *Okay, he's off to a good start.*

"It's beautiful," I murmur.

"You want to learn about us?" Ivan asks.

I nod.

"Somatic therapy will teach you more than any words."

"Somatic therapy?" I swallow hard. "Let you test to see if you can trigger memories. Something held by my body that my brain can't register?"

"Exactly. But remember, I love you so much." His voice is coming closer. "I would never do anything to make you uncomfortable. Trust me please."

I could tell him I need to check on Richelle. Run away and delay this for a few more days. What if this works though? He warned me the other day before he touched my face. That was cool. He seems respectful. Still. My runner's legs are twitching to take off.

"What are you going to do?" I ask.

"Give me a hug. That's it. It'll fix most of our problems."

I puff my cheeks. "That's it?"

"Yup. Don't look at my hideous face. I'm going to stand here, unshielded. Give me a hug when you're ready to learn about us."

My feet seem to be stuck in the cement. I stand, staring at his boots. Why does this feel so awkward? I've hugged people before. This is just such a strange request. Hugging a friend or family member is a mundane activity. Hugging Ivan? That seems high stakes.

I picture the rugged, smiling face from his laptop last night. That's waiting for me, inches away.

Showing his remarkable self-command yet again, he waits, silent. *Just try it.* I step forward, looping my arms weakly around his waist.

"Ready for me to hug you back?" he asks.

Did this just take a turn? I spin my engagement ring, prepping to push the panic button. "I'm kinda scared."

"Don't be. I'm a man of my word. We're starting with a hug only." *Starting with?* One hand grips my upper back, the other grabs my waist, holding me. "Relax, wife. We were closer than this riding Obsidian on day one."

I try to adjust back to a respectful distance, like you should maintain when hugging someone for the first time. Apparently, that's not how we hug.

He bends me like a piece of clay into a Story-shaped mold on him. Oh. Okay. This is better. There's a slight chill in the morning air. Ivan is solid and warm. He's a wall built to keep me safe. I take a calming breath, testing how it feels to be in his arms. He pulls me tighter, pinning me against him. I don't panic. If anything, I take a genuine breath of relief.

"I assume Obsidian is a horse?"

As if a map of Ivan lives in me, my cheek slips into the middle of his chest. What is this? Can't explain it, but I'm resting somewhere familiar. His heart thrums wildly. He's nervous too. And yet, we fit perfectly. It's in the way you only feel with someone you love and trust completely.

Something, not quite a memory, hits. I've been here before.

"Correct. Your dad sent me to rescue you from the forest wardens. Long story. I'll tell you tonight in bed."

"That's big talk from someone who's only allowed to hug me."

"I have faith that I'm a very convincing hugger, Mrs. Rhys." He scoffs. I can't help but laugh.

His chin rests on top of my head. The weight is like a shield to keep anxious thoughts away. I grin when his short beard scrapes through my hair. Even that feels like something I'm used to.

He readjusts me, gently swaying. We must have spent many moments twined together like this, in happy harmony. Probably not by a waterfall. Or wait... maybe, yes, by a waterfall?

"Please don't hate me if I'm wrong again. This could be a fake memory with Nathan. Being with you like this by a waterfall, seems like something that really happened?"

Dumb question, Story! Probably ruined his whole thing.

"That was me for sure. You and I are *big* fans of waterfalls since our wedding. We did our own little ceremony and celebration, just the two of us on top of one."

The warm, comforting air we share ignites a glimmer of something. A reminder that here in his arms is my home. "Can I tell you something weird?" I ask.

"Always."

"I have a purge symptom none of you are talking about."

He makes a questioning, "Hmm?"

I run my fingers down his arms. "You feel that?"

"Fingers? Yes."

"No. Do you feel it?"

"I'm kinda confused. Explain please."

"Nathan kissed my cheek the other night. I've hugged Dad, Richelle. They're just regular-skinned people. But you? It's hot and feels like my fingers are well, it's like my fingers are striking a match."

"I *hurt* you?" He leaps back several inches.

I smile. He must really love me for the thought of hurting me to repel him like that.

"No! You know when you strike a match, and it doesn't work, so you automatically try to do it again? I can't explain it. It's a muscle memory, before a conscious thought. You're a match that won't light. I'm drawn to get back into contact with you the second my fingers let up."

"Interesting. We're going to have to do a lot of testing."

I laugh and melt closer. "Ivan, I'm serious."

"So am I! You're back, aren't you, my love?"

"No. You're a stranger."

"Story Rhys, you lie."

"I don't know you, but my body sure seems to. I think I do belong with you after all?"

"That's what I've been saying!"

"This is what we do, isn't it? We fix each other?" I ask.

"We do. By the way, did you do CPR on me this morning?"

"No. You only needed an emergency mask."

"Phew. Was gonna say you'd really taken a liberty there." He breathes out a soft laugh. "You wanna go back in now?" No! I shake my head fast. "Me neither. I know I said I just wanted to hug you, but can I ask a favor? Tell me no if it freaks you out."

Shut up, heartbeat! "What?"

"Can I feel your little baby bump? I miss sharing moments like that with my wife, my best friend."

I'm a fan of how he thinks. I drop my arms and turn, leaning my back against his chest. He rests the heels of his hands on my hipbones, lacing his fingers together across my lower stomach. It rocks me back towards him, holding me in place. Not a bad way to watch the falls.

"Hey kiddos, be nice to your mom. She's got a big day ahead. She already saved a bunch of people this morning. You wouldn't believe how hard she's working to get better. Hope you're doing well. Love you, babies. I can't wait to meet you." He laughs a little. "This is your dad again, by the way."

My heart nearly bursts. This is it. This is why I rushed to marry him. He's not just a good man. He's the best. Purge or not, I'd marry him again right now.

"You're really good at giving hugs, husband. I suppose I do love you after all."

"I love you. Close your eyes. Time for a more advanced therapy technique."

In a blink he dips me back over his arm. It's fast enough to steal my breath, but his grip is so sure and steady that I know I'm safe under his power. I don't remember him, but I *know* him. I know *this*.

Whatever our marriage has been surges to life, unshaken. It's like I've stepped back into something that has never fully let me go. The air itself crackles around us, and there we stay—suspended in this perfect storm we created.

Until his phone goes absolutely crazy in his hip pocket. It's buzzing like a mini-jackhammer and loud rings are punctuated by even louder message notifications.

He grumbles and gives me a final kiss.

"Baby, I have to tell you something before we go back in. No panicking, promise?"

"I'm calm." *Except for the lightning you left running in my veins.*

"I kinda got...stabbed like the tiniest bit yesterday."

I forget about the purge and lean up to look at him. He clamps a hand over my eyes, blocking my view of his face. "I'm fine."

"What happened?" I squeak.

Don't freak out! This isn't about me. Show him I'm trying to be his partner in life.

"An ALICE attacked me. Honest, it's practically just a scratch."

I *can't* lose him again. Keeping my head and shoulders turned so I can't get a full view of his face, I grab his shirt and pull it up, sliding my hands over his chest and shoulders.

"Where?!"

"I'm not telling you. I've missed your busy doctor hands. You gotta find it."

"Were you even really stabbed?" *Found it!* There's a rubbery hydroseal dressing on his left flank area. I lunge behind him to inspect it.

"How did that somatic therapy stuff not hurt you?"

"They seeded my incision with pain relief gels. I won't feel anything for weeks."

Peeking out from the bottom of his bandage are a couple of hesitation marks. Looks like it kept coming and he twisted to get away.

"Incision?"

"Well, yeah, they took me straight to surgery."

Ignore the lump of anxiety in your throat. Shove it down. Don't be too fragile to handle life with him. "Why didn't you tell me last night?"

"I wanted both of us to get a good night of sleep first."

I hold his hand, and kiss it, squinting in the now bright sunlight. How long have we been out here? He's made me lose all sense of time.

"At the top of another waterfall, I want you to make a vow to me, husband."

"Anything."

"You have to tell me, in a timely manner, every time you get stabbed, shot, or injured. I'm talking papercuts, all of it."

"Done. Same for you, though. Don't hide stuff from me. Like that grin when you saw my face last night. You know you hit the jackpot." His singsong voice makes me smile.

"I did."

He laughs. "I wanna see it all with you."

"Deal. I think we've been out here longer than two hours. We gotta go in."

In the hall, we run into our group of newly discharged, healthy friends. Richelle, Henri, and Nathan are on their way to the INES lab.

"Hey," Ivan says. "We need to test a hypothesis. I need Story to touch you to see if it has the same effect as when I do it."

"Seriously!" Henri guffaws. I nod.

"What do you need?" Nathan asks.

"I need you all to take a turn holding Story's hand. And give her a hug. Say, ten or fifteen seconds," Ivan replies.

"Richelle, show them how it's done." I step close and hug her. I laugh as she counts like an opera singer. This feels exactly the way hugging her always has. Friendly, but nothing like Ivan.

"Fifteen! Try holding my hand," she says. Her hand is cold.

"Nothing. Richelle, you don't electrify me." I make a bored face.

"Thank heavens! Same here."

I look at Nathan. "You don't have to. I know I made it weird."

"I'm game. Ivan, can I hug your wife?" Nathan asks.

"For science," Ivan says.

Nathan's hug feels like hugging an ironing board. Cold, stiff, and wrapped in cottony fabric.

"Story, you feel it with him?" Ivan asks.

Nathan jerks away. "Feel what?!"

"Electricity," I say. "And no."

Nathan holds my hand. It's cold. No spark.

"Baracu. You're up." Richelle gives him a friendly slap on the shoulder.

Henri hikes up his belt like he's about to run a sprint.

"Hugging is for children or old ladies. I'll try," he says. Then he crushes me, seeming like his goal is to restrain me. *Has Henri ever hugged anyone?*

"Gosh, is this how you think children hug? Never touch the twins," I rasp over his shoulder. I'm feeling very Goldilocks right now.

Henri releases me from his crushing embrace. "Hand, please." It's as cold and hard as granite, like the rest of him. I shrug. "Nothing."

I extend my hand a fourth time. There's no waiting, it's caught by Ivan. His grasp kindles the tiny inferno I've been searching for.

"I've got you, my love."

He really does.

Two Steps Forward, Ten Steps Back

~ Ivan ~

"She's baaaack!" I tell David. I'm in the farthest corner of the INES lab. Story's on surgery number three of the day.

"You fixed the purge? Get it shipped to everyone," David says.

Ha, no. Nope. "I didn't fix the purge yet per se. But Story is...she's Story Rhys again. That's for sure." I grin.

"How'd you do it?" Henri asks.

I spin my chair in a circle, tossing my water bottle in an arc, then catching it. "I gave her a hug."

Glad I'm on a video conference. David would strangle me if I was within reach. "You're saying your *hug* is the cure? Have you lost your mind?"

"That's proprietary information, property of IC." I point my water at him with a flourish.

He'll send a drone for me if I tell him the full story of my somatic therapy stunt. I'm speechless that it worked. It was such a long shot. Bodies are so weird. Brains are even more of a mystery.

David shakes his head. "In the spirit of a real update, from someone doing actual work, Darrow has several topics to cover."

"We need you to get the Tallulah people in a room to go over the report I emailed you. Woods worked on it. The way he found the culprit this morning was genius." While Darrow speaks, I open the file he sent and read over the Action Items. "Happy to say you're safe there now. You should sleep good tonight knowing that."

"I'll be sleeping well in my hotel," I mutter.

"Your what?" David squints.

"I've been here what, five days or something?" Darrow, David, and Henri nod. "The second we landed, Story got the purge. Bots going wild in this Helm. The dudes from your report tried to kill us. Story *needs* some fresh air and sunshine. IC's security team set us up in a swanky hotel in Atlanta. Super secure. Has a huge balcony if we need a secondary exit. Sully can fly us from the hotel to here. It'll take him ten minutes, tops."

"No." David glowers.

"You sure about that? Because my hotel is right next to one of the purge care facilities. A big one! Maseko and I were chatting travel plans, hotels, the whole thing...before she had me book it. She wants to get some positive press for The Bastion. Asked if we can go to the purge people there and do stuff with them."

"You talked to Maseko? Before you talked to us?" The Lancaster Helm fire suppression might have to kick on to extinguish David.

"It was Richelle's idea. She told me to ask Maseko if Woods could handle Lancaster for a day. You fly down here and play in the Georgia sun with Richelle. We've got a pool!" I grin.

David leans forward. "I don't like this, Ivan. Private security? That's never happened in all the years we've worked together."

"In those same years, the world has never fallen apart, David. Times change," I say. Life changes too. If it was just him and I on this call, I'd tell him to knock it off. As soon as I mentioned Richelle, he was in. He's too deep in the day-to-day of SC to realize he's not a bachelor anymore.

"What day are we doing this?" he asks.

I look at Henri. "Tomorrow?"

"Sure," Henri says. "Alan, Amelia, and Lark arrive tonight."

"What? No!" I miss my water bottle as it arcs back down. It lands with a crunch on the floor. Surely it can't be too late to cancel their flight.

"Richelle approved it. Lark was upset they hadn't let her see Story since the purge. She was begging to come."

Curse you, Richelle! Gonna have a chat with her later.

"I'll arrange things here with Woods so I can travel," David says.

"Delac?" I arch an eyebrow at him. He pauses, waiting for me to continue. "Story was happy to save your curmudgeon-ly self. Lemme take her to Atlanta in peace." I point my water bottle at him. He looks up and sighs. "By the way, I have been doing real work. When I saw the effect of my hug on Story, IC found Dr. Mori. He leads the top team of trainers for neuroscience models. Take it away, please, sir."

Mori begins speaking in an elegant Japanese accent. "Greetings, Irontrace. It's an honor to work with you." *Love this guy!* "My associates and I work in cognitive, sensory, and relational neuroscience. I specialize in studies on how touch activates our somatosensory cortex."

David and Darrow lean in.

"Tactile information, or things we learn by touch, become part of our remembered experience. Those work with other senses to build a web of multi-sensory networks to encode and retrieve memories. Touch isn't just a social signal. It becomes part of our history, our identity."

He screen shares a quadrant of paused videos.

"The purge is an emergency. I took a liberty. Forgive me. We conducted a blind experiment. Ivan said Story doesn't respond to other people holding her hand the way she does to him. Please watch."

A massive warehouse has a wall dividing the room. There's a series of small doors cut, about elbow high, just large enough for a forearm to go through. Cameras are placed above and throughout, panning around. One screen shows about fifty adults milling around on the left side of the wall. Another screen shows a similar number of adults on the other side of the barrier. They're wringing hands, bouncing on feet, heads darting around.

Miro speaks. "There are fifty doors. One purge victim will put their hand through the small testing door. The other forty-nine testing doors have an unrelated nurse who will place their hand in the test environment. We tested to see if Ivan and Story are correct. Is the relative's touch able to trigger memories in the purge victims?"

"Purge patients. Line up at the back wall, please." An ALICE voice broadcasts in the warehouse. Some take a stance like they're ready to sprint. It looks like one of those old movies where a coach blows a whistle, releasing school kids to grab dodge balls to blast each other in the faces. I'd love to have gotten to play that.

"Line up against the back wall please, relatives." They form a long, single-file line around the edges of the room.

"Patient one, approach the wall. Give each hand sticking through the doorway a three second handshake. Move on. If you feel you may have found your relative, silently raise your hand. Do not speak to or interact with the person behind the wall."

I already know what's gonna happen, but I can't sit still. The patient walks along, trying several hands. On the eighth one, their shoulders jerk back like they've been hit. They raise a shaky hand.

"Remove your hand, relative." The hand disappears behind the wall. The AJA slams the small door shut, then orders, "Go sit on the bleachers. Wait to be called for results."

We watch several more rounds. The mood on the relatives' side of the wall doesn't change. But the patients? They're smiling. Every new patient that rushes to the bleachers is welcomed with smiles and fist pumps.

Miro pauses all four video feeds. "It worked. A one hundred percent success rate."

David slaps the conference table. "Extraordinary! Why?"

"We triggered tactile memory." The conference screen changes to a series of MCDI brain scans. "The results are astounding. We can't fully explain them yet. Areas of the brain linked to emotions, attachment, love, and bonding lit up. They've been homesick to the point of physical distress. But a familiar hand? One young woman said it gave her the same feeling as being tucked in her warm bed on a cold, snowy night. Another said it hit them with a sense of relief and safety, like they've been drowning and that hand pulled them up from freezing water. Others said it felt like home. Peace. Comfort."

"What happened when they looked at their relatives?" Darrow asks, hope making his voice bright.

"We haven't tested that yet. We're waiting until Ivan's contacts are delivered to try a face-to-face introduction." Miro looks at his watch, "They'll be here in ten minutes. Maseko gave the go-ahead for us to do large-scale testing. I'll report back soon. My colleagues are saying the contacts have worked great on test patients."

"Thank you, Dr. Give our sincere thanks to your team." Darrow grins. He hasn't smiled since his wife was moved to a purge care center.

"Thank you. I have a lot of work to do. Goodbye." Miro disconnects.

"Rhys! What is wrong with you?!" David angrily bursts. "You couldn't have led with Dr. Miro?"

"I have to keep you on your toes." Honestly, I was so happy about my reunion with Story that I still can't think straight. "I better go box up some contacts. Later."

They wave, and I end the call. I creep over to check on Story. They're about halfway through this one. North is primary. Wylie's assisting. Story's watching and answering questions.

I send David a quick message. *We'll be ready in two hours for our grand reveal of the culprits from this morning. -SC Rhys*

"Henri, I need a confidential favor," I say. "I need you to go to the biomed lab next door, please. Grab the seven glasses off my printers. Carefully put them in a box, load them on a cart, and bring 'em in here."

"On it, boss."

I better build some kind of barrier to keep Story from seeing what I'm doing. If she sees the glasses, it might get her hopes up. Story keeps a wary eye trained our way while Richelle and I shove library shelves around. We put them in a U-shape to create an alcove.

"Where do you want these?" Henri asks, pushing in a cart with my precious cargo.

"Leave it there, thanks. You two keep eyes on Story. I gotta work here for a bit." From the lab fridges, I grab a load of cranial simulation models. Each is a generic looking face, with a neck and a bob of convincing hair.

"This is so disturbing," I mumble.

I hate plugging these things in. Their eyes blink to life. Nostrils flare. Lips and cheeks twitch. Gives me the heebie-jeebies! Anything for Story though. My morbid row of seven heads is arranged and turned on, facing a screen. I put a pair of glasses on each head.

"Screen on." I stare at the person who appears on the screen, watching their faceless void shift and reach. It doesn't faze me to watch it twist and change, but my limbic system is in order, as far as I can tell.

"Alright, decapitated dummies. Wow me." I stand, hands on hips. Their vital signs are okay. Temp of the glasses is stable. I'm going to leave them for twenty-four hours and check back. Honestly, no one would wear them for a consecutive twenty-four hours, but I'm testing them the same as I did the contacts.

Back to hunting Moulson with DNA. Or should I work on the real purge fix? Normally I could decide in a flash, but Story's got my head all turned around from this morning. *Story.* I'll go check on her. That's always the right solution.

She's discussing edits they can make to the Agora recovery timeline. Words tumble out in her melodic teaching voice. It's bright and warm, the kind of voice that makes her students feel safe asking questions.

"Story, you done? You got a video call!" Richelle yells from the desk.

"Be right there. Who is it?" Story asks.

"Maseko."

SHOOT! I neglected to tell Story what I had Rosa do. This was a conversation for after Story and I were back in love. One where she could look in my eyes and see my reasons. If she can't see I did this from a place of concern, she's gonna be big mad.

Story tips her head. "Who?"

"Architect Maseko!" Richelle yells back.

Story pauses then steps out of the sterile field. She tears off her gloves and gown in a practiced pull. "Never heard of him," Story says, bouncing down the platform steps.

She knows Maseko!

Wylie laughs. "Do you live under a rock?"

"No...I..." Wifey can't see she's right in front of me. "Ahh!" she squeaks into my neck when I lean down and nearly put my lips on her ear.

"Shh, it's me," I whisper. "Tell Wylie and North you know Maseko."

"But-" she stammers.

"TELL them you know Maseko!"

She pushes me back and does an adorable, thoughtful twirl. "Richelle, sorry, you said Maseko?" she asks.

"Yep. Ar-chi-tec-t Ma-se-ko," Richelle replies.

"Ah, I was too focused on the next surgery. Let me go get cleaned up, then I'll join the call." I follow like a shadow towards the bathroom in the back of the lab. She freezes with her hand on the door. "Ivan?" she whispers.

"Yeah."

"Come in with me, please. Tell me who Maseko is."

She works through her post-op cleanup routine while I talk. "Maseko is the current leader of The Bastion. She's a sharp lady. She's on Project Ilex with us."

"And I know them?"

"You definitely know her." I clear my throat. "Can I come out of my shield so you can be distracted by my biceps while I tell you bad news?"

She drops her towel in the trash can. "What bad news?"

"Shield? No shield?"

"Just tell me."

"Maseko wanted you to be the head of ASTRA. You told her you'd do it so you could come operate on Darke. But it wasn't official yet."

She's tucking little flyaway curls into her surgical cap. Not focusing.

"When I realized you had the purge, I was desperate to protect you. I knew you'd be crushed if you couldn't keep working towards saving Lark. Story, listen." I catch her hand. "I had Rosa evaluate the contracts. She said they were good to go. I forged your signature and sent the contract to the BBA. Maseko is calling from the press conference to officially welcome you as the head of ASTRA. I'm not sure what this means for Ilex. It shouldn't change anything."

She drops her hands and stares at her reflection.

"It comes with certain protections. If you're head of a huge agency like that, they-"

"I have brain dam-well, I've been purged!" Her chest heaves.

"I took care of that. I made them add a short-term disability clause. Just tell them you need some time off."

She tears off her scrub cap and shoves it in her pocket. "You said you're someone I can trust. Someone I'm safe with." Her fingers fly, loosening her braid. "You're supposed to be looking out for me, not missing the point. You're missing the point!"

"What point?"

Is her brain deteriorating in real time before my eyes?

"You still don't see it? I'm done. Call David. I'm going back to Lancaster." I'm at a loss. I've never seen her abandon the surgical cap and hairdo in the middle of the day. "Call David or I'm pushing my panic button."

"Baby don't leave! Hear me out."

"Come out of your shield." I flash to standing next to her. "Ivan. I...Maseko? Rosa? ASTRA? Ilex? It's the worst thing yet...This changes things. Do you know what it all means?"

You hate me and are going to fling yourself at Nathan?

"It means I'm the dumbest man alive? I'm so sorry. If I could go back in time, there's no way I would have taken this liberty. I'll *never* do something like this again." She wraps around me so tight it takes my breath. The apologies are working. Keep going. "I love you. I respect you. Again, I'm sorry. I had reasons, but no reason is good enough to make you feel like you're not safe with me. I'm so sor-"

"Stop." Her soft cries transition to helpless sobs. "How do you still not get it?"

"I'm so sorry. I'll do anything to fix this. I love you."

"I don't know Maseko. I didn't know about the ASTRA thing. What or who in the world is Ilex? Rosa? I give up. No more surgery for me. I'm a hazard."

My heart stops beating for a full five seconds. She's worse than any of us thought. I was too caught up in the ASTRA paperwork forgery. My brain glossed over this escalation in her symptoms. Keep her calm.

"You've just got some memory gaps."

"I thought you were the only gap. What if an emergency happens in surgery and I can't remember what to do?"

Don't let panic sink its teeth into her. I pry her hands loose from my ribs and turn her back against my chest. "Let's try a breathing exercise." I lay one hand on her chest, one on her stomach.

"No! I'm not panic...panicking. I'm just sad!" Sob, sob, sob. "And scared. I'm so scared."

Me too, baby! "Is there anything else you've heard in the last few days that felt off? Something we all know that you should know. Anything?"

"Do we have a dog?"

Birdy has been lost in the purge too! This is a terrific opportunity to get rid of that small devil before the babies are born. I can't do that to Story though. She loves that furry little menace.

"Yes. Birdy. She's obsessed with you."

"Who are the people we went to a funeral for?"

Why would Moulson purge Travis and Talia from her? "They were two young, but very capable Irontrace I'd appointed as your guards."

"Did Moulson kill them because they were helping me?"

"He killed them because he's a monster."

Richelle pops the door open. "Ivan! What did you do to her?" She rushes over, laying a hand on Story's back.

"We need some more time, Richelle," I say.

"Story, is he holding you hostage in here?" Richelle steps close to me, squaring up. She whispers to Story, "Is he...did he *bother* you?"

Story shakes her head fast. "No!"

"Richelle, can you tell Maseko to call back later?" I ask.

"No can do, boss man. The whole BBA is on the call. Maseko said she's got an announcement. Let me get my makeup kit. You need to be glowy and camera ready in five minutes." She ducks out.

"What if I forget the kids?" Story clings to my shoulders like she's dangling from a cliff.

"You won't." *She might.* I pull up the hem of my shirt and wipe her teary, snotty face.

"Gross." Her protest turns into a hiccup cough combo. "I'm sorry. Your shirt!"

"Don't worry about it. I've been wearing your biological glitter since the second time I saw you." I press some tissues into her hand.

Another sob escapes. "What does that even mean?!"

"Tears, baby. I wiped your tears then too."

She blows her nose on the stack of tissues. "What if I panic on the call?"

"I'll be prepped to knock the internet out."

"That sounds illegal."

"Layer eight issues happen all the time." I stroke her cheek. "Sorry things are worse than we thought. You *WILL* be okay."

"Here, put a cooling cloth on your neck. I'll start with your hair." Richelle deftly finger combs Story's curls to the side and lays a cool pack on her neck.

I'm useless for hair and makeup. I disappear into my shield.

Story sits on the edge of the sink, staring at nothing. Richelle bustles around her, bumping into the shell of my wife. She's still warm, breathing. But not *with* me. No freckled face lights up when I walk in. No shared memories to laugh about. If she keeps forgetting things, I'll be the sole witness to our life. I've been shot, stabbed, burned. The ache in my chest looking at Story's blank face? Ah. Way worse than any pain I've felt.

"Story, I love you!" I lean in and kiss her cheek. *Please, see me, my love.*

Her shoulders sway a bit in surprise, but she doesn't look for me. "Love you, Ivan."

It's all I can do to not tear the mirror off the wall. It would get out that overwhelming burn to crush or destroy something. Instead, I go back into the lab.

Henri stands next to my Burt fortress with a fire extinguisher. The simulator heads, glasses, and my wall screen are covered with blue fire suppression foam.

"Five out of seven overheated. The glasses lit their hair on fire," Henri says. "This round is a total bust. Sorry, SC."

I pick up one of the heads that didn't have fire damage. The glasses look fine. Maybe they would have worked, but Henri ruined them. I can't continue to use them now for sim testing.

"Get CLEANRs in here for this mess, Baracu."

The skull makes a sickening crunch when I hurl it in the medical waste bin.

Time to give Burt some extra printing speed. I type in the parameters for him to print several copies of the good glasses that didn't catch fire. They'll be ready in an hour to resume testing.

"Burt, work fast." I hit send on the order to print the files when an idea slaps me in the face.

Lark's on her way! Fifty percent of Moulson's DNA is being hand-delivered. He did this to Story. I'm going to make sure he pays. No one else can find him. I can. What paperwork would Alan and Amelia have to sign for me to get a DNA swab on Lark? I could run it and build a profile to hunt Moulson. No, I don't want to pull them into this. That would make them accomplices.

What if she happens to leave a stray hair somewhere? Then I happen to run it through my DNA sniffer program? That wouldn't implicate anyone else in what I'm doing. Rosa would slap me upside the head for the person I've turned into. I don't care anymore.

32

Sharp applause rings out from the lab speakers.

"Dr. Rhys, would you like to say anything to your new employees?" Maseko asks.

"Thank you," I say. I made it through the video call without panicking. Maseko did a whole dog and pony show about how extraordinary I am. If they only knew how broken I am. She'd gleefully burn my contracts.

I should be excited. I'm not.

I should be mad at Ivan for this ASTRA thing. I'm not.

I should be worried about Lark. I'm not.

What am I? I'm nothing. I can't muster a single emotion. That in itself should make me scared, but it just makes me tired.

Maseko blinks. "Sorry, your mic cut out. We can't hear you."

"Thanks." I force my lips into a smile.

"A woman of few words. We'll let you get back to work." Maseko grins. Clapping breaks out again. I slam the laptop shut.

"Dr. Rhys, when should we start the next surgery?" Dr. North asks. "Looking forward to getting the guys here at my Helm done."

"When my dad gets here," I reply.

"Oh, we thought it would be sooner," North says.

Ivan lays a hand on my shoulder. "Richelle changed the schedule due to Maseko's meeting. Surgeries will resume tomorrow morning. Good day, Dr. North, Dr. Wylie."

He disappears into his shield. "Go in SAM. Let's take a walk."

A walk will make me more tired. No thanks. I frown and lean back.

"I got ya, baby." Ivan turns on SAM then puts one arm behind my shoulders and one under my legs, lifting me from my chair. "Door, Richelle."

I don't protest when he carries me into the lab next door. It's full of computer consoles, manufacturing robots for medical equipment, and rows of empty desks.

"Sit here for a second."

I can't control what's going on with my brain. Now my body rebels too. Some primitive survival reflex kicks in. Ivan's arms are the only thing keeping me alive. Instead of letting go, I wrap tighter around his shoulders.

"Ooppff, baby, gosh!" He nearly takes a header trying to keep his feet, but somehow, he does. "You're right. Sticking together is better." He laughs, shuffling me higher in his arms.

Yep, instincts were right. It's nice here.

He walks to a counter with a bunch of 3D printers. I burrow my face in the hollow under his chin. I close my eyes so his beard won't poke them. If I stay blind to the world here, and can only feel Ivan, maybe whatever has snapped in me will heal.

"Look, I'm printing glasses. You'll be fixed soon." He walks slowly, inspecting every pair. "I'm happy with their progress. I have to test them out for a day or so, but I can't wait to give you a pair."

I give a bitter sigh.

"What? Are they ugly?" he asks.

"Glasses won't fix me."

He rubs his cheek on my forehead. "They're just step one. This batch looks good. Sorry, I have to go to the control room."

"Take me with you."

"Of course. Not letting go of you for a second now that you can tolerate me. You comfy, or squished?"

"I'm comfortable. But I can walk."

"Nonsense. Been a proud member of the weight room's fourteen-hundred-pound club since I was nineteen. You're literally nothing to carry. Just kick that door open for us, please."

On the walk, he told me about the testing he'll put the glasses through before I'm allowed to try them.

The control room is full, but quiet.

"Is Rhys here yet?" David asks as we walk through the door.

"Getting settled in now," Ivan says, sitting in a chair in the farthest back corner. "Staying in my shield."

"Where's Story?" Henri asks.

"Somewhere safe." Ivan answers.

He props his feet up on the desk in front of him and leans back. Much better. My cheek is on his shoulder. My bump is in a safe little hollow space between us. Once I quit wiggling, he drops his arms to the armrests.

I whisper, "You sure they can't see me? I thought they had contacts."

"I restricted all access to SAM. I'm the only one who can see you."

"Let's get started. Woods. Baracu. Take over," David orders.

"We've taken Commander Nichols and King into custody," Baracu starts. "He and Councilman King had been working to gather information on Story's location for, well, a few groups of people."

"What kinda people?" Ivan rolls his shoulders and tucks me closer. It's not lost on me when he casually folds an arm across his chest, laying his hand over my ear. Again, I don't care. I'm not annoyed by his overprotectiveness. I'm not curious what Baracu has to say. I'm tired. And these babies are making me so hungry.

"Bad actors interested in using her skills for monetary gain. A few creeps. And of course, Moulson's org. They were running quite a bidding war. He'd arranged Story's news interview as proof they had her for the bidders," Woods says. Ivan's chest rattles an angry groan. "Moulson and Nichols hacked the AJAs. They were so confident in their plan that when Sully and the Titans arrived, they got into a bit of a dogfight with a heli-drone. It was waiting to fly Story and King to..." Woods pauses, looking at his laptop. "Tybee Island."

"What's on Tybee Island?" Ivan asks.

"Dunno. We sent the Titans to find out," Baracu says. "The stuff he piped into the rooms was a mix of chloropentath and ketafol."

"This Helm is the worst!" Ivan whispers.

"The ALICE attack on Darke Ivan stopped, was that Nichols and Moulson too?" David barks.

"Yep. Darke is one sharp SC. He realized something fishy was up. Started a shadow audit trail on the whole Helm. Max is proud of his little brother."

"Darke sounds smart like you," I say.

"I'll add him to Project Ilex," Ivan whispers, quickly adding, "I'll fill you in on it later." His left hand is between us, thumb tracing slow arcs across my stomach. "Why don't you go to sleep for a bit?"

"I could never sleep in here."

He gives an amused snort, then whispers, "You underestimate my husbandly powers." He tangles his free hand up in my curls and alternates pulling on them with rubbing my neck. I guess I *could* sleep.

"Nichols and most of the people that hired him are in custody. Moulson, of course, isn't," David says.

"Who's looking for Moulson?" Ivan calls out.

"We have a task force on it," Darrow replies.

Ivan follows up with, "What methods are they using?"

"Standard Irontrace procedures," David says.

Ivan clears his throat. "No enhanced search methods?"

"Like what?" Darrow asks.

"I say nothing is off the table. Throw everything we've got after him," Ivan suggests. "I've got some ideas."

David cuts in. "No. We follow existing protocols. We'll find him."

"I'd like to know what Ivan was going to suggest," Darrow presses.

"No. We stick with proven, safe methods or we're no better than him." David abruptly changes the subject. "Let's talk purge progress."

It's cold in here. I snuggle down tighter. They continue talking for what feels like ages. I don't focus much on what they're saying. It's about neurons missing a protein that acts as a bridge for something.

At one point, Maseko said that whoever finds it, gets to name it, and would be awarded fifty million dollars. Everyone unmuted at once to assemble teams of doctors and engineers. Ivan didn't join one, even though lots of people begged him to. He said he's already got a team.

He's so warm. It's like being cuddled by a comfy couch that loves me. The control room conversation drifts to MCDI scans, but his heartbeat drowns it out. One of those awful sleep shudders hits that made me feel like I was falling off a cliff. I jerk up to a sitting position. A fire poker of pain burns in my right lower abdomen.

"What's wrong?" Ivan steadies my sudden wakeup panic.

Where in the world am I? I'm in the control room, sleeping *on* Ivan? The pain in my side is fading into an ache. I use both hands to rub it. Ivan puts his hand on my side, massaging my hip bone area.

"That feels really good. Thank you." I point to his hand.

"I'll keep going until my hand falls off." He kisses the side of my head. The tiniest spark of happiness cuts through the fog I'm in.

Darrow is droning on about some task force called IC from a huge monitor down front. Then he switches to talking about the horrific complications some people are having from the purge.

My happiness is extinguished. Thanks, Darrow.

"Are you okay?" Ivan asks.

"Yes." I wish my side would stop having these weird spasms.

"You sure, my love?"

"I think I need to drink some water."

"Okay. Let me wrap up here."

I slide off his lap and work through a series of overhead stretches. They don't make the pain come back. Must've been a fluke.

Wait. My brain is much worse than we thought. Am I losing more information each day? I start a mental inventory of what I know right now. Ivan's debating with Darrow and David about a hotel in Atlanta's security. Now's a chance to leave myself some reminders. I snatch a fine-tipped permanent marker from the desk and push up my long sleeves. While Ivan's talking, I scribble some things I don't want to forget on my arm then pull my sleeve back down.

"Ready?" he asks. "We need to put the glasses on fresh sim heads."

"Sure." I fish around in the air until he catches my hand.

We carried eight sim heads into the INES lab and got them hooked up to a computer he called Burt. When he was ready to turn them on, he told me not to look at the screen in case it made me panic.

I wander up the ramp for my operating platform, hand trailing the rail. Will I ever get to do surgery again? The smell of cold, sterile metal is comforting. The INES tool arms are in their beautiful silver honeycomb above me. Its console is turned off, waiting for my voice.

"Bye," I whisper, tapping the frame of the console.

The lab door slams open and a luggage cart rolls in, pushed by Richelle. She glances around before jogging to the back. "How did we miss that Story's-" she blurts. Ivan spins from Burt.

"Story's fine, Richelle," he hisses.

"No, she doesn't even-"

"Richelle she..." His voice fades. She glances in my direction while he mutters rapidly.

"Well, here's your bags. Come on. Sully's back with your new BFF's." Richelle scurries over to the platform. "Sorry. Didn't see ya, girl. You're in for quite the treat tonight."

The treat better involve a messy bun and pajamas. "Cool."

"Don't sound so enthusiastic." Ivan laughs. His boots scuff as he bounces up the platform steps. "Let's get out of this Helm before it tries to kill me again."

He laces his fingers through mine and guides me towards the ramp. I turn, looking over my shoulder at INES. My extra surgical cap covered with constellations peeks out of a drawer by the console. I yank it out of the drawer and toss it in the trash.

"Get me out of here, husband."

33

At the end of the hallway, a group of seven grizzled men with grey hair are standing at attention. They all have a similar demeanor to Ivan. Shoulders straight. Sharp eyes sweeping the area. Carrying quiet authority in their tight jaws.

"Gotta come out of my shield, baby. Keep your eyes off me," Ivan whispers.

"Senior Commander Rhys, Dr. Rhys, meet your new secure transport team," Sullivan says.

"Pleased to meet you. I'm Michael Sullivan, call me Mike." A bald man built like a bulldog steps forward and shakes our hands. His grip feels like a vice. He juts a thumb towards Sully. "He's my oldest kid. Taught him everything he knows." He grins. "Looking forward to getting to know you both a lot better."

Ivan drapes an arm across my shoulders and follows Mike and Sully. The other men fall in, surrounding us. I tuck closer to Ivan. Mike launches into a round of introductions to the PrivSec Team. They're a group of friends that retired from elite special forces units. They work for Mike's private security company now.

"When we heard IC was looking for a security team, I knew Dad's company was the one to go with," Sully says.

IC is another mystery. I shuffle along next to Ivan, eyes glued to the floor. The men talk and laugh, engaging Ivan occasionally, but I'm barely listening. Why bother trying to pay attention? I might wake up tomorrow morning and not remember it anyways.

"Story, right?" Mike asks, stepping close. I nod. "How you doin'?"

"Good."

"You seem quiet."

I nod again.

"Hopefully we can be friends," he says with a smile.

I give a quick smile. I don't need friends. I need a functioning brain.

"I heard you haven't been feeling so great lately, huh?" he asks.

Did they tell these strangers I'm pregnant? Or that my brain is broken? Either way, it's none of his business.

"You ever been to Atlanta?" he asks. Gosh, this guy is persistent.

"No, she hasn't," Ivan says. "Have you?"

"Just passed through until today. We've been at The Continental Peach since this morning setting things up for you two."

I must have slowed down, because Ivan gives me a little wake up nudge on my shoulders.

"Mike, can you go fill Richelle, Story's assistant, in on the plans?" Ivan asks.

My right ear feels like it's going to catch fire from Mike's burning stare. "Mmmkay, boss. Nice talkin' to ya Story."

Ivan kisses the top of my head. "We're going to stay in a fancy hotel. I don't want us in that Helm aside from surgeries."

"Thanks." I bump along beside him into the bright sunshine. The white and gold helicopter cuts a sharp contrast against the lush dark greens around us.

"You wanna sit by the window?" Ivan asks.

"No, you can." I crawl into the middle seat and put on the plush white restraint harness. For the short flight into the city, Ivan goes back in his shield. We watch the transition from a sea of green slopes and rugged cliffs into a grey metropolis. The city is massive. It's like other urban areas, a woven patchwork of green spaces and vibrant living walls on the buildings.

We descend towards one of the tallest buildings of the skyline. It's a copper and glass skyscraper that glows a faint peach color in the setting sun. There's a crescent-shaped piece missing from the northwest corner with a helipad on it. When we land, a bustle of activity breaks out. Mike and his team surround us in the rushing gusts of wind.

Ivan clings to me. "Feels like we're in a tornado, I love it!" His rich laughter makes me smile, but I don't think it's exciting. If anything, it makes an uncomfortable pull in my stomach to be so high.

The streets are nothing more than black pathways with cars crawling like ants. Clouds and the warm glow of a sunset make pink and orange streaks across reflective glass towers over the city sprawl.

"This is amazing!" Ivan twirls me to his other arm from pure excitement. "You scared up here, baby?"

"No."

The wind whips my curls into a frenzy, and I catch them in one hand. That's going to take forever to detangle. Mike swipes a keycard to take us into a rooftop elevator. I scurry into the corner and pull Ivan's broad back in front of me. Maybe they won't talk to me. He makes a perfect wall. The only part of me peeking out is my fingertips that I slide into his side belt loops.

"Where's Story?" someone asks.

"Back there," Mike says.

"She doesn't talk much, huh?" a PrivSec guy asks. "My wife and daughters never shut up. She should teach them her ways." He laughs, and I hear the thud of someone being punched hard in the arm.

Ivan reaches back and rests a hand on my left hip. "Good thing we're not paying your team for your conversation skills then," he says.

Mike snorts. "Eddie, shut it."

The elevator opens and they file out, forming a barrier around us.

"Welcome to the penthouse," Mike says. "Sully is on his way with your friends. They'll be here in about ten minutes."

Eddie opens the door and we're ushered into more of a palace than a hotel room. It's all clean lines and soft light. A huge wall of floor-to-ceiling windows opens to a private pool that shimmers like liquid sapphires. Leather chairs, wicker rockers, and a massive pillowy white sectional couch are all dripping with blankets in a variety of fabrics and textures. The polished wood tables and well-appointed dining area hint at sophistication. This is a place you come when you don't need to lift a finger. Is Ivan rich? I don't have money for a place like this.

"Ivan...this is..." My stomach growls.

"Would you like to eat our welcome charcuterie board on a giant swan pool float? We could relax and look out over the city," Ivan says. *But the pajamas? And the messy bun.* "No. Forget it. Dumb idea." He hoists his laptop backpack on his shoulders. At least ten bursting gift baskets sit on a huge marble island. "Hey, PrivSec guys, help yourselves to whatever you want."

"All clear. See you kids later," Mike says, appearing from a side room. His team happily tears into the gift baskets full of meats and cheeses.

I wander into a massive bedroom suite. It's got a sitting area, bed, bathroom, and a huge balcony that joins the pool area. Safe to say this is like its own mini vacation home.

Ivan comes in behind me and locks our bedroom door. "What would you like to do?"

"Eat welcome snacks on a raft in the pool." I force a smile, looking out the wall of windows. Maybe I can muster some fake happiness so Ivan won't feel like I'm a depressing cloud in this beautiful place.

He clicks his tongue and throws himself on the bed. "Shame. I'm not in the mood to do that anymore. I'm thinking we should put on comfy clothes and eat snacks until Richelle orders a dinner feast." I smile for real. "You and me?" He props up on an elbow while he's talking. It's so hard not to look at his face, but I'm keeping my hand up to block it out. "We'll stay locked in here. Richelle can slide food under the door like we're prisoners. I owe you some stories."

"In bed?" I ask.

"Obviously. I'm not moving," he says with a laugh.

"Can we float on rafts tomorrow?"

"Whatever makes you smile like that, my love. I'll do anything."

My smile nearly slips, but I keep it plastered on. I want to tell him to have an opinion. If he always goes with what I want, I'll never learn about him. I barely know what I want anymore.

"It's a date," I say.

This place is fantastic. A white satin pajama button up shirt with shorts sits on the bathroom counter. The last button was uncomfortable on my small baby bump, so I gave up and left the bottom two buttons flapped open over the shorts. Ivan said he nearly died from the cuteness.

He kept his word about our evening plans. Henri, Mai, Cherise, Richelle, Nathan, and PrivSec all hung out in the living room.

We stayed locked in our little refuge, talking for hours. Ivan set our suite's air conditioner to what had to be a few degrees above freezing, turned on the fireplace, and put on ocean sounds with classical music. I turned it loud enough to drown out the laughing party atmosphere beyond our door.

"So, the nurse in the forest clinic? Then attempted execution by The Bastion? Why does everyone keep trying to kill me when you're not around?"

"You see now why I don't want to let you out of my sight? I'm getting PTSD from people taking or hurting you."

I've put him through so much. I should take better care of him. He's laying in his shield beside me. "Your surgical dressing needs checked. Can you roll over, please?"

The bed rocks while he adjusts, then he appears facedown, resting on his arms. His dressing is sealed, clean, and dry. I'll leave it. His tan back is scattered with scars. They read like a survival manual written in flesh.

I clear my throat. "Looks really good."

He laughs. "I'm sure you mean the dressing?"

"Mmhmm." I put my fingers on the edge of a healed bullet wound on his left shoulder.

"September 2047. Tactical sim gone wrong," he says.

I trace down to another series of scars on his left ribcage.

"January 2040. One of my first battles at The Helm."

I tap two chest tube scars.

"October 2042. Elle escaped the boundary. I found her and had a stroke trying to get her back."

These scars show where life hit hard and he wasn't defeated. My wounds are fresh, but invisible. If I could just scar like him, toughen up, life wouldn't be so hard. I'd have a fresh, smooth shell to show people *I'm healed, I'm better, I survived!* They'd see it and say, "Wow, you're so tough, an inspiration!"

People don't do that when you have mental health issues like anxiety. I know it. I've seen it. A suffering person shows Herculean strength to pull themselves free from a spiral and the best some people can do is give them a dismissive smile. That icky smile. Not genuine. It has daggers behind it. A false congrats that you did what everyone else can do. Bravo to you for doing the bare minimum. I'm not even doing the minimum yet.

Dad, Richelle, David, everyone, gives me a smile that screams I'm a busted mess. They don't mean to, but it speaks louder than their words. I don't know how Ivan used to treat me. In the last few days, his is the only genuine voice I've heard. I wish I could see his face. Does he give me a pathetic smile like they do? Or does he look at me with an actual smile, like the man I've seen in pictures?

I don't blame him if he can't muster a real smile. This anxiety of mine has taken on a life of its own. It's shifted, broken my brain to the point of apathy. I want to scar. I want to get better. I want to be Ivan's Story again.

I'm tough. *I think.* I'm salvageable. *I think.* Maybe I'm not. Maybe I'll never be. If I keep getting worse, maybe I'll forget to feel sad or stressed and stay in this limbo forever. Not happy. Not sad. Not scared. Not brave. Just alive. Able to exist in moments like this with Ivan.

I stretch out beside him, putting an arm over my eyes. "Who's Elle?"

He rolls over, facing me. "Keep those eyes closed, baby. Elle was my little sister."

That hits like a punch to my gut. I cross my legs and toss them over his hip. He scoots me closer, closing the space between us.

"I'm sorry I forgot."

"You didn't forget. It was taken."

"Do you want to tell me about her?"

He sighs. "Can we have that chat on another day?"

"Of course."

"It's a terrible story. I've had my fill of sad lately, sorry."

"Nah, don't feel bad. Sorry for what I've put you through. Someone said even before the purge you had to help me with panic attacks. You deserve a wife who can be your equal partner in life. Not one who's always falling apart."

"Do you think people with anxiety are weak, my love?"

I AM. "No. People with anxiety aren't...No. But in my case, yes."

"Since you were thirteen years old, you've been pushing yourself to save Lark. Being her rock, smiling. Helping your parents. You met me. Decided I needed fixed. You helped Richelle. You saved Birdy. You're a pillar, a support for everyone in your world. Moulson saw your wonderful self, taking care of everyone, with no one to take care of you. You're the strongest link. He hit you the hardest. He took so much. Anxiety isn't from being weak. It's from being too strong, for too long. It's a chemical and physical reaction you can't control."

My face, my neck, his chest, his neck, are slick with my tears.

"Don't ever say you're weak again, my love. The strongest people—you—bear the weight, the burden. Anxiety like this? It means others need to carry the weight. Let me."

"Ivan! You made me cry!"

"I'm so sorry, I didn't mean to." He grabs tissues from somewhere.

"No! You made me cry!" I blow my nose. "I've been numb. I thought I was losing my mind even worse."

He grabs me in a hug. "So, the crying is good?"

"Very!"

"Ah. You scared me."

"Wait, one more thing. Who's Richelle?"

He freezes, lips on my collarbone. "Richelle?" I wish I could see his face. But even if I open my eyes, he'd be a faceless monster. "Richelle. Richelle is-" his voice is heavy.

I cut him off. "My cousin! I'm messin' with you."

"Story Rhys! You better get-"

He jumps up on his knees, and must have hit a lamp, something crashes into a bookcase. A chain reaction of knickknacks, vases, and books clatter to the floor.

"My bad!" he says.

We both crack up laughing. He's doing it. Ivan is scarring me up.

Someone bangs on the door. "You guys good?"

"Yeah!" Ivan yells back.

"Open the door. We need to get eyes on Story."

"No!" I call out.

"Open. The. Door!" Nathan knocks again.

Ivan sighs. "I can't be mad at them. I trained them too well." He unlocks the door and it swings open. Nathan and Richelle step in, looking around. Richelle's eyes settle on the broken glass and mess of bookcase items between the bed and wall.

I'm on my knees on the bench at the end of the bed, mostly hidden behind shirtless Ivan. I peek around his hip and smile.

"Awww! Baby bump is popping. Look, Nathan!" Richelle dances in place with excitement.

"Congrats?" Nathan looks like he's about to jump out of his skin.

"You guys hungry? The Mexican food's gone." Richelle waves for us to follow. "Mike's team is hilarious. We're playing games. We got pizza."

I flop on my side in bed. "I think I'm getting the flu. I'll be in here."

Ivan coughs. "Same."

"You poor thing," I say, forcing a frown.

"I'm outta here." Nathan nearly leaps through the door.

Richelle rolls her eyes. "You two are so antisocial. It's repellant." She waves and walks out.

Ivan locks the door behind her then dives into bed behind me. "Soooo...?"

The doorknob rattles frantically, "Story! It's Lark! Openup openup openup! I wanna see you. Dad said you're pregnant!"

"Oh, for the love," Ivan groans, dropping his head on my shoulder. "Any chance I'm imagining that?"

I can't help a small laugh. "You can stay in here. I just want to go see her for a few minutes."

"Story! Can you hear me?" Lark bangs on the door.

"I'll go too." He disappears into his shield, then leans over, caging me in with a kiss.

Lark keeps beating on the door. "Ivan! Is she asleep? Are you asleep? Open up!"

He does a fake sob on my cheek. "We're really not getting out of this, huh?"

"Come on, Invisible Ivan." I wiggle free and open the door. A white, furry rocket darts in, dancing around my feet.

"No, that dog hates-" Ivan blurts as it launches into the bed. Birdy? I assume, snarls, snaps, and mauls at something I can't see. It turns out his cloaking shield really doesn't prevent things from hurting him. "You little rat. Stop biting me, stop!"

I fold over from laughing as he makes her into a seething dog burrito. She's all teeth and growls in her duvet swaddle on the foot of the bed.

"Story!" Lark clings to my waist, hugging me. "Dad and Mom said you're having TWO babies! Why didn't you tell me?"

"I am! Don't worry, I'm working on getting your surgery approved. The babies haven't distracted me. I've missed you. How was Germany?"

"Great! Mom and I have so many pictures to show you. And I want to talk so much about the babies!"

She drags me into the living room. To my satin-clad horror, it's a full house. I plant my feet and pull back to retreat and grab more clothes, when Ivan drops a fluffy white robe onto my shoulders.

"Thank you," I whisper.

"Keep your eyes off my face," he murmurs.

Birdy sprints out of our room and paws my legs. "Hey, pup." I pick her up, mostly to keep her from biting Ivan.

She goes wild, wiggling in my arms, licking my neck and chin. She's comically tiny. "Settle down, Birdy." She keeps wagging her tail and trying to lick me, so I cuddle her tight like a toy. That soothes her hyperactive nervous system, and she snuggles into the folds of my robe.

"Hey, honey!" Dad kisses my cheek. "How are you feeling?"

"Good, thanks."

"You're good? No lie?" Mom asks, giving me a long hug that squishes the dog.

I haven't seen her since the purge. I'm sure Dad told her I lost my mind and my marriage had fallen apart. "No lie."

"I'm happy with her progress." Ivan lays an arm across my shoulders, tucking my head so I can't look at his face.

"How'd you pull this off?" Dad asks, squinting.

"Ivan's smarter than Moulson," I say.

"Yeah, but what did Ivan *do* to fix you?" Mom asks.

Conversations all stop; we're the center of attention.

"He reminded me where I belong," I say. He kisses my head, leaving his bearded chin woven with my curls.

Mom glares at Ivan. "So, you haven't actually done anything to help her. Your wife and kids need you. Do better. Why are you sitting here instead of working?"

"Amelia. I've got this," he replies.

Nathan interrupts the growing tension. "Alan, how long are you here for?"

"Not sure yet. I need to talk to Ivan," Dad says. "Can we go chat?"

Ivan nods. "As long as I can do it from right here."

"It's kind of..." Dad raises an eyebrow. "We should talk privately."

Ivan sighs. "I'll give you ten minutes. Nathan, Henri, get by Story." He leans close. "I'll be back. Love you, baby."

"Love you," I whisper back.

Nathan and Henri step to either side of me. Mike and a couple of his guys sit across from me. So much for personal space.

"No. Move. I'm sitting by my daughter," Mom snaps.

"Sorry, Henri," I say with a quiet laugh as he trudges to a new spot.

"Mom and I have so many pictures to show you," Lark says, swiping at Mom's tablet.

"Lark, that can wait a few minutes," Mom says, taking the tablet.

I'm very aware of my right side. Nathan sits by me, ramrod straight. I tuck my bathrobe along my leg to make sure no part of me touches him. Mom is squishing me on the left. Birdy is in a warm cave in my robe. Lark is on my knee. Henri's on the coffee table in front of me. Mike is opposite me in a recliner. I take a chance, flicking my eyes to find Ivan. *Where did he go, twins?*

"Story, how's pregnancy treating you?" Mom asks.

Really? In front of all these men I don't know. No thanks, Mom. There's a non-zero chance Nathan will cover his ears and hum if I start talking baby bump and ultrasound pics.

"I'd rather hear from Lark about Germany," I say, grinning at her.

Lark launches into a long explanation of what she's been learning, her favorite horses, and what their Helm is like. She and Dr. Ryland have become buddies.

"How many days left until my surgery gets approved?" she asks.

"I'll talk to the people from ASTRA and see," I tell her. Oh, that's me. I don't have the heart to tell her I took myself out of surgery.

Lark grabs the tablet from Mom and swipes to open it. "Oh cool, Mom's on my pics from the alpine coaster."

She holds her tablet about two inches from my face and rapidly flicks between pictures. "Look! We were so high, and then we rode it down to here. This place had the best pretzels and so many yummy dips."

I'm trying to follow along, but she's pausing for about half a second per picture.

"That looks so fun," I say.

"It was my favorite," she chirps.

"Look, we didn't need tickets for the coaster, they ran off QR codes." Mom taps a finger on the screen to pause it.

The pictures had been moving so fast, directly in front of my nose. Now the pause on the black and white pattern almost makes it swim in front of me.

In a nearly blinding wave, a headache crushes my skull from all sides. I look at Nathan and squint an eye.

"Hey, you okay?" he asks quietly. I lift a shoulder. The tiny motion makes me nauseous. I lean forward and hug Lark.

"You want a drink, Lark?" I ask. "I do." Not really. I'm going on a scavenger hunt for something to help my head.

"Yeah, the flight was super long." She jumps up. "Can we go swimming tonight?"

"Maybe, I'll talk to Nathan." I scoot and a little dog tumbles in the fabric of my robe. "What on earth?"

I place the little dog down and stand. My first two steps wobble.

Henri steadies me with a hand on my arm. "Story?" he asks.

"Thanks," I tell him, then turn to Nathan. "You wanna go swimming tonight with Lark and I?"

"No. Story. Again?" He lays a hand on my shoulder, fixing his eyes on mine. I love those green eyes. "Someone get the SC right now," he says softly.

Henri bolts to his feet. Mike and his men do too.

"Come on, let's get you that drink." Nathan leads me to the kitchen. Henri runs into a bedroom suite and slams the door.

Ow, my head. There's got to be a first aid kit. I open all the cabinet doors. Just tons of fancy dishes and kitchen supplies. Nothing for my head. Oh well.

"Gonna go lay down," I say, kissing my silent Nathan's cheek.

"Okay, *sweetheart?*" Why is he saying it like that? I trail a hand down his face and walk towards my room.

The little white dog sticks on my heels. This is so weird. Wait. Where in the world are we?

I freeze. This isn't our house. Or our Helm. There's a balcony. Maybe some fresh air will help. I walk to the door and slide it open. Nathan slams it shut.

"Go to bed, Story, I'll be in soon," he says.

"Nathan." I lean close to his ear. "Where are we?"

The Nuclear Option

~ Ivan ~

Alan and I are discussing the awful new update on Story's symptoms.

"Why is she worse off than the rest of them?" Alan asks.

I shrug. I'm playing it as cool as I can with Story, but inside? I'm losing it. She's worse. Why? This all seemed bad before. Now I'm filled with dread. Panic. What if it's permanent?

Henri and Mike burst through the door. Henri takes a knee in front of me. Mike clicks the door shut gently.

"Rhys," Henri hisses. "Listen. Don't go running out there, causing a whole thing. Your girl just broke again."

"She what?!" She's not even fixed yet. How can she break again? I jump to my feet and disappear in my shield.

I sprint into the living room, followed by Alan, Mike, and Henri. I'm just in time to see her kiss Nathan on the cheek then try to escape to the balcony. Thankfully, he stopped her and sent her towards the bedroom, directly in my path.

Assess her. Her eyes are dazed. That means her head hurts again. She's clearly confused about a very enthusiastic Birdy, leaping between her feet. Amelia and Lark are digging through the fridge. Mike's guys shift uncomfortably. They know something bad happened but aren't sure what.

Story steps into the master suite.

"Alan, keep an eye on her." I yank Nathan into the den by his arm. "What the heck, man?" I bark into his face.

He looks at the ceiling and sighs. "We were looking at pictures from Germany. Then she turned and I could tell she was gone."

Twice. Twice she's fallen apart with Nathan. What do I know about him? Been at the Lancaster Helm with me for eleven years. Aside from David and Josh, he's the one I've worked closest with. I consider him a good friend. He wouldn't be the first Irontrace to betray the team. Is he working with Nichols? Henri, Richelle, Mai, Cherise, Mike, and his men are gathered around us. The only voice is Richelle hurling lots of blame his way.

I interrupt Richelle. "Commander Cantone. I'm trying *really* hard to give you the benefit of the doubt. But my wife has-"

Nathan interrupts. "Ivan, knock it off. I didn't do this!"

"Been injured, on two separate occasions, in a very specific way while next to you," I finish, raising my voice over his.

"I was there too this time," Henri says.

Nathan is the factor. He was there both times. I can't take any chances. How bad will she be broken this time?

"Baracu. Voss. Take Commander Cantone into custody," I say.

"You can't be serious," Mai says flatly.

"Cherise. Once he's in custody, notify David we need an AJA." I turn to Nathan. "She *saved* you, man! If you fail that AJA interview-"

Just shut up.

Henri steps towards Nathan, pulling cuffs off his belt. "Ivan, wait! Listen." Nathan dodges Henri and grabs my arm. I yank away from him. Nothing he can say will fix this. Richelle puts an arm around my waist, and we walk towards the door.

"It's pictures!" Nathan blurts. "It has to be pictures. From Amelia. On the plane, she sent Story pictures. Now this with her tablet. It's Amelia."

Richelle whips around. "You think my Aunt Amelia did this to her own daughter? Don't blame that sweet woman!"

Nathan blinks. "I can't say it was Amelia. But both times it happened after pictures? Maybe someone has corrupted her data?"

Henri pipes up. "It might'a been a picture. They were holding that tablet like an inch from Story's face. Could you see what was on it, Cantone?"

"A German mountain coaster, tickets to it, and food. Ivan, I was watching. I would never let her get hurt. I didn't even tell her she's confused again. I can't stand to see her panic like on the plane."

Is she gonna panic again? I gotta get out of here.

"Mike and team, watch him. Henri, Cherise, Mai, get that tablet. Clone it to Lancaster Helm. I want Delac and Woods on it. Figure out what happened."

Richelle takes several shuddering breaths. "Do we have to start all over with her?" Sounds like she's about to have a panic attack of her own.

It may kill me if Story's back to square one. With the blank face that stares at nothing. The terror, the guttural screams tearing her throat.

Mike speaks up. "What exactly happened? Explain like I'm ten."

"You know the purge that broke everyone?" Mai asks. Mike's whole team nods. "Moulson hit Story with it too. He takes the person she loves the most. Ivan. One full look at him and she panics so badly that she has to get sedated and help to breathe. It's destroying their life. It makes her believe she's married to Nathan."

Mike screws up his face. I don't want to stand here anymore. I can't.

As I walk to the door, Mai adds in a whisper, "Plus, with being pregnant? I don't see how the twins will get through many more of those episodes."

We're not going to let her get like that again. Nathan's sitting there, face tilted towards the floor. I grab the cuffs he's wearing, yanking him to his feet.

"Know what? You're gonna come make sure my beautiful wife is happy." Nathan nods, rubbing his cuffed wrists together. "Henri and I are going to be in there in our shields. You do one thing that I think looks sketchy...*one,* and I'll throw you off that balcony myself."

"Rhys, don't say anything you're gonna regret," Mai says.

"Voss, it's *Story.* Nothing is off the table." I pull Nathan forward and uncuff him. "I mean it, Cantone. When we go in there, first thing you do? You go open that balcony door. Have it prepped and ready if I need to use it."

Nathan looks me straight in the eyes. "I didn't do this."

Henri and I disappear in our shields and walk in the master suite, Nathan trailing us. She's wrapped in blankets, laying on her side. Birdy is nestled by her cheek and growls softly. The sound machine is back on.

I crouch a few feet from her. She's out. I creep closer. Birdy rumbles more growls. "Good dog. Bite everyone. That's the spirit," I mutter. It works. The little dog keeps her dark eyes on me without another peep.

"Story?" I whisper. Nothing. I reach under the sheets. "Good, Birdy, keep her safe." Birdy doesn't bite my hand as I gently feel Story's radial pulse. Steady, normal rate. I lay a hand on her ribs. She's taking deep, even breaths.

"She's okay, Birdy. We'll watch her tonight." I slide in the bed behind her. Ah, I've missed this. She rolls to face me, dragging Birdy in her arms like a stuffed animal.

"Can we go?" Henri whispers in a voice just above an exhale.

"Yeah. We're fine." I pull my phone out, mute it, and turn the screen brightness as far down as it goes.

I text Henri, Mike, and David directions that Nathan is to be cuffed, fully interrogated, and to get everything they can from Amelia's tablet. Then have an AJA interrogate her as well.

David sends me a sad face. Henri sends me a thumbs up. Mike sends, *Message received, will do.*

I pull my shirt off and wrap an arm under Story's neck, pulling her close. She melts against me. Time to tuck us away in SAM.

"I've got you, baby. I love you," I whisper.

Burt has a computer code editor linked to my phone. This is a good chance to get some programming done. Every thirty minutes, a timer buzzes for me to check her vitals in the SAM dashboard. She's okay, snoozing like a champ.

I spent the next five hours coding and running it through Millenia test suites to make sure my DNA hunting program is ready to use.

A text flashes in from David. *SHOCKED you had Nathan AJA'd.*

Thrilled to report that he passed with flying colors. Amelia was an emotional wreck in hers, but that's expected. A barely passed is still a pass. Nathan was right. Photo albums had some kind of code embedded in them that held the purge program. Woods is reverse engineering it now. I'll be there soon. -Delac

By 4:07, my eyes feel like they're bleeding from staring at the tiny screen. Birdy's been between our chests the whole time. The little monster isn't so bad.

"We did it, dog!" I mouth, giving her a friendly scratch. No need to worry that Story will see me if she wakes up. I'm in my shield, inside SAM. I guess in this turducken of shields, I'm the chicken-y middle.

I've got to get some sleep. I'm picturing myself as a poultry stratum.

"Keep sleeping good." I gently press my lips to Story's forehead.

Those were the best forty-two minutes of sleep I've had in ages.

I jerk awake when Story rolls off my arm at 4:49. Pins and needles flood my finally non-compressed arm and fingers. "Gah." Flexing and wiggling them doesn't help. They're dead for now.

Story sits on the edge of the bed in the nearly dark room. She stands and stretches, rubbing her eyes when she turns on a lamp. Birdy runs through some doggy yoga of her own then hops down behind Story.

"Where did you come from?" Story's curls tumble in lovely nighttime disarray when she bends to pet her.

The faithful little dog bounces and paws at Story. She takes a couple steps toward the bathroom then stops, rubbing her stomach.

"Twinsies, what happened?" she mumbles. When did she start calling them Twinsies? That's the cutest thing I've ever heard. "My head got hit by a truck. I know you guys are okay, but oof, I do not feel good."

Stay there, baby! Let me do a sweep in the bathroom.

I dart around her and look into the huge bathroom. Ceiling and walls are fine. Shower and tub empty. Cabinets are too small for a person to hide in. I slip out. She's turned on a light and is studying her arm.

"What is this?"

I step close. When did she write on her arm? No idea how I missed this yesterday when we were together. It's her writing though. The words start a few inches below her left armpit. There are two lines of tiny, printed words.

Story <u>Rhys</u>, you LOVE <u>Ivan Rhys</u>. Moulson gave you the purge. You're not married to Nathan!

Don't trust yourself. Trust Ivan. Let him clear the fog and bring you back. Do whatever Ivan tells you.

"Ivan Rhys?" she whispers. Come on, you know me. You can do it, baby! Her lips twitch down. Cripes, she doesn't remember.

"Nathan?" She walks to the living room door and peeks out. "Dad!" She runs out and drops to her knees in front of him. "Wake up! Where are we?"

His eyes fly open and he sits up. So do several of Mike's guards. Story shrinks down by the couch. I drop her robe on her back. She looks at the ceiling like it's raining bathrobes, then rams her arms in the sleeves.

"Story, how's it going with Ivan?" Alan asks. "Did you panic?"

"What does that mean? Dad, I need to get to the INES lab. I have surgery."

"No, honey, you don't," he says gently. "Life has changed. I need you to sit and listen carefully."

Nathan wandered in from the den where he slept. While he drifted from the balcony and back in, ordering breakfast and coffee from room service, Story's eyes followed him. The second he'd glance her way she'd look at the floor or Birdy.

Alan kept talking. And talking. And talking. I'm going to fall dead asleep if he doesn't give it a rest. Mike and his men, Nathan, Richelle, my Irontrace, even David. They're all here, lounging in chairs or on the floor, backing Alan's words up.

She sat, absorbing every word. No tears. No questions. When he was done, she held her arm up, showing Alan and Richelle the writing.

"Yes, that is all fact," Alan says.

"When you let Ivan hug you, it triggered some memories. It helped a tiny bit." David hands her a tablet. "Read. Miro's team in Japan are having explosive success with a clinical trial based on touch. First paragraph. Look. The current theory on how to fix the purge started with a patient, *SR,* you. With her husband, *IR,* Ivan Rhys. Moulson must've gotten mad when this report came out and attacked you again."

She swipes fast, devouring the research paper.

"Is this Ivan person here?" she asks.

Alan looks around. "Ivan?"

"Yes," I say, from her side. She reaches a hand my way to gauge where I am. I catch it and kiss it. "Good morning, my love."

She scoffs, pulling her hand away. "Richelle, can we chat?" Richelle plops on the floor in front of her. She leans forward and they begin a volley of whispers.

Richelle knows how this went last time. I know she wants, more than anything, for Story to get better. Richelle unlocks Story's phone and points at my photo on the lock screen.

"Nathan. Ivan. Come here, please." Story shuffles Birdy to the couch and stands.

We line up in front of her.

"Husband, can I do surgery today?" She crosses her arms and stares at Nathan.

"I'm really not your husband. You have to believe us. Moulson hurt you badly. I'm sorry. So sorry," Nathan says.

"Do you think I'm capable, mentally, of surgery right now?" she asks.

He shifts between his feet. "No."

"Dad says a hug shows who I love. Would you be willing to give me a hug?"

A hug-off! This will be over in two seconds.

"Story..." He balks.

"No, that's fine." She waves a hand, dismissing him.

"Wait. I really want you to get better," he says.

"This is the craziest thing I've ever seen!" Richelle bounces in place, rubbing her hands together.

He bends forward at the waist, putting his arms behind her shoulders, giving her the weakest, saddest pats. Story grabs him in a frantic hug, tipping him to the side. She's clingy. He's floppy.

I vote we call him Cold Fish Cantone after this. I'm gonna make him a shirt or a hat with his new nickname.

Her arms drop and she raises an eyebrow. I wish it would have gone like this last time. No panic starting us off on a bad foot.

She raises her arms, twitching her fingers in a silent command for me to hurry. "Ivan. Your turn."

I'm not waiting around for her to quiz me. I'm getting my wife back. I refuse to wait days this time. Show her who she is. Who I am.

"Don't be afraid," I say gently.

She looks towards my voice, brows knit. Her squinted eyes tell me her head still hurts, but her open, curious face makes my breath catch. She's strong. So strong to take on this hunt for facts.

Her hands drop to her hips, and she juts her angry little chin my way. "I don't fear you. Don't love you. Don't know you. You're nothing to me."

"You're everything to me," I say.

"Do whatever you want. Say whatever. Hug me until your arms fall off. Just get me back into surgery."

I bite back a laugh. Ferocious Story. Ready to tear me apart to get back in the OR.

"Close your eyes. I'm coming out of my shield." She sighs but does. One arm on her upper back. One arm around her waist. She's hesitant as I shift her in my arms, bending her against me the way she likes.

She's always said how much she loves my voice. I speak low, just to her. "You can do surgery. You can do anything. You're amazing. We built INES together. It was your idea. I made it come to life. INES? It means Ivan's Nifty Excision-bot-for Story. I know, I suck at acronyms. But no one's better at loving you than me. It's okay if you can't remember. I'll help you. Trust me. *Relaxxxxxx.*"

I run my hand down her spine. Her whole body shivers. She leans into me, testing how it feels to surrender. No part of her is pulling away. If anything, she's settling in.

"Everything you touch is better because of you. I love you more than my life. It's yours. Take it. *I'm* yours." I speak into her red cloud of curls. Her shoulders drop the tension they're carrying. I take a risk and press a kiss to her cheek. "I can look at you across a room and read you. Your head hurts. I'll get you some pain meds that are safe for you and our babies." More of her settles against me. "That tough stance you were in? You did that to hide your shaking hands. You're scared. Let me take care of you. We're the real thing. Feel it in these bones." I give her ribs a soft squeeze.

She's hanging on every word. The whole room is frozen, pinning us under their stares. I scoop her up in my arms, spinning so her reaction is hidden from them.

She squeaks in surprise, grasping my neck. Her freckled cheeks burn red.

Ha! Those cheeks. That squeak. This is over. I've got the purge on the run. Time for the nuclear option—I'm gonna be a polite jerk.

"Should I put you down and retreat to sit by your other rejected husband?" I ask softly.

"Stop," she whispers.

"Oh, stop holding you?" I shift forward like I'm going to put her down. Her nails cling to my shoulder and arm.

"Don't."

"You want back in the OR?" I ask. She nods, leaning closer, ready for the secret to get back in there. "I'm your ticket there, baby. Those labs? Those robots? They're mine." She smirks at my words. "So. Play nice if you want a scalpel."

Her eyebrows shoot up over her closed eyes and her jaw sets. I did it. She's just mad enough to accept my challenge. She lays a palm on my cheek. Must be checking to make sure I've got a real face instead of the void Alan warned her about. Her fingers pause on my lips. She draws her thumb across them, then trails down my neck.

"Nice to meet you, Ivan Rhys."

"Right back at ya, Dr. Rhys." Even though she's set every nerve in me on fire, this is sufficient. I don't want to overwhelm her. Until she has a proper assessment, I'm unsure if she's more vulnerable than usual.

I won't risk taking advantage of her trust.

Shifting her up in my arms, I rest my cheek on her forehead. She presses back against me and smiles. I turn to the expectant crowd.

Hope and fear are etched on every face.

"Story? You good?" Richelle asks in a tight voice.

"Say it. What's your husband's name?" I ask.

Story clears her throat behind a rosy-lipped grin. "Ivan Rhys."

Richelle squeals, nearly choking David with an overenthusiastic hug. Birdy assumes we're under attack and darts around, looking for someone to maul.

Alan lets out a low whistle. "You've done it again, Rhys!"

"That's my second divorce this week," Nathan jokes.

"NOT how to fix the purge, but, bravo, dude." David laughs.

"Richelle, Mai. Go guard Story while she gets ready." I give Story one more kiss on the cheek before gently placing her on her feet. She takes an unsteady step. I grab her waist. "You better open those eyes before you fall. I love you."

She shakes her head and laughs, walking away.

Everyone is staring with a mix of curiosity and congrats.

"Get the docs on a videoconference. Everyone is too focused on the limbic system. I vote we look at them like retrograde amnesia patients," I tell David.

"Will do. Let's meet with them and Maseko today," David says.

"Amnesia?" Alan asks.

"We need to keep leaning on implicit memories to activate cortexes and systems to ground them. It might bring back who they are at their core," I say.

Alan's eyebrows go up. "I want to be on that call."

Amelia and Lark come out of the side hallway. "Morning!" Lark calls, catching Birdy when she runs up her legs.

"Hey, honey," Alan tells Amelia, hugging her. "Story's okay, Ivan fixed her again! It was amazing, and a little bit disturbing to watch as her dad. You could see him take down her walls and make her relax."

Amelia grabs me in a hug, sloshing my coffee all over the island. "We can't thank you enough." She went from zero to a sobbing, blubbering mess real fast. "Our girl! You brought her back!" She completely loses it, hyperventilating between sobs. "I…"

I look to Alan for help.

"Amelia, she's okay." He pulls her to his side.

Lark sits on a stool by me. "I want to go to the Atlanta Aquarium too. Did you know they have whale sharks there? Can you and Story take me with you today? Please, please, please?"

I ruffle her hair. "I'll see what we can do." When I pull my hand away, a stray hair dangles between my fingers.

If I cross this line, I can't go back. I could do all this work to fix Story, then end up dead for stealing DNA from a kid. This will work. I can get Moulson. He'll never hurt anyone again.

"I'm gonna check on Story. Later." I walk into our room, waving for Richelle and Mai to leave. Story's still in the shower. I go straight out to the balcony and inspect the hair in the bright morning sun.

One white-blonde hair, thirteen inches or so in length. Did it break off or did I get my prize? I squint. There's a club-shaped root intact on the end. Bingo. I tuck it in a glove in my backpack's med kit. I'll process it in Burt's lab once we get to The Helm. Sorry, Lark. Please don't hate me forever.

A billboard advertising a local baseball team at a stadium in front of our hotel goes black. Green letters twenty feet high scroll across the dark screen. *I didn't purge Story. I need her to save my daughter. Someone much worse than me is after your family. The purge fix is simple. Restore plasticity. Add proteins back to neurons, you dolt.*

Moulson! He didn't purge Story? Who could possibly be worse?

Keith Landon #45 pops up on the screen, smiling, with a bat swung over his shoulder.

34

Richelle wouldn't let me leave without a purge survival pep talk.

"You've been through so much. If you think something might make you happy, do it," she told me while she put my hair in double French braids. "Plus, Ivan doing that 'come back wife' trick every day? You're literally living the dream!" She tugged hard on my right braid. I grinned. "Go. Have fun with him. Ignorance is bliss or whatever, babe. Be blissful. Embrace being dumb. Just for today."

I'm trying.

When we got here, Ivan took me in a lab next door to check on glasses he's making. His voice was bright when he told me no heads caught on fire overnight. That doesn't exactly inspire confidence in his skills. Then he messed around doing something with a computer named Burt. He was quiet for that. I asked more than once if he'd left.

I listened to him fight with my dad about me scrubbing in as surgical attending. Dad insisted, nicely, that I'm too stupid now and can't be trusted. Ivan said I get to do whatever I want. I chose surgery, obviously.

Ivan seems cool. People respect him. They get quiet and lean in when he speaks. I wish I could watch him speak too. Dad and David made me promise I wouldn't touch any patients. Dr. Ryland is on deck to help if someone needs it.

There's been some kind of purge war room happening in the back part of the lab all day. They're staying far enough away so they won't interfere with the sterility of the operating platform. Ivan's in charge of it. A group of about twenty doctors, council members, and Irontrace have listened while he speaks from behind a wall of bookcases.

They unfurled a floor-to-ceiling theater screen that's about thirty feet wide. ALICE trainers from all over the world are gathered virtually.

Snippets occasionally drift my way. Ivan explained that my implicit memories aren't being blocked. He told them the first meeting had wired panic in place, making me associate him with terror. But working through it allowed me to lessen the purge symptoms. Now that we met a second time without that initial panic, I'm handling it better.

"Are you suggesting that we purge their brains again to give them a fresh start?" Councilwoman Kim asked.

A unanimous, raging chorus of *"No!"* made me jump. Good thing I don't have my hands in a patient.

"That would work though, right?" Kim insisted. "What about using the ALICEs for a partial second purge to make them into blank slates like Dr. Rhys?"

"Let me tell you this in as clear of terms as possible!" Miro shouted. "You purge their brain a second time, and who knows what chain reaction of damage that would ignite. No. We can't do that to them!"

"I want to be absolutely clear. I'd never, under any circumstances, suggest or implement a second purge," Ivan said. "Find whatever the missing piece is. We need to promote reconnections to bring them back. It's there, it has to be."

Boo. This is not making me happy!

Wylie left with our patient for recovery. I want to test my dexterity and decision-making with one of our training programs.

So now I'm actively working to ignore the purge meeting.

Where are my earbuds? I swear they should be in my bag. Shocker. Another thing I forgot. I'll use some of the old-fashioned wired ones from the patient supply cart. I snatch a pair and plug them into the charging port on my phone. My beach tunes playlist roars, blocking out the purge conversation or arguments, whatever you wanna call it.

I fly through ability tests on the surgical training simulator. Peg transfers. Knot tying. Following a precise path. Resecting only diseased tissues. Response time drills. Using mirrored arms. Navigating instruments via camera feeds.

My results pop up. *Surgeon scored higher than average on psychomotor performance, visual-spatial processing, and advanced decision-*

making under simulated intraoperative stressors.

Not good enough. Is there such a thing as a perfect score? I'm going for that.

When can babies hear music? It's never too early to share something that makes me happy. I tuck my shirt on the bow holding up my scrub pants. "Here you go," I whisper, looping a headphone in my waistband.

Hmmm, how loud? *Enjoy some Niko Moon, Twinsies. He's my favorite.*

I restart the skills simulator and get totally lost in my work. The results make me grin. *Surgeon shows mastery of advanced...*

"Better, I did better." I look around. I'm alone. This can't be right. Dad said I'm not allowed to be alone. "Twenty minutes until prep time," I mumble. Not enough time to do another sim. In moments like this, paperwork is my constant companion. I sign in on my laptop and pull my standing desk up to work on planning.

My favorite song plays. I'm humming, trying to stand still, but the happy, slow song is irresistible. I can't help swaying. I'm probably alone anyways.

Ivan's voice beside me nearly makes me throw my laptop. "You're not having my kids listen to something horrific like the news, right?"

I smile. "No. Music."

"Good. Care if I hear a sample? I'm curious if you still like the same songs."

"Only if you come out of your shield. I hate it. I wanna see you."

He clicks his tongue. "You have to obey the rules of the purge. I'll only come out if you swear not to look at my face."

"Pinky promise." I hold my left pinky out.

A broad chest in a black shirt appears in front of me. His tan finger engulfs mine.

Don't look up. Don't do it.

He steals the headphone from my waistband and puts it in his ear. Bold move, Ivan Rhys.

He starts singing along with the chorus quietly in a deep baritone. I tip my head down to hide a grin when he sings about dancing and spinning together, taking a chance on someone.

"Do you know what this song is?" I shake my head, keeping my eyes trained on his black belt buckle. "You told me this is our unofficial wedding song." He wraps an arm around my lower back. "Well...would you like to dance with me?"

I loop my arms around his waist in a sloppy semblance of a dance position. He readjusts my arms, then twirls and steps with me for the rest of the song. Impressive. We do know how to dance together.

"I like you. Quiz me on things your wife should know," I say.

"I love you. But I don't think you'll enjoy that game."

"Please?"

He spins me, then disappears into his shield. "Alright, I'll play. Who's the head of ASTRA?"

"Dunno. Tell me."

He laughs. "It's you."

"No way!"

"How long have we been married?" he asks.

"No idea."

"What's my mom's name?"

I burst out laughing. "Do they make awards for this? I really am the worst wife in the world. Can you make me a trophy or something?"

"Hey. Stop. Why are you in such a good mood?" He freezes.

I shrug, pulling on his hips. "Dance."

A song starts about how ethereal life is and he begins dancing again. "Story, I'm worried this is a new purge symptom."

"Am I not normally such a delight?"

He kisses my forehead. "Of course you are. What's the first thing you remember when you got a headache yesterday?"

"A wave of love for Nathan. It hit hard. Sorry."

"Who is Nathan to you?"

"Meh, hard to say. I have all these memories with him, jumbled up through the years. But when he talks, it's, bleh. When *you* talk? Your voice does something to me."

"Fact check, who's your husband?"

I lean back in his arms, feeling very carefree. "You. SC Ivan Rhys."

"Do you love me?"

"Not particularly. Sorry," I admit. "Are you feeling loved right now?"

"Not particularly. Sorry. How would you describe me?"

Passionate. Strong. Funny. Kind. Safe. Bearded. Magnetic. Chiseled. "Warm." I shiver closer to him.

"Would you say I'm a monster?"

"Not in my experience. Are you?"

"No, I'm not. Should you fear me?"

"No."

"Where am I sleeping tonight?"

I give him a test squeeze under the ribs. It feels perfect, like he's all mine. "You're some kind of giant snuggly bear man. Wanna sleep next to me?"

Now he laughs. "I'd love to. This was surprisingly helpful."

"Brr. Please help me find a sweatshirt." I tug on the hem of his shirt.

"Sure." He threads his fingers between mine, leading me to the lab next door. "So, you don't see me as a faceless monster?"

"No. Honestly though, I'm tempted to peek. Can't be that bad."

"It *really is that bad* when you look at me. How are you feeling? You and the babies okay?"

"My head feels fuzzy. I think I'd like to lay down after the next surgery. How are you?"

"I'm great. And yes to the nap date. We love those." He grabs a sweatshirt from his backpack and lays it on me. "Here. Hang out for a few, please."

He works from inside his shield for several minutes. "Done. Six pairs of glasses passed that round of testing. Any winners and you can try them tomorrow. Come on, cutie. You've got surgery."

Dr. Wylie did a flawless first half of the surgery on Commander Hugo.

"I'm gonna take off. We made a plan to get through this Helm faster. Dr. North and I are going home to rest for a few hours then we're coming back to do two more surgeries tonight," Dr. Ryland says. "You two good in here?"

"Absolutely," Dr. Wylie replies.

Thirty-six more hours and the first round of patients at this Helm will be done. I step into Ryland's now-vacant spot.

"Here we go. Draining veins controlled. Removing the nidus."

We continue chatting about her time growing up in Miami. She drops the center mass of the Agora onto a back table tray. My eyes lock in while she paints the protective polymer on the neural chip tendrils. They're razor sharp and can cut through nearly anything.

I stare at the live angiogram feed.

What is that?

"Dr. Wylie, do you see-" I start to ask.

INES cuts me off. "Abnormal angiogram alert." The angiogram flashes red and yellow.

"What's bleeding, INES?" she asks.

The screen zooms in and several new monitors light up with magnified angiogram and myo-hem images.

"How?" Dr. Wylie blurts. "Did I miss a neural chip tendril?"

"Looks like one of the tendrils needs more polymer. Don't pull it out!" I tell her.

She panics and yanks the whole neural chip free, flinging blood across my surgical gown and face.

Fatal error, Wylie!

I snap a sterile towel up to clean my surgical glasses. The surgical field fills with blood.

"Oh no!" Her voice shakes. "I've never...what do we..."

"You've practiced for emergencies. Go. Follow protocol," I say.

"Initiating cell salvage and blood loss protocols," INES says. Wylie stands, eyes bulging at the oozing blood.

"Wylie!"

She takes huge steps back. "Take over!"

"No! You've practiced!"

She rushes down the steps, leaving a trail of smeared blood.

I lunge forward on autopilot. "INES, I need more visuals and pressure sponges."

Blood spurts with each pulse, occluding my vision further.

"Story! Don't touch that patient!" David yells from across the room.

"You've got this, baby!" Ivan shouts.

Harsh conversations break out.

"Alan! Scrub in!" David barks.

I ignore them. Commander Hugo will be okay. I'm here.

"INES. Take over cell salvage and control the bleeding." I'm pulling the incision to the side with a small retractor, trying to get a better view. INES dabs a pair of forceps with a sponge.

"Subclavian artery injury!" I exclaim.

"Reviewed surgical footage. A neural chip tendril tore a 2.3 cm section of the subclavian artery."

I was right!

"Why was it even over there?" I mutter.

"I've killed him!" Wylie wails through sobs.

"Story, you promised you wouldn't touch patients!" David hisses.

"David, I'm not going to just watch him die," I say.

INES works fast to expand the incision. Hem-stop gel on the injured scalene and trapezius muscles slows the bleeding to drops.

"I've got the proximal end clamped. We need to find the distal injury." INES and I follow the artery until we find a healthy section. "INES! Clamp here." I take a deep breath before issuing more orders. "Clean up the blood. Adjust volume expanders by patient body weight to keep him stable."

"Yes, Dr. Rhys."

I stare between the arterial segment in my hands and what INES shows on screens. The neural chip shredded it.

"Prepare an ARTER-HEAL graft. We can't repair this. We're going to remove the damaged segment and replace it with the graft. It's going to be difficult from this angle. We'll need extension tools and cameras."

New arms whir down. "Are you suturing or should I prep to?" INES asks.

I look at my tray with an array of fine vascular sutures. "I am."

Sighs and voices murmur. "Silence!" Ivan orders.

The field is irrigated. INES cut out the unhealthy section of artery. "INES. Make as much space as you can for me on the distal end. Anchoring it now." A small piece of tissue extends from the clamps. I place a series of continuous patch sutures. "Careful." Hugo has enough problems without me tearing these fragile vessel edges. "Flush test."

Holding the unattached end of the patch up, I squirt a small flush of saline with yellow dye in. I clamp the unattached end of it and gently move the artery.

"Suture line intact. No dye run," INES says. I stare at the angiogram. Nothing came out. I roll my shoulders and stitch the other ends of the vessel to the patch. Time to test the flow.

"Story. I can take over," Dad says from my right elbow.

I shake my head. "No."

"David said-" he starts.

"Dad. You *know* I'm doing this right." I release the distal clamp. "INES, release the proximal clamp. Restore ten percent flow as a test."

"Yes, Dr. Rhys." The arm beside me quietly whirs. I freeze and stare at the angiogram.

"I'm here if you need me," Dad says.

My attention flicks between the angiogram and myo-hem images. No fresh tears. My patch is holding.

"Fifty percent flow, please, INES." No leaks. It's filling up but handling it well. Imaging looks good. "Restore normal flow." Perfect! "INES, check both arms. Compare flow and function."

"Normal blood flow, muscle, and nerve function in both arms."

"Thanks. I need monitoring on that area for the rest of surgery. Remove the arterial repair arms. Prep for muscle repairs."

"Yes, Dr. Rhys." I carefully work through any micro-repairs to the scalene, relying on the myo-hem images. "Normal muscle and nerve function per myo-hem testing," INES reports.

"Thank you. On to the intermediate muscle repairs." I silently work until we're ready to close the incision. "INES, initiate closure protocols."

Twenty minutes later, Hugo is done.

I've been in the same spot for an hour and a half. My surgical booties make a gnarly *Scrht* sound when I do a calf raise from the dried pool of blood under my feet.

"INES, call the ICU and tell them he's on Agora recovery protocols."

The room erupts in applause.

35

Back at the hotel, Ivan and I laid down for a one-hour nap. Richelle woke us up three hours later. My instincts were right. His cuddle game is unmatched. I don't recall ever sleeping that well. Ha! Doesn't mean I don't sleep like a baby next to him every night.

"It's too tight…" I complain to Richelle, inspecting my black dress with a gold zipper in the floor-length mirror.

"Well, when you got this dress for the funeral, we couldn't have guessed the twins would have popped out like this. Then we all just wore Irontrace clothes to the funeral." She hands me a pair of black wedge heels. "You look absolutely stunning, babe. I promise. No one is going to be looking at your bump."

"*You* look gorgeous," I tell her. "You never had to dress like this on the farm, that's for sure."

She looks like some beautiful creature from the ocean. Her bright blue ankle length dress has yards of flowy fabric that seem to move, even when she's still. The sequins on the fitted top half catch the light, looking like sun glinting on the waves.

A woman from the hotel salon came to give Richelle and I fresh blowouts. Her blonde hair hangs in loose, tasteful waves. My red hair is swept to one side, a gold and pearl comb holding it over my left shoulder.

"We Ross girls clean up okay. I gotta tell you, thanks so much for sticking with me through all this. Love ya," I say, linking my arm through hers.

She takes a few more pictures of us then says, "Thanks for bringing me to The Helm. The purge has been really hard on Ivan and me. David too. We love you so much. Tonight's a party though. Enjoy. Let's go blow our SC's minds."

When we walked into the living room, Lark greeted us in her flowery, flouncing dress. "You two look like princesses! I can't wait to get to the aquarium. Let's go."

David and Ivan are on the balcony with their backs to us, looking over the city. They're both in black tuxes. The view from behind him nearly knocks the wind out of me. His wall of shoulders. The cut of his jacket. His stance radiates authority.

Richelle taps on the glass and David turns towards us. Ivan blips out of sight into his shield.

Stupid purge! I want to see the way he moves, talks, and smiles.

David rushes in and whisks Richelle to his side. Whatever he's saying makes her smile and arch an eyebrow. I stand, waiting to see when Invisible Ivan will make himself known. He doesn't.

"Lark, you ready?" I smooth her long ponytail.

Maybe Ivan isn't a fan of my dress? I knew the bump looked stupid. Not enough to actually look pregnant, just bloated.

"Yes, let's go! I'll put Birdy in her crate so she doesn't get hair on your dress." Lark squeaks a toy and throws it to catch the dog's attention.

Ivan speaks from behind me. "Sorry. I saw you and needed a minute." His voice sounds weird. Shaky? "I know you don't know this, but you're new-ish to me too." He clears his throat. "I've never seen you dressed up like this. I'm astounded. Speechless. You're *so* beautiful."

My flaming red cheeks probably look delightful with my black dress. "It's too tight."

"Is it uncomfortable?" he asks.

"No. But...look. Is this burritos or babies?" I point to my abdomen.

"As long as you're comfy, I can assure you, that dress is perfection. You're radiant. The passion in your eyes, the confidence in these shoulders." He runs a hand firmly along my back. "The poise in your step, these hands that I watched save a man today. How did I ever convince you to marry me?"

I chew my lip. "I wish I could see you."

"Tomorrow. Okay? I'll put the tux back on and do a little

performance." I crack up. He tilts my chin gently in circles like he's dancing. "Gonna practice it tonight after you're asleep."

I lean up to surprise him with a kiss but miss, catching a mix of lips and beard.

"We'll work on that later." He plants a real kiss on my lips. To him? It was probably nothing. Just part of our daily habit. But that five-second kiss makes my wedge heels wobble. I catch myself on his arm. We laugh. "Don't fall."

"Your ride's here!" Mike announces.

No! Go away, people.

The Atlanta Aquarium is decked out like nothing I've ever seen. The building stands several stories tall. Dozens of drones hang in the sky around the aquarium like mechanical stars. They're projecting video of a colorful coral reef onto the aquarium's smooth concrete exterior and grounds. The middle section has words made of seaweed in a colorful shifting script, *Welcome, Ilex Corporation!*

Lark chatters beside us, asking Ivan and I about the fish species that swim along on the building.

"Speech time, SC. Need to rush." Henri bumps Ivan's shoulder.

Aquarium staff greets us and leads us through a back hallway. They're all grinning, moving in a wave around Ivan and I. PrivSec keeps them from getting too close, but they're all demanding Ivan's attention. Several people shouted thanks to him. Two women tried to talk to him and started crying. A man tried to hug Ivan. Mike restrained him. This is a weird night.

Ivan's unaffected. His left arm is draped heavily across my shoulders. The way he subtly shifts me closer several times betrays he's not on a casual walk. That arm is a shield. He's my personal guard.

At the end of the hall, he whispers, "I'll be right back. Hang out here for five minutes in SAM." He kisses my cheek, then speaks louder, "PrivSec." They snap to look at him. "Counting on you guys. Keep her safe."

A very enthusiastic man in a navy suit leads Ivan onto a stage.

"Thank you all for coming, whether in-person or virtually. I'm Dr.

Eric Griffin. Tonight, we'd like to introduce you to someone incredibly special." He stops. "My wife has been living in a purge care facility for the last several weeks. Due to the man standing beside me, my kids and I welcomed her home last night." His voice cracks. "Senior Commander Ivan Rhys has been committed to keeping you all safe since he became an Irontrace at age nine. Lately, he's worked tirelessly to find a way to reunite loved ones. As founder and CEO of the Ilex Corporation, he's done it with his optic filtering contacts."

The banner on the sign was to welcome Ivan! I thought this was just a gala to tell purge people not to give up. Turns out my husband is a very cool person. He should've told me this party is for him.

"As of right now, fifty million patients are wearing his contacts from the comfort of their homes." As Griffin speaks, screens showing videos of people hugging, waving, and having parties fill the wall behind him. Many of them are holding signs to thank Ivan. "SC Rhys, the world is indebted to you. Please. Come say a few words."

A deafening roar of applause breaks out.

"He did it!" David cheers, crushing Richelle and I in a hug.

Griffin waves Ivan to the podium.

"Good evening." Ivan's deep voice fills the room. "First, let me say, I'm so sorry for what you're going through. The purge has united the world in the worst imaginable way, through pain and through fear. We've been scared, separated, unsure. The days have been long and lonely."

Ivan's been feeling alone? A weight settles in my chest. I did that to him. Wait a minute! Screens don't make purge people panic. I push my way to Mike.

"Find me a screen! I want to see him." Mike whips to look at Henri. He gives us a thumbs up. PrivSec walls me in, pulling me through the tight crowd.

"These times are also full of hope. By trying to save someone I love very much, I've worked with a remarkable team to bring these contacts to you. If you're still out there, waiting to get back home to your family, know this: The purge may be strong, but love is stronger. *That's* what fuels my work. We won't get through because it's easy. We'll get through because we keep holding onto each other, in big and small ways. When we look back on this someday, we won't just see the pain, the fear, the hardship. We'll see how we pulled each other through and showed up every day."

Ivan! There he is. My hands fly over my mouth. I lean forward to inspect the monitor Henri parked me at. Ivan wears a soft smile. His dark eyes are kind and passionate. Tears spring to my eyes. I see his face! I'm not panicking. He pauses, a crooked smile spreading.

"To my darling wife, who's still waiting on her purge fix, hang in there, my love. Our someday will come. Have a wonderful night, my friends."

He gives a grin, but it's laced with sadness. *His face!* I love it. It lights me up. He jogs towards the edge of the stage. In a flash, he disappears when he hits the top step. He's coming for me.

"C'mon, c'mon, c'mon." I exit SAM and wait for him.

"We're heading to see the new exhibit next," Mike tells me. "Or would you rather get food?"

"Um, are you and your guys hungry?" I ask.

"We're working. We do whatever you and boss man want."

I lay a hand on his arm. "Mike, I'm so grateful to you and your team. Please find out their favorite foods. I want to throw a thank you dinner tomorrow night to show them."

"What are you showing?" Ivan asks over my shoulder. "Why no SAM, wife?" There he is! I grab into the empty air, catching a handful of tux jacket, yanking him close.

"I saw you!"

"How?" He tries to push me back to look at me, but I cling to his ribs. What if I lose him again? I won't survive. "Story, are you okay?" His voice demands an answer.

I nod fast and mumble an "mmhmm" over his heart.

"Your girl's so smart. You were up there talking, and she had me run her to a monitor. Said she wouldn't panic if she saw you on a screen. Been in this happy trance since," Mike says with a soft laugh.

"You got all those families back together. I'm so proud of you!" I say in a rush, bouncing against him in an overjoyed hug. "I got to see you. I'm happy, I'm *so* happy. I don't know you, but I miss you. I want to know you, and seeing your face?"

"The monitor was a great idea." He gives me a happy squeeze. "Sorry I didn't think of that."

"Senior Commander Rhys!" A teenager sprints through the crowd, followed by several aquarium employees. "Basketball!" the boy yells, continuing at us full speed.

Two PrivSec guys step directly in his path, lurching him to a stop. The aquarium staff grab the back of his shirt, unleashing a flurry of apologies at us, telling him how much trouble he's in.

"What's going on?" Ivan asks, shifting to tuck me under his arm.

"There's a pickup game by the new exhibit! Can you come play?"

"Leave him alone! He's not here for such-" a staff member barks. The boy's face drops.

"Never played," Ivan interrupts, sounding intrigued. "Baby, do you care if I go play with them for a few minutes?"

I care very much! Means I have to let go.

The boy grins. "You're my hero. My mom put on your contacts and came home last night. I haven't seen her in...a long time. Dad and I have been taking care of my little sister. She's sick. You wouldn't believe the look on my sister's face. Mom doesn't remember us, but she's trying. You brought my mom back, SC Rhys." He goes quiet.

"Go play basketball," I tell Ivan.

He kisses the top of my head and unbuttons his jacket. "Just for a couple minutes, I promise!" He sprints off like a big kid.

I really *like Ivan.*

To add to the excitement of the Ilex event, tonight's the debut of a new tank exhibit. It's an indoor reef with a six-hundred-foot-long viewing area.

The Atlanta Medical Hub did a random drawing to invite purge patients that were given the contacts. I sit, wearing Ivan's coat, on the end of a bench on the edge of the crowd. Mike, his PrivSec team, and our

Irontrace surround us, only letting a few people near me at a time. I've watched grinning kids cling to their parents as they wander around.

Lark happily chats with groups of purge families as they enter. She points to me, and I hear her say, "My sister has the purge."

"Did she forget her kids too?" a little girl asks.

Lark gives me an up-down look, ignoring the question. Ivan warned her not to tell anyone I'm pregnant, even though my dress is a blabbermouth. "My Uncle Ivan made those contacts for everyone. He's that tall one playing basketball in the white shirt."

"Everybody knows who Ivan is," Sara says in a *duh* voice at Lark. "My brother 'bout went crazy when he heard Irontrace were here."

"Lemme know if you want to meet Ivan," Lark says. I'm fairly sure having family in the Irontrace will rocket Lark to the top of the fourth-grade social scene.

A woman has been standing a few feet from us. "Hello, I'm Jen. You're his wife? The creator of the contacts?" she asks.

"I am."

"Did he say you've got the purge too?"

Mike and Henri step close on either side of me.

"Yeah," I say quietly.

"The contacts didn't work on you?" she asks, voice thick with sadness.

"I can't wear contacts," I reply. Henri smiles approvingly.

She frowns. "How awful, to save the world, but not your own wife. He must be heartbroken. Please tell your husband thank you."

Her eyes cross the room to where he is. I wish I could look too.

"I will. Nice to meet you, Jen. I'm glad you're home with your family."

"Lark, next group of people coming through," Richelle announces, pulling Lark to her side. "Tell Sara bye."

"How you doing, Story?" Mike asks.

Furious I'm trapped in the purge. I want to go home. Ivan's been playing basketball for thirteen minutes and it feels like seven hours.

"I'm absolutely fantastic." I'm not taking my eyes off the far-left corner of the tank. Any minute, a manta ray the size of a van should cut through the deep teal water.

"Matthew's not our only kid, you know. Our daughter is about your age."

The manta ray's back. I follow its journey the length of the tank. It looks so free, flapping gently, swooping through the water. That must feel beautiful. Nothing relying on you. No demands. To float with no worries.

It's a lie. This ray is as trapped as I am. It's in a gilded enclosure with no hope of returning home. How sad. This ray's life is ruined. I gotta stop watching this before I ruin my makeup.

"Got any parenting tips?" I ask.

"Stick together. You'll figure it out as you go. Like billions of parents before you."

"Stick to Ivan." I snort. "I'm trying. I keep getting taken from him. Any advice on that?"

"Stop lettin' your brain get purged, for a start." He laughs when my jaw drops open in protest.

A woman steps beside me and a hush falls over the room.

"Hello, Story." She sits on the bench across from me. "After today, I'm more excited than ever to work with you."

Who is this mystery woman? I look at Mike, Henri, and Richelle. They smile respectfully at her, but don't give me any clues who she is. Come on, guys! Help me out.

"Story?" she asks.

Ivan speaks from behind me. "Architect Maseko. Thrilled you could make it."

How does he do that? He's always got my back. Literally. He throws a leg over the bench and scoots against me. He must have been giving his all in the game. His chest is hot, and he's just a little out of breath.

"Hey, baby," he whispers in my ear. His breathless voice makes it sound like he called me "BB," and it's the cutest manly whisper I've ever heard.

He's your husband. Enjoy. I settle back like he's a recliner. He seems to like it and rests his chin on my shoulder.

"Hey, SC," I whisper.

Maseko continues, "You were unbelievable in surgery today. We've never seen anything like that in real life. All the council members and docs I've talked to have been saying the same thing on repeat. Why did we ever take patient care from humans? You're single-handedly return-ing the future of healthcare to human hands."

Is she serious right now? I shrink back onto Ivan. "She's right," he murmurs.

"Thank you," I manage to say. "Have we discussed where you see me taking the future of ASTRA?"

She perks up. "No. What do you see for it?"

Curse you, Story! Why on earth would I ask that before putting any thought into it? Ivan loops an arm around my waist and rests it like a shield across my lower stomach.

Ivan! Ivan made INES. It's cool. More INES?

"Robot's advanced tools in the hands of a skilled human? That's the sweet spot we need to chase. Speed and precision of the bots, coupled with reasoning and compassion from human surgeons. You've heard complaints from people for years. Amputations they weren't consulted on. Consent is a checkbox to ASTRA, not a conversation. Also, it's no-torious for choosing second-best surgical approaches to shave seven minutes off the surgery time." I can't tell from her furrowed brows if she likes what I'm saying, but I keep going, "I vote we build off INES and create robots to assist human surgeons for each surgery practice."

I drop my arm across Ivan's. Talk about human connection. Pretty sure he's holding me up more than my spine is at this point.

"Excellent. Assemble whatever team you want to get that done. I want you in the office full time ASAP," Maseko says.

Ick. No. "I'd like to keep doing surgery."

Her eyes flick to my stomach. "You sure about that?"

Ivan must have seen it too. The way he puts his other arm around me turns him into a protective cage.

"I'm sure," I say. "I wouldn't have these ideas if I wasn't in the OR, learning. Experience is the best teacher."

"When I offered the job to you, I said you could make your schedule. I thought you'd be in an office. Focused. Not in the OR."

Just when I was getting excited about the possibility of leading AS-TRA. Now she wants me to change my whole life.

"I have to spend at least half my time in the OR."

She taps her chin, making a gorgeous stack of gold bracelets rattle softly. "Dr. Rhys. We appointed you for your ideas. To be the face of a fresh, young approach to ASTRA. We didn't hire you to continue cutting people open. You'll have a much bigger impact in the role I've defined for you. Don't mess this up."

"You've given me a lot to think about," I tell her. Maybe that will buy me time to think.

"So, I'll see you in London on September twenty-second to get your office set up?" she asks.

"London!" Ivan blurts. "Next week?"

"Yes. That's where ASTRA will run from for the next fiscal year."

"This isn't a remote role?" I ask.

"It is. From your home residence in London. Is that a problem?"

I've got to have freedom to be where Lark needs me. "I'm not moving to London. At least half of my time will continue to be spent operating."

"I see you've put a lot of thought into what your role looks like." She looks at something above my head and makes a gesture, sweeping her hand. Her guards fan out in a large circle, forcing the crowd away from us. After a glance around the now empty area, she goes on, "It's a shame you're hiding things. It'd be a good start if you finally admit you're going to require...family leave, we'll call it."

I nearly scream. Ivan tightens around me. "*If* Story would require such leave, I'd like to know how you obtained that information?"

A half-smile pulls her lip up on the right.

"It's part of an ongoing investigation we're working." Ivan snaps his fingers. David looks up, and Ivan waves him over.

Maseko's eyes drift to the Irontrace assembling around her. If it comes down to it, I'm not sure if Maseko and her guards or the Irontrace would rank higher.

"My mom was a midwife before the war." She leans forward, speaking fast. "She passed her gifts on to me. I can practically smell the hormone shift. Glowing cheeks. You can't keep your hands away from your stomach. It's natural. That instinct there's something precious there. But that behavior draws attention. Ivan's always got his massive paws all over. It's practically a flashing billboard."

"How long have you known?" I ask.

"Our first Project Ilex meeting."

I tap Ivan's hand for help. "So, you've known about this nearly as long as we have?" he asks. Maseko nods.

"Do you see this as a weakness?" I ask.

She leans forward and lays a hand on my knee. "I'm really trying to help you out here. We could be great friends."

Her words sound wrapped in a warning.

"Friends," I say.

She leans forward and smiles. "Now, tell me when you're due to have that baby."

David holds up a hand. "I'd like you to go have an interrogation by the aquarium AJA. Cantone, Baracu, please escort Maseko."

"You're joking," she says, shooting a glare at Nathan as he slides to her side.

"I don't joke about the safety of my people," David says tersely.

Her eyes burn at Ivan over my shoulder. "They're wrong."

"I trust an AJA about as far as Story could throw one," Ivan says, and I scoff. "I want to interview you myself, right now."

Oblivious, happy purge patients dart around the tank viewing area with their kids. The PrivSec team and Maseko's guards make a solid wall of bodies around us. No one speaks, waiting on Maseko's response.

"Bring it on," she says.

The focus narrows to her and Ivan's game of verbal ping pong.

"Are you aware a bomb was sent to our apartment?"

"Yes."

"Did you send it?"

"No."

"Do you know who sent it, or have even the foggiest idea of who did?"

"No."

"Have you had eyes on Story's lab work?"

"No."

"You want to know when she's due for the *baby*?"

"Yes, I want to know for staffing purposes." Maseko narrows her eyes.

"Has anyone on your team expressed a particular interest in my wife or her affairs?"

"Every one of my guards has an interest in Story." Ivan tenses at her words. "She's been a huge point of discussion with my inner circle. We had to vet her. But I'm not as touchy with my guys as you are. We aren't a family. If I found out any of them did something to hurt her? I'd push that final med myself. No AJA needed."

"Harsh," Ivan says.

"Don't you want harsh people in your corner to protect Story?" she asks.

"I do. Are you worried pregnancy will affect her job?"

"No, that's why I agreed to the short-term disability clause you attached. Clever."

Ivan sighs, puffing my curls.

"Maseko's in the clear, David. She doesn't know about the twins." Maseko's eyes go wide. "I really want to know who got those labs from Alan's computer."

"Twins? You two are in for it." She laughs. "I'll see what I can do about the labs. Consider this my official congrats. This was a productive chat. Also, Ivan. Extraordinary work with the contacts. Don't stop. Figure out the next step. Fix the purge for real." She stands, smoothing her skirt.

"I will, good night," he says.

Her guards silently engulf her in a wall of khaki. Ivan moves to stand. I clamp my arms on his, stopping him.

"Wait. Do you want to move to London?" I whisper.

"Do you?"

No! I want to fix Lark. I want to watch the babies grow up on a mini farm in Ohio. I want my identity back. My memories. For people to stop looking at me like I'm not a real person anymore.

"What would your Story want to do?"

"You *are* my Story." *Good answer, hubby.* "I think you'd want your family to stay together. Whatever that looks like, you'd make it happen."

Lark's running along the tank wall with a group of kids, chasing a loggerhead sea turtle. Yes. I want my family to be together. That sounds right.

"Hmm. Looks like you do know me," I say.

He turns on SAM then piles my curls over my right shoulder. He trails several kisses along my neck. My thoughts scatter.

"Sure do. Right now? You're hungry."

I nod, his beard brushing my neck. "Starving."

A happy rumble vibrates through his chest into my back. Whatever kind of electric power he has over the purge makes his growl feel like an unspoken "I love you."

He shuts SAM off then untangles his arms from mine. "Let's go get some dinner."

I frown. For the walk to the cafeteria Lark chatters nonstop to Ivan about the aquarium. I only catch a bit of what they're saying. Most of my thoughts are on Ivan, wondering when we'll get a moment that's just ours.

In the cafeteria, there's a catered array of international foods. Each section is divided by a mascot dressed as an ocean animal. Cartoony sea creature cutouts drip from everything.

"Hey, purge people, sorry your brain broke and your family is now your worst nightmare, can we offer you a lobster crown?" Richelle jokes.

"Like a lobster crown could actually help?" I drop a whale shark crown on my head. "Maybe a whale shark is the fix?" I spin towards Ivan.

He snaps a hand over my eyes. "Story! Don't test the purge!"

I laugh and pull his hand down. "I don't know what you like to eat, Ivan, sorry."

"I'll eat anything, seriously. Lead the way."

There's an Indian food table that smells divine.

"Is this okay?" I look at Richelle and she makes a weird fast nod, looking very much like a bobblehead toy.

"Sounds great," Ivan says.

An event volunteer stares at Ivan with fangirl eyes while she loads a plate full of some kind of red-sauced chicken, rice, veggies, and pita for me. He orders a vegetarian dish. I'm surprised he's built that wall of a body with only veggies.

We settle in at a table, and a group of teens approach us. They unleash nonstop questions at Henri, Nathan, and David.

The food tastes as good as it smells. I don't want Ivan to go back in his shield, so I'm keeping my eyes down. Everyone else is talking and laughing. Every time I peek over, Ivan's moving food around his plate, not really eating.

I lean my shoulder against his. "Aren't you going to eat?"

"I am. How does your food taste?" he asks.

"Great, thanks."

"Purge Story is more adventurous than the real Story, huh, Ivan?" Richelle asks, tearing off a chunk of pita and dipping it in the vibrant sauce on my plate.

"Purge Story is the real Story, Richelle," he snaps.

Aww, thanks, Ivan.

"What's that mean, Richelle?" I ask.

"She means that you're typically a picky eater," Ivan says.

That's news to me. "Really?"

"You brought me chicken and noodles when I got the injury that left this scar on my face. You transferred every single shred of chicken onto my plate from yours." I wish I could remember what he's talking about. "You filled up on noodles and salad that day."

"Aren't you a vegetarian?" I point to his plate.

"Not even close. I got this as a backup meal for you."

"Here, take the rest of mine. I'm full," I say.

"No. You eat."

"I'm full!" I dump my plate onto his.

"Wife, eat." He laughs and dumps it back on mine.

I stab a couple chunks of chicken on my fork and aim it towards his head. "If I could look at you without dying, I'd shove this in your mouth. Now, eat!"

He pushes the fork towards my mouth, "You eat it."

I lean back, pushing the fork at him. "Eat it, Rhys!"

He disappears into his shield and pulls me against his chest. "No! Open that little mouth, Rhys," he orders. I don't. I hide my mouth against his chest. "Right now!"

We're both laughing hysterically. I'm working so hard to avoid the fork it knocks my hair comb loose, springing my curls free.

"Would you two knock it off before someone gets a fork to the eye?" Richelle tries to scold us, but she's laughing too.

All our Irontrace and PrivSec have turned to us. We must be causing quite a commotion. A lady in a café uniform places two full plates of the chicken dish on the table in front of us.

"Ah...wow, thank you," Ivan says, clearing his throat.

The woman goes pale at the voice coming from his seemingly empty seat.

"Sorry, that's just an Irontrace," I tell her.

She raises an eyebrow, not taking her eyes off his seat. He flashes into view. Her hand flies to her chest. "Hi, hello, uh, Mr. Contacts Guy." She turns and scurries away.

We all crack up.

"Gosh, Ivan, settle down," I say behind a grin while I fight my hair back into its comb.

"I can't around you," he whispers, taking the hair comb and pinning my curls back. "Let's eat real quick, then we'll go hang with more purge victims for a bit."

More people in our space. Just what I wanted...

Poor guy. Every time he starts eating, a new purge family approaches to tell him thank you. He stands to shake hands with each of them, hear the story, and take pictures with those who asked. I hid in SAM.

A voice broadcasts through the loudspeakers, "The Aquarium event will close in thirty minutes."

Ivan wraps an arm around my shoulders and peeks at the line that's formed around the cafeteria of families waiting to talk to him.

"There's so many of them, Story."

"They want to tell you thank you," I say. "Look how happy they are. You did that. Go. Talk to your fans."

"PrivSec," he says. They all look at us. "I want Story to meet them too. Can you please go ahead and behind? Turn on a dead spot. Make sure no one films her or broadcasts anything."

"Yes, boss." Mike nods. "Fan out, guys."

We met so many victims. Ivan's contacts shut down their panic. Grateful families shed happy, hicuppy tears while thanking him. Sad groans broke out when the aquarium staff dimmed the lights and told us it was time to go. I nearly jumped for joy. Hotel time with Ivan away from these people? Yes, please. I'm ready to have him all to myself.

The lobby has a huge line to exit so we took some time to explore touch tanks and smaller exhibits. Neither of us let go on our walk. There was a quiet heat connecting us and I wasn't going to miss out on a second of it. If my memory never comes back, I know I can be happy, genuinely happy, with him. We can start fresh from here and be fine.

Lark sprints up with her face glowing. "Story! The aquarium doctor person said we get to go to the gift shop once everyone is gone and get whatever we want! Can we go?"

"Of course. Go tell Mom." Before I can finish speaking, she's running flat out towards my parents.

"I'm glad she's had a good day," Ivan says.

"Me too. I had a good day too. I learned something today. You're a really good person." I bump into his chest as we walk into the glass topped lobby. Fake constellations project onto the ceiling and twinkle like we're under the Milky Way.

"You are too."

I want to go home. But I want to stay here. I've never been so conflicted. Today has been like some kind of emotional oasis in the desert of the purge. It's given me strength to keep going.

"Ivan. I'm terrified to go to sleep."

"Why?" He stops and turns SAM on.

"Because I love you."

He rests his hand on the back of my neck. "I love you too."

"If I already love you this much in one day, imagine how much I could love you if I stopped forgetting. What if I wake up and I don't remember you?"

"I'll bring you back."

"Promise?"

With the fake stars twinkling above us, he leans in and reminds me as only he can that for now, I'm here with him and very much in love.

And that's enough.

sudo rm -rf ~

~ Ivan ~

I couldn't lie to Story. If she gets purged again, and tonight goes badly, I won't be there to bring her back.

It's been a day of waiting. They're coming for me. I used Burt for something stupid. It's what I had to do to protect my family. So, I don't particularly care. I'm worried about how she'll react when I get arrested.

I told David when I give him the signal, he's to get Story out of here, fast. He better not try anything stupid to protect me. I met with Nathan and told him he's to take care of her if she gets a purge reset again. He complained, but he ultimately agreed.

There's a tiny chance the brazen stupidity of my stunt is enough to make it come full circle and I won't be in too much trouble. It was a stroke of genius to do it the day my contacts were released. I might be the world's favorite person right now. Executing me would be heavily frowned upon.

Story looks happy. She's laughing, playful, touchy. She's not holding back or scared. Our perfect moment under the fake stars was interrupted when I saw them come in. Behind Story, I saw David whip toward the group of AJA arrest units with aquarium security guards.

I pulled back and wrapped my tuxedo coat tighter around her shoulders. "Can you run with Lark and Richelle to the gift shop? Look for some cute baby stuff. Fish socks or a whale blanket to match your crown?"

"Okay." She gives a content, rosy-lipped smile.

"I have to run with Henri to do something. If he takes a long time, go back to the hotel with our Irontrace and PrivSec, okay?"

Her smile drops. "No."

"You have to, just for a bit, okay?"

"Please. No. I want to stay with you."

Run. Take her. Have Sully fly us away. David, Richelle, and Lark appear at my side. Running would be the coward's way out. If I can pull this off, the whole world will be safer in about an hour.

"Baby, I need you to go with David now, please."

Fear and worry make her look much younger than she is. She's so strong and wise for her age. But right now? She looks small and scared.

"I really do love you, you know," she says.

"I love you more." I kiss her forehead and take off in a silent jog. Richelle wraps an arm over Story's shoulders. She turns her head, trying to see me, but I'm in my shield.

Keep going. I have to draw them away from her. I run to meet the AJAs before they can sound an alarm for a search. I lean against a wall, projecting calm. David shuts the gift shop doors and tips his chin at me. I'm about a foot from one of AJAs human escorts. The man nearly screams when I flash out of my shield.

His face hardens and he grabs my arm. "Senior Commander Rhys, we need you to come with us."

"Why?" I ask, giving him my most charming smile.

"We'll explain in the security office."

We walk out of the viewing area and another guy that's at least a foot shorter than me puts a hand on my chest. "Extend your arms for cuffs, please."

"Why?"

He tilts his head. "SC Rhys, we're aware of the advanced tactical training you've had. Maseko said this will keep everyone safer."

Mirror him. I tilt my head. AJA doesn't have normal cuffs. They have built in electro-inhibitors. Try to break your thumb and escape? You'll be shocked until you're reduced to a blob, foaming at the mouth. If you withstand the shocks and keep fighting? Spikes come out to punish you.

"Will do, boss man." I hold my wrists in front of me. It's hard not to rip the cuffs out of his hands, but I know I'm in enough trouble already.

The cuffs snap shut. He grins. "Ready."

A dozen ways to wipe that grin off his face run through my mind. I smile down at him.

They lead me along the west wall of the lobby. On the left is a souvenir-making area attached to the gift shop. It's a collection of photo booths, coin press machines, and various medallions to purchase.

Lark! Shoot! She's coming out of a photo booth.

"Turn on my shield, please?" I ask the guards around me.

"Not happening," short man hisses.

"Now!" I bark. The cuffs are magnetized to my belt buckle. I can't shift my hands enough to hit the button and turn it on.

"SC Rhys. Knock it off!" an AJA barks. I crouch and tilt my head away from the souvenir alcove.

"Hi, Ivan!" Lark yells. I crouch more. Story turns towards me. I whip my face away so fast I nearly tore something in my neck.

"Turn on my shield. NOW!" I order, trying to run in a low crouch to make it into the hallway. The AJAs and officers press tightly against me.

"Rhys. We'll happily use force if you don't walk normally," the warthog man says.

I could fight the cuffs and get shocked, then cut. But those cuts go *deep.* "I have to avoid letting my face be seen by a person of interest to our seven o'clock."

Kinda. They don't need to know the full story of Story.

"Unlock the office, Cramer," the short jerk-face says.

I stay leaned down; head tilted to the side. I can't go without making sure Story's okay. Keeping my face hidden between chests and AJA pieces, I sneak a one second look behind me. I catch her side profile. She's holding Lark's hand, looking up at a live stream of an alligator pond.

"Didn't see me," I breathe as they lead me into the office.

Focus. Get out of here. Story will be waiting at the hotel.

Loose lips shorty gave a vital detail away. Maseko's involved in this. If she's involved, I *should* be fine. The tricks come easily to seem trustworthy.

Relaxed posture. Feet grounded. Don't shift or fidget. Lean just enough forward to look engaged. Keep my hands still in the cuffs. Natural, small smiles only. Eyes soft. Slow nods to signal active listening. Keep my breathing even.

I've taught AJA what to flag people for. I'll be fine. Well, I'm like ninety-seven percent sure I'll be fine. They've got six arrest AJAs trained on me.

Someone is freaked out. One arrest AJA is beyond normal human capacity to subdue. Six? Total overkill.

If I think about how Story's doing, my heart rate will go up. I lean back in my chair. There's a fish border going around the room. The acrylic painted fish are kinda unprofessional. It doesn't really scream *you're in trouble* if they bring you in here. Granted, this room is probably only used as a holding spot for lost kids until they can find their parents.

The fish aren't so bad, I guess. I'd want Huck and Holly to see goofy fish and smile if they were lost and missing us.

Finally, the door opens and the short lil muffin man comes in.

"SC Rhys, thanks for your patience." He sits across from me.

"Anytime, bud. What can I do for you?"

"Begin the interrogation," he says. A wall panel slides out of the way, revealing an AJA interrogation model.

"SC Rhys. Please state your full name," the AJA says.

"Ivan Rhys."

"No middle name?"

I shrug, smiling. "Not officially. My wife calls me Ivan Nicholas Rhys when I'm being annoying."

"Why are you here today?"

"I'm Founder and CEO of Ilex Corporation. You know, the one I made the contacts under? To save the world and reunite a billion purge victims with their families."

Shorty scoffs so hard he coughs. It's a gross, wet sound.

"No, why are you in this interrogation?" the AJA presses.

"Oh. No clue. Why am I here?"

"You haven't done any recent work involving air quality AI models?"

"I have for sure."

"Why?"

Stay relaxed. Keep eye contact, but don't stare it down. Pretend you're talking to a very dumb person. "I was looking for Anthony Moulson. I found him, by the way. Could you please let Maseko know?"

Shorty turns flaming red. I'm seriously worried about this dude's blood pressure. He looks like a fire hydrant.

"You!" He jabs a finger my way.

"It's okay if she doesn't answer. I've already made sure a press release goes out in..." I struggle to look at my watch, "thirteen minutes. It details The Bastion being made aware of his precise location, how I found him, and how we can keep eyes on him. You know, lots of stuff that will make me famous for saving the world yet again."

I give what Story calls my cocky grin. The blood drains from Shorty's face. He's really got something going on with his cardiovascular system. Crimson to ivory in less than ten seconds? That can't be a sign of good heart health.

"Sir, do you need a doctor? My wife's an *excellent* physician."

The door swings open and Maseko walks in. The lady is the picture of poise and grace typically. Right now, she's shaky, eyes darting, breathing too fast. I need to give her some lessons on being cool under pressure.

"Turn the AJAs off." She sits across from me. "Rhys. What'd you do?"

"Found Moulson. You're welcome."

She pinches the bridge of her nose. "Good j...Excellent job. You sure did. I sent units to pick him up. He was camping out in a nowhere town.

Luray, Ohio. Near an old data center. Sucking up the remnants left behind by a huge cloud provider that was taken over years ago."

"What's wrong?" I ask, shifting forward.

"You used DNA. We *don't* use DNA." She stabs at the table with a perfect, turquoise gel nail.

"We *haven't* used DNA," I say. "And look where it got us? How many patients are in the ICU from cardiac complications due to his purge?" She doesn't answer. "Upwards of four thousand now. They can't even try the contacts in their condition. Is that okay with you?"

"Of course not!"

"Remember those men that died, trying to visit their wives?" She nods at my reminders. "How many do we have now with non-epileptic seizure activity?"

"Guards." She points to shorty the fireplug, "And you. Out. All of you, out." One of her guards hesitates. "Out!"

They leave.

"Do you have a SAM on you?" she asks.

I narrow my eyes. "Nope."

"Shame. We'll use mine. It's similar." She walks to the door and opens it. "Delac. Baracu. Darke. Come in."

None of their faces have two eyebrows. Just one angry line of eyebrows joined together on their foreheads. Freaky. They flop into chairs around me. Baracu's knee bounces like a small earthquake. David's about to chew a hole through his cheek.

"Where's Story?" I lurch, stopped by my cuffs.

"With her other husband," David mutters.

"We're in my shield now. Why? Rhys? WHYYYYY?" Maseko nearly launches herself across the table at me. "You...you had better spend some time on your knees thanking whatever you believe in that I'm on your side."

"For what?"

"Your little DNA sniffer program? Did you even *think* to check and see who his relatives are?"

"Of course I did. But I haven't had a chance to see the result yet."

I know it won't show Lark. I had her hair loaded, ready to go for a DNA analysis. Then a crisis of conscience hit. I couldn't do it. She's like my little sister. I'm grateful to have a real family. I checked and the DNA database had Moulson in there from his Columbus arrest. All I had to do was edit my program to find him from the Columbus DNA swab. I'm sure that's what got me in trouble.

It was quite the tradeoff. Running her DNA with that hair through my sniffer would have kept my hunt in phantom-mode. Checking the Columbus database left a blaring trail pointing right at me. I built this audit trail into their system as a safeguard.

I didn't expect to get myself arrested someday.

While I was in there messing around, I removed the key linking him to Lark. She's free from him, at least from a data viewpoint. I got to throw her hair away with a clean conscience. My code edits took up so much time I didn't have time to see if anyone else popped up.

David knees me in the thigh with his patella like it's a bayonet. "Ivan, stay calm."

"Let me guess, he's my real dad. That'd be a riot." I laugh dryly.

"You're having twins? Twins typically run in families," Maseko says. "Does anyone in your life remind you of Moulson?"

I look at David. His eyebrows got worse. Think. "No one at The Helm. Alan's not his twin. He'd have killed him in the womb. No council members seem similar. But?" Something is nagging me. Who's around Moulson's age?

Faces and bodies flash through my mind like a movie. Jaws? Eyebrows? Noses? Posture?

My jaw drops.

Amelia! She's got the same chin. The catlike way she moves reminds me of how he slinks around. Story is Moulson's niece? Our kids will have shown up in the DNA database, linked to him.

Is this part of the reason Lark ended up with Amelia and Alan? Moulson had to have orchestrated it. That's why she let him in Lark's ICU room. Alan. My friend. My father-in-law. There's no way he knows. That man is goodness in human form. This will break his heart.

"Where is Story?" I slam the cuffs on the table like an idiot. An immediate shock jolts my forearms. Stars flash across my vision.

Henri leaps to my side and unfastens the cuffs. He speaks evenly, laying a hand on my knee. "Mike and PrivSec are lookin' for Amelia. Funny thing. Maseko said the DNA result came in at 2302. Last time we've seen Amelia on any surveillance? 2304, in the gift shop. Lark's fine. Sully brought in Rosa. She's with her now." Mom's got Lark. That's a relief. Rosa's practically a nuke with all the weapons I've shoved in her over the years. "We put Rosa in protect and defend mode."

"Story needs more than just Nathan!" I yank on the doorknob.

"She's also got Cherise, Mai, and Alan," David says.

"Have you told her yet?" I ask. The door's locked. I rip its control panel off the wall and start fiddling with the wires to spring it open.

"No. And we're not going to," Maseko says. "Sit down. We have a couple more things to talk about before you're allowed to leave."

"David. Go watch Story. If I'm not there, you need to be," I say.

"I will soon." He puts a hand on my shoulder and squeezes a pressure point like a jerk.

"Talk fast," I say, twisting away from him.

"Thank you for finding Moulson. You used DNA," Maseko waves a hand, "at this point, The Bastion doesn't care. You need to be glad I'm the Architect right now. I'm your ally. I still believe in The Bastion. In the Kernel. In the Irontrace. I want Project Ilex to help me fix it. We can't do that without trust. You should've trusted me."

I stare at her. I have to get to Story. If her mom gets to her again and breaks her worse while I'm trapped in here...

"Again. Thank you for finding Moulson. I didn't get to be voted in as Architect by being bad at engineering and data management. I personally erased all connections in the WW_DNA_DB to your family. No one will ever know. Story is no longer his niece in the DB. When you ran Moulson's DNA, it created a key to attach your kids to him as a relative. I made sure that link no longer exists."

"I checked. She did," David confirms.

"We have Moulson in custody. He promises to cooperate but says only if he gets to talk to you first," Maseko says.

I huff. "Let me guess, you told him yes?"

She twists her lips and nods. "I did."

"Five minutes. Then you have to let me go to Story. Deal?"

"Thank you." Maseko opens a tablet and rolls her chair to my side.

Moulson. There he is. Sitting at an interrogation table, much like the one I'm at. The room narrows to just him and me. No one else speaks.

"Ivan," he grins. "How's your lovely wife?"

I crack Maseko's tablet in half. Glass and plastic rains onto my lap.

"Ivan! Settle down!" David roars. "I'm so sorry, Architect Maseko." He pulls out another tablet. "After working with Ivan all these years, I came prepared with a backup."

"He has no right to ask how she is!" I throw the chunks of tablet at the fish border so hard it dents the drywall.

"The faster you shut up and get this done, the faster you get out of here," David says. "I'm joining the feed with him again. Behave."

Behave, seriously? That's what he's going with. I'm starting to think maybe Moulson has bribed David too.

"Why? Why do I have to do this? He's insane. It doesn't matter what he has to say." My fingers twitch to break David's shiny new tablet.

"He said there are things he has to tell you before he'll talk to AJA. He's been sitting there silent, no matter what we do," Maseko says. "We're going to try this again. Please. Help us."

David props the tablet in front of me.

Moulson grins at me from the screen. "You're back! I know you've been dying to talk to me."

"I've been dying to introduce you to an AJA. They've got a shot for you."

"You're in a bad mood today, Ivan."

"Maseko, I'm done." I turn from the tablet.

She mouths, "Talk."

"Rhys," Moulson says. "You need to keep Story safer."

My eyes nearly pop from their sockets.

"Let me tell you what I mean. This goes way back. There's no official record of it, but Amelia and I were abducted when we were fourteen. She was never the same. Once we returned home, life was a fiasco. One by one, things began, shall we say...coming to a depressing end on our property. I didn't want to blame Amelia. She'd been through the unimaginable. After a particularly sad morning discovery in our chicken coop, I couldn't stay silent anymore."

"No. Amelia's maiden name is Taylor," I say. This is some power trip he's dragging me along for.

"It is. Anthony *Taylor* was wiped from existence anywhere that matters by The Bastion. Same as the Irontrace. Ivan Rhys. David Delac. Henri Baracu. We were all phantoms, removed from the pages of history by our fearless leaders. Until you went on the news about Irontrace."

I hate to admit it, but he's right.

"When I went to my parents, they suspected the same things I did. They confronted her. She exploded. When I got to school the next morning, school resource officers were waiting for me. They'd discovered things on my computer that I lacked the skills to do. I was sent to a juvenile detention center. Amelia had done it. I tried to tell them. She came to see me on family visiting day and threatened our parents if I told anyone."

"*Amelia!?* Seriously?" She had me fooled. Maybe this is a trick too. I wouldn't put it past him. He ignores me, lost in his memories.

"While in the JDC, they found I was good with computers. They sent me to a national tech institute. That's where I met the team I built the original Kernel with. A real messed up group of people. That's why I've never believed in it. They used desperate, scary people to build it, then handed it off to people who didn't understand its power. Giving it to the Irontrace was the only hope to keep the world safe."

I'm not listening to this anymore. I scoot my chair to stand.

"Wait," Maseko says.

"Speaking of safe." He glares into the camera. "I've kept a very close eye on Story since she was born. I had to make sure Amelia kept her venom from affecting that girl. I did *NOT* purge Story. Yes, I built the purge, I admit that. You're welcome for the confession, Maseko. Amelia twisted it. Made it worse, then hit Story with it to get to you. When she found out about the twins, she became desperate to remove you from Story's life. The bomb. Replacing you with Nathan. She knew you'd try to save Darke from that ALICE. The gas. She will not stop while you're still standing. Guarantee she thinks the twins are some weird do-over she wants to control."

"I'll never let that happen," I say.

Moulson's lips draw in a tight line. "And that's exactly why she wants you out of the way. Story will be putty in her hands."

"This doesn't make any sense. You knew your sister was like this?" I ask and he nods. "Surely, you've known all these years she had Lark."

"When Lark completely disappeared, I assumed Amelia had her. I reached out. Amelia promised to keep Lark safe. She has. She's got an odd loyalty directed my way since she ruined my life. Immediate target on the back of anyone who works against me. She'll get you. If not now, someday. Watch yourself. Watch Story. Nothing is off limits to her."

"How do you suggest we handle Amelia?" I ask.

He smiles like he knows how this is going to end. "You can't *handle* Amelia. If the world was scared of me? It should be terrified of her."

"Why are you telling me this?"

"Cover your ears, Maseko, lest what I say shock you," he says. Maseko doesn't move. "Ivan. I trust you. Do the right thing. Bastion, The Kernel. They have to be brought down. If you won't do it, Amelia will."

I'm mentally reviewing every interaction I've had with Amelia these last few months. Yeah, she's a very emotional person about her kids. But she's the definition of a meek housewife, dedicated to her family.

"Please tell Story I'm proud of her. The things she's done with AS-TRA, INES. I think if the world wouldn't have wounded Amelia, she'd have been like Story." Moulson cracks. He finally seems real. "You? Safe to say I dislike you to my core. But Story? In my own way, I love her like she's my daughter. Tell her I tried to stop this from hurting her."

I rub my chin. That might be the only honest thing he's said so far.

"I've got a date with an AJA. Bye, Rhys."

I jab the icon to end the call. "I'm going to find Story."

Maseko exhales in a short burst. "Don't let him get in your head."

"He didn't," I say. *He did.* "You need to confirm his story though. Find a way. I'm leaving."

David lays a hand on my shoulder. "Listen, The Bastion doesn't care if you used DNA." He takes a shuddering breath. "Irontrace do. You ignored our process and disobeyed protocols. SCs took a vote. It was close, but you're out."

I don't want to be SC anyways. I hate this job.

Darke pipes up, "I voted to keep you." I'm sure David voted against me. Irontrace search protocols are oxygen to that man.

"Thanks, Darke. Don't worry about it. I hate being SC anyways. I'm fine being back in the control room as a grunt." More time for Story and the kids.

Henri looks like he's going to vomit.

David's eyebrows go up. "No, Ivan. You're *out*. Of Irontrace."

Henri slams a fist on the table.

This has to be a joke. Irontrace is a lifelong sentence. Or privilege. It depends on how you see the work. To me, Irontrace is who I am. How I met Story. A way to be creative and really make a difference.

"David, law enforcement has used DNA for years to identify criminals," I argue.

"I-den-ti-fy. Not hunt. You went after him on a level showing blatant carelessness for legally established guardrails. People already feel like they're living in a surveillance state. You just proved them right."

He's staring me down like he has for years when we disagree. But it's different today.

No blood vessels in his neck or temple pulse with fury. He's almost relaxed? I've stood in front of his storms of anger before and never once backed down. This isn't a storm. It's more a gentle, refreshing rain of anger. Time to tell him exactly what I think of his archaic views on how to hunt for madmen.

"Why are you such a-"

Angry fists beating on the door drown me out.

Someone yells, "Maseko! Answer your phone!"

I pause, preparing a fresh argument to roar at David.

Maseko rises so fast her metal chair legs scream on the porcelain tiles. "Stop. Ivan. I'm so sorry." She lays a hand on my arm. "An ambulance is here for Story. She's in bad shape."

I lurch towards the door. Forget Delac and Irontrace. My wife. My home. Has she been taken for real this time?

36

Too much beeping. It's a seriously excessive amount of beeping for an aquarium. Maybe a tank burst. What if the manta ray thought it was free, bursting out of its glass cage, back into the ocean, but it's flopping to death on the carpet beside me?

No. I've done the touch tanks at the Aquarium in Columbus. A ray would feel slimy. I'm not wet. Or slimy.

There's something on my face though. A featherlight cool pack lays across my aching forehead. Not the faintest idea why it's there, but it's not helping. A hand—not mine—rests on my stomach.

"Hi?" I whisper, hoping I'll recognize the owner of the hand's voice.

"Hello, hey my love. I'm so sorry I wasn't there."

It's him. His warm body fills the bed beside me. I try to scoot closer, but the movement makes a splitting, white-hot pain sear through the left side of my head. Nausea freezes me in place.

Please don't puke. I'll choke to death. I can't turn my head.

"What can I do for you?" he asks.

"The babies?" I ask.

"They're okay."

"Why am I here?"

"You had a seizure."

My head wouldn't hurt like this from a seizure. "Why?"

"You should rest." He laces his fingers through mine on my stomach.

I will myself to open an eye. How am I supposed to rest? "Why?"

"Your symptoms from the purge are getting worse."

"Oh."

"Can I ask you a question? If you don't know the answer, it's okay."

"Yes."

"Who am I?"

"My husband, Ivan."

"Oh, baby. Yes. Yes, I am." His deep voice cracks.

"I'm not feeling well. Can you stay with me?"

"I won't leave you for a second. Never again."

I wriggle my shoulders over towards him, careful not to jar my head. *Still not close enough.* I lift my feet a few inches. He slides a leg under them, then rests his other leg on my shins. I'm warm, safe, and squished in all the right places.

When I wake, my head still hurts on the left. I reach my hand up and gently feel the area. There's a squishy lump that makes me cringe when my fingers brush it. My hair hasn't been shaved though, which means no surgery.

Ivan is holding me. *Remember him, come on brain!*

Grasp some vague memory of him from before a couple of days ago. Wedding. Babies. Dating. How did we meet? I've got nothing. My brain is useless. He's mostly a stranger. But at my core. I know him. We're rooted together.

I had a dream last night that there's a precipice in me, somewhere between the light of life and the dark chasm of oblivion. He pulled me out of it. He was my bright shield from the darkness. I'll do anything to stay in his warm light.

I peek an eye open. Mai and Richelle are playing with their phones.

"You're up!" Richelle slides from her chair and snatches the water off my table, holding it out for me.

"Is it morning?" I rasp.

"No," Mai says. "How do you two sleep like that? I'd be crippled."

"How's your head?" Ivan asks, groggily.

"Getting better." I sip the water Richelle gave me.

"I've been dying to wake you up!" Mai hisses in a loud whisper, bouncing on her tiptoes. "Maseko's been all over the news." Richelle turns on the TV but mutes it. Parades show signs with the Irontrace logo and Ivan's face. "Maseko told the news you caught Moulson, man. They're saying the Contact Creator tried to save his wife and stumbled into saving the world too. You two are like the most famous people ever. Look! I bought an Ivan phone case for you, Story."

She lays my phone screen side down on the overbed table. Sure enough, it's in a case with a picture of Ivan. He's in his tux from the gala. But they removed his tie and the top couple of buttons are undone on his white dress shirt. There are red and pink hearts framing his handsome face. I smile. Whoever made this phone case is going to be rich.

"It's a good day!" Richelle exclaims behind a huge grin. "Story's awake. She knows Ivan. He got Moulson. Party time! I ordered cake."

"What happened last night?" I ask.

"We were getting souvenir coins pressed and Lark saw Ivan. You glanced his way but seemed fine. Kept watching the screen with me, then you did this wild move where you put your arm up." Richelle does a ballerina twirl while she talks. "I thought you were waving at someone. I turned to see who it was, then I heard Nathan scream 'No!' I looked, and you'd taken a tumble towards concrete stairs. Nathan threw himself under you to catch your stomach, but you hit your head hard. Then started seizing."

Richelle rubs her face, as if trying to swipe away the memory. "I've been with you for the hyperventilating, panic freak outs. But the seizure was worse. To me at least. Mai counted and said it was-"

"Two hundred and twelve seconds," Mai supplies. "Nathan and I rolled you on your side and sat with you."

"While I was sitting in a room sixty feet away. Unaware. Useless," Ivan murmurs.

"That's our cue. We're outta here. Love you, girl. Get well soon," Richelle says, kissing my cheek.

"Can't believe all this is happening," Mai croaks.

"Richelle, Mai, thank you." I catch their hands and give them a squeeze. "I really appreciate your help. Love you both."

"Yes, thank you both. Later, ladies," Ivan tells them. "How are you feeling, my love?"

"Happy. I'm super happy." I grin. *Why am I so happy?* There's pure sunshine glowing within me. I poke myself in the cheeks, trying to make them relax, but they stay rounded from smiling.

"I'm glad, baby. Your dad is on his way with breakfast."

"Where's Lark?"

"Tallulah Falls."

"I'm going to get ready before everyone gets here." I use the bed rail to swing myself up in a sitting position.

"Whoa, careful!" Ivan steadies my chest and waist.

"Ugh. Bad idea." A wave of pain hits my head and neck so bad it makes me nauseous.

A hard knock on my glass door and the curtains swing open.

"Morning Rhys'sssssssssss...Story, oh, goodness!" Dad's jaw drops. He stops so fast that Nathan, Cherise, and Henri run into him.

They stare.

I stare.

A sharp crack of someone getting an invisible slap to the gut cuts the silence. It snaps Dad back to the moment, "We brought you breakfast and coffee. How are you, honey?"

Head is killing me. Nauseous. Not allowed to walk.

I grin. "I'm great!" *That was not what I meant to say?*

Nathan and Henri make big eyes at each other. Everyone starts muttering about how glad they are I'm okay, blah, blah, blah.

For ten minutes, they chatted while we answered questions about what happened. It's too loud and they're hurting my head.

I interrupt Nathan's report on where Moulson's being held. "Nice of you all to come. Thanks for breakfast. But get out of my room. Now."

They freeze.

"Thanks for coming guys. We'll catch up later," Ivan says.

I can't stop smiling. *What is going on with me?* I hold my coffee cup in front of my lips to try to hide it. I'm smiling, yet so incredibly annoyed. I could burst into tears any second.

"Okay. Glad you're doing well. You scared us," Dad says. They gather backpacks and computers and hustle out.

The door clicks and we're alone.

"Ivan?"

"Right here." He scoots my table over with its bagel, yogurt, and fruit on it.

"I can't stop smiling."

"I can see that. But you look exceptionally beautiful."

From the way Dad looked when he saw me, I doubt that. I hold up my phone camera.

I barely look human. Around my eyes is dark. My face is puffy. The left side of my forehead has a bruise. Richelle and Mom must have abandoned trying to do my hair. My curls are smashed flat in a tangled ponytail on my left shoulder. I have to get this mess washed as soon as I can. I wonder if they've got me on a med that's making me swell. What meds could do this? Ah, I can't remember. I drop my phone.

"Am I getting worse?"

"Your doctors will see you soon. Try to eat some breakfast."

"Okay."

My face still won't relax. I know there's a medical term for when your emotions are all messed up, but for the life of me, I can't think of it. What's that called? Afflict...admit...reflect. No, none of those are right. I'll ask the doctor.

I picked at fruit until my ALICE monitor turned on. A not quite human, robotic female face greets us. "Dr. Rhys, how are you feeling?"

"Good."

"No skull fracture. You have a scalp hematoma. You'll be released this evening. Any questions?"

"Why can't I stop smiling?"

The ALICE smiles. "Don't worry. We're monitoring you."

"There's a word for it. What's it called? I can't show how I feel."

"Dr. Rhys, don't get worked up," the ALICE orders.

Stupid robot! My grin grows. I massage my cheekbones with my fists, trying to force my face to relax.

"Affect, baby. You have what's called an inappropriate affect," Ivan whispers. *YES! That's it!* He speaks louder to the ALICE, "I'm worried. This is a new purge symptom."

"We can't possibly predict when her new symptoms will occur."

"You're working toward a treatment plan, right?" he asks.

The ALICE screen does a small glitch to the right. "If you can't manage her care, we can secure a spot for her in a purge care facility."

"Power off, ALICE." Ivan sighs.

I clamp my hand over my mouth. *Don't laugh, don't laugh, don't laugh.* It won't stop. My chest and shoulders shake. I lean forward and bury my face in my hands, willing my throat to choke it back.

"What's wrong, baby?" Ivan lays an arm across my shoulders.

No sense hiding it. I drop my hands and let him see me. The laughter jostles me too much and makes my head hurt. I put a hand on my goose egg, in a useless attempt to splint it.

"Oh, you're laughing," he says.

"Life is just so stupid right now!" More laughs. "Isn't it?"

"Yeah, it is. This is pretty bad."

"You should laugh more, Ivan." I trail my hand up his invisible arm to his face. "You seem very serious today. Have some fun with me."

He presses my hand to his lips. I think he's probably laughing now. He's kinda shaking with me.

"Baby, don't hurt your head." He lays a hand over my heart. "Let's breathe." *Get it together! You're scaring him.* Try as I might, I can't do it. His hand on my chest is so awkward, the weight of it makes me laugh even harder. "Deep breaths. In through the nose, out through the mouth. Please, Story. You can do it."

A quick knock raps on the door and Richelle walks in. "What on earth?" She takes in the tears streaming down my face and looks at Ivan.

"Story can't stop laughing," Ivan says, in a voice that's too bright.

"We thought you were celebrating," Richelle says.

"Guess what?" I take a breath through my nose, trying to get control. "They said my purge symptoms are just like unfixable," I throw up my hands, "I can go in a purge care prison if Ivan can't manage me."

I won't be able to sleep next to Ivan in a purge prison. I'll be too cold. It'll be dark without him. Fear seizes my chest. The laughs end. "Don't let them send me there. Please? I'll stop laughing. I won't laugh anymore. I promise I'll try not to."

A torrent of tears falls. The sobs hurt my head much worse.

"Story, I won't let anyone take you." Ivan folds over me, holding me tight. He's so warm. I can breathe again. "I love you. Keep breathing with me."

"Help. I'm disappearing," I whisper into his neck.

"Not to me. I see you. You'll be the love of my life no matter what."

Richelle sobs beside us. An alarm screeches on Ivan's phone. Something on my neck faintly vibrates. She leaps to my side, "Wait! Is that the thing?"

Ivan leaps up, and a drawer on the stand flings open. "Baby, I have to give you a shot in your-"

37

"Alan, it doesn't matter how I'm doing," Ivan says in a faint voice. He's holding my hand too tight. It hurts.

"You can't keep going on like this," Dad says.

What's Ivan going like? Why was I asleep again?

"You're one to talk. You can't either."

Silence.

"How long was that one?" Dad asks.

"Twenty-two seconds. The seizure alarm worked. It went off and I gave her an injection of Kepfetal." Ivan's voice is flat and sad.

"She's getting worse, fast." My dad can barely get the words out.

Silence.

"You go sleep. I'll stay with her," Dad says.

I didn't think it was possible, but Ivan grips my hand tighter. I'm going to have a bruise for sure. Will he listen to Dad and leave me? I wouldn't blame him if he does.

"Rhys. Go eat and drink, or I'm starting an IV on you," Dad's voice has an edge to it.

Ivan's grip on my hand relaxes. "Alan, I'm not leaving her."

Thank you. "Drink something, husband," I say.

"Story, can you hear us?" Dad asks.

"Yes."

"You had another seizure," Dad says.

I wave a hand to stop him. "No. No, please. Only happy things. The babies?"

"They're doing well. You're stable," Ivan answers.

"I want to go home."

"You can't-" Dad starts.

Ivan cuts him off. "To The Helm in Ohio or our hotel?"

"Our house."

"You don't have a house!" Dad says, not trying to conceal his panic.

"What kind of house do we have?" Ivan asks.

They probably think I'm confused-er. That's not the word. There's a doctor's word. I can't think of it. "We don't have a house. I want one. Can you buy us a house?"

"Where?"

"Ocracoke Island," I say.

"Where Ryland lives?" Ivan asks.

"Yes." I nod.

"Why?" Dad asks, giving me a shocked face.

I hold Ivan's hand on my cheek. "Please. Take me somewhere with sunshine. The ocean. People who are real doctors."

"Okay," Ivan says. His free hand throws a thick menu at the door. It makes a fluttery thud on the glass. Richelle and Mike burst into my room. "Call Ryland. I'm taking Story to Ocracoke. Ask if he has a place we can stay."

"You can't be serious?" Dad glares Ivan's way.

"On it." Mike pulls out his phone and ducks into the hall.

"Hey, babe, how are you?" Richelle asks.

"*Stable.*" Ivan seems like he knows medical words. I steal the word he used for me. We sat and caught up for a couple of hours. If I sit here any longer, I might explode.

My head doesn't hurt now. I test sitting up. No nausea, but I'm pretty dizzy. "Can I get up?"

"We'll meet you all down there for lunch later," Ivan says, dropping my bed's rail.

Dad and Richelle both give me hugs then leave.

Ivan steps in front of me and helps me to my feet.

"Get your balance, first, baby." Ivan stands, hugging me gently to him.

How long have I been in that bed? I'm not sure, but I need to get a shower immediately. My matted mess of curls is about to crawl off my head. I'm pretty sure I'm a fall hazard. So. This is gonna be an awkward ask.

I speak softly, unsure if I even want to say it. "Hey, have you ever untangled curls with conditioner?"

He laughs a quiet breath in my ear. "I'm practically a pro when it comes to your hair. Let's go."

There's an arboretum on the Atlanta medical hub grounds. It serves as an outdoor food court. Several restaurants and food trucks line the pathways. We chose a little taqueria and got platters of veggie and fajita nachos. By the time our group joined us, our damp hair had mostly dried, and my knees had lost their wobble.

I flip up the armrest separating my chair from Ivan's. "Is it too hot to lean on you?"

He scoots me closer with a quick arm around my waist. "Get over here, baby."

"What day is it?" I ask.

"Tuesday, September twentieth," Dad says.

"Where's Mom and Lark?"

"Tallulah Falls," Dad replies.

"What are we doing today?" I ask.

"Resting," Ivan says.

My shoulders drop. "No. We can't. Fix me, please."

"I've been working on it, don't worry. Darrow and Maseko put together a team for me. They're working at a biomed facility for IC in Lancaster."

"Don't you want to see how it's going?" I ask.

"Yeah, I want to get up there soon. Your glasses are ready. I can send Sully to get them. Your dad and Ryland are hosting the next wave of surgeons to start training tonight at Tallulah Helm."

I smile. "Can we go meet them?"

"If you want, baby. I need to pick up some stuff from the lab there."

When we got to the Tallulah Helm, things are humming along. Dad and Rylan had finished the rest of my surgeries. Ivan said David spent a full six hours yelling at the Irontrace here until "he had no voice and they were fit for Lancaster." No idea what that means, but it struck me as funny. I laughed for a solid ten minutes about it.

"What are you going to work on today, head of ASTRA?" Ivan asks.

"Coloring shapes in the SketchGeorgia toddler app. I'm not fit for anything else." I flash a dazzling grin his way.

"Get it, baby, make your team a whole new logo. I've got a handoff meeting in the back corner for a few minutes. Nathan, Henri, the whole PrivSec Team are here with you."

A sharp cramp hits my right side as he turns away. I've been laying down too much. I'm all scrunched up inside from days of no activity.

The pain creeps across, settling in my lower abdomen. Walk. Sip water. Walk. I try to look busy tidying.

Ugh. My stomach. Where's Ivan? He's talking on a video call with the team in Lancaster. Something important sounding about replenishing proteins on neurons to get my memories back. I don't want to interrupt him for a stomachache.

And anyways, terrible things can't keep happening to me. The universe isn't that cruel. It has to go pick on someone else at some point. Right? I'll try some stretches. I sit in my office chair and do some breathing and gentle movements. It works! The pain lets up.

"Better. I'm okay. We're okay Twinsies," I whisper.

The INES platform is empty. I hop up the steps and sign into the console. I navigate to the Agora removal surgical outcomes dashboard to see how the data is shaping up. Between Germany, Australia, and the U.S., we've done fifty-one Agora removals.

No one has died. No severe complications.

We need forty-nine more surgeries until Dad can submit for official approval for Lark. How is hers different again? I stand, trying to piece together why she hasn't had surgery yet.

Crud. I forgot. I'll do some research. I project an image of an Irontrace Agora onto the whiteboard, then overlay it with hers.

Whyyyyyy?! A fiery cramp hits, nearly knocking me to my knees. I grab the console to steady myself and accidentally fling a tray of sterile packages on the floor.

Mike jumps to his feet. "You good?"

"Yes. Clumsy. Sorry." I bend to pick the packs of drapes up and silently scream behind a curtain of curly hair. Do a check-in with the twins. I put my hands on my stomach and stand, studying the Agora scans on the screen.

Come on, babies, how are we doing? Normally I get a little happy thrill when I focus on them. Right now? Nothing. If anything, I feel a pit of loneliness. *I need something, body. Hormones? You got anything for me?* Nothing but a growing, icky despair. Something's wrong.

Ivan, where are you?

I strain to listen to him.

"I see. That narrows it down. Stop testing for that protein. Here, I'm sending you the next in line. We need to talk about this one now," Ivan says, staring at his laptop.

There's no reason to interrupt his work. He's too important to stop him on a hunch.

I fiddle around on the platform for another minute, taking deep breaths. Keep it chill, don't make your guards panic. Most of them are watching. I can't even take a minute to assess myself. How can I get out of here without them following me? There's a fresh delivery of scrubs in a laundry cart by the steps! I grab an armful of shirts.

"Gonna try these on, be back," I tell Nathan. He nods. I try to look casual as I walk to the lab bathroom. "We're fine, little ones."

By the time I get in there, a sickening sensation hits. They're not fine. This can't be right. My brain has broken. My eyes are lying.

"Holly, Huck, what's happened?" I lean against the wall to hide a sob in my elbow. "Ivan!" His name dies in my throat. I want to scream, to shout for help. He's huge. He's strong. He has to be able to do something. Panic chokes me. I can't force his name out. Breathe, breathe, breathe.

Breathing won't stop this. Why bother trying to stay calm? Go full panic. Flip out. I finally have a real, honest to goodness reason to. Panic. Get help. Move. I'm frozen. All I can do is clutch my stomach. Where's my phone? It's on my desk. Of course it is. Should I push the panic button on my ring? What if that calls PrivSec and all the guys in here? I'd die.

I sit, begging the stupid universe to help me when there's a faint knock on the door.

"Story?" Mike says quietly. "You good?"

No Mike, I'm not. I don't answer.

"Story, answer me within three seconds or I'm getting Ivan."

One...Two...Three...

He'll come for me.

Broken Glasses

~ Ivan ~

Done! I slam my laptop shut. That meeting was annoying, but every time we rule something out, I guess in a way we're one step closer. Speaking of getting closer to fixing her, the glasses have passed several rounds of testing. They're ready.

I was going to give her this pair tonight as a surprise when I tell her I got fired. She's had such a bad few days. I'll give them to her now. Wait, where is she? What is Mike doing? He's talking to the bathroom door like he's defusing a bomb. Henri, Nathan, and his guys are staring at him.

Something's happened.

I sprint over right as Mike turns, crashing into me. The glasses fly out of my hand and shatter.

"She's been in there awhile. I'm worried," Mike hisses.

I steel myself for the worst and swing the door open. Okay, she's not passed out or seizing on the floor by the sinks. That's good. This stupid fancy bathroom blocks my view. The stalls don't have the usual gap under the doors. It's more like a row of walk-in water closets with floor to ceiling walls.

Only one door is closed. I tap on it. "Story?" She doesn't answer. "You've gotta let me know if you're okay," I say.

Nothing. I make a fist, deciding where to hit the door.

It opens a crack.

"I'm in my shield. Coming in." I grab the top of it and muster all the self-control I can to slowly open it.

Her pitiful, blackened eyes stare up at me. She's as white as a sheet. "I think I'm...I'm losing or lost the babies," she sobs.

Screws rain down on the tiled floor. The door is suddenly heavy in my hand. I ripped it clear off the hinges.

I throw myself down beside her. "Are *you* okay?"

She doesn't answer.

What do I do? Who do I call?

"What...pain? Bleeding?" Deep breath. I'm no help to her if I can't stay calm. I'm ready to rip Moulson, or anyone really, limb from limb. I have to get perfect control before I dare touch her. Ready.

I put my hands under her arms and help her stand.

"Get a doppler. I'll wait here for you." She creeps to the sink and leans forward, splashing water on her face.

Me?!? Get a doppler for this? What is she thinking? I can't do this. *I can't make the call if our kids died.* There's no way. I'm not the person for this. I wipe my sweaty palms on my pants. "Story, let's go to the clinic, baby?"

"No!"

"I love you so much, but I...we need someone to help us."

"Ivan, NO! You. You have to be the one to tell me."

Hug her. Hold them together. My family can't fall apart before we ever got to meet each other. No, that's not how it works.

"Go. Please. Go," she sobs, shivering into my chest.

How I feel doesn't matter.

"No more sitting or lying on the floor, that's gross." There's a low bench. She should be okay on that. I unbutton my outer shirt and lay it on the bench for her, then gently guide her to sit on it. "Can Nathan or Mike come in with you?"

"No! Don't tell them."

Ah, she's making this difficult. She's probably in shock. "Sit here. I'll be right back, okay? Two minutes, tops." She draws her knees up in front of her and leans her forehead onto them.

I thought the purge choking her was going to kill me, but this is so much worse. She's completely broken. The last few weeks have reduced her to this tangle of tears and trauma in her turquoise tank top and running shorts. How can I leave her? She's been through so much. But I have to spare her any embarrassment. How can I determine if she's medically okay? What do I do if there are no heartbeats? What do I do if there's still one?

The door slams into the nine faces pressed against it when I exit.

I bark out orders as they rub their heads. "Henri! Find Richelle and Alan. Mike, tell Sully we're gonna need a ride. PrivSec, pack our hotel up for the trip to Ocracoke. Make sure we have a secure place to stay." I pull Nathan toward the bathroom door. "You're on Story duty. I don't care how you do it, keep both eyes on her."

I didn't know he had it in his wiry little frame, but he wraps me in a rib-cracking embrace.

"Sucks, man. Our girl's really down this time," he says.

I clear my throat and back up. *I will NOT cry in front of Nathan Cantone.* I dash out of the lab, past several doors, and into the main clinic. The oldest volunteer I've ever seen looks at me like I'm a madman. I shove an ALICE out of the way with a palm. Found it, Central Supply.

"Imaging, imaging, where are you?!" Second row, third pillar has a sign for it. I run to that section and crouch, looking for a portable ultrasound and doppler. "Got 'em!"

I jump up and run out.

"Ivan! Help, in here." Amelia's voice sends rage I've never felt coursing through me.

"Amelia! Where are you?" I shout, clinging my treasures to my chest.

"Nathan just carried her in," she says, stepping out of a clinic bay. She points to the first room. This has to be a trick. Nathan would've yelled for me.

"She's seizing again, Ivan!" Alan yells.

I dodge around Amelia and poke my head in the room.

Huge mistake. No Nathan. No Story. A laptop. A loop video plays Alan's voice, "She's seizing again, Ivan!"

Something like a gunshot slams into my neck. No. I've been shot enough times to know it wasn't that. I grab my neck and whip to see a syringe retreating into an arrest AJA arm that lurks just enough behind the curtain that I missed it. Great, Amelia hacked one to turn it into her buddy. Which one of the seven meds those carry did it hit me with?

"Amelia. She needs us," I say, reeling against the glass door.

"No. She *needs* me. Her mom. Not you."

My vision's getting spotty. I slam my hand onto a panic alarm on the wall. It doesn't light up. I try again. Nothing. *Bad. That's bad.* I reach for my phone, but my arm is too heavy. It feels like I'm moving through sludge. I try again and grab it.

"You purged her! You did this! Why? She's your daughter. She loves you."

"You won't stop Ivan. She's how we can stop you," Amelia says.

Who's the we?

I look at her and her pupil makes a wave-like pattern with a silver glint I'd know anywhere. This is not Amelia. It's a robotic clone of her. That's how she got in here unnoticed. That psycho is watching this all play out from somewhere.

"Story!" It comes out a whisper. My stupid tongue is too heavy.

I grab the bed rail and try to stay on my feet. My vision's down to maybe twenty-five percent. Nothing hurts though. Not even the injection site. Means she probably hit me with a SubDu shot AJAs use to knock out dangerous people for transport.

Think, Rhys. Get to Story. You've got about twenty seconds. My left knee gives out, and I fall on my hip against the bed. *Where are all the people in this stupid clinic?! What did she do with the staff?*

"Amelia, where are you? The real you? Story needs help," I try to force the words out. But I can't pronounce the letter sounds for S or E. She probably can't understand me. Right leg gives out. I'm down. My phone is too far. "Help her!"

I love Story so much. I can make it through this. This is doable. I've been through worse.

"I've been dangling her in front of you since I arranged that stupid trip to the Hocking Forest. Why won't you stop going after Anthony?"

Amelia set us up? There's no way. I have to be in some kind of hypoxic state. Nothing makes sense. The clinic lights go out. Or did I die? I tap my watch onto my lips, and it lights up. I didn't die. The clinic power is out. Story's probably so scared. She was already terrified. If I die, please someone purge her again.

Amelia, do your monstrous trick once more.

Make her forget me.

Make her forget today.

Make her forget the kids.

A fresh start.

Move on, baby. Be happy.

My face is dripping something onto my hand. Blood? I don't think I'm bleeding. Tears. It's tears rolling down. For Story. Her loss. Pain. What she's been through. What she's going through right now without me. And rage I can't get to her.

A call from David makes my watch buzz, lighting up the floor around me. I try to tap it on my lip and answer, but I can't move. My stupid eyes won't stay open anymore.

It's too bright behind my eyelids. Way, way too bright. No need to open my eyes. The scent of damp forest fills every breath. I'm next to another waterfall. Not wet though. That's a small bonus. So much for laying paralyzed on the clinic floor.

I squint my eyes open. The sun is burning down through the little valley I'm in. It's beautiful.

I wish Story was here to see it. She's so beautiful, like a princess. She'd hate to be called a princess.

"Why be a lowly princess when you can shoot for queen?" I hear her say. She's laughing. She's right. Princesses usually seem helpless. Not my Story. She's a force of nature. Fighting the purge to come back, time after time.

No matter what Moulson does, Story keeps going. It's killing her. I should make her rest. Get up and go make her rest.

I feel *weird*! Why am I napping next to a waterfall?

I stand. A rush of memories nearly knocks me down. Amelia. Drugged me. Had an AJA throw me off a balcony. Falling. I'm dead, I have to be. Or is this a nightmare? I look up at the falls. There's no way I survived that fall. I'm an actual walking corpse.

Story. Get back to her. *Move.* I wonder which Story is waiting for me. The newest Story that can't stop laughing and thinks she had a miscarriage? A Story that's been freshly purged again by her mom? Heck, maybe even the original Story will be back.

I don't care. No matter who she is, she's my favorite person. I fell down that cliff, but I feel good. I'm a bit sore, but no real pain. No clue how I'm alive. Super glad though. Now that I'm awake, I just have to get back to Story. No big deal, get hiking. I do believe falling was the easy part of my day.

I've known something like this was coming. There's been a suffocating feeling around us lately. Now I know it was the weight of death lurking, inevitable as the sunrise. Gotta say, it took me by surprise that death came for me wearing Amelia's face.

I really, really hate Georgia.

38

"Where is he?" I rock on the bench, muttering onto my knees.

Someone knocks on the door.

"Story?" Nathan says softly. "Story, I'm coming in."

I don't care anymore. I need help. He pushes the door open and sits on the bench beside me. I scoot away from him, making sure we're not touching.

"Hey, what's goin' on, ex-wife?"

I stay under my hair like a shield. "Where's Ivan?"

"I'm not sure."

I can't just sit here. I'm a mess. "Find him."

"Story, I need to get you to an ALICE."

"No. Ivan's coming." I push my hair back and look at him. "The memories with you are a lie. You're a trick. Ivan's real. I need him."

"Those memories are fake. But I'm your real friend."

"Where's Ivan?"

"If you let me take you to an ALICE, we can look for him. You really need to see a doctor. Your face is too pale. I'm not exaggerating. I'm not like Ivan. I don't know medical things. I have no idea how to help you."

I lay my cheek against the cool wall. "How long has he been gone?"

"Fifteen minutes, at least."

He wouldn't leave me by choice. Has the purge gotten him too? It's my turn to find him. I wrap his shirt around me the best I can. A sudden rush when I stand makes me wobble. I grab Nathan. "I'm sorry."

"I've got you." He locks an arm around my ribs and guides me to the door. "Turn on SAM."

The INES lab is empty.

"Should I push my panic button?" I ask.

"No. You're safe with me in SAM."

In the hallway, there's a security barrier down. *No!* It's blocking the way we need to go. I launch myself out of Nathan's arms and punch the steel wall.

"He's behind this. He has to be. Get us through," I plead. Fighting the wall made my vision swim.

"I don't have authorization like an SC would to override it. There's an overflow clinic. Let's go this way." He pulls my shoulder, but I cling to a metal maintenance handle. "If you want to be healthy enough to find him, you have to take care of yourself." I drop my hands. "Come on, Story, good job."

We silently walk to the tiny clinic. One teen girl sits at the desk. She has earbuds in, swiping on a tablet. I turn SAM off.

"Excuse me," Nathan says. The girl looks at me and drops her tablet. "I have a patient that needs to see an ALICE."

She stutters, "I. I gotta. Need to call my SC. One sec."

"You okay?" Nathan asks me. I shake my head no. "I'm going to put her in room two." He leads me into a room and flips on the monitors.

An ALICE and ORION whir in, hitting me with a barrage of questions that are none of Nathan's business.

"Want me to go out?" Nathan asks.

My brain's a jumble. These aren't his kids, but at the same time, they feel like they used to be? I hate my life.

"How about I hide behind the curtain, and you'll have a friend if you want one?" he asks.

This should be a quick abdominal ultrasound. "Thank you, yes."

The ALICE unceremoniously presses a transducer arm on my stomach. A video appears on the screen.

There's a bouncing, twitchy baby with a rapidly flickering heartbeat on the left. A little life! This one is okay. They're still with me. *Baby! You're okay. I love you. So much. I can't wait to meet you. Please hang in there. I bought you your first outfit last night.*

Joy transitions to a horror I've never felt. The purge can't possibly be worse than this.

The small form beside it is completely still. No racing heartbeat, not even a slow heartbeat. Nothing. *No! How? Why?* Grief sucks the air from my chest. For once, I don't get palpitations. My heart would have to be beating for that, and I'm sure that in honor of this loss, my own heart stops beating for several seconds.

ALICE immediately speaks. "Twin A has no heartbeat. Estimated fetal demise was two hours ago. Twin B has a regular, normal heartrate. Crown to rump length is consistent with expected size for eleven-weeks four days gestation. Sorry for your loss. We'll send you home with information on Vanishing Twin Syndrome. Let us know if you need additional grief counseling. Congrats on Twin B!"

The ALICE wheels out.

I can't take my eyes off the ultrasound video. It repeats in a four second loop.

Holly is Twin A. Holly *was* Twin A. Her tiny heart stopped two hours ago. What was I doing two hours ago? I think I was eating nachos with Ivan in the sun. I was sipping frozen lemonade and listening to him catch me up on what my broken brain has missed lately. Did I eat or drink something that caused this?

How is the whole universe not screaming with me in protest? Our baby. Just gone. Why? With no warning, no goodbye, a quarter of my family has been wiped out.

No raven-haired little one to read stories to after bathtime. No second car seat. I won't be going on coffee and bookstore runs with my daughter, Holly, someday. The yellow seahorse socks Lark got her at the aquarium won't be worn by Holly's little chunky baby feet. I bought her the most beautiful tiny sweater last night. The knitted wool is so soft it's almost silky. It's light blue and has rainbow sea creatures embroidered on it.

What do I do with them? Throw them away? Burn them? Keep them as a painful reminder to myself? Put them on Huck and pretend they were his all along?

My arms are going to feel lopsided. What will I do with my empty arm? I bet that arm will freeze while I sit and cuddle Huck. Huck! Will Huck forever know there's a void in his life? The person who may have been his best friend didn't make it.

"Story?" Nathan whispers.

"Where's Ivan?"

"We can't find him."

"Go! Find him!"

"I'm not allowed. I have to guard you."

"Nathan," I beg. "Find Ivan!"

One quick knock, then my dad bursts in. "Honey!" He hugs me. "Nathan called me. What happened?"

I point to the monitor above the doorway. "Holly." I sob.

The color drains from his face. "Is Holly A or B?"

"A."

"I'm sorry. So sorry. How are you?"

"Where's Ivan?"

"He was attacked. We can't find him."

"Another AJA?"

His face crumbles and he shrugs, wordless.

I dial a number on my phone. Dr. Brown answers right away, "Hello, Dr. Rhys?"

"Dr. Brown. Access my ALICE records and tell me if I can be up, walking around. It's an emergency."

"Okay, I need a few minutes please."

Jazzy piano music comes from the speaker.

"Where's Mom and Lark?"

"Rosa flew down and is watching Lark. Your mom is busy with something for Maseko."

My mom is working for Maseko? "Tell Mom about Holly."

"I will, honey. Can I get you anything?"

"Ivan! Please, find him," I beg.

"We're trying," Dad says. I've never seen my dad cry this hard.

Dr. Brown returns and walks us through a much kinder, but still heart-shattering version of what ALICE told me. "Take a few days. Rest." Oh no. My stupid, broken, brain. I'll never forgive myself. "Cry for Twin A. Be excited for Twin B. Don't smash your feelings down."

No chance of smashing purge brain feelings down. It's taking over my chest, a shaking, rattling that won't relent.

"Do whatever feels right in the moment for you to cope in a healthy way," Brown says.

I shove a pillow over my face right as it hits. Uncontrollable laughter. Dad looks at me in horror.

"This is supposed to be tears!" I choke out through laughs. I'm the worst person in the world. "HELP!" I can't stop. My laughs border on hysteria. "I'm so sad. Why can't I just be sad?"

I lean forward, hiding my face in the pillow.

"Alan, how long has she been like this?" Brown asks. I think that's what he said. I can hardly hear over my horrendous whoops of laughter.

My baby! I want Holly back. Ivan told me this morning she was going to be his look-alike. I want to hold her. I want to teach her to walk. To ride horses. Ivan would teach her to swim. I just know she would be kind like him.

"Holly!" I halfway wail.

"Story. Calm down. You're going to get all amped up and have a seizure again. Stop this crazy laughing!" Dad shouts.

"She's having more seizures?" Dr. Brown yells.

"Yes, I am." Laughs have turned to sobs that splinter my throat. "Did the purge kill her? Is it going to get Huck next?"

"This is a serious escalation of symptoms," Dr. Brown says. "I'm convening an emergency treatment panel to discuss this."

"Call Limon from IC!" Dad tells Brown over my sobs.

Nathan peeks in through the curtains, I try not to look at him. He swings them out of the way and comes straight for me. "Breathe. Ivan would tell you that you can make it through this. He'd say you can do anything. Fight the purge. For Huck."

He holds my hands, drawing in, then blowing deep breaths. He's been my best friend for years. Lean on him to get through. No, that's not right. He hasn't. I shake my head. I see Ivan's face smiling from my phone screen. Ivan's my best friend. Nathan is a trick. The trick is helping. His familiar green eyes calm me. We breathe while Dad talks to Brown and after a few minutes, I'm back to crying like a normal human being.

"Thank you," I say, sniffling.

He smiles, then retreats back to his corner.

Dad hangs up my phone. "You heard him. Rest."

I close my eyes to gather myself. "I'll rest from the control room, or I'll walk the halls of this Helm until I find Ivan. I have to do something."

"No," Dad says.

Nathan sticks his head in. "I texted SC Darke. He said we can have a workstation with a couch in the control room. You can keep your feet up."

"To the control room, then. No laughing this time, I think...I think I won't laugh anymore. I'll cry in SAM. A lot."

Dad and Nathan agree to let me go in a wheelchair.

The control room is in a video call with several other Helms. There's an emergency alert out to find Ivan. The last surveillance image of him is when he's sprinting out of the INES lab to get an ultrasound.

Why did I make him do that? I should have just seen an ALICE. We could've stayed together. Instead, I sent him away. He'd been telling me he'd keep me safe. Never again. I'm going to stick on him like a second shirt once he's back. *Come back, Ivan!*

Henri lays my phone in front of me. Forty-six missed calls from my mom. What on earth? No voicemails. Just calls. Maybe she heard about Holly. I don't want to hear her cry about it right now. I mute my phone and lay it face down. The edges light up with a fresh call.

"We're in hour four of the search for him. It's not looking promising after what we found in the clinic." Darke tells David. An image appears of a patient room with several items on the floor.

His wedding ring.

An ultrasound.

A doppler.

His broken watch.

A pair of cuffs.

His shattered phone.

"We've got nothing," Darke says. "There was a surveillance outage that hit as soon as he left the INES lab."

David jabs a finger at the screen. "All Helms need to have a team on this until he's found."

My phone lights up again.

"Aside from Ivan, Woods is next best at hunts like this. He's in swarm breakout room two if anyone wants to join," David announces.

"Let's join and see what they've found," Nathan says.

We sit and listen for a few moments. An uneasy realization hits. If Ivan's gone too, half my family will be dead. I'm barely a person. Huck will have nothing. The odds are very stacked against him.

My phone lights AGAIN. Forty-one more missed calls from Mom. "What!!" I answer in a whisper-yell.

"Rosa and I found Uncle Ivan! The Helm is in lockdown, and we're stuck in our apartment!" Lark shrieks. "Rosa. Come show her." A GPS point appears on the phone screen.

He's in a gorge? Far down. I rush to send the coordinates in a blast chat to the whole room. A wave of dizziness nearly drops me to the floor when I stand too quickly. I plop back onto the couch.

Sorry, Huck.

"David Delac!" I shout.

"Story? Where are you?" he calls out, looking very confused.

"Lark and Rosa found him!"

"Where is he?" David fires back. "Send a team. Right now!"

"Ivan built a DNA thing for dogs but found out it can locate people. Rosa used a drone bee to fly to their hotel and steal his hairs from him and Story's bed and then we found him with the DNA sniffer. He got thrown off a thing. Don't tell Maseko, she'll take my computer away!

Story, look, my tooth fell out." Lark pulls up her lip and aims the phone camera at her gums.

"Good job, Lark!" I choke out.

"Delac!" Woods barks. "I've restored the surveillance. You're never gonna believe it."

A crisp video takes over the monitor wall.

"Story, don't watch," Nathan says.

"I want to see what happens."

He clamps a hand on my eyes. "The purge. It might get Huck."

"I can watch videos of Ivan."

"Story! Do NOT watch it!" Nathan steps in front of me, bending to fill my line of vision. "Talk to Ivan first. I am begging you."

I'll do anything for Ivan and Huck. Even if it means not looking.

"Take me to his GPS location then."

He looks me up and down, thinking. Pausing on my abdomen.

"No. But the second the rescue team brings him to the top of the gorge you get to hold his hand."

Standing too fast nearly took me down, a hike to get to him would knock me out.

"Let's go."

I sneak a peek at the screen. It's changed to the back silhouette of a woman, walking beside an arrest AJA that carries slumped Ivan. Her hair looks familiar. Ivan's head flops to the side and I turn. Nathan's right. I can't watch that.

39

A mini rescue chopper lands on a clearing at the top of Hurricane Falls. Nathan holds onto the back of my tank top like he's restraining a kid from chasing a ball into the road. As soon as the rotors stop spinning, I run across the heli-pad.

They slide the doors open and Ivan's reclining on a stretcher.

"Close your eyes!" Nathan hisses from behind me. "I'll take you to him." He pulls my arm until I bump into the stretcher.

"Ivan, I love you! I love you." My hands assess what my eyes can't. His neck is in a brace. An oxygen mask covers most of his face. He's sticky with mud or blood from shoulder to waist.

"Are you okay, baby?" he asks. I shake my head. Fresh tears slip out. He fumbles for my hand, pressing it to my stomach. "Tell me."

"Stop." Nathan orders the Irontrace pushing the stretcher.

I lean by his ear. Of course he wants to know, but there's so many strangers around us.

"Holly died."

He doesn't react. If he didn't hear me, I don't think I can say it again. Then his hand tightens in my curls, anchoring us together.

"I'm sorry I wasn't there. I'm so sorry, baby," he whispers.

I'm crushed, too weak to walk back in. I step on the stretcher frame. Ivan holds me, bound against his chest and neck. Grief shudders through us as if we share one soul.

"Push them in. Let's go," Nathan says.

After the clinic made sure Ivan was stable, PrivSec flew us to our ho-tel. Dad, Dr. Brown, and Dr. Ryland helped us get settled in.

"*Mom* is Moulson's twin?" I ask Ivan and Dad.

Dad nods. "She's on the run. She's the one who accessed your labs and sent the bomb. Ivan was her target. She thought he'd gone home to sleep while you were in Lark's room."

"Mom is on the run. *My mom*? The woman who won't walk in a dark parking lot by herself? The one who wouldn't let me take a self-defense class in college because she said the best preparation for conflict is to avoid it?"

"I'm struggling with it too." Dad's voice comes out harsh, broken. He stands. "I have to go meet Lark and Rosa. I'm so-, I just. Really heartbroken too about Holly." He loops an arm around Ivan and I, gripping us in a group bear hug. "I love you both. Night, honey."

"Love you, Dad. Night." I run a hand through my hair.

Dr. Brown bid us good night too and left with him.

"I want to know how you survived that," Dr. Ryland says, giving Ivan an ice pack and a suspicious look. "No human could have survived that fall. They found you ninety-six feet down."

"Don't underestimate what I'm capable of for Story," Ivan says mysteriously.

Ryland's face hardens. "No. How?"

"Tuck 'n roll, Ryland."

"You're really not gonna tell me?"

"Tuck. And. Roll. We're going to bed. Night." Ivan stands, then extends a hand for me to follow. He locks the door after we're in our room and drops into the desk chair. "Gotta do something, really quick. Sorry."

I head to the bathroom to get ready for bed. The woman in the mirror is someone I don't recognize. She has my bone structure and jawline. Fading yellow bruises frame the left side of her face. Worn creases make hollows around her eyes. She's pale. Not go to the beach and get a tan pale. It's an unhealthy, washed-out color.

"Be gentle with yourself," everyone told me.

"Take it easy," Dr. Brown said.

Gentle? Easy? Those aren't words I'd use to describe anything lately.

Maybe that's what life is. Making a conscious decision to find the gentle parts of your day. But how? When life is overwhelming, it's like a mental wall goes up around the good things. The bad stay withing reach, within view. I can't even remember what I'd find gentle, easy, or happy.

Ivan steps into the bathroom. *It's him.* He's my gentle, easy, happy thing.

"Hey, I'm waiting on a call, but wanted to give you something. Close your eyes."

I hesitate.

"Please."

I let my eyes flutter shut.

"I'm going to touch your face." He slides stems of glasses over my ears, then adjusts them. "Okay. Open up."

Now is not the time for this. I'm barely standing. I pull them off and open my eyes, staring at the floor. "It's too much today. I can't."

He sighs. "I promise, it's safe. They won't hurt Huck."

I frown. I didn't even think of that. I knew Ivan wouldn't put these on me if there's even a tiny chance of it hurting one of us.

"Baby, it's okay. You can put them on. They'll block your panic."

I can't. "Ivan...Holly *died*."

After what must have been a full minute, he replies, "I'm sorry."

"I laughed."

"Hmm?"

"They said she died. My heart was torn from my chest, but I couldn't stop." My words pour out. "It broke me. I couldn't understand—I still can't understand—how I survived that news. I was happy...*so* happy for Huck. How could I be happy for him? I was so, so, so, sad for her. I am still so sad for her. This will never go away." I lay the glasses on the counter. "I *laughed* when they said our daughter died. I've been turned into something I hate by this purge. I'm glad you weren't there. You'd hate me too. And you might hate me now for telling you this. It's okay. You can tell me if you do. I probably won't remember tomorrow. Just leave me and move on."

He picks up the glasses. "Please. Just put these on." I shake my head no. "I haven't gotten to look in your eyes for eleven days. Two hundred and sixty-four hours. Today, something precious...our *kid*...was lost. I need to look in my best friend's eyes."

"She wasn't a kid yet. She was a concept." That's not what I meant. Why can't I get the right words out?

"A concept?" His breath cuts out, hard. "You're right. A concept. Definition: a future possibility. Potential. That baby was those things."

I nod, agreeing. He's putting into words what I can't.

"If I was there and heard you laughing? I wouldn't have hated you." He kisses my hand. "I would have seen exactly what I see now. Your heart hurts. But you're sick. And you aren't sure how to show it. You're grieving, baby. I see it. I see you."

He traces a thumb along my cheek. "My chest aches," I say.

"Mine does too. Not for someone we knew. But for who that baby could have been. It would have been a beautiful life, all of us together. I *need* you to look in my eyes, to see me."

I keep my eyes closed and slide the glasses on. *Please work, glasses.* After what the purge has put him through. I owe him this. He built SAM. He built INES. These will work too. When I finally meet his eyes, he's not the man I expected. The Ivan from my phone's lock screen and from the Ilex gala looked joyful and confident.

This Ivan has dark rings around his eyes. Worry lines crease his forehead. He's got a bruise on his neck. I lay a hand on his cheek. His jaw is clenched rock hard.

"Do the glasses work?" His thick lips press into a hard line.

Oh no. Laughter is bubbling up. "You look horrible."

His mouth drops open. What is wrong with me? This perfectly handsome man has probably never had anyone tell him such a mean thing.

"Like, black face tendrils horrible?"

I cover my mouth, trying to fight the laughs. "I'm sorry. No. They work. You just look wrecked, absolutely terrible!" I point to my face. "I look like crap." A tiny smile touches his lips. "What happened to us?

We're beautiful in the picture from May." I kiss him between laughs. "Now I've got brain damage. Our kid died. I want to crawl in a hole and rot. What has life turned into? Can you believe this?"

He grins, trying to kiss me back but I can't stop laughing. Slow laughs rumble in his chest. His laugh is wonderful. It soothes something in me. He's not scolding me. Not telling me how broken my brain is. He's meeting me exactly where I am.

I'm loved! Few people can say they've ever been in love. Yet I'm completely and totally loved, even when life is at its worst.

He catches my chin and holds me, studying me. "You're still as beautiful as you were in May."

I stare in his eyes. *Come on, brain. Remember this man.* Nothing. His unfamiliar eyes are a peculiar color. They're so dark they only register as brown when they catch the light. Exhaustion is worn deep in a way sleep can't fix. His piercing gaze gives my heart a thundering flop. I freeze, grounded to him. My laughs stop.

"There you are, Story."

I can't imagine what it's been like for him since we got to Georgia. "I love you. I'm sorry. I really love you."

"I love you. Never apologize. This is not your fault."

"How will we get through this?" I sit on the bathroom counter. I'm exhausted and weak and don't trust myself to stand here any longer.

"The same way we always do." Ivan doesn't hesitate. He scoops me in his arms and carries me into our bedroom. "We'll take care of each other. Lock the world away until the pain isn't so loud."

The night, day, and another night passes in a sleepless haze of words, memories, future plans, and shared heartache during my waves of discomfort. He's with me through it all.

His computer rings loudly on the desk, jarring us awake. Before I can form a full thought, his hand flies to my glasses, making sure they're on.

"Morning," his gruff voice says. "No. Good afternoon."

His sleep-wrinkled face makes me smile. "Afternoon," I say.

"We have to answer that. You'll want to talk to them. I have a theory on how I survived the fall, but I want to hear it from my rescuer."

He answers the call. Lark yells. "It worked!"

"It did. You're my hero," Ivan says.

"Did you tell Story?" Her little voice is pure sunshine.

"Nope. You tell us," he says, pulling me onto his knee.

"Hi, Story! You got glasses. I love them. You look so pretty. I bet Ivan made them. So. Listen. Rosa and I were hanging out in the apartment and she got real still and said there was an alarm and I said well we have to find my family, and she said we can't go out there and I said don't worry, Ivan has a way to find people."

He holds up a finger. "About that. How did you find my DNA sniffer program?"

A devilish grin spreads across her face. "You wrote the doggy DNA program one day and then I heard someone say you got arrested for hunting people with DNA and then Dad said you got fired for it, and I thought to myself, that stinker, he used Birdy's DNA thing to find people. So, Rosa woke Burt up-"

Surely Lark didn't just say Ivan got fired. I imagined that.

"She what?" Ivan snaps.

Rosa pipes up, "Son, you've rotated the same twelve passwords since you were nine. Baaaaad boy! I taught you better. Hacking into your Burt was too easy."

He looks at me, speechless.

Lark continues, "She woke him up and we had him find you and we saw you were in bad shape with an AJA. WHO DID THIS TO YOU, IVAN? No one will tell me." He grips my hand but stays silent. "Someone needed to protect you. You always save everyone. Rosa said we had to do something, and I said I wished I could throw a SAM on you, and Rosa said yes, let's throw a SAM on him. But we couldn't get it figured out until right when the person was having an AJA drag you up on a stone ledge and then Rosa launched a SAM shield out from a drone, and we caught you in it. You would not *believe* how hard you bounced down that gorge thing. I almost puked from the SAM video flinging around. But then Rosa got really grumpy and turned off the video and said something about Story needed help instead and we called her two hundred times."

I force my voice to stay calm. "Thank you, Lark. Thank you, Rosa."

"You're welcome!" Lark chirps.

"Mom, Lark, you guys ran my DNA through the program?" he asks.

"Yes, Rosa said you have a whole big family out there Ivan. Can we meet them? Am I in trouble for the DNA thing? You seem mad I did that."

Ivan pinches the bridge of his nose and laughs. "Not at all. It was just that you running my DNA made me laugh. I've thought about running some family DNA myself in the past few days. Thanks for saving me. You're my hero."

"Can I come swim with you tomorrow?" Lark asks.

"Lark. Go do your lessons," Rosa says.

"Rosa," Lark whines. "I'm talking."

"No. Go finish your math lesson, then you can talk." Rosa points to her bedroom. Lark pouts but marches off and shuts the door. Rosa leans close to the camera and lays a hand on her chest. "My loves, I am so sorry for your loss."

I whimper softly. Ivan kisses my cheek. I'm never leaving this hotel room. I can't have this conversation with everyone we know.

"I'll keep Lark busy. Happy. Educated. You two take your time. Ivan, you look terrible. Story. You look strong. Healthy. Keep doing what you're doing. I'm proud of you."

"Strong?" I sob. "Healthy?" Ivan wraps me in his arms.

"Anyone else wouldn't have gotten out of bed after day one of the purge. They'd have gone to a purge care house and be doing puzzles twelve hours a day in padded rooms with the other patients." She checks for Lark, then leans forward, narrowing her dark eyes. "You haven't stopped. Ivan, *make* her stop. She's strong, but tired. She needs healthy food. Sunshine. Fresh air. Sleep."

He nods, his beard scratching my forehead. "I will."

"I'll be watching to make sure you do."

"I'm sure you will. I'm changing my password."

"To what? Sup3r_Iv4n_Rhy5 should be next in your rotation. Make a new one. You're too predictable, my boy."

He gives me an exasperated sigh. I should get him out of here.

"Love you, Rosa," I say, collecting myself.

"Aww, love you, my girl. It'll hurt the worst these next few days. Sleep and hope are medicine. Use them both." She wags a finger at Ivan. "Hold your woman close. Plan for good times with Huck. He's okay. I'll watch him for your first date night in April." She grins. "Bye my babies."

The screen goes dark.

"Did Lark say you got fired?" I smooth his black wave of hair back.

"Yes. Sorry. I know you loved the whole SC Rhys thing."

"No. I love the whole you're Ivan Rhys thing." Did I used to be some awful, shallow person who wanted him to be an Irontrace boss man? "If the old me made you feel you had to stay SC for me to love you, I'm really sorry."

"That was a joke. You hated that I was SC."

I let out a long sigh. "Sorry my mom tried to murder you."

"Sorry my mom is a robot."

She's what?! I frown and give him wide eyes. I can't have heard him right. Then the laughs come back. Holding a hand over my mouth does nothing to stop them. It just makes me short of breath. I lean over to hide my laughs in a couch pillow.

He kisses the side of my head and pulls me up. "Lunch time, giggle pants."

Seashell-Colored Glasses

~ Ivan ~

"Don't drop that one!" Story's arms are full of seashells. She's using me as her extra set of hands. I'm shocked at how difficult it is to carry olive shells, but they're her favorite today.

We've been in our borrowed three-story beach house on Ocracoke Island for four weeks. Lark hasn't asked much about where Amelia is. As far as I see it, that's a good thing. I was about Lark's age when my family betrayed me. I know Rosa can nurse Lark's sad heart back to health.

"Good work, you two. These colors of nature themed purge glasses will be a hit," Richelle squeals, grabbing my stack of shells and dropping half of them.

"All of the glasses designs are a hit." David reaches to pick up the fallen seashells.

We found out some other people wanted glasses like Story instead of contacts. When Richelle saw I designed the purge glasses to be black, she had a fit.

"Ivan, you are not putting those poor, depressed people in black glasses!" Richelle pulled Story to a chaise lounge and they worked for hours. They gave me a rainbow of colors, designs, and interchangeable wraps to manufacture the glasses in. Today they're sketching shell ones.

"What color do you want, baby?" I asked Story.

"Black." She laughed and bumped my shoulder affectionately.

Those laughs. They have a mind of their own. As unsettling as it is, I prefer it when her laughter won't stop. It's far better than when she can't stop crying. She's had six more seizures. She wears a heart monitor now. Her occasional palpitations have progressed to runs of tachycardia that take her off her feet.

Dr. Brown is giving her the purge cure tomorrow. David and Richelle came for moral support. She'll be the first patient in the world to get it. I'm terrified. I don't know the last time I slept more than thirty minutes. All night I jerk awake to lay a hand on her chest and check her heart, to make sure she's not seizing, to see if her glasses are poking her since she won't take them off.

"My boy! You look worse every time I see you! I'm sending you more soup," Rosa yells at me on our nightly calls.

When Story's awake, I watch her constantly. She doesn't like to go more than an arm's reach from me now. I've caught her as she went down for five of the six seizures.

We put an INES in the tiny island clinic. She religiously does two sims per day. Ryland's team of surgical mentors here worship her.

She's taught them how to use robots to sharpen their skills and move faster. They've taught her to rely less on INES and more on herself. She gets frustrated and forgets medical terms, but we know what she means and remind her.

Good thing I'm not an Irontrace anymore. Running IC has taken up every bit of brain power I can spare. It's turning into the real deal. The contacts and glasses belong to IC. INES belongs to IC. Rosa and Burt do too.

My goal with Project Ilex to change the world for the babies took a sharp left turn. I can't be mad though. Instead of making the whole world a better, safer place, I've made sure *my world,* Story, is kept in a better, safer place. These last few months have taught me lessons I needed to learn. Lofty goals are admirable, but some days the most important thing you can do is make a sick person smile. To make her feel loved. Safe. If that's all I can accomplish right now? It's enough for me. And by the smile on Story's face while she falls asleep in my arms at night, I can tell it's enough for her too. Maybe I'll change the world next year.

David and I have a frosty agreement to not mention Irontrace when we talk. He broke it when he landed in Ocracoke yesterday. "It's nice you have time for Story and Huck. No Irontrace to divide your focus anymore, Mr. CEO." His eyes flashed like voting me out was a favor, not a punishment.

Maseko and I came to a friendly agreement to destroy my DNA sniffer program. We both stood and read the code a bit too long before deleting it. Pretty sure she memorized it too. Never know when you'll need to fight dirty and find a murderer.

The PrivSec team has become like extended family. Several of their families joined us in Ocracoke. I'm grateful for them. Story thanks the group daily for their love and support. We keep her surrounded with safety, sunshine, homecooked meals, and snacks.

Every glimpse I get of her growing baby bump makes my heart skip. Overall, she's surviving. I'm trying to make moments for her to not only survive but *live* a life she'll enjoy.

Tonight, we're having a bonfire on the beach. It's chilly in late October, but I'm not complaining. Gives me a reason to hold Story tighter.

We lay on a plush blanket, away from the laughing crowd. David's playing his guitar, Richelle's singing an old song about fishing in the dark, and everyone else is singing along.

"I want to sleep out here every night, looking at the Milky Way with you," Story says. My arm is under her head, and her legs are tossed across mine.

"I do too. Makes me feel so small."

"You? Small?" She laughs and squeezes my bicep.

Please don't die tomorrow.

Please don't have a seizure tonight.

Stay in a normal heart rhythm.

Just make it. Live.

I don't care if you forget me, but you have to make it through the purge fix.

Please, please, please.

I breathe my silent wishes into her curls.

"Are you ready for tomorrow, baby?" I ask.

"Yep. It'll be fine. They took your idea and made it real. You're so smart," she says forcefully.

While she faded in and out of sleep the first few days in Atlanta after she lost Holly, I went a touch crazy. She would tell me all the time how electric it felt when I touched her. The docs from IC and I threw ourselves into researching touch. I laid beside her in bed and worked. I sat beside her when she was up and worked. Until I found it.

The protein we'd been hunting for. I named it Rhysase0524. It connects touch with memory. Touch is converted into a signal the brain interprets as safety. The more tests we did, the more we understood how to translate physical contact for purge patients into emotional regulation that could override their panic. The purge mutated the protein, giving it a stronger than normal effect.

That demonstrated how cruel of psychopaths he and Amelia are. They turned the touch of the most loved person in your memory bank into something you *craved*. Purge patients didn't just miss their loved ones, they were withering, shrinking as their protein levels slowly depleted. Then he made sure that seeing the person they loved most would detonate panic in their limbic system. Conscious thoughts couldn't intervene to save them. Reason couldn't override it.

They couldn't survive without their loved one's touch—and he made it so they couldn't survive seeing the person who could replenish a natural supply of the missing protein.

She has to get the fix, before the creeping shadows of gliosis on her MCDI brain scans become permanent.

"Are you ready for your old Story to be back tomorrow?" she asks.

"My love, you've never stopped being my Story. I'll be yours forever, no matter what."

"Ha! A shooting star went over. Now you're stuck with me."

"Better be."

Please let me be with you forever.

40

"I just drink it?" I smell the small plastic cup Dr. Brown handed me. "Gross, it's cherry? Come on, guys, it should have been like coconut iced coffee or something adult-y."

Ivan's bloodshot eyes stare into mine. He's been "toughing it out" for the last several days. I know he can't wait for me to be back to normal, even though he won't admit it. He's got to miss the Story he lost in September. She's dead now. Even if I remember my whole past life when I drink this gross stuff, I won't be holding Holly in April.

"Yes, you drink it," Ivan says, staring at the cup like it's radioactive.

David sits in a chair in front of me. Richelle is perched on his armrest. Dad promised to video call us, but we haven't heard from him.

"Next time I hand you a cup, it better be ice chips when you're having that baby." Brown laughs. "Never had to oversee a clinical trial to prescribe a patient a protein repair syrup with a healthy dose of oculo-limbic stabilizer."

From the looks on everyone's faces, I'm gonna guess they're with me on the emotional tilt-a-whirl I'm feeling. Fight. Don't laugh. My chest shudders and my shoulders lurch while Brown and Ivan talk about how to test if this worked.

Bite your lips. Hold your laugh in. I clap a hand over my mouth to stay quiet and then swipe it up, making it look like I'm adjusting my glasses. I've had enough of the purge. I'm done. I can't help them if I stay a useless victim. Might as well drink up.

I smell my amniotic acid syrup cup again. *No.* Amniotic is wrong here. I giggle. That's not what it's called. Amniotic is something baby-related. Proteins...ah! *Amino* acid syrup. I can't remember what it does, exactly. But everyone is extremely excited. Another laugh threatens to escape.

I look at Richelle, giving her a grin. She shakes her head. I've worn her patience thin. There's no time like the present to get better, I suppose. Bottoms up! I tip the cup up and the nasty cherry liquid fills my mouth. Gross. I swallow it as fast as I can.

"Story!" Ivan shouts. "I wasn't ready!" Why is he so upset?

"I'm fine." I smile at him. Everyone else is quiet. They're just staring. "What?" I shrug.

They freeze. Hmmm, did time pause? The room looks weird. No one is moving. At all.

David is mid-leap, resting in some kind of frozen squat, holding the arms of his chair. He looks mad! Someone's in trouble. I've seen that face. He's about to ruin someone's day. He makes that face at Ivan a lot.

Richelle is mid-run. Frozen with one foot in the air, arms reaching for me. She'd love to see her hair right now. Her bouncing action has given it perfect lift from her scalp. Looks like she's rocking a fresh, blonde blowout.

Ivan's eyes are wide and his mouth is stuck open in a weird 'O' shape an inch from me. His right hand still holds my shoulder. His left hand is about to tear out a chunk of his hair. He better not. I *love* his hair. It's one of the first things I noticed when he found me in the woods.

Dr. Brown's eyebrows are up and his tablet is...stuck? He's paused in some kind of yelling or exclaiming, I don't know. The tablet's not falling. It's hanging in mid-air. Between his hands and feet.

How did they do this?

"Guys?" I snort.

Is this a trick? What's up with the tablet? I kick my foot at it, but it stays suspended in front of me. Why am I holding a medicine cup? I smell it. Cherry something. Weird. Definitely not an adult med. I throw it towards the trash can but miss.

"Guys!" I yell. Nothing. They're frozen.

That's it, I'm gonna fight dirty. They think this is hilarious. I stick a finger in Ivan's gaping mouth. He's really into this charade. He doesn't move.

"Ivan Nicholas Rhys!" I yell. Ah, something on my face bumped into him. Glasses? Why am I wearing glasses? I pull them off and it's like a bomb went off in the room.

"Story!" "Baby!" "NO!" "Honey!" "Dr. Rhys!"

Everyone is screaming. The tablet hits the floor, bouncing a few times.

"What!" I snap. "Why are you all yelling?"

Ivan lays a hand on my chest. "Baby, are you okay? Talk to me. Please, lay back for a minute." I resist his gentle push backwards, but his onyx eyes are panicky, so I relent and lean back. He looks rough. He's lost weight. These couple weeks as SC have really taken a toll on him. The lighting in here must be intense. "Talk. Talk to me, please," Ivan begs, kissing my cheek.

"About what, handsome?" Wait, why am I here? I pull him close. "Ivan, what's going on?"

"Humor me, what's your name?" Ivan whispers.

"You're being weird," I say. Richelle holds her face like she's staring at a car crash. "Richelle? You okay?"

"Babe. Name. Now!" Each word from her is a squeak.

They're serious. "Story Caroline Rhys," I say.

Ivan collapses his head onto my chest and heaves a content sigh. "Who's your husband?"

"Are you okay? Have you had a collective Transient Ischemic Attack? Do you need me to get you some antiplatelet therapy?" I snort a laugh, but no one else does. Tough crowd today.

"Story. Excellent job remembering TIA's," Dr. Brown says. "But we really need you to tell us your husband's name. Now."

Forget them being on the brink of panic. I think they're all confused.

"Ivan Rhys," I say, stroking his cheek.

David drops his head between his hands. Ivan stares at me. He's smiling, but cautious, guarded.

"Bear with us. Please continue to answer all questions," Dr. Brown says, pointing to Ivan. "Look closely at his face. Do you see anything strange? Does he give you shortness of breath? Palpitations?"

I widen my eyes and pretend to study his face, then give a soft laugh. Come on, he's Ivan. Do they really want to hear the things I feel for him? That list could go on and on…

"I see Ivan."

Dr. Brown, David, and Richelle hound me with the strangest list of questions for a few minutes. Ivan sits quietly with his keen onyx eyes trained on mine. I tell them about Birdy, Agora removals, Project Ilex, when and where Ivan and I got married. Fairly sure they're going to bust out champagne and hand me a cup of apple juice any minute.

Ivan finally throws his arms around my waist in a hug. "You're okay! The glasses are gone, and I don't scare you anymore."

Why would Ivan scare me? I love him. *And too tight, baby, ouch!* Those glasses. Why was I wearing glasses? I have perfect vision. I've got a growing list of questions to spout back at them.

"Ivan Rhys! Let go. You'll squish the twins!" I hiss.

"Twins?" Dr. Brown asks, worry rising in his voice. "You're having twins?"

I smile and nod at him.

"Story, I can't. Help guys?" Ivan says, dropping his arms.

I swear he's lost twenty pounds and aged ten years. I knew going from Commander Ivan Rhys to husband and dad of twins was gonna make him crack. Did Moulson do something to Ivan and we're here for him? He didn't look like this a little bit ago in the control room.

"Story, I need you to tell me what day it is," David says. I screw up my face at him. "I'm serious. Tell us before Ivan faints."

I lay my hand on Ivan's cheek. "Today is September tenth, 2050."

Richelle screeches, nearly making me jump off the table.

"Dr. Brown, take over." Ivan waves for him to step closer.

"Story, why are you here today?" Dr. Brown asks.

"My first OB appointment."

Brown narrows his eyes. "Tell me about your pregnancy."

"I'm nine weeks six days pregnant with twins. A boy and a girl." If

Ivan wasn't having a medical emergency before, he is now. His face takes on a grey-ish green hue. "What's wrong?" I jump up to steady him. "Whoa, the twins have POPPED since this morning. I look four months pregnant!" I point to my noticeable bump and grin at Ivan.

He doesn't smile back. "My love, we're going to the beach now. Okay?"

That's a very odd request. "Why?" I ask as he lays a black and pink plaid flannel shirt over my shoulders.

"We need to have some difficult conversations. I'd like to have them in a beautiful place."

"You want us to go too?" David asks.

"No," Ivan says. "This is just for Story and I. Brown can you please drive us?"

I asked him dozens of questions as we wound our way out of the little clinic. We're in North Carolina! I've taken some kind of trip through time and space. Ten minutes later, the floor of Dr. Brown's minivan is covered with a carpet of tissues.

Brown parked at the north end of the island, near an abandoned ferry dock. Ivan led me through the chilly sand to a little seating area with chairs and a simple porch platform.

Moulson is my uncle? Mom betrayed me. She's hiding in some un-disclosed cave location. I don't understand why the cave thing made Ivan so mad, but it seems extra upsetting to him that she's avoiding air filters. No clue what that means. Rosa has stepped in to help Dad with Lark.

Then he told me about Holly. I didn't know the human body could sob this hard without dying. Surely I have internal bleeding from the way sobs have shredded my chest and stomach in the last hour. Ivan tried, unsuccessfully, to keep it together.

It's too much bad news; it's making me physically ill. There's a swishy, bubbling spasm I keep getting low in my abdomen. *Please be okay, Huck, please.*

"Your nightmare!" I finally manage to say. "It came true."

"What nightmare?" he asks.

"In my lab. You had that nightmare Holly was gone."

He tangles his fingers in my shirt, gripping me like something is going to steal me away any second. "You're right. I forgot about that. You remember! We're going to be okay."

Are we? I'm feeling far from okay.

"I do have a bright spot for you," he says. "Lark's surgery is scheduled." A confused, happy gasp breaks through in my sob. "Three weeks from now. We've got the data and approvals."

It's too much. The pivots between devastation, loss, and relief for Lark have given me emotional whiplash. I'm reeling. And my lower stomach still feels weird, like it's flopping.

"We come here every evening to watch the sunset," Ivan says. "Come look at this. You wanted to build a memorial to Holly. This is stuff we found on the beach."

We walk to an extraordinary web made of sea glass, shells, and driftwood hanging between two low scrubby pine trees. It's beautiful. Delicate. From the top hangs a pinkish tan chunk of seashell, pounded by the ocean and sand into a heart shape. I tuck it in my palm.

"When will we know if my seizures are better?" I ask.

"We can do an MCDI scan in a couple of days. I've been broken these last two months. So have you. There were times I was sure we weren't going to survive." My heart hurts for him. "We literally almost died. And Holly-" He shudders.

"Feels like I did die. I don't...I have no memories of the last seven weeks," I say. "I'm sorry you went through all that sadness without me. It's cruel."

"It wasn't all sad. Every time, you drifted back to me through the purge."

I press our foreheads together. His dark, sad eyes pull me in. The ache in my chest for Holly fractures in half. I'm not carrying this alone, he's devastated too. He's not asking me to be okay. He's right here, choosing to carry the hurt with me.

The heart-shaped seashell I'm clutching is sharp against my palm. I'll cherish this bit of her memorial forever. *You changed us, little one. I'll love you endlessly whether I'm awake, asleep, or that place in-between.*

Someday, this bleeding wound on my heart will scar. Someday, Ivan won't be wrecked by living in nonstop emergency mode. Someday can start well, someday. Not today. For now, I'm alive. Here. With Ivan. That's enough.

I've heard that grief has no time limit. But wallowing should. I'm going to give myself until Lark's surgery to be a mess. Then I'll start putting in the hard work to heal.

What is going on in my stomach? Wait. I'm like sixteen weeks pregnant now.

"How long have we been able to feel Huck moving?"

"We haven't. Not that you've told me at least."

I press his palms to my stomach and we stand, waiting to feel it together.

"There!" I say.

We jerk happily at the just barely there, but definitely there swishy little feeling. He's healthy. He's getting stronger. We can go home and wallow together. Ivan was right. Eventually, we'll be okay.

"Come on, Huck. Do it again, please. Come on, come on kid." Ivan presses his hand deeper.

We hold our breath.

Then Huck does it again.

Ivan lets out a shaky sigh. "Hey, hi little buddy! Please hang in there."

"He'll be okay. He has to." Ivan doesn't respond. He just breathes quietly, holding onto Huck and I like he's never letting go. "Hey. How are you?" My voice wobbles.

What fresh wounds has the purge left on my beloved Ivan?

He leans in like he's going to kiss me but pauses. "I'm warm. You've brought the sunshine back in my life."

Blackout

~Ivan~

"Stop bouncing baby. You're gonna rattle Huck around." I cuddle Story tighter under my arm. She stops bouncing her leg and traces little circles on my hand with her thumb instead.

I'm not sure if we're fools or optimists for thinking it would happen, but our "three weeks until Lark's surgery" plan went sideways. Her Agora removal didn't get scheduled in November. Or December. Or January.

So now I'm sitting here on February 17th, 2051, holding my very beautiful, *very* pregnant wife in the surgical waiting area. There's a massive screen on the wall in front of us. Lark's patient code is 0711.

0711 Status: In the OR.

Lark's been in there with Ryland, an INES, and a pediatric surgery team for three hours.

"I can't sit still anymore." Story walks (well she kinda waddles if I'm being honest, but I'd *never* tell her that) to get another cup of tea I know she won't drink.

Alan stands. "Okay, we have at least two more hours before we get an update. Let's go downstairs and eat."

Story opens her mouth to tell her dad no. He wags a finger at her.

"No, honey. A trip to the cafeteria. Get some real food. Protein. Whole grains. Veggies. And you're eight months pregnant now. You need to walk and pump those calf veins then put your feet up on the couch."

With Amelia gone and Lark's health worse than ever the last few months, Alan has turned much of his focus to Story and Huck. Story raises a hand for him to stop. None of us can handle another pregnancy health lecture right now.

He shakes his head. "You know Rosa will come get us if there's a message, right Rosa?"

"Of course," my mom replies. "But there will be *no* message. Lark will be out soon. I already placed the order and told MPort Cafe to have our little dinner party here no later than 6pm. They're bringing all her favorites."

Story sighs and shrugs. "A BLT does sound pretty good."

"That's the spirit!" I lay my left arm over her shoulders and drop my right hand on her stomach to guide her in the hallway. "I was about to chew my arm off. I'm starving."

PrivSec follows us like silent shadows. Down the elevator. For our slow walk (waddle...). They ate lunch with us. Then back into the elevator to head up.

Story and I are leaning against the elevator wall when my phone blasts a sharp chirp I haven't heard in months.

What OR is Lark in? -Delac

I type a quick reply. *No clue. -Rhys*

You have to give me something to identify where she is. I'm serious. -Delac

I sigh. I haven't heard from David since December. Now this? What is going on?

All I know is her patient code. 0711. Why? -Rhys

Where are you? -Delac

Been walking around the hospital to keep Story calm. -Rhys

You hungry? -Delac

No. Just got lunch. In case your next question is what I'm wearing: dark blue jeans and a red shirt that really sets off my eyes. You? -Rhys

The elevator stops. Two floors below where we should be. We shuffle to make room for whoever is getting on. But the doors don't open.

Rhys. It's time for SWEETS. -Delac

SWEETS? Surely David did *not* just send me our "worst case scenario" code word we invented when we were twelve. *Nope, nope, nope.* I will not panic. That would scare Story. PrivSec wouldn't care if I gave them a heads up, but I can't risk saying anything in front of her.

"Excuse me cutie," I shift Story back a few inches and press the *Door Open* button.

Nothing.

I push it again. Nothing. I jab it several times knowing the stupid thing is dead.

"Boss?" Mike steps close and looks around the elevator. He knows me well enough to see something is up. "Is everything okay?"

I meet his eyes and give the tiniest shake no.

He stiffens. The other PrivSec guys do too. Alan looks between all of us and narrows his eyes.

Why, David? -Rhys

His typing icon pops up, then disappears. Shoot! I'm too late.

No, David! We're in an elevator!!!!!! -Rhys

It goes dark. Not even a pinprick of light from the ceiling or wall panels.

Then my phone dies.

"Ivan? Baby...what happened?" Story gasps, trailing a hand up my arm.

I pull her close and step to the middle of the elevator car. "I'm right here. I've got you."

I know where this is going—and I hate what comes next.

To be continued in **Malpractice**, *book three of The Irontrace Saga...*

The Irontrace Saga

Malformation told how they fell in **love.**
Malice asked how much the heart and mind can **endure.**
Coming Summer 2026:
Malpractice will dare them to choose **hope.**

Follow T.S. Night on Instagram for more updates:
irontrace_saga_books

Acknowledgments

Thank you to my lovely group of friends across the medical field who were references for this story. (JK, TH, JL, AS) Your expertise on anxiety, amnesia, and anatomy were invaluable. To those I interviewed who spoke candidly about panic, intrusive thoughts, and the quiet ways to prevent stress from taking over your life, I'm indebted to you. Your words helped me understand this experience more deeply. If someone can learn a few coping mechanisms from this book, I'd be over the moon.

Here's a few that worked for Story that might help you: slow breathing, grounding techniques, name what you're really feeling, give yourself gentle reality checks, and move your body. If your anxiety continues, there are many resources and doctors willing to help you find other therapies or treatments that can help you feel better. **You're not alone in your struggle!**

So. Let's talk about Ivan's skillset. A biomedical engineer turned senior software engineer? It may sound outlandish. However, let me assure you, Ivan's career transition is based on a person I had the privilege of working with (and learning from!). Hearing them discuss the biomed lab they used to run while live coding to help the whole team level up was an unforgettable experience. Nothing like discussing genomes and querying languages in morning standup while hiding a dropped jaw behind my cup of sweet tea.

Now to show some gratitude. As always, thank you to my husband. You're my best friend. You keep me breathing, smiling, and laughing every single day. Can't wait to see what our tomorrow brings. Thanks for bearing with me when my brain blips out mid-conversation because a new idea struck. You're the kindest, most patient person I know. I love you forever baby.

My kids, you're seriously the greatest group of humans in the world. It's a true joy to be your mom. I'm continually in awe of the people you're becoming. Let's keep planning our next adventure. There's always a new one right around the corner. Love you always, my wild and wonderful crew!

Thank you to my siblings for your support and questions. My sister: I love when you find a plot hole that should've smacked me in the face. Himmy: the golf cart biz *will* be a reality someday. To my other brother: looking forward to the next chat about tech news :O

Mom, thank you for the constant, unwavering support since day one! Thanks for not being an Amelia...

To my readers, thank you for your time. It's a resource you can never get back. I appreciate you spending time with The Irontrace. **Stories matter.** This Saga exists to tell some important ones. There is so much more to come. Hang in there with me. The first Irontrace trilogy will wrap up this year. Yes. I said the *first* Irontrace trilogy.

I can't wait for you to read Malpractice! It sets the stage for the second trilogy and has some wild twists and turns. If you've made it this far, consider this a little call to action. Reach out to me on social media. I'd love to hear from you, and I'll make sure you get a proper welcome to The Irontrace.

My editorial team from MMP, you were wonderful to work with. Thanks for cutting this down by ~20k words. I have no hope I'll ever be able to keep my first drafts under 150k. I write. We chop. Thank you for your guidance.

Thank you to my engineering team. I appreciate your willingness to teach and explain things clearly so we can level up and pull others with us. Here's to hoping we'll never be the layer eight issue.

To any families out there who know the quiet (yet loud) grief of miscarriage, this book was written with deep respect for your loss and resilience. You are not alone.

<3, T.S.

Endnote Trigger Warning

This story contains themes involving pregnancy loss (miscarriage). If this is a sensitive subject for you, please read with caution and care for yourself as needed. Supporting resources and loved ones can make a difference—you do not have to carry your grief alone.

There are also scenes involving memory loss in which a main character fears harm from someone close to her and reacts defensively out of confusion. These moments and their aftermath may feel intense for readers.

About the Author

T.S. Night lives with her boisterous family in Ohio. The Hocking Hills region holds a special place in their heart. Having worked in careers from nursing to engineering, she wants to create clean stories that grab hold of you and won't let go. You'll never find cussing in her books. Any elements of romance are written from a place of respect, emotional connection, and humor rooted in her values.

When not building worlds where love is the only thing that can help you beat the odds, she's most likely reading with one of the family's many pets, swimming, hiking while loudly complaining about bugs, cuddled up with her 'Ivan', trying not to break an ankle playing sports with the kids, or testing how many cups of coffee it will take to get the next plot twist typed out. She believes in cliffhangers, characters we can relate to, and that the chaos in fiction will never hold a candle to the chaos we all live through daily.

9 798999 864929 5